Foxen Bloom

PARKER FOYE

CONTENTS

tailed stag. Human legend promised the stag would grant a wish if it were caught, but the stag could not be caught so long as the forest stood. So the birds sang. Though how they knew the forest's inner workings, Fenton didn't ask.

Summer breathed colour into the forest. Puddles of dappled light dotted the trails made by hoof and paw, and for much of the morning the hunter kept to the paths that time had made. She advanced quietly, carefully, her hands steady on her short, curved bow. Sweat made her skin glisten as the sun grew tall, but she remained alert as she tracked flashes of the stag through the trees. She smelled like metal and wheat.

Fenton followed from above. Birds chittered when he jostled their branches, chastising and coaxing in equal measure. He was too big to perch in any of their trees for long, but they never chased him away; sometimes he wore feathers to show his kinship, and curled his claws to talons, but the birds always whistled him back to his usual shape. Now, they chirruped as he shifted his weight to leap and land and leap again, calling to one another to warn and celebrate, even as he tried to gentle the impact of his presence. He hollowed his bones with a thought. His company was a burden he wished to ease.

The hunter glanced up as the birds gossiped in their pretty voices, but she didn't stop. She moved sleek and cautious as she stepped off the trail to follow a glimpse of the stag. What she thought was the stag. She stepped into the inviting gap between rises of the thorny guardian thicket and disappeared temporarily from view, the stave of her bow subsumed by shadow. The thicket closed behind her.

Fenton gripped the branch he perched on, holding it between the curved claws of his feet, and watched for the hunter to emerge again. He would have to follow on foot, but the thicket liked to play catch with his vines. Fenton scratched his throat where the thin vines tangled, grimacing when his scratching made one of the skinnier

PART ONE:
OLD NAN HAD TWO SONS

The bow hunter came in summer, entering the for
on leaf-light feet. It had been many seasons since
humans crossed the boundary. Fenton had woken to
excited chatter of birds and followed their voices to
westernmost part of the forest, away from the heart o
wood, where he scaled to the tops of the trees to watc
hunter's progress. The hunter riffled through the scru
examined the overgrown trail, then pushed onward.

The hunter tracked the white-tailed stag.

Fenton knew the forest to every root and l
knew the stream and the thicket; the trail and the
and he spoke with every creature, all those of fea
and fang. All but the white-tailed stag. He knew
only from glimpses seen from the corners of hi
tracks pressed to mutable earth, and in the storie
told.

Most creatures of the forest were lik
remaining within the forest's bounds, but the b
as they pleased, and they sang their stories t
they would to a chick from another nest. I
Fenton of the humans and their ever-stron
and of the stories humans told each other ab

threads break at the root. He flicked it away and dropped from the branch, his landing as easy as a sigh of rain. Hunching small and thinking his vines tight-tight-tight, Fenton moved loam-soft and water-quick through the thicket, which deigned to turn its thorns at his entreating. He let his claws skim over the nearest leaves in thanks as he passed and left the thicket behind.

Rabbit warrens vibrated with activity beneath his feet and Fenton listened to their heartbeats as he stalked forward, in case any messages needed to be carried across the forest. He often passed days and moons that way: noting the gossip of birds, scenting the news of foxes, watching for the stag's white tail. Blood-warm sunlight seeped through the forest as he listened to the rabbits and set roots. The day grew long.

Fenton blinked slowly as he returned to himself. The hunter. The stag. Fenton sent his shadow to search ahead of him, stretching across the forest floor, as day bowed to evening.

He caught up with the hunter kneeling by the stream that tripped over a cluster of rocks into a wide pool, near the spot where sunset flowers grew thickest. She had laid her bow down. Her hands were raised to her lips. Fenton watched the hunter drink from the cup of her hands until they were empty. He willed his vines to lift in turn, mimicking her. He shifted his weight, trying to move as she did, but unexpectedly she turned toward him. Her eyes grew wide. She cried like a fox in the night and blood bubbled forth with the sound. Blood slicked her chin and the sweat sheening her face stained red as her veins spidered to the surface of her skin and burst free. She shuddered and made the fox noise again, and blood burst in her eyes and wept from her ears and then she was dead. The stream continued to rush into the pool.

Fenton's shadow curled around his trunk like another one of his vines and tightened. Crossing to the dead hunter, Fenton crouched and traced the shape of her with his eyes. He inhaled the death-blood-sweat stink of her, letting his mouth hang open to gain a fuller scent. For a time, he sat and breathed in the place where she did neither. Night came. When he knew her, as best anyone living could, he waded into the stream. Fish butted his legs. Reeds tugged his claws.

By the time Fenton waded out the other side, he could smell wheat. He glanced over his shoulder. Reddish gold sheaves fluttered in a tender breeze, a great stretch of them, in the space where the bow hunter had been. Moonlight limned them.

Fenton turned away. Ahead, the flash of the white-tailed stag.

Summer passed in a long stretch of warmth as the new wheat grew tall. When days were at their hottest, Fenton dozed beneath the shade of the golden stalks; there was always a breeze whispering in the wheat. Little paws pattered over him from time to time, bringing berries and stories to share. His vines flowered. When he walked through the wheat, he left petals behind.

The next hunter came in autumn. He wore a long knife at his belt and a rope wound over his shoulder, and his footfalls crunched dry leaves as he stalked the white-tailed stag. He kept to the trails, but his eyes flitted over the hedgerows and through the trees, his head tilted to the side as if one ear were better than the other. When birds chattered overhead, whistling to Fenton, *come and look, come and see,* the hunter paused, one heel lifted. Listening.

Called to the boundary from his slumber, Fenton stood among the trees and looked as he was bid, his vines coiling and flexing. A sharp wind rushed through the forest as he his eyes. He inhaled the death-blood-sweat stink of her, letting his mouth hang open to gain a fuller scent. For a time, he sat and breathed in the place where she did neither. Night came. When he knew her, as best anyone living could, he waded into the stream. Fish butted his legs. Reeds tugged his claws.

By the time Fenton waded out the other side, he could smell wheat. He glanced over his shoulder. Reddish gold sheaves fluttered in a tender breeze, a great stretch of them, in the space where the bow hunter had been. Moonlight limned them.

Fenton turned away. Ahead, the flash of the white-tailed stag.

Summer passed in a long stretch of warmth as the new wheat grew tall. When days were at their hottest, Fenton dozed beneath the shade of the golden stalks; there was always a breeze whispering in the wheat. Little paws pattered over him from time to time, bringing berries and stories to share. His vines flowered. When he walked through the wheat, he left petals behind.

The next hunter came in autumn. He wore a long knife at his belt and a rope wound over his shoulder, and his footfalls crunched dry leaves as he stalked the white-tailed stag. He kept to the trails, but his eyes flitted over the hedgerows and through the trees, his head tilted to the side as if one ear were better than the other. When birds chattered overhead, whistling to Fenton, *come and look, come and see,* the hunter paused, one heel lifted. Listening.

Called to the boundary from his slumber, Fenton stood among the trees and looked as he was bid, his vines coiling and flexing. A sharp wind rushed through the forest as he threads break at the root. He flicked it away and dropped from the branch, his landing as easy as a sigh of rain. Hunching small and thinking his vines tight-tight-tight, Fenton moved loam-soft and water-quick through the thicket, which deigned to turn its thorns at his entreating. He let his claws skim over the nearest leaves in thanks as he passed and left the thicket behind.

Rabbit warrens vibrated with activity beneath his feet and Fenton listened to their heartbeats as he stalked forward, in case any messages needed to be carried across the forest. He often passed days and moons that way: noting the gossip of birds, scenting the news of foxes, watching for the stag's white tail. Blood-warm sunlight seeped through the forest as he listened to the rabbits and set roots. The day grew long.

Fenton blinked slowly as he returned to himself. The hunter. The stag. Fenton sent his shadow to search ahead of him, stretching across the forest floor, as day bowed to evening.

He caught up with the hunter kneeling by the stream that tripped over a cluster of rocks into a wide pool, near the spot where sunset flowers grew thickest. She had laid her bow down. Her hands were raised to her lips. Fenton watched the hunter drink from the cup of her hands until they were empty. He willed his vines to lift in turn, mimicking her. He shifted his weight, trying to move as she did, but unexpectedly she turned toward him. Her eyes grew wide. She cried like a fox in the night and blood bubbled forth with the sound. Blood slicked her chin and the sweat sheening her face stained red as her veins spidered to the surface of her skin and burst free. She shuddered and made the fox noise again, and blood burst in her eyes and wept from her ears and then she was dead. The stream continued to rush into the pool.

Fenton's shadow curled around his trunk like another one of his vines and tightened. Crossing to the dead hunter, Fenton crouched and traced the shape of her with tailed stag. Human legend promised the stag would grant a wish if it were caught, but the stag could not be caught so long as the forest stood. So the birds sang. Though how they knew the forest's inner workings, Fenton didn't ask.

Summer breathed colour into the forest. Puddles of dappled light dotted the trails made by hoof and paw, and for much of the morning the hunter kept to the paths that time had made. She advanced quietly, carefully, her hands steady on her short, curved bow. Sweat made her skin glisten as the sun grew tall, but she remained alert as she tracked flashes of the stag through the trees. She smelled like metal and wheat.

Fenton followed from above. Birds chittered when he jostled their branches, chastising and coaxing in equal measure. He was too big to perch in any of their trees for long, but they never chased him away; sometimes he wore feathers to show his kinship, and curled his claws to talons, but the birds always whistled him back to his usual shape. Now, they chirruped as he shifted his weight to leap and land and leap again, calling to one another to warn and celebrate, even as he tried to gentle the impact of his presence. He hollowed his bones with a thought. His company was a burden he wished to ease.

The hunter glanced up as the birds gossiped in their pretty voices, but she didn't stop. She moved sleek and cautious as she stepped off the trail to follow a glimpse of the stag. What she thought was the stag. She stepped into the inviting gap between rises of the thorny guardian thicket and disappeared temporarily from view, the stave of her bow subsumed by shadow. The thicket closed behind her.

Fenton gripped the branch he perched on, holding it between the curved claws of his feet, and watched for the hunter to emerge again. He would have to follow on foot, but the thicket liked to play catch with his vines. Fenton scratched his throat where the thin vines tangled, grimacing when his scratching made one of the skinnier

PART ONE:
OLD NAN HAD TWO SONS

The bow hunter came in summer, entering the forest on leaf-light feet. It had been many seasons since any humans crossed the boundary. Fenton had woken to the excited chatter of birds and followed their voices to the westernmost part of the forest, away from the heart of the wood, where he scaled to the tops of the trees to watch the hunter's progress. The hunter riffled through the scrub and examined the overgrown trail, then pushed onward.

The hunter tracked the white-tailed stag.

Fenton knew the forest to every root and leaf—he knew the stream and the thicket; the trail and the loam—and he spoke with every creature, all those of feather, fur, and fang. All but the white-tailed stag. He knew the stag only from glimpses seen from the corners of his eyes, in tracks pressed to mutable earth, and in the stories the birds told.

Most creatures of the forest were like Fenton, remaining within the forest's bounds, but the birds roamed as they pleased, and they sang their stories to Fenton as they would to a chick from another nest. Birds warned Fenton of the humans and their ever-stronger weapons, and of the stories humans told each other about the white-

watched, making the birds raise their voices in response. The hunter started forward again, moving faster but just as guardedly. The white-tailed stag skulked ahead.

Leaves didn't crunch beneath Fenton's feet. As his shadow passed over them, they curled into crescents of red and gold, then crumbled to dust as he moved on. Trees shuddered in the growing cold of the year and Fenton pressed his hands to their trunks as he followed the hunter, listening to fragments of slow stories as he wove his way through the forest. He left a trail of dust behind him.

The hunter came to the field of wheat. He paused, his fingers twitching at his sides, then ducked his head and threaded through the stalks toward the stream. Fenton slowed, his vines coiling tight, but the hunter didn't pause to drink. He followed the course of the stream toward the pool and the sunset flowers. There, his progress slowed, as if a weight pressed upon him. He had stopped looking through the trees and stopped listening to the birds. They were whistling to him, now, *don't go and see, don't go and look*, but the hunter didn't heed their song.

Fenton watched the hunter near the sunset flowers. Idly scratching the inside of his elbow, Fenton plucked a vine that had started to itch. Thorns bristled on the vine. Blood beaded on their tips. The hunter reached toward a sunset flower.

Don't go and look, a fat little robin perched on a nearby branch sang to the hunter. *Don't go and see!* the robin cried with all its might.

Startling, the hunter looked toward the robin, and saw Fenton for the first time. A sunset flower fell from the hunter's open hand. The hunter touched his hand to his chest and opened his mouth. Fenton raised his own hand but kept his mouth closed. He licked his fangs as the rope around the hunter's shoulder unspooled itself and threaded rabbit-quick around his throat. Though the hunter wrestled with the rope until his nails broke bloody, his efforts were in vain. The hunter dropped to his knees, then to his side. His movements slowed. Something popped. Something cracked. His flat teeth smeared in blood. Fenton looked away.

The fat little robin went quiet. Fenton flicked aside the vine he'd pulled from his elbow. He touched his finger, as light as breath, to the robin's bowed head. He had no claws. Claws would have offered no comfort.

Wheat whispered as Fenton passed through the rows. He brushed his hands over the stalks in apology. When he reached the hunter, Fenton rolled him onto his back. He didn't look anything like the summer hunter. He smelled like blood and leather. Crouching, Fenton cupped the fallen sunset flower in his hands and blew softly on the fist-sized bloom. Petals scattered on the obliging breeze until only the two largest and glossiest remained. Those, Fenton placed over the hunter's glazed eyes.

Fenton's shadow passed over the hunter. Dust sighed in its wake.

Winter came, and with it, snow. The white-tailed stag slept. Fenton, too, dozed beneath the loam, spreading roots as his shadow carpeted the forest floor. Winter fed darkness, leaving all else lean and hungered. Old Nan had taught Fenton about the dark. She'd told Fenton stories then sent him off with a pie hot from the stone.

Someone else had been there. A bright slash of lightning.

Sleepy-eyed, Fenton worried thorns from his sides and lined them across his torso like ants marching home. He hadn't thought about Old Nan in a very long time.

The third hunter came in midwinter, when the days were dark and short. She shivered. Though Fenton had passed innumerable winters sleeping in the roots of the forest, the recent turn of seasons had left him restless, exquisitely aware of their passing. He already watched the boundary when the hunter came to cross. Her moon-pale face was gaunt and her hands were fisted tight in the threadbare fur of her cloak. She strayed from the trail almost immediately to follow old tracks through the trees. The sour scent of hunger dogged her heels.

There were no birds singing. No rabbits drumming. No white-tailed stag to tempt her, and yet the hunter ventured deeper into the forest and deeper. Fenton shadowed the hunter, stepping where she stepped, leaving snowdrops and bluebells in the indentations from her boots.

When the hunter reached the wheat, still lush and gold even in midwinter, she didn't falter. Her shoulders stiffened but she pushed past the stalks with nary a glance. Behind her, Fenton made a silent game of leaping from boot print to boot print.

Next came the stream and the sunset flowers. Frost made petals glitter like stars across the blanket of night. The hunter paused, and her hands twitched at her sides, but she didn't reach for the blossoms. She mumbled something, a quick burble of water, and passed the flowers, heading to the other side of the pool and into the thick of the forest once more.

Fenton rubbed the heel of his hand against the throbbing beneath his eyes, then let out a sharp hiss when something prickled. Lowering his hand, he discovered blood painting the thorns of his palm. He'd caught his vines on the hooks. Had that happened before? Raising his hand a second time, more guardedly, Fenton ran his fingertips across his vines. They bristled. The sensation itched. Fenton dug his nails into his vines and tugged, but no vines came free. He pressed harder to his face. His skin. Where there had been a tangle of vines, his fingers found only flesh, sore where his thorns had struck.

A white flash. A glimpse of antlers. Fenton dropped his

hand and frowned at the forest. When he didn't see the hunter, he sent his shadow in pursuit and followed after. He could smell something unusual, something new, that made his roots twist. The trees moaned and reached their branches toward him, nearly catching his loose vines as he passed, oblivious in their distress. Fenton's thoughts were rabbit-nervous and cuckoo-odd. His shadow unspooled like an inky river before him.

The hunter recoiled when Fenton stepped into the clearing, and he quickly shrank himself to hunter size. Her acrid scent eased. She sat on a large stone with her hands outstretched toward a small bundle of sticks and the flames dancing over them.

Fenton hadn't seen fire for a very long time. His vines coiled away from the heat. The deadwood of his heart creaked.

The hunter spoke in her waterfall voice, scarcely blinking as she pointed her face Fenton's way. She paused, as if awaiting a response. Fenton didn't know how to tell her she was going to die. When he stood silent as the stones in the circle in the heart of the forest, the hunter gestured toward the fire and burbled again. Though her body was held tight, and her face scarred with winter, her eyes were gentle as dew.

Fenton eased into the clearing. The hunter watched him with all the caution she should have given the forest. Fenton's shadow tucked underneath his feet as he crouched by the fire and watched the hunter in turn. Her skin burnished gold as wheat in the firelight. He studied the movement of her hands, the tilt of her face, the way her legs hinged. Sometimes she burbled at him, or perhaps to herself. She held her hands toward the fire. Once, she flashed her teeth at him.

Fenton stayed until the fire went out. Until the dew of the hunter's eyes cracked with cold.

When Fenton dreamed, he dreamed of stone hearths and clay ovens and the scent of fresh bread. His roots stretched out like searching hands. Thorns prickled through his tongue and eyes and ears and fingertips. He had no claws in his dreams.

He had a sibling, though. He knew their laughter. He knew the hummingbird flicker of their expressions and the mutable storms of their temper. The agile tricks of their shadow. They fought one another, in Fenton's dreams. In Fenton's dreams, he lost.

Winter began to wane. The forest thawed. The white-tailed stag ran.

The last hunter came on the first day of spring. Fenton sat astride a high branch in the trees at the edge of the forest, looking out through the unfurling leaves, a sunset flower in his hands. He had been spending more time on the edges of the forest of late. The hunter was winter-lean but his stride was strong, and he held his longbow easily in his hand. He smelled like fern and fear. His hair shone like river-slick wood. He kept to the trail. Fenton watched him until the hunter took the bend of the trail, moving deeper into the forest.

A squirrel scampered up the tree trunk and chattered at Fenton about the hunter, as if Fenton hadn't noticed his presence. He snapped his teeth at the squirrel. The squirrel flicked their tail at him and used his legs as ballast for their jump. Fenton let the petals of the sunset flower float down from his fingers. Rustling in the canopy of leaves, the wind brought a question. Fenton could not answer.

Fenton dropped from the branch and landed soft as a leaf on the forest floor. He followed the hunter on the trail, his shadow stretching behind him.

When the white-tailed stag flashed through the thicket,

9

the hunter paused. He stood strong, planted like an old tree, and watched the forest for a handful of slow, measured breaths. Unseen behind a friendly tree, Fenton watched the hunter likewise. One of Fenton's vines broke through the skin of his wrist, curious; he nipped it between his fingernails and dragged the vine from his skin like a wriggling worm from the earth, tugging it free in a hot splash of blood. The vine writhed on his palm.

The hunter stepped off the trail.

Hissing between his teeth, Fenton followed the hunter in the direction of the stream. Fenton moved soundless as an owl in the night, walking in the clever-mouse steps of the hunter. Rich scents filled the air: ripe wheat, clear water, and the heady musk of sunset flowers. Fenton's insides crawled like insects over carrion.

The hunter met the wheat. He brushed his hands over the stalks, his eyes and mouth pinched. Fenton's fingers flicked at his sides. When the hunter moved on, Fenton hurried to press the same stalks, soothing in the same motions, seeking the hunter's touch for his own fingers. Wind tousled his hair and made the vines in the strands shake.

They reached the stream, and though sweat laid on the hunter's neck as the sun crawled high, he didn't stop to drink. And though he admired the colourful fists of the sunset flowers, he didn't touch. Flowers turned their faces to the hunter as he passed, entreating with their scent, but he shook his head and rounded the pool, moving faster now. Fenton followed behind, snake-weaving and fox-skipping, and brushed his fingers in the air above the sunset flowers as he passed. The flowers whittered to him, their voices light with laughter.

Ahead, the flash of the white-tailed stag.

The hunter pushed into the other side of the forest. Fenton listened to the birds but they continued happily gossiping among themselves as he and the hunter ventured deeper into the trees. Fenton's shadow twined around the ancient trunks and sank to their roots, chasing rabbits in their warrens and rattling acorns in hidden hollows. The hunter didn't notice the company at his heels as he kept walking, his gaze focused ever ahead.

The hunter reached the clearing with the little pile of sticks and the bigger pile of rocks. They'd been heavy, the rocks, and Fenton had broken claws and thorns as he carried them, leaving scattered parts of himself behind. Snow had frozen his flowers brittle. His new, rounded, fingernails had grown in the colour of broken ice floes.

"Winters must be vicious here," the hunter said as he reached toward the rocks and rested his fingers on the topmost. He left tiny indentations in the frost-tipped moss.

Fenton edged forward. Between the trees blinked a flash of the white-tailed stag. The hunter's hand tightened around his longbow, but he didn't leave his place by the rocks. His shoulders set firm. Fenton learned the taut lines of the hunter's back from his hide in the dark of the trees. His shadow curled at his feet like fox kits in their den.

Rain began to whisper in the air, spitter-spatters almost too fine to feel. Water misted around the hunter, catching in the weave of his clothes, the waves of his hair. He made a huffing noise, then in a sudden flurry swung his longbow from his shoulder and brought it to his side. Before Fenton needed to act, the hunter used his leg as a brace to lever the bow's string from the notches that held it. He slid the string into the pack he wore slung over his chest.

Fenton's hands knew those movements. He stared at his palms, where no thorns grew.

"My name is Prior. I have come to ask for your aid," the hunter said.

Fenton started. He expected to find the hunter—Prior—looking directly at him, but instead found Prior's back. Prior stood with his face tilted to the sky and his arms spread wide. He had set his bow beside the rocks. Rain drummed on the leaves of the trees that had bent their heads to keep Fenton dry. Prior turned slightly on his heel and Fenton moved instinctively in kind, like a—a dance. Like dancing. Fenton retreated between the trees until his back hit a sturdy trunk. He felt like a mouse in the thicket. Something hunted him. Trees murmured comfort as Fenton's shadow clambered the nearest trunk and coiled around it in another ring of age.

Did Prior await a response? Fenton had none to give. When Prior completed his rotation, he lowered his arms to his sides.

"Didn't suppose it would be that simple, but it was worth a try."

Rain made his hair slick, and he had to keep swiping it from his eyes, but Prior didn't seek shelter. He rummaged in his pack and began arranging items in a rough circle: a candle, a shallow dish, a clay cup, a knife. He settled onto his knees. He bowed his head. Fenton traced Prior's profile against the forest; his proud nose, his strong chin. The dark sweep of his eyelashes.

He looked cold. Fenton glanced at the canopy of leaves keeping him dry. He considered the squirrel who poked their head from their burrow and wriggled their nose when rain fell on it, the spiders and the birds and the brooding sky. He caught raindrops in his palm and rubbed water between his fingers. The rain could fall later. Fenton flicked his fingers at the clouds.

The rain eased. Prior grunted and shook his head, as if clearing away a fly. A vine curled around Fenton's ear, and where once he would have plucked it free, he instead twined it around his finger. Prior took a deep breath. The trees sighed toward him.

"It has been a difficult winter, and a dry summer before that, and the winter before that as hard as any I can remember," Prior told his circle of things. He touched the candle, the dish, the cup, the knife. "Livestock wither in the fields. Crops turn to ash at the harvest. Where once we would have traded away our excess, now we scarcely have enough to feed ourselves. And of late... of late there is a sickness. Folk in my village sleep and do not wake." Prior's jaw clenched shut. His brows creased. He rubbed the seam of his mouth as if to unstitch it. "My sister has not woken these past three days."

Prior stared hard at the ground between his knees. Fenton coaxed his shadow to murmur toward the hunter, only to summon it back when Prior began to pull more items from his pack. He poured something into the dish, sloshed something else into the cup. He withdrew a flint— Fenton stiffened—but merely held the flint in his hand before clicking his tongue and returning it to the pack.

Prior picked up the knife. He lay the flat of the blade on his open palm. "My sister Sylvie adores fairy stories. Tales from the wood best of all. When she was small, I used to nag the elders for stories when I should have been in the fields or tidying the cottage. As many stories as I could, all to tell her after. I missed supper so many times for shirking my chores." His lips quirked. "I'd do it again."

Falling quiet, Prior tapped the knife against his hand. Fenton wanted to snatch the thing away, throw it in the stream, bury it in salted earth. He did nothing. He couldn't move. His shadow wrapped around his legs like a second skin.

Prior continued. "Some say a god has cursed the land. Perhaps that is so. There seems no other reason for this spreading darkness, but I cannot accept it as merely our lot. I refuse to accept it. But no healer, nor hedgewitch, nor any of the wise folk I have found can offer aid. So what else am I to do but ask another god for help?" He lifted the knife and traced the lines of his palm with the tip of the blade as he spoke, almost idly. "Since I was a boy, I've heard tales of this place. Warnings. In my village, they say a mage coupled with a wicked spirit and gave the child of that union to the forest, to live in the roots and the breeze. On the far side of the moorland, they say it was a virgin and a fairy princess. I've heard some say about changelings, and children left for exposure raised by wolves. Powerful things, all. And all surely strong enough to break a curse." He held the knife point-down to his palm and raised his brows. His fern scent thickened. His mouth twisted. "If curse it be."

Prior adjusted his position on his knees; the ground must have been cold. He spoke again to the knife in his hand. "Our grandmother came from the land in the north, where they have different gods, and she told us about Old Nan and her two sons." As he continued, Prior set the knife aside to count on his fingers, his voice lilting like birdsong. "One son to the rivers and one to the land. One to the sun and one to the moon. One to the sea, one to the sky, one to the day, and one to the night. One to shadows, one to life." He huffed out a breath and wiggled his fingers, all ten of them. "That's more than two, you'll note. I was always so pleased to point that out, as if my grandmother had never noticed ten to be more than two. She'd just smile at me and say again, 'Old Nan had two sons'."

Prior picked up the knife. Fenton's shadow snaked up his body, pressing close, smothering. Protecting.

"Sylvie used to talk about the white-tailed stag," Prior said.

In a single swift motion, Prior sliced the knife across his palm. He hissed between his teeth as blood welled a shocking red from the wound. Clenching his fist, he squeezed his blood into the dish, the cup, and over the candle, then set the knife back into position. He wrapped his hand in a strip of cloth drawn from his pack. The actions had taken but an instant.

"An offering to the heart of the wood in hope of your assistance with the curse," Prior said. He scratched his jaw. "If you care for that sort of thing. And if you care to help at all, I suppose."

Fenton prised his fingers from the tree trunk and soothed a touch over the indentations until they cleared. His shadow unclenched from its chokehold around his throat and oozed down his chest like sap. Vines uncoiled. Fenton finally exhaled. Birds began once more to sing.

The forest smelled like Prior's blood. Fenton opened his mouth to taste it.

"Can you hear me? Do you understand me?" Prior shook his head and pressed his thumb firmly to his wounded palm, as if in reprimand. Red spotted the cloth. "Asking a god if they understand what I'm saying. The *arrogance*. Not like any of this will do a damned thing. It's not enough to break the curse." Prior began to mutter beneath his breath, too quiet for Fenton to understand.

Old Nan had told Fenton about curses. Blights, she'd called them. To her, the world was a garden that required tending, and she held the shape of it in her wrinkled, green-thumbed hands. Hard winters and dry summers were necessary seasons, for all those living through them might wish otherwise, but for a sleeping sickness to enroot as Prior claimed? That might indicate a blight at work. It was possible.

As he considered asking Prior about the blight, a rush of words lodged in Fenton's throat like a guardian thicket. Which of them to say? And to what purpose? Prior had spoken of the white-tailed stag but he was no hunter: he had unstrung his bow, put away his flint, and harmed only himself. Prior did not seek a wish. He sought a god.

Fenton worked his jaw and plucked a petal from the corner of his mouth. His feet rooted in the welcoming earth. He curled his toes into the dirt. He said nothing, and his silence weighed on him like a stone.

When the sun began to sink like a burning torch through the trees, Prior rose to his feet and gathered his things into his pack. He picked up his bow. His tread sank heavily into the moss. Fenton asked the forest to watch over Prior as he returned to the boundary.

After Prior left the clearing, Fenton knelt in the same place Prior had, his knees filling the same depressions. He traced the places where Prior's blood had spilt, though there were no remnants but for in memory, and drew his fingertips to his mouth to taste the ghost of Prior's sacrifice to the white-tailed stag. A fox kit nosed at Fenton's other hand and he rubbed the kit's head gently with his knuckles. The kit butted Fenton's hand and cheeped at him, then bounded away through the trees, into the drawing dark of the forest. In the direction Prior had taken.

Ahead, the flash of the white-tailed stag. Despite himself, Fenton darted a glance toward the flash—then froze. The stag had remained in place. It looked back at him.

Fenton had never seen the stag in anything but passing. Yet there it stood, twice as tall as Fenton, shadow-black eyes set in the rugged bark of its face, two bone antlers proudly jutting from its skull. Fur didn't cover its body, but rather a fine layer of moss, and in places gorse shone a shocking yellow. The true-white fur of its tail was as snow. A deliberate signal. A taunt.

Seasons upon seasons had passed since Fenton first woke in the forest. Kits had weaned and grown and died in the time between. Fledglings had left their nests and returned with songs from far-off places. Even the hunters had changed; the intricacies of their clothing, the art of their weapons. Fenton didn't note the passing moons or changing stars, but he knew them nonetheless. And more and more, since the summer's hunter. What had changed? The blight?

Perhaps like called to like.

Fenton considered the white-tailed stag. He considered Prior, and all the hunters who had come to the forest and never left. Then, rising to his feet, he left the stag behind and tracked Prior's path to the pool by the sunset flowers. Hooves echoed his steps. At the pool, Fenton regarded his reflection. He raised his hands—so like the hunters' hands—to his face—so like the hunters' faces. Similar, if not the same. Not bird nor fox nor bear. No muzzle. No beak. Fenton pressed the ridges beneath his eyes, the protruding banks of his collarbone. A vine curled from beneath his hair and he wound it around his finger, where it bloomed. White flowers studded his dark hair in a ragged crown.

A fish leapt from the pool and shattered Fenton's reflection. He jolted back. On the other side of the pool, the white-tailed stag waited. It wore no crown but the weapons of its antlers. Fenton bared his teeth at the stag. His shadow tensed. The stag lowered its head. Moved away.

Fenton left the pool for the sunset flowers. The flowers turned their faces to him, their musk rising in heady clouds. Fenton rubbed a petal between his fingers and thumb until his skin stained dusk. He carried the scent of the sunset flowers with him to the stream, where he drank from his cupped hands. He brushed his wet, stained, fingers over the tops of the golden wheat, where the stalks reached for the sky. Night birds sang their hunts to him. Foxes barked a greeting as he passed. His shadow clung to his heels.

When Fenton reached the threshold of the forest, in the place where the world began, he stopped. Warning sang in him. The boundary did not permit him to cross. Fenton was not bird or fox or bear. He was not— A hoarse bellow demanded his attention.

Fenton faced the white-tailed stag. He raised his hand and the stag bowed its head, pushing into Fenton's palm. Moss felt nothing like fur. Fenton sank his fingers into it. He learned the shape of the stag's bone antlers, the coarse living bark of its legs, the springy moss of its hide. He saw himself in the black pits of its eyes. His deadwood heart ached in his chest.

The stag made a noise like wind in the trees. Pain lanced through Fenton's skull and he flinched back, dropping to one knee, his eyes screwed shut. A whine escaped his clenched teeth. His shadow rushed over his skin in a cool caress as the pain crested, and finally passed.

When Fenton opened his eyes, the stag had left. He pushed shakily to his feet and faced the boundary once more. No warning sang. Fenton pressed his fingers to the nearest trunk, hard enough to imprint the ridges into his skin. Trees breathed him in. Fenton exhaled. He crossed the threshold and followed Prior out of the forest.

Flowers bloomed in his footsteps.

Prior hadn't intended to speak to a god, the day he'd set out with a knife in his hand and an ache in his heart. It had been many years since he'd prayed more than idly. Most of Ashcroft was the same: war had taken the village's prayers, while the subsequent lean days and bad harvests had seen to everything else. Seasons had been long and hard, and as unbending as the trees in the forest.

A small village, Ashcroft sat at the southern edge of the moorland, close to the Great Road that ran from the port of Spear Bluff all the way north and had allowed several rich estates to sprout across the territory. The walled city of Northrope took most travellers' business, but some passed through Ashcroft on their way east to the coast, or on their return, bringing enough custom to sustain an inn and a full-time smithy. Most folk in Ashcroft were farmers or hunters otherwise, and went to Northrope's market to trade for what else the village needed.

Travellers made life in Ashcroft richer than many other of the moorland settlements, and not only in coin; Sylvie still remarked on the elfkin family that had hurried through one summer when she and Prior were young, which had inspired her stories for nearly a year. More frequent visitors were merchants and others who made their living from the land. During the past winter, a hunter had visited the village, her face as lean as the season, a short bow in hand. She sought the white-tailed stag, she'd said, for the wish it would grant her, and had come to Ashcroft as it sat close to the trail to the forest. Most eyes had turned from her, then. Ashcroft knew of the forest—all of the moorfolk did—but none ventured there that had anywhere else to go. Even the great creatures—griffins, centaurs, and the like—had abandoned their territories and moved north rather than hunt near its borders.

Yet determination had scored every line on the hunter's face. She had passed the evening at the tavern and asked for stories, though received naught but warning songs; perhaps she had come to Ashcroft for some cheer, or hope, but it had been seasons since any in Ashcroft had good feeling left in their stores. Betta, the innkeeper, had sold the hunter hardtack at twice the usual price, and refused to sell the last of her mead; a step too far, she'd said, to host a living wake. The hunter had scoffed and promised to visit on her way home.

Winter had settled into Prior's bones like marrow. The hunter had not returned.

Then spring had approached, and with it had come the sleeping sickness. The village had sent for healers and hedgewitches from surrounding settlements, and even some of the estates, but none could help. Many were falling to the same sickness. Prior had heard tell a mage worked in Northrope, but even the consulting fee would be far beyond Ashcroft's pockets, let alone any kind of cure.

Weeks had passed and the sickness had shown no sign of stopping. Prior had tended their small patch of land, finding ever more stone than arable soil, while Sylvie had mopped the brows of the sick until Prior called her home.

And then one day Sylvie did not wake.

Lying restless that night, listening to his sister's slow breaths, Prior had thought about Sylvie's stories, and the wish of the winter's hunter, and the forest that darkened the far side of the moors. He had decided he could not lie still and wait for Sylvie to die. He had to try what he could to help her, and the rest of the village.

Standing with his back to that same forest, Prior sighed. He rubbed his face and grimaced as the action pulled at his wounded palm. "At least Sylvie won't know what I tried to do."

For as the scent of heather filled him—so much richer outside the forest, as if the forest had not been in the moorland at all—he dared wonder: what if the rumoured god, be they stag, or satyr, or whatever other creature, had *answered* his prayer? He simply hadn't thought that far ahead. Desperation did not make for a forward-thinking bedfellow.

Prior cast his gaze to the cloud-bruised sky and the rising moon. The night absorbed his worries and shone them back a hundredfold. If Sylvie's sickness progressed as the others' had, she would be dead in days. Prior hoped he'd fall sick before he had to watch her die.

"I heard you."

Prior whirled around, nearly tripping over his own feet as he stumbled back. He tightened his grip around the stave of his bow, readying to use it as a staff, and cursed himself a fool for not restringing it. Yet he saw nothing. No one! Trees and trees and trees. For several rapid beats of his heart, he wondered if the forest itself had spoken, and only the numbing grip of fear prevented Prior falling to his knees. If he moved, if he fled, *it* might give chase, whispered the frightened animal of his heart.

Then something changed—the forest, the night—and a man stood at the threshold of the trees. Prior flexed his fingers around his bow, but then lowered it. The creature's gaze didn't flicker. Prior didn't present a threat.

"I understand you," the man—the creature—continued. Wind creaked in the branches of his voice.

The creature—the man—was of a height with Prior, and slender in a way that suggested physiology, as opposed to Prior's skipped-meal leanness. The man wore no shirt, and no shoes, and his legs were tightly encased in a material like none Prior had ever seen, which ate light like a shadow. He wore a crown of snowdrops perched atop his pointed ears.

The ears might have indicated elfkin, but the rest of his demeanour suggested the man was nothing so benign. Though the night limited Prior's vision, he could see the wildness shining in the man's dark eyes. It hunted in the fox-like shape of his face. When the man tilted his head in assessment, he wore a crow's curiosity. Living vines moved in the unkempt mass of his long brown hair. He was as beautiful and dangerous as a frozen stream when spring approached. Prior needed to watch his steps.

Prior gripped his bow tightly to hide the trembling of his hands. With a sick jolt, he realised the creature—the man—the god?—had been answering the questions Prior had asked the forest, when there had been none but birds to hear. Fear hammered Prior's heart in his chest. He ducked his head and wondered if he shouldn't bow.

"Are you the god of this forest?" he managed to ask, his eyes cast firmly to the ground. The creature could be none other. Yet Prior hadn't expected a god to be so... to be such a man.

He should have, probably. In the stories, gods fought and fucked just as humans did, though on a scale as a stag to an ant. But Prior didn't feel like an ant. He felt... Well. Prior shifted, out of sorts.

The god, if he was such, thankfully didn't seem to notice Prior's hastily stifled reaction. "I am called Fenton. Someone taught me about blights, once. A long time ago. You came to my forest for aid."

"Y-your forest?" Prior stammered.

Fenton made a low, humming noise, and then fell silent. Prior dared to look up and nearly choked on his sharp intake of breath. Directly behind Fenton stood an enormous stag with dark wells for eyes and antlers the length of a man's arm. The deep colour of its strangely textured fur made Fenton corpse-pale in contrast. The stag

21

towered over Fenton with a solemn mien. Prior stood transfixed.

Following Prior's stare, Fenton glanced over his shoulder—how had he not noticed the stag's presence?—then hummed again and stepped to the side. The stag advanced. Prior's heart beat furiously in his throat. Sweat gathered in the creases of his palms and made his wound burn. An almost overwhelming scent of wet earth and old blood surrounded the stag; it settled on Prior's skin. He would never be clean of it. His gaze fixed on the knife-like tines of the stag's antlers. He waited to die.

With a noise like the cracking of a lightning-struck tree, the stag abruptly lowered itself to the ground, kneeling front then hind legs. The movement should have seemed absurd, awkward; Prior had seen horses kneel and remembered the unsteady buckling of their legs, the precariousness of the action. Yet the stag lost none of its stateliness.

Prior checked Fenton for a cue. Though Fenton was as unnerving as the stag, he had spoken, at least, and thus might provide guidance. But Fenton had attention for the stag alone. He watched it as children watched stars.

Prior couldn't meet the stag's eyes. He well remembered Sylvie's tales of the forest and the white-tailed stag, and the bitter remnants of his own desperation lingered on his tongue and pulsed in the wound on his palm. Prior had scarred himself for hope, and in so doing, had made himself more vulnerable still. Yes, he had left Ashcroft in search of a god. He hadn't expected to *find* one.

Certainly, Fenton had to be a forest spirit of some sort, and Prior could accept that—there were dryads in the moorland, some said, and as a boy Prior had heard the coarse cry of a griffin as it hunted—but the white-tailed stag was old as the moors. Older. Prior's grandmother had gifted him the stories of Old Nan and her sons, the land and the sea, and here knelt one of their emissaries.

Another guise, perhaps, and from stories Prior had not yet heard, but. *But.*

How had he not already been slain for his temerity? No lost waif nor wronged princess seeking home, Prior had entered the forest for selfish purpose. Tales didn't end well for people such as he.

"Can I— Is there something you would request of me?" he asked, and waited to hear his judgement.

"You did not drink from the stream."

Wrongfooted by the non sequitur, Prior looked up, then stilled. Fenton had reached out his—its?—long-fingered hand toward him, close enough he could surely feel Prior's breath on his skin. His fingers were not tipped with claws, as Prior might have supposed, but were as round as Prior's own. As Prior watched, scarcely daring to blink, Fenton turned his hand over and cupped his palm, but then drew his hand back. His eyes flickered from Prior's mouth to the sky, and fixed there. A vine unfurled from behind his ear, tiny red flowers studding it like gems.

Prior shifted in place. Loosened his grip on his bow, his injured hand stinging hotly at the release of pressure. The night grew chill. The stag continued to kneel.

"Should I have drank?" Prior asked, when Fenton remained content in silence. Tales told travellers to take nothing from the forest not freely—and clearly—given.

Fenton returned his gaze to Prior. Another crow-tilt. His crown didn't shift with the motion. "You did not take a flower."

Prior frowned. "I took no flowers, that's true. There are many beautiful flowers in the forest, of course, but I can admire them with my eyes equally as well."

He tried to recall the stories his grandmother had told when he and Sylvie would sit before the fire, those long summer nights together. His grandmother's gods had been capricious but playful, storms and children both. This creature of the wild with his careful words seemed as a storm locked in a box. Prior wanted to retreat, in case the weather changed or the lock broke, but his feet were stuck in the soft earth.

"And you did not light a fire," Fenton said, as if concluding an argument.

"I did not."

"Yet you hunted the white-tailed stag."

It wasn't a question. Yet Prior had to disagree, even as nausea roiled within him at the concept of disagreeing with one so beyond his understanding. "If you heard my—my prayer, then you know that isn't true. I sought the stag's aid." He dared to glance at the stag, still silent on the grass. "*Your* aid. There is a curse—"

"A blight."

"If you would." If Fenton wanted to debate vocabulary rather than rip Prior's spine through his mouth, Prior would cede every ground. He tried again. "I sought the aid of the forest. A witch, a devil, a fairy prince, whomever might answer! My sister is dying and I cannot afford to be particular. I did not, in my heart, expect a god to heed my prayer, but know I will pay any price." Fenton hissed between his teeth and Prior hurried to finish speaking, entreating stag and Fenton both, as bold as he could force himself to be. "Any price you ask, I swear it. I request only that I see Sylvie saved before you— Before whatever it is you will do."

Prior had not consciously decided to bargain with his life, but as he spoke the words, he knew the offer to be sincere. He would not renege. If Fenton or the stag could save Sylvie, they would be welcome to what remained of Prior. The wound in his hand throbbed, surely painting the stave of his bow with blood. Prior wanted to present the bow as a promise of more blood to come, whether from within his body or without.

Fenton turned his eyes to the sky once more, becoming still as a wolf watching the herd. It seemed as if he intended to simply ignore Prior's speech and his offer. Prior breathed shallowly and willed his heart to slow from its frenetic beat. He had been plain. More words would muddy the water.

Insects clicked. Wind blustered through the trees. Clouds drifted over the moon, masking Fenton's face in shadow, until he flicked his hand dismissively and the clouds departed like unwelcome guests. Prior's breath caught. Moonlight coated Fenton's crown with silver.

Fenton's gaze slid to the stag. With a thoughtful expression, Fenton raised his wrist to his mouth, then ripped across his vulnerable inner wrist with suddenly vicious fangs. Prior cried out as blood wept freely from the wound, but Fenton only swiped his other hand in the mess, and then flexed his fingers with a moue of irritation. Vines emerged from the ragged mouth on Fenton's wrist and lashed around his arm, wriggling and twisting as they sealed the wound. Nausea rushed hotly in Prior's throat.

Nausea that intensified when Fenton swiped his bloody hand along the length of one of the stag's antlers. Blood smeared grey in the colours of the night. The wet earth and old blood scent of the stag redoubled to near choking and then, with another harsh lightning crack, the stag crumpled, all at once, to nothing more than dry and broken wood.

Prior staggered back. "What? What was—" His voice shook. "Did you— What did you do? What are you *doing?*"

Because Fenton had raised his hand to his mouth and clearly intended to lick away the blood that remained. At Prior's shrill question, he stopped and looked placidly between his hand and Prior. He showed Prior his palm, as if that could possibly answer Prior's question. As if anything might.

"Not *that*," Prior said, voice going high. He gestured toward the kindling that had once been a god. "That! The white-tailed stag is no more and—"

"The stag is sleeping," Fenton interrupted, unbothered. He wiped his hand against the peculiar fabric of his trousers.

Sleeping? Well. Prior supposed gods might sleep. His mind slid to the memory of Sylvie's unnatural rest, his entire reason for standing before Fenton and the forest. A weight pressed on his chest, or perhaps he remembered how it rested there, and in remembering it became all the heavier. He took a deep breath to alleviate the weight. Though he knew the answer, he owed Sylvie the asking.

"Then I will find no aid here? For the curse— The blight?" he asked Fenton.

Wind rustled the trees, making a sound like many voices whispering. A bird called. Prior shivered. His knuckles ached in the cold where he still clung to his bow, contrasting with the heat of his wound.

Fenton's eyes narrowed, and Prior felt the weight of his regard.

"I will help you," Fenton said.

Prior exhaled in a rush. He scarcely dared speak, to push his luck, but he had to know. In the stories, people never asked, and while he knew he would pay the cost, he wanted to know the price. He had to know.

"And in exchange?"

Fenton smiled. It was not a terrible smile. He showed no fangs. Yet Prior's blood went cold nonetheless.

"You said Old Nan had two sons. I, too, have a sibling. You will help me find them. You will help me kill them."

After they had been walking for some time, when Prior's heart once more beat a steady rhythm in his chest, he chanced a look back at the forest. It was gone. There remained only the low rise of a perfectly ordinary gorse-dappled hill, a stream with starlight caught on the surface, and what might have been a pile of old and broken wood.

Swallowing thickly, Prior turned around and continued walking. The forest walked beside him.

THE HAND THAT REACHES
FROM BENEATH THE WAVES

A diamond drowned in the dark. They had known the sea once, known the rich texture of its hidden places and all the many rivers that reached from its depths like branches from a colossal tree. Not that the diamond thought much of trees, when they thought at all, but in the dark they grasped for what they knew. Clung to familiar refrains.

For one long lifetime, the diamond had known the sea and the sky and the promise of the moon. Islands rose and coastlines quivered and tempests thrashed at their command. The diamond had choked miserable trees with rain until they drowned as they should.

Then into the vastness of blue forever, lightning struck, and stone hands and dirt bodies piled upon the diamond in the crash of a leaden wave. The diamond didn't shatter beneath the blow. They couldn't shatter. Simply refused to entertain the notion. Earth smothered and choked the diamond, and they shone all the more brilliantly in the muck, but shining when there were none of note to see became exhausting. Time passed and the diamond's light dimmed. Their shadow grew.

Sometimes they remembered scratches scoring their

face.

Sometimes they remembered a forest.

They thought of trees more and more. Did trees still grow, somewhere beyond the stone? Did roots yet learn the hidden waterways of the earth?

More scratching. More stone. Locking tight like a pearl in a shell, the diamond gathered their shadow to protect the truth at their core. When lightning struck again, it tore away the diamond's shadow and the diamond *screamed*. Stone scorched. Blood boiled and flesh bubbled and sloughed away and then there were two where there should only ever have been one, and the diamond let themself be buried in the grave that had been made for them.

Yet water always found a way. Through stone and dirt and shadow, water oozed a determined course toward the diamond in their grave. The stale, brackish trickles might have been insulting to one who carried tides in the many facets of their splintered heart, but the trickles had touched the sea once. They carried salt and secrets. They were welcome as floods. Cupping their shaking, bloody hands, the diamond drank eagerly. They swallowed the tears of the world.

They learned that the forest had woken, and laughed.

PART TWO:
NO HEDGES ONLY OAKS

A night and a day stretched between the forest where Prior had found a god and Prior's village. The distance felt vaster, the path darker. He had left Ashcroft buoyed by the twin fervours of panic and hope, but he returned with a sunken tread, not least because he'd scarcely slept in days. Light from the bold near-full moon transformed the world into a silvery landscape, like something from a dream, though the aches in Prior's body were a decidedly corporeal concern. His muscles were rigid from the constant tension of walking side by side with a being able to— Well. Prior didn't know what Fenton could do, exactly, but where there once stood a forest, one stood no longer, and that had been demonstration of power enough to make further questions foolish.

Though Prior spoke no questions aloud, they spoke themselves in his mind as he struggled to comprehend what he'd seen. If he'd seen anything at all. He shied from the memory; it seemed his feelings swung from fear to disbelief with every step he took. From awe to doubt. The cut on his palm seemed sufficiently convincing, yet perhaps he'd been overtired, and had imagined— Then he'd glimpse Fenton in his periphery and know he couldn't imagine such a man. Such a being. Sylvie had ever been the one of them with a skill for stories.

Prior kept walking. They were progressing along a worn trail toward Ashcroft: behind them, the trail led to coastal settlements favoured by merchants and wreckers, while in their current direction it would eventually lead to the walled city, Northrope. Between their feet and Northrope, however, lay little but superstition, moorland hamlets, and land with too few hands to farm. Ashcroft alone offered a beacon to Prior, and even then, year on year the light grew dimmer.

On either side of the trail, scrub rolled outward until meeting the untamed spread of the moors. The season was too early for much gorse, besides those forest spirit strains, but by midsummer there would be butter-yellow spread to the horizon, and soon after purple heather would dapple the higher peaks. Grazing animals had occupied this part of the moorland when Prior was young, but war had seen to the farmers, and opportunity taken the beasts to other pastures. The Aspinwick Estate had claimed much of the surrounding land but had placed no urgency on tenanting it. Rumours said Aspinwick had gained its fortune from wreckers on the coast, which could well be true, but Prior didn't see how that led to leaving good land fallow. Surely more wealth would be favourable to less.

The combination of neglect, the season, and the trail's position on the lower belt of the moors meant the view offered little but tumbling stone boundary walls and scrub grass until they reached Ashcroft.

In truth, Prior would have welcomed the distraction of scenery. His legs ached and his feet burned. Rain had softened the ground and the weight of clinging mud made each step heavier than the last. The leather of his boots was cracked and his toes were going numb. Night stretched before him like a yawning creature, Prior stumbling unheedingly up its tongue. It would consume him whole.

If Fenton didn't first.

Prior dared a sidelong glance at his companion. Moonlight cast Fenton farther still from quotidian and into fantasy, paring him to the truth of a fox-faced spirit with unblinking eyes and ceaseless energy. They had marched through the night, but Fenton's pace hadn't faltered; his narrow shoulders were rounded, his head forward, and his easy lope unflagging. The strange black fabric encasing Fenton's legs shimmered in the moonlight. Fenton wore no other clothing save a crown of snowdrops resting on his pointed ears, but he demonstrated no awareness of the chill lingering in the dark.

How could Prior explain such a being to his village? Fenton had promised to lift their curse. Would that be enough to excuse his oddness? Prior wasn't naive enough to imagine none would pass comment on his companion; Ashcroft wasn't so big that strangers went unnoticed. The rest of the moorland held a handful of smaller villages that had long eked by largely on the contents of each others' pockets, and war had made their lives smaller still. Prior's life had never been destined for largeness.

Yet he walked with one who wore the guise of a man cut from starlight. Nerves knotted Prior's stomach and he clenched his hands around the stave of his unstrung longbow, needing the familiar touch. He checked the uneven ground as best he could in the dark, then looked again to Fenton, drawn like a mouse to a snake.

And like a snake to a mouse, Fenton caught Prior's eyes. Vines moved in the shadowed mass of his hair. "Your eyes flutter like a bird seeking a place to land. Why is this?"

Prior nearly stumbled over a rock and had to tear his gaze from Fenton to concentrate more fully on the ground; his vision had adjusted to the night, but it remained limited. Heat crawled across Prior's nape and bit the tips of his ears at Fenton's question. How to answer? Prior watched Fenton because Fenton was terrifying, and because Fenton was beautiful.

Think of Sylvie.

Prior's gut churned with shame. How dare he think of anything other than his sister? She might be dead as he wasted time admiring a pretty face.

She wasn't dead.

Prior gritted his teeth and redoubled his concentration on his surroundings, digging deep into what energy remained in him. Long as his journey had been thus far, he couldn't allow further delay.

"Prior." Fenton said Prior's name like a rock dropping down a well.

Prior upped his stride. "I'm tired, that's all. I haven't slept. I can't sleep."

"Are your people near?"

"We should reach Ashcroft after noon. Soon after. We can walk through the night, it's no matter."

Fenton grunted, a low, almost animalistic noise, and resumed his loping pace. Prior pushed himself to match it, battling his body as each step shocked up his legs and made his empty stomach lurch. His eyes burned. His tongue grew thick in his mouth. Darkness crept into his vision as if the night were falling anew. He blinked it back. Pushed himself. His hips hurt. His fingers cramped around his bow.

The next time he stumbled over a rock, Prior crumpled to the ground and there remained. The relief of stopping muted sensation for a moment, but then the sharp pain in the back of his head, the throbbing around his ribs, and the hot twist of his ankle all made themselves known. He trembled at the impossibility of having to stand. Having to walk. He couldn't walk any farther. Prior lay flat on his back and glared at the moon as if it were at fault.

Fenton—having not paused when Prior fell—finally returned. He blocked out the moonlight as he loomed over Prior like a heron at a pond.

"You have stopped," Fenton said, as if Prior hadn't yet

noticed.

Prior huffed a laugh, then winced as his ribs protested. "I have indeed."

Fenton inhaled deeply, his mouth hanging slightly open. When he inclined his head, the night-grey buds of his crown shifted. Perhaps, if Prior were able to see Fenton's eyes, he might recognise the look as predatory. He was glad for the dark.

"You bleed afresh," Fenton said.

That would explain the wet sensation spreading across Prior's scalp. Head wounds made themselves known with high drama. Yet his vision didn't blur and his ears didn't ring, and when Prior took a steadying breath nothing in his chest objected. Cuts and bruises only.

"Might you help me up? We can be on our way." Prior reached out in expectation of aid.

Prior's hand went ignored. Fenton's attention drifted away and he raised his head, one pointed ear toward the sky. Prior's hands went clammy. Blood treacled his scalp. He moved to push himself up, bracing himself as best he could, and Fenton's gaze swung back to him. In a swift movement, Fenton grasped Prior's hand—Fenton's skin was shockingly warm—and heaved him upright with no apparent effort. Prior staggered as he found his feet, but Fenton clasped him firmly, his other hand going to support Prior's waist.

Prior swallowed. "Shall we go—"

"No." Fenton's stare pinned Prior into place. "You will sleep." His speech picked up speed, as if the wheels of his voice had been greased. "There is a burrow. You will sleep. Heal."

"There's nothing here but dead grass, I don't..." Prior trailed off as Fenton pointed to an oak tree that had appeared from nowhere, and yet the roots rumpled the ground beneath Prior's toes. "I don't understand," Prior said, weakly.

It would take at least six adults with arms outstretched

to ring the tree, so huge it was, and the mass of aboveground roots did, indeed, appear to form some kind of shelter. Prior glanced inside, as much as he could in the dark, and confirmed the space held either a burrow or a pit. Yet neither tree nor burrow had been present before Prior fell; he would have had to walk right past it. He would've seen it on the horizon as they approached.

Prior pressed his free hand to his head. The coolness of his skin helped calm his rushing mind.

"Prior." Again, Fenton spoke Prior's name like some threw rocks. Straight into the back of Prior's head, where it sat for him to trip over the memory. "You must rest."

"I can't, I have to get to Ashcroft!"

"If you die before you arrive in your village, do you imagine I will continue on alone?"

Ready to argue that he wouldn't *die* from lack of sleep, the rest of Fenton's words sunk their claws into Prior's ears, and he snapped his mouth closed hard enough his teeth clacked. The indifference of Fenton's tone utterly snuffed the heat of Prior's protest. Fenton was right. As much as Prior loathed the idea, he alone had gained Fenton's agreement to lift the curse: without Prior to reciprocate his end of the deal, why would Fenton keep to their bargain? Nothing compelled him.

Prior wasn't entirely sure why Fenton had decided to help him at all. He shouldn't encourage Fenton to question his motivations likewise. Prior rubbed his face. He mightn't die from lack of sleep, true, but Sylvie wouldn't survive if his mind were a dull blade instead of a sharp knife when he needed to wield it. Sylvie needed him to be at his best. She would tell him as much, when he saw her again. As she would chastise him for being woefully underprepared for the situation in which he found himself; but if anyone *could* have been prepared for Fenton, Prior would dearly like to meet them.

Or, on second thoughts, perhaps not.

Conceding to Fenton with a tight nod, Prior allowed

himself to be helped to the burrow and lowered onto the surprisingly soft moss blanket nestled in the roots. Fenton rested Prior's bow beside him.

"You will rest," Fenton said, his tone somewhere between command and question.

"I will rest," Prior agreed with a sigh.

He curled up as best he could, and slept.

The human was still bleeding. Fenton could smell it. Taste it. He watched Prior snuffle in his fitful rest. Did his wounds pain him? Fenton curled his fingers into fists. Vines nudged through his hair, one more insistent than the others; when he pulled it around to see, he found jagged leaves and small clusters of white flowers. A healing plant. Humming lowly, Fenton plucked the flowers and chewed them slightly, then applied the crude poultice to the wounds on Prior's head and palm, setting Prior's bandage aside. Prior twitched but didn't wake.

Fenton withdrew his fingers and licked Prior's blood from them. Fragile creatures, humans. Easy to hurt. He cleaned all traces of Prior's blood from his fingers and ran his tongue across his teeth, trying to taste all he could of Prior, to learn the unexpected places where Prior was weak so that Fenton might know where to be strong. The urge confused him and the knot in his chest drew tighter. He had forgotten so much of the world.

He pressed his hand to the tree he had borrowed from the forest that he now contained within himself. The tree murmured in its deep slumber, its leaves barely rustling. Its branches were empty of birds—the birds didn't belong to the forest, nor anywhere of the earth—but the air thrummed with clicking and chirping and the calls of bats to their fellows. Fenton wasn't lonely. He didn't know how to be.

He didn't want to learn how. As he had walked beside

Prior, Fenton had become aware how thin the ice of his guise, and how volatile the waters beneath. He didn't want the ice to break. He scarcely remembered a life before the forest. Pies from the stone and fighting with his sibling, but little more than that, and no notion of period or place. Memories were as a story a bird had told him. He saw no reason to change that.

Yet with each step taken into the world, he stretched himself into a new—or perhaps old—shape. Already his speech came more quickly, as if the river of Prior's company were wearing Fenton's rocks smooth. His hands no longer seemed outlandish without their twisting vines. He didn't expect to see talons on his feet. The forest had been a place outside of time, and within its borders Fenton had been a thing outside himself, but Prior had asked for aid and the white-tailed stag had answered with Fenton. Or Fenton had answered with the white-tailed stag.

He glanced at Prior, and away with a grunt. Prior had released the lock on the cage Fenton hadn't realised trapped him. For that, watching over Prior's sleep was the least Fenton could do.

Fenton circled the tree once, and then again, and on his third pass sat with his back against the trunk, on the opposite side to where Prior dreamt. His shadow stretched out from where it had been covering his lower limbs, and Fenton charged it with guarding Prior's dreams. Inhaling Prior's pleasant fern scent and relaxing into the embrace of the tree, Fenton let his mind take flight.

The magic in the world outside his forest held the familiar texture of the small magic of living creatures, but as Fenton stretched his senses he found a vastness of intent: large workings of charms and spells, influence both overt and covert, flecks of superstition and prayer, and chirring resonance from huge, enchanted undertakings for which Fenton couldn't fathom the purpose. Magical noise clattered his senses and made him unable to be certain of malignant influence at work, much less a possible source of Prior's blight. Perhaps the surfeit of magic was simply the world's truth, now.

Yet he could also tell the dew had become brackish, animals he encountered carried the first scent of rot in their living flesh, and greenery that should have been flourishing at the promise of spring remained sleeping with winter, or else had rushed to mulch. Focusing his mind, Fenton consumed the ghosts of petty magics and tried to taste their living shapes. The truth in the rot.

The dryad came to him between one breath and another. They tweaked one of his toes and darted away before Fenton opened his eyes.

"Caught you napping!" the dryad sang, twirling in place with their arms raised above their head. Leaves whisked around them in a playful, sweet-scented breeze. "Lazy fox. Lazy vines. Dance with me!"

Fenton rubbed the ache at his temples as he watched the dryad dance. Their dappled green fur was winter-thick, and of a lustre that indicated they were of good health, and though their flower garlands were few—showing their youth—the yellow daisies and pink hyacinth were flush with colour. There had been no dryads in Fenton's forest, but he knew their kin of old; the knowledge sat deep in the deadwood heart of him.

"There is one sleeping," he told the dryad, for what little it would matter to them. "I cannot dance with you tonight."

"Then another night?" the dryad asked, their tone comically sly.

"Perhaps."

They twirled and hopped their way closer to him, exclaiming as they did. "I shall take that as a promise! You promised! No one has danced with you for moons and *moons*, we ain't seen a single twig of you, not a solitary tuft of fur. Why is that?"

"Perhaps none of me was fit for seeing." Fenton lowered his voice pointedly. "I mentioned the one sleeping, did I not?"

"You did." Seeming to accept that Fenton did not intend to move, the dryad ceased their dancing and plonked themself beside Fenton's outstretched legs. They poked him in the knee. "Is this a new shape? Got no fluff nor tail, and nowhere to hide, neither."

"An old one."

"And your sleeper?"

Fenton hummed. "A new one. I think. I do not recall having met them before."

"You think? Aha! I have a thinking dance, would you like to see it?"

"Not now."

The dryad flopped onto their back. Leaves gusted up with their extravagant sigh, then floated down again. They kicked their heels in the air. "No one said you were *boring*."

Fenton had grabbed the dryad's leg before he registered the impulse to move. Vines erupted from his palm to bind the young creature's lower limbs and began crawling over their body, knotting leg to leg even as the dryad struggled against his hold. Black hellebore bloomed on the vines as the dryad thrashed, their fur bristling and their leaves buffeting in an eddy that failed to dislodge Fenton. He combed through their fur with his claws, not pressing in, not yet. The dryad trembled. Their flowers began to pale.

"I'm sorry, your most fragrant foxliness! Your high oak fearsomeness!" the dryad babbled, their voice shrill.

Fenton snarled into the belly of the night. Birds and bats and insects silenced. The dryad ceased struggling. Fear shivered through their fur and their scent turned acrid as they bared their throat for the fangs that gleamed in Fenton's muzzle. The dryad's blood would be thick as sap. Fenton licked his lips.

He tasted Prior's blood.

Snarling again, Fenton wrenched his vines loose from the dryad and banished his claws and fangs. Working his jaw, he leaned heavily against the tree and flexed his fingers, kneading his hands against the damp grass. Insects cautiously renewed their chittering, but the dryad continued to lie in place, trembling. Fenton considered them. Dryads held an immense store of magical energy, such that Fenton might require to lift Prior's blight, and many green-furred siblings danced in the woods of the world.

Prior snuffled. When Fenton stiffened, his shadow relayed to him Prior had but changed position in his sleep. Fenton returned his attention to the quaking dryad, their scent sharp with fear. Huffing in sudden frustration, Fenton plucked a snowdrop from his crown and flicked it at the dryad.

"A gift, since I will not dance with you," he said, relaxing against the tree. Gifts were how he showed favour, and by the light in the dryad's eyes, they recognised the significance.

Moving quickly, as if afraid Fenton might change his mind, the dryad grabbed the flower and stuffed it into their mouth, chewed ferociously, and swallowed. They licked their lips to chase all remnants of the gift. Then they leapt to their feet and patted themself down, watching Fenton keenly as they did. Their checks completed, they stilled. Their scent sweetened.

"Do you want my name?" they asked in a whisper.

"If you would give it freely."

The dryad darted forward and dropped to their knees beside him, leaning in so close his vines twisted away. Their fur held the scent of honey and snow.

"Burdock is what they call me," they said.

Fenton inclined his head. "Then Burdock is what I shall call you."

Flushing a lush green, Burdock pressed a chaste kiss to Fenton's cheek then cackled and somersaulted backwards, ending with a flourish and a hop that brought them upright. They opened their mouth as if to crow, but snapped it closed with a fearful flicker of their eyes toward

Prior.

"Will you search for dance partners elsewhere, Burdock?" Fenton asked, hoping he wouldn't have to entertain the youngling through to dawn.

Their expression sobered. "No one wants to dance of late. There's ill magic here, and all manner of metal and death what turns creatures away from their nature. I seen a village clear gone to sleeping. My siblings and I are leaving the moorlands and travelling southerly. You should leave as well." Burdock's leaves rustled with agitation. "If'n you want to, I mean, your magnificent foxliness. Your supremely handsome treeful—"

"The blight is why I am here," Fenton interrupted. Burdock hadn't asked his name and he didn't care to hear every version the dryads had exchanged among themselves.

"You're intending to break it?"

Fenton found himself glad Burdock had not assumed Fenton had caused the blight. He hadn't known he held the worry.

He nodded. "If I can."

Burdock whipped up their arms, conjuring a dance of leaves, and grinned as gaily as if Fenton had never bared fangs at them. As they hopped, they turned, and their voice travelled to him on the breeze as they danced away into the night, all chastising about volume forgotten.

"You can!" Burdock yelled to the moon and whoever else listened. "You can, you will, you shall!"

Fenton snorted. Such groundless faith. He knew little of himself, but more than enough to know he was not the type people asked favours from, merely attempted to placate. He steepled his hands together and tapped his fingertips, each tap causing a bud to burst from his fingernails, flourishing into colour before closing their faces again. He plucked one of the flowers from his thumb and chewed it, thinking. Burdock's claim of "ill magic" proved the blight bothered more than humans. Fenton

40

needed to learn more if he were to have any chance of breaking it. Prior and his village would provide more information.

Could Fenton break the blight? Certainly, in time all things were possible. A river could destroy the largest boulder, given time. Fenton picked a stray petal from his lips and considered it. He rubbed the silky petal between his fingers and inhaled the musky fragrance.

In truth, he couldn't be certain of his ability to break the blight, not without more information. Just as he couldn't be certain the bargain he had struck with Prior— to break the blight in exchange for assistance killing Fenton's sibling—was anything he wanted. But it had been the first notion that found his tongue. Did that make it a truth of the heart?

Perhaps. But Fenton had deadwood where a heart should beat.

Fenton ate the petal. He rested his head against the sturdy trunk behind him and listened to the song of the night, and to Prior's steady, sleeping, breaths.

Prior woke as dawn touched the horizon, the thin sliver of sky he could see misty with morning. For a handful of breaths he savoured the lingering peace of sleep as he watched the thin sun rise through his half-closed eyes.

Then he remembered Fenton, and shocked awake. The roots of Fenton's tree were reluctant to release him, but Prior managed to shove himself free of the grabby foliage and crawl from the burrow. Breathing hard, he finally looked up, only to recoil on finding Fenton crouched not an armlength away, watching Prior with a serene expression. Fenton had not, Prior was sure, been there a moment ago.

"G-good morning," Prior offered, while discretely flexing his fingers and toes to check all were present. As he did, he frowned, and glanced at his hand: where he'd sliced across his palm for the ritual-that-wasn't, nothing remained but a raised red sliver, appearing days old rather than hours. "Did you heal this?" he asked, the words forming strangely in his mouth. "That is— I mean, thank you. If you did."

Fenton blinked. Then he thrust out his hand and Prior jerked back again, narrowly avoiding cracking his head on the tree trunk. The vines in Fenton's hair flickered, distracting Prior briefly from the bloodied... something... Fenton held in his hand: a lump of pallid flesh, split open to reveal bones and a mess of organs. Blood smeared from Fenton's fingertips halfway to his elbow, glittering in places. Prior swallowed thickly.

"Eat," Fenton said. He had blood on his teeth, at the corner of his mouth.

Despite the hard seasons and poor harvests that had dogged the moorlands, not to mention the stress-thin meals he'd barely eaten since Sylvie had fallen ill, Prior suddenly found himself absolutely replete. Yet could one refuse the gift of such a being as Fenton? Was this a trick?

He eyed the flesh in Fenton's hand. The speckles of light dotting Fenton's bloodied skin were scales, Prior realised; Fenton had been fishing. Prior had thought the river all but empty, another consequence of the curse.

Prior licked his lips. He met Fenton's eyes. "I thank you, but I can't— Humans can't eat fish like that. It needs to be cleaned and cooked."

Fenton's gaze slid to the fish, then back to Prior. He withdrew his hand slowly, as if Prior might change his mind, then ducked his head and shoved the fish into his mouth. His teeth flashed once. Bones cracked and Prior quelled a flinch. Didn't people choke on fish bones? Another crack. Prior rubbed his face and glanced surreptitiously between his fingers toward his pack; his knife glinted in the open mouth, clean as it had been the day before. Fenton hadn't borrowed it. Not that Prior would have objected if he had. He merely observed that Fenton had apparently caught and torn apart the fish with his hands.

An interesting observation. That was all.

Finished with his breakfast, Fenton licked the side of his hand with broad swipes of his tongue, cleaning it of watery blood and scales. He licked in swathes as Prior struggled with where to put his attention, shifting uncomfortably.

"There's water in my pack, if you— No, you're happy with the licking, I see." With effort, Prior tore his gaze away and rose to his feet, where he dusted himself off briskly for what little good it served. He couldn't spend all morning staring. He had to return to Ashcroft.

Drinking sparingly from the waterskin in his pack, and eating some of the provisions he had rationed for his journey, Prior then gathered his bow and stepped pointedly onto the westerly turn of the trail. He couldn't bring himself to hasten Fenton along verbally, and though Prior knew that the presumption in even the minor action should make him wary, he felt removed from it. Indeed, he felt only nebulously connected to his body at all, as if he had not truly yet awoken, and his actions were but a dream. Perhaps the entirety of the past few days were but a dream, and Prior lay sleeping beside Sylvie, and neither of them would wake.

"What can you eat?" Fenton asked, suddenly from behind him. He had moved silently, and the pressure of his presence at Prior's back taught Prior the exquisite fear of a prey animal.

Prior closed his eyes. "I have provisions in my pack."

"I would provide."

I would provide. What did that mean? Prior opened his eyes and stared hard at the trail ahead, forcing his words steady. "It's early in the year for gorse, but there might be chickweed or dandelion growing nearby. Or—"

"I understand. I will go."

The weight of Fenton's presence lifted and Prior exhaled hard in relief. He didn't look after Fenton, but set out shakily westward, his bow propped over his shoulder. Another careful sip from his waterskin did little for his dry mouth, but the village well would be cool when he reached it. And he *would* reach it. Prior let his conviction draw him onward, and tried not to jump at every darting shadow that moved in the hedgerow hugging the trail.

After half a mile or so, Fenton caught up with him, and silently offered a handful of wild carrot and dandelion. In return, Prior gave him the last strip of salted meat from the pack, and they both ate as they walked. Rest—and possibly Fenton's intervention—had solved much of Prior's hurts from the day before, but the morning chilled his skin, and he walked more briskly in an effort to escape it. Fenton didn't exhibit any concern over the cold, if he even noticed it. He spent the morning ranging across the land near the trail, away from Prior and back again, as if Prior were a tether.

Each time Fenton rejoined him, Prior noted another aspect of his companion: the vines in his hair, sometimes still, sometimes in motion, but also the odd-shaped scar on his shoulder, the sculpted curve of his calves, the unconscionably intriguing slope of his back. Fenton's semi-undressed state kept surprising Prior, and as they drew close to Ashcroft he wondered if they shouldn't wait for the cover of night; Fenton wore little but his strangeness, and it made him seem vulnerable. Then Fenton returned from one of his wanderings with blood on his teeth and reminded Prior of the truth: Fenton mightn't wear much clothing, but power cloaked him like the promise of a storm.

Now Ashcroft waited mere paces away, bright noon buffing the village to a generous shine. Prior drew to a stop and rested the tip of his bow on the top of his boot. Children played a game of sticks and bones in front of the inn while a skinny mutt lolled at their feet. He could hear some folk nearby whistling, perhaps pinning out washing, while rhythmic clanging from the smithy acted as discordant accompaniment. Smoke curled from chimneys, and one of the Greaves boys stood on their roof, yelling at his brother. The thatch must need patching again.

In truth, most of Ashcroft needed some kind of tending. A generation ago, war had marched along the Great Road and left little in its wake; Prior could still read the resultant neglect in Ashcroft's tired thatch, on the scarred walls, and swinging from doors loose on their hinges. In empty buildings that would have been taken by newlyweds, had not so many of Ashcroft's children gone to war, like his and Sylvie's parents had. Those too young to fight had been left in the care of those too old; his grandmother had refused to speak of the war, as if silence were a ward, while Sylvie and he had spoke of little else, until they grew old enough to comprehend the chasm of their loss. Until silence warded them as well.

Sylvie. The heaviest weight on Prior's body. At the far end of the village, past the inn and the Greaves boys and the well and the falling-down statue of a long-dead lord, Prior's sister might be dead, the fire of their cottage gone cold. He blinked furiously and firmed his trembling lip, yet couldn't bring himself to lift his feet. Another step seemed impossible. At the threshold of the village, Prior lived in ignorance of Sylvie's fate. He could turn, now, and leave. If he could move.

Prior might have stood there forever, but a bleating noise drew him toward Fenton, whose latest venture had taken him to one of the goats that had the run of the village; they ostensibly belonged to the smithy, Baltair, but in truth Baltair belonged to the goats. Fenton crouched by a gruff, grey creature and was humming at it. The goat bleated again in response.

At any other time, Prior might have laughed, but at the edge of the village where he stood, in that moment where he waited, Sylvie lived. He dared not find joy in anything else in case it diminished the profundity of that.

"Do you wait on me?" Fenton asked Prior, glancing over his shoulder.

Prior sniffed. He shook his head. "I wait on my courage. I find myself overcome."

A huff of breath. An assessing look. Visibly dismissing Prior as not his concern, Fenton rose. He made for the village proper, his long strides quickly eating up the distance. The children paused their game as he passed and the dog rolled over to watch. People elbowed each other and turned hard eyes on Fenton's oblivious back. Ashcroft was more used to passing travellers than elsewhere in the moorlands, but that didn't mean all were welcome, and Prior didn't want to chance Fenton being where the line was drawn. Prior cursed and jolted into motion, grabbing his bow and hurrying to catch up.

He puffed as he drew beside Fenton. "*What* are you do— Good morning, Goodwoman Hilde," Prior said, slowing to duck his head respectfully at the woman beating a rug in front of her cottage. Goodwoman Hilde harrumphed in her typical manner, not pausing in her work. Prior reached for an explanation and hoped Goodwoman Hilde's attention did not stray to Fenton or his vines. "This is a, ah, a friend of mine. A traveller from the north."

"Your half-naked friend know there's a sickness? Better off back where he came from," she said, delivering the rug a particularly violent thwap. Dust steeled her fading hair.

"Yes, Goodwoman Hilde. Thank you." When they had passed the property, Prior lowered his voice to grumble. "Thank you for your typical friendliness and ever-so-useful advice."

Fenton eyed Prior sidelong but didn't comment. Prior's cheeks heated. He'd known the sharp crack of Goodwoman Hilde's wooden spoon on his knuckles, and the bruises remained, indelible, in his mind. Her pie had definitely not been worth it.

Thankfully, most villagers were in the fields, sowing or tending to whatever they could grow in the grip of the curse, and weren't around to gawk at Fenton. They did pass another group of children, too small to be working, who stared with rounded eyes at Fenton, one reaching for him only to have their arm tugged back by another. Prior didn't begrudge their caution, only hoped it went unfounded. As he followed Fenton through Ashcroft, the loping stride that had suited the moorland seemed sinister among the familiar confines of the village, and Prior worried if he hadn't opened the village to something worse than the sickness. He and Fenton had struck a bargain, true, but what defence did that offer, in the end? Life for death. The thought chilled him.

He couldn't think on it. Not yet. He didn't have capacity in head nor heart for anything but Sylvie; a mere sliver of unbruised flesh remained, and it winnowed away beat by beat. There would be ample time later for regret.

Fortunately, Fenton was trying to pick up a goose, which provided sufficient diversion to the maudlin turn of Prior's thoughts.

"Put her *down*! Bloody flux, don't you know those beasts have teeth?" Prior whispered furiously, swatting Fenton's arm to make him drop the goose.

The goose fell, snapping its beak but otherwise none the worse for wear. Prior, however...

Prior's hand remained on Fenton's elbow, where he'd swatted him. Where he'd thoughtlessly swatted a forest spirit like he would a misbehaving child. Like he would argue with his sister, ready to duck her inevitable retaliation. He wouldn't be able to avoid Fenton's retribution.

Fenton regarded the offending hand dispassionately. The absolute stillness of him made Prior clammy with fear. Sound rushed in his ears like he had water stuck in them.

"I need that hand to kill your sibling," Prior said quickly. He didn't snatch his hand away—moving seemed counterproductive to keeping his fingers—but he thought about motion very, very strongly. The fingers of his other hand twitched around his bow so violently he dropped it. "Please. Sorry. Please."

The goose honked rudely.

Fenton blinked. His eyes, Prior noticed, were the colour of grave dirt. Fresh, wet earth. He tried not to interpret the colour as a sign. The vines in Fenton's hair curled around his crown of white flowers, readjusting it as a nervous man might his hat. Thorns sprouted from the interwoven stems. Beauty and danger blossomed on Fenton. A living rose. Prior couldn't look away.

Fenton's gaze flickered to Prior's dropped bow, then to Prior's hand, still on his elbow. Without changing expression, he patted Prior's hand twice, then pushed it away. Wordlessly, he plucked Prior's bow from the ground and continued on through the village.

For a long moment, Prior held one hand in the other, cradling himself as he might a wounded bird. As if beseeching. Could Fenton hear prayers? Prior couldn't recall making one, but perhaps the terror in his heart had sung out and Fenton had heard. Yet Fenton's indifference suggested Prior had only imagined giving offence. The vast chasm of understanding yawned between Prior and Fenton. Prior didn't know how to approach crossing it.

He wrinkled his nose. Best not question his luck. Sylvie always said—

"Fuck. *Sylvie.*"

Prior ran toward their cottage at the edge of the village, which Fenton had somehow found unerringly: Prior saw Fenton's back as he slipped through their open door. Why was the door open? Had the village already emptied the property with no one to occupy—?

"Sylvie!" Prior burst through the door, and cursed as he almost tripped over another damn goose.

A firm hand caught Prior and righted him before he could fall. Grave-dirt eyes caught his and buried him.

"Hush." Fenton inclined his head toward the bed by the window. "She sleeps."

Prior swallowed against the knot in his throat. Sylvie didn't appear to have moved since he left for the forest. Her stillness on the narrow bed—beneath the window, so she might see the sun—made Prior think Fenton had attempted kindness in saying she slept, until he saw the thin blankets rise. The air smelled thick with stale sweat and the lingering char of smoke. He swallowed to clear the dryness from his throat.

As he went to the bed, Prior noted a clay cup and shallow bowl at Sylvie's bedside, both empty: Baltair had been by with food at least once, then. Prior must thank him for taking the risk. The sickness didn't seem contagious, but no one knew for certain and Prior had traded on his friendship with Baltair for Sylvie's sake. He owed the man. Prior's debts were growing breath by breath.

"She looks cold," Prior murmured. Sylvie's freckles were like ink spots on her pallid skin. The curls of her hair stuck to her sweaty brow and he gently brushed them away, then readjusted the blankets more closely around her. "Should I close the window? She prefers it open. But should the wind carry sickness—"

"The window matters not," Fenton interrupted, his voice low.

Prior glanced over his shoulder. Fenton had set Prior's bow against the wall and he was examining the inner side of the open door, head tilted, hands on his slim hips. As Prior watched, Fenton stuck out his tongue and licked the scratches on the door, then pulled a face like a child trying a new food. His vines rippled in his hair. Prior opened his mouth to ask what Fenton had expected a door to taste like, but he thought better of the question. Fenton might answer.

Prior found himself smiling at Sylvie as he imagined what she might make of the peculiar visitor to their home.

She had loved their grandmother's stories.

Overcome with sudden fury, Prior swiped roughly at his eyes. Sylvie *loved* those stories. *Loved*.

Prior's hands shook as he adjusted Sylvie's blankets again. He watched her breathe, shallow but even. With each breath she took, he managed another of his own.

"Why doesn't the window matter, then?" Prior finally thought to ask, voice swampy in his ears.

He started when Fenton appeared at his shoulder, close enough to feel the heat rising from Fenton's bare skin. They needed to find him some proper clothes. Prior caught sight of the mud caking Fenton's feet and added boots to his mental list. The surmountable task was pleasing to consider, if asinine. He clung by his fingernails to normality. Shirt, boots, perhaps trousers if Fenton desired. They were of a similar size, and Fenton the smaller, so Prior's old clothes might suffice—

"The mark on her throat. What is it?" Fenton asked.

Prior frowned. He had seen no mark. Leaning closer, he moved the blanket he had tucked over Sylvie's neck. A faint discolouration, almost like a fingerprint, bruised her skin.

"Dirt?" Prior suggested.

Fenton made an odd noise through his teeth, like a bird call, if the bird had been trapped in a barrel of nails. He leaned over Sylvie and for a terrible moment Prior thought Fenton would lick her, and he didn't know how to prevent it from happening, but Fenton only sniffed deeply and withdrew. He wrinkled his nose. His eyes grew distant.

Impatient, Prior raised his eyebrows. "What is it?"

Fenton tilted his head. "Salt and ash."

Salt and— It was like speaking to a rock but somehow even less helpful. Fenton had no sense of urgency. Sylvie was dying and he didn't *care*.

Taking a fortifying breath, Prior reminded himself that Fenton *didn't* care. He released his tight hold of Sylvie's blankets. Smoothed them flat. Fenton was not like him.

Prior needed to remember that.

"What does 'salt and ash' mean? Is it the curse?" Prior asked.

"Of a kind. This place reeks of my sibling's magic," Fenton replied.

"Y-your sibling? A sister? A brother?" Prior hadn't thought to ask before. It didn't matter, but he couldn't parse the implications of Fenton's statement.

"Sometimes."

Prior blew out a breath. It didn't *matter*. Fenton could be as obtuse as he wanted, if only he would break the curse. But then Fenton jolted, so slightly Prior only noticed due to their close proximity, and squinted into the middle distance. He slid his gaze to Prior.

"You may call them Lorcan, if you must."

Lorcan. A name it seemed Fenton had just remembered, though surely that couldn't be the case. Prior nonetheless filed the name and Fenton's odd reaction away for future consideration.

"Thank you for telling me," he said.

Fenton returned his attention to the window. To the world beyond Sylvie's sickbed. "I must find them. There is something untoward in their magic, and if this blight is left unchecked, it will surely drown all in its path."

Prior spoke through gritted teeth. "You will go *nowhere* without first healing Sylvie."

A muscle flickered in Fenton's jaw. He didn't meet Prior's eyes. Sunlight burnished him in gold, when it had left Sylvie a ghost of herself. Flowers bloomed in his hair in a spring garland. The sight struck Prior like a slap. He commanded himself to calm.

He spoke again, when Fenton did not. "You said you would save her."

"I cannot," Fenton said.

Prior's knuckles split open on the wood of Fenton's face.

Pain and blood and salt. Pain glazed Fenton's cheekbone, blood smeared his teeth, salt saturated the air of the little dwelling. Prior had shed many tears inside these thin walls. Fenton swallowed the memory of them as he swallowed his own blood. He reset his nose and licked his teeth clean. Then he helped Prior to sit on the edge of his sister's bed and knelt at his feet. Prior cradled one hand with the other—that hand had touched Fenton twice, now, which was twice more than any human hand he could remember—and blood daubed his skin like sunset trickling toward the horizon. Fenton wanted to smear Prior's colours on his own skin. His hands twitched on his thighs. The sight, and his reaction to it, unnerved him.

Prior was speaking but Fenton wasn't listening. He plucked a cluster of shepherd's purse from the vine insistently prodding his temple, and chewed the flowers before applying the poultice to Prior's knuckles. He had already healed this hand once; application was easier than the first time. Fenton hummed as he worked, pleased. He held Prior's hand in his.

"—are you doing? What is this?" Prior's harsh questions pricked Fenton's contentment. Prior tried to tug his hand free but Fenton held him firm.

"Hush." Fenton finished applying the poultice and tucked Prior's hands together on his lap. "Be still."

"You put your—your hair? Is that your hair? Into my open wound! I will *not* be still!"

Fenton's hands flexed around Prior's. "There were no ill effects following the first occasion, I do not understand why you prot—"

"The *first* occasion?"

"After you fell."

Colour rushed into Prior's face and his eyes lit with fire. "I *knew* I shouldn't have healed that quickly! I knew it! What else have you done?" He yanked his hands free from

Fenton's grip—Fenton let him go—but then sat in expectant silence, waiting for an answer.

He would be waiting a long time. Fenton surged to his feet, quelling the urge to steady himself as he did; tainted magic had soaked into the walls of the little den, expelled by the woman's exhalations and forming a miasma that hung in the air. Even brief exposure made Fenton's head throb. Humans were fortunate to have such limited senses. The door stood open, and the sole window, but that altered little. Magic seeped through cracks in the walls and thatch, and like gossamer it went unseen until tendrils caught in his vines.

The woman was very ill. His sibling's mark on her skin showed how close she drew to death; sigils only showed in the final stages of such things, as the body fell utterly to the other's influence, its own energies depleted. Likely other victims bore a similar mark, but to the human eye it would seem as simple bruising. The sigil proved beyond doubt that magic had splintered within her, as it had across Ashcroft and the surrounding land, seeding a rotten crop.

Fenton recognised the shape of his sibling's magic, as he recognised something had forced it from true. Like recognised like: Fenton may have remembered Lorcan but recently, and more recently still their name, but he knew the shape of their magic as he knew his shadow. He recognised Lorcan's magic like a human might know their fellow's voice over distance, yet the language Lorcan spoke was unfamiliar. Wrongness dwelt within Lorcan's magic like a poisoned seed and every branch had grown out of true as result.

Fenton was now certain the blight could be broken, but the task would not be a simple one. He needed to find Lorcan, or the rotten seed itself, and rip one or the other out. He might be the only one who could. He remembered no other sibling.

But first, Fenton must save Prior's sister. Death clung to Sylvie like honey on a comb, rot-sweet and spreading.

"Are you listening to me?" Prior demanded. Whatever awe had previously held him had fled. He shook his bloody hand, then winced. "You keep drifting away to the window. Is there something out there? More goats?" He hissed. "And what even is this potion?"

"Have you truly never encountered a poultice?" Fenton snapped. Were there not more important questions?

Prior jerked his head back. "I have, but—"

"Then leave it be and ask no more questions."

"Y-yes. Of course. I'm sorry."

The cowed demeanour had returned. A sharp ache made itself known between Fenton's ribs. He wanted to ease it with his knuckles, but what would be the purpose? The ache sat on the edge of a bed and watched him with imploring eyes, begging as fruitlessly as a fish to a hook.

"I cannot lift the magic from your sister, but I can prolong the days she has left to her. Gift her the days until the moon is dark again. That should permit time to find— To lift the blight," Fenton said, with care. He had never explained himself before. Had never been punched in the face before, either; he and his sibling had reshaped landscapes with their fighting, made the earth quake and the sea roil, but base physical confrontation, flesh to flesh, was a new experience. What a strange time.

Prior addressed his hands. "Then you can do nothing for the curse at all?"

"Not with the elements present here. That magic requires more."

"More what?"

Fenton's shadow pulsed around his legs as he quelled his instinctive response to lash out at Prior in frustration. His lack was not Prior's fault. He drew a breath and considered the messy fingerprints marring his sibling's magic.

"Who is the most powerful in this region?" he asked.

"The most powerf— Magic user, do you mean? There's a hedgewitch in the next village, she saw to it when one of

Baltair's goats went near lame last summer. Reasonable prices, too."

"No. No hedges. Only oaks."

Prior finally looked up from his bloody knuckles. He frowned. "'Oaks'?"

"Bigger. Stronger."

"I see. Then you need a sorcerer, or a mage, or—"

"Those are all *words*." Agitation made Fenton's vines twitch. "Who is nearby? With whom may I speak?"

"I don't know. I'm sorry. Sylvie might—" Prior cuffed his eyes as sobs blurred his words. His shoulders bowed and he covered his face with his hands.

Fenton cut his eyes away as an unfamiliar sensation washed over him, like the grime of stagnant water. Prior's sniffles were loud. Fenton wanted to climb a tree. He curled his toes, dithering, then huffed out hard. With jerky motions, he plucked buds from his vines and dropped them into the shallow bowl he grabbed from Sylvie's bedside, then crushed the buds into mulch with his knuckle. He coaxed a young, thready vine from the bend of his wrist and bit it in two, using the viscous sap to bind the concoction together. Humming lowly, he licked his thumb and swiped the last remnants of blood from his face, then pressed his thumb to the paste in the bowl and massaged the blood into the mix.

At first, Prior continued to sniffle as Fenton worked, making Fenton's vines twist, but gradually curiosity began to conquer his sorrow and Prior's miserable salt-scent threaded with lively fern. The questions were irritating, but far preferable to tears. Fenton found himself drifting toward Prior, that he might better see.

"Ack! What was— Is that your blood? Was that a vein? I don't unders— Oh no, you're doing it again. That's definitely blood this time. ...I think I shall be sick."

"Move aside," Fenton said, nudging Prior away from the bed before he could either vomit or protest further. The man spoke as incessantly as birds sang. "She must drink."

"Chew, I think you mean to say. Wait, you can't give her that!"

Fenton dug his claws into the bowl. "Then she will surely die."

"I mean— I can do it."

"You cannot. This is poison to you but the blight protects her. To touch it would make you gravely ill." He didn't know if he should throw away the bowl, even.

Prior blanched. "You're giving Sylvie poison?"

If the woman had been but sleeping, she would surely have woken at the shrill pitch of Prior's question. Fenton closed his eyes briefly, commanding his fingernails back from claws.

"She can take this poison and chance to live, or she can die, and most certainly, from another kind. Choose now."

Prior rolled his lips inward into a tight line. Sweat beaded on his brow. Blinking, he stepped away from the bed and unease lurched in Fenton at the retreat. Frustration followed, though whether at Prior or himself, Fenton couldn't tell. Trees did not question. Rivers did not chatter. Birds and foxes did not weep nor rage at their own limitations.

Fenton kept meeting the boundaries of his experience, yet Prior was the one bruised from the impact. Were Fenton's failures a result of his time in the forest, or the reason he had languished there in the first place? His hands tightened around the bowl.

When Prior protested no further, Fenton carefully fed the tincture to Sylvie, coaxing her throat to swallow, then set the bowl aside and sat back on his heels. His shadow twined around his legs with comforting pressure. Splinters of sour magic worried through the air, drawn by the change in Sylvie, and crumbled as they met Fenton's rising aura. He watched the bruise of his sibling's mark on Sylvie's skin until his vision blurred and he had to rub his eyes to clear them.

The day grew long. Prior paced. A goose wandered into the house and out again. Prior sat. He opened his mouth, but closed it without speaking. Outside, voices rose in argument over a goat, a woman, gods, and gambling. Fenton kneaded his hands on his thighs. His muscles were tight. The sun finally bowed its head and Prior lit a stubby candle, making shadows snarl across the walls. The window grew dark with night.

Sylvie opened her eyes.

Prior found Fenton kneeling in the fields behind the cottage, communing with a goat. Possibly the same goat from the day before, Prior couldn't tell. Setting his bundle by the crumbling boundary wall, he perched atop of the wall and crossed his legs, content to watch Fenton as the morning stretched across the fallow field. More warmth emanated from the sunlight than he had felt for many days, easing the last traces of sleep from his bones. Someone whistled merrily. It wasn't him—Prior couldn't carry a tune for love nor money—but he appreciated the second-hand joy.

The night had been a fitful one. After Sylvie had awoken, blurry and exhausted from long days of fever, Prior had made a thin broth from their equally thin stores and sat with her, exchanging words for spoonfuls. Fenton had left almost the instant Sylvie awoke, taking the goose that had been waddling around the room with him. Sylvie hadn't asked after Fenton's presence; she'd been confused, at first, and Prior wondered if she had reckoned the half-naked man with vines in his hair to be some kind of fever dream.

To his shame, Prior had considered—only for a moment—not mentioning Fenton's involvement at all. But he and Sylvie had never lied to one another and he couldn't bring himself to start, not even for both of their comfort.

Thus, when Sylvie had entreated Prior for explanation of her recovery, he'd relayed what little he'd understood of events, including Fenton and his remedy. But when it came to the question of Fenton's nature, Prior had hesitated, not knowing how to answer. In the end, he'd said Fenton was a creature of the forest, and clearly had magic at his command, but whether for good or ill he'd been unable to say. Sylvie had accepted the non-answer, as she had wearily accepted Prior's admittance that she had not been cured of the sickness, but that her fate had merely been postponed. At the latter, disquieted understanding had lit Sylvie's tired eyes and she'd pressed her fingers to the not-bruise on her throat; she could feel the magic, she'd said. She had known it lingered.

They'd slept, not long after that. If he dreamt, Prior did not remember.

By the well, he watched as Fenton carded his fingers through the goat's ruff, then plucked a flower from his crown and offered it out on his flat palm. The flower was not one of the snowdrops Prior had become used to, but something else, and hopefully something edible. The goat bobbed its head, almost like a bow, and judiciously lapped the flower from Fenton's hand. Something loosened in Prior's chest; watching as Fenton lost his fingers to a goat would have been a poor way to start the day.

After scratching the goat about the horns, Fenton rolled fluidly to his feet and loped over. Shadows clung to the hollows beneath his ribs and Prior frowned. Had Fenton become leaner, or was it Prior's imagination?

"How fares your sister?" Fenton asked, pulling Prior's attention.

Prior shrugged. "She's awake, which is more than I had hoped, and she seems no worse, which is more than I'd expected. The fever left her weak, though, and the mark remains on her throat. She said she can feel it there."

"The sigil will linger until the blight is lifted."

"About that..." Prior rubbed the back of his neck. "This morning, I asked Sylvie if she could remember when she took sick, in case that might offer clues about the curse."

Fenton frowned. "It is my sibling at fault, I have said."

"And I heard you. Believe me, it's not the kind of thing someone can forget. But Sylvie said she distinctly remembered feeling faint out by the old well. She'd been hunting for mushrooms and they used to grow that way, so she thought— Anyway," Prior cleared his throat, adjusting course as Fenton's frown deepened. "Sylvie said she lay down that evening and didn't get up again. It's worth investigating, surely? It's not far."

They didn't know where to go next, anyway. Fenton could wander all over the countryside searching for his sibling and Sylvie would die while he searched, unless they could find some strong magic user before the moon went dark. An "oak", as Fenton had put it. Prior had asked Sylvie to ponder possible leads while he showed Fenton the old well. Distracted him, in other words. He didn't intend to mention that interpretation to Fenton. It seemed counterproductive.

"Show me this well, if you must," Fenton said, a shade imperiously.

Curious, Prior asked, "Can't you sense it? Like you knew which was my cottage?"

Some emotion crossed Fenton's pointed face—a tightening of his lips, some shade moving in his eyes—but perfect blankness wiped his expression clean before Prior could hope to name it.

"I followed your scent," Fenton explained. His vines twisted. "Water is not my domain. Might you show me this well?"

Prior relented. "Of course. But first, here." Prior grabbed the bundle from beside his feet and tossed it at Fenton, who caught it neatly. As he stared in confusion at Prior's hand-me-downs, Prior recognised the feeling bubbling in his chest as fondness. Unexpected, uninvited, and potentially dangerous, but fondness nonetheless. He quashed the feeling without compunction and jerked his chin at the clothes. "Sylvie said you can't go running around half-naked. It'll put people off their work, she said."

Whether because people would be distracted for better or worse by the spectacle, Sylvie hadn't clarified. When she'd found Prior unearthing old clothes and asked the reason, she'd raised her eyebrows at Prior's stuttering explanation, and, with a tone reminiscent of their grandmother, directed Prior to dress Fenton "before anyone gets ideas". She'd left Prior with the understanding that he, specifically, was "anyone", and that the ideas would be bad ones. He'd scoffed even as he gathered the clothes, because who got "ideas" about forest spirits?

Watching as Fenton donned Prior's tired blue tunic, Prior realised Sylvie's warning had come too late. In truth, it had been too late when he met Fenton, and only Prior's fear had kept him oblivious to his feelings until this moment. It was difficult to fear someone who saved his sister and then looked so striking in blue. Prior turned away.

After shuffling fabric and making a disconcerting wet sound that Prior chose not to wonder about, Fenton stepped beside Prior.

"The well," he said, expectantly.

"The well," Prior repeated, mostly so he didn't say anything else.

Dressed in a tunic that reached his thighs and a pair of trousers too short for Prior, Fenton somehow seemed more naked than he had wearing nothing but the odd black trousers. Which had completely disappeared. Prior glanced back at the field but found only goats. He dismissed the question. More important was wondering how Prior might focus on anything but the absolute knowledge of Fenton's vulpine beauty.

A human sort of foolishness, that the simple act of putting on clothes had brought Fenton—albeit undoubtedly temporarily—into the sphere of Prior's comprehension and softened the extreme edges of his otherworldliness. Abruptly Prior comprehended Sylvie's warning, more fully than she could have from her removed position: to dare imagine Fenton as anything other than a destructive force, to have the sheer *temerity* to fantasise about Fenton as something touchable, would kill Prior. He knew it as he knew the sun rose in the east. Yet he lingered on the newly covered parts of Fenton, on the too-long sleeves draped over his hands, at the familiar worn places of Prior's trousers made newly strange on Fenton's slender legs. On Fenton's bony feet curling into the long grass.

"No boots?" Prior asked, without meaning to speak aloud. He'd given Fenton his spare pair, battered though they were. Sometimes Sylvie wore them when it rained.

Fenton grunted. "Too heavy."

Before Prior could ask for the return of the boots—or decide how best to ask—Fenton rolled his shoulders, then leaned slightly away from Prior. When he straightened, he silently offered Prior the boots. Half-expecting to see a goat wandering off, Prior saw a slick blackness slink around Fenton's legs like an affectionate cat before fading away and leaving Prior to doubt the evidence of his eyes.

He tightened his hands around the boots, making the leather creak. All the questions he dared not ask crowded behind his teeth.

"The well is this way."

Boots in hand, Prior led Fenton to the edge of Ashcroft, not far from Goodwoman Hilde's property. Given the early hour, they passed few people, as most had already headed to till what they could from the fields or else were still abed. Those they saw gave them no mind, focused on their own day, but tension made Prior stiff nonetheless: he'd told Sylvie to keep her head down, being that she alone had woken from the sickness, but she'd insisted she would visit Baltair to thank him for his tending. Prior had cautioned against it, but Sylvie knew her own mind and Baltair was popular enough. He and his smithing tools would be good protection, should Sylvie need it.

Prior hugged his boots more tightly. He didn't want his sister to need protecting.

"This is it," he said, when they reached the boarded well, inlaid in stone. "This used to be the main water supply, back when Ashcroft was smaller, but it ran dry years ago and they started using the one over where the marketplace is now." He toed the dusty ground. "Can't see anything growing here, Sylvie must've been feeling optimistic." Or desperate.

Fenton hummed. He trailed his fingers along the tired stone of the well, then rubbed fingers and thumb together and darted out his tongue to lick his fingertips. Heat rushed to Prior's face. He cleared his throat.

"Taste anything?" he asked, then wished he'd kept quiet. *Taste anything?* What a buffoon.

"There is… Here."

With a quick motion, Fenton prised his fingers beneath one of the planks covering the well, where the workers had left a gap, and lifted the plank free without seeming to exert any effort. A rusted nail dropped onto Prior's boot as he stared.

Tossing the plank aside, Fenton reached into the dark mouth of the well, apparently unconcerned by the possibility of falling headfirst as his arm and shoulder nearly disappeared beneath the remaining boards. His toes curled into the dirt for purchase. Prior exhaled in a heave of relief when at last Fenton drew back with something held in his hand—no, something held in the vines that extended from the inside of his wrist. Prior had grown used to the vines in Fenton's hair, but seeing them protrude from his skin was newly captivating. He watched as the vines retreated into Fenton's flesh and disappeared beneath his skin, dropping bones into Fenton's waiting palm as they shrank. Bones and flesh and scraps of fur, which were better than bones and flesh and scraps of cloth, if Prior were pressed to choose.

Prior closed his mouth. Blinked his dry eyes. Then, gathering his courage, he peered at the contents of Fenton's cupped hands. "What's that, then? Too small for goats, too big for chickens. Rabbits? How'd they get into the well, though?"

"A fox kit," Fenton said. "Parts of one." He cradled the remnants of the kit in his hands and smoothed the rotten fur with his thumb. Prior desperately hoped he wouldn't lick it afterward. "You said this well ran dry a long time gone?"

Prior nodded. "Before I can really remember. Is it related to the curse?"

"This death came at some child's hands. A shameful secret hidden in a forgotten place." Fenton regarded the pitiful bones in his hands. "Flesh carries memory. This kit walked across nets of my sibling's magic, and the poison is pungent within it. There is another at work here but I cannot yet see their shape." A muscle flexed in his jaw. "I must find the source."

"But you'll break the curse first," Prior reminded him on reflex, his mind still processing the rest of what Fenton had said.

"As you say."

"And to do that, you need to find a mage, or a sorceress, or— Words, yes, I know!" Prior hastened to add, before Fenton's sombre mood could twist toward anything sharper. "Very well. Leave the remains of the poor beast here, and let's ask Sylvie if she has any notion of where we might head next."

He'd expected Fenton to drop the bones back into the well—there was little else to do with them, as Prior yet held out hope they wouldn't be licked—but instead, the strange, slick blackness he'd seen before oiled out from beneath Fenton's sleeve. It disappeared the bones into the chasm of itself, then dripped from Fenton's hand onto the stone rim of the well, before oozing into the dark beyond.

Prior watched the well for a moment, then decisively turned his back. "Come on. Best we were on our way."

Prior explained the situation, and Fenton's wish to find a magic user, in more words than Fenton thought necessary, but when he finished, Sylvie furrowed her brow in thought. Her eyes flickered between Prior and Fenton, liquid with worry and sunken with exhaustion from the sickness that had continued to fade from her, though she would not be truly well while the blight remained. Wrapped in blankets, she sat by a dismal fire that failed to warm the cottage. Fenton nudged power into the flames as he waited. Heat would help clear Lorcan's influence more quickly.

Fenton had taken a position leaning against the wall by the door as Prior paced and Sylvie tapped her forefinger against her teeth. Weak sun shone through the window, making the room glow. Fenton eyed the thatched roof. It would hold another season.

At last, Sylvie spoke. "There's always— Well. You say healers and hedgewitches are no good? What about an apothecary? There's one in Spear Bluff."

Prior made a sharp gesture across his throat, as if cutting it. His eyes darted to Fenton and away. "A strong magic user. That's what we want. Need. That's what he needs."

Sylvie's fingers twitched over her blankets and her scent spiked with fear at the reminder of Fenton's presence in the room. Since their brief introduction, when her polite smile had frozen to a rictus, she had been doing her best not to look his way. Fenton pressed himself closer to the uneven surface of the wall, his vines coiling against his skull. He had not intended to return to the cottage, but Prior had insisted, and Fenton had been curious about her recovery.

Sylvie cleared her throat. "If it's strength you're after, then you need a mage. The hunter that came through last winter, you remember her, she mentioned a mage in Northrope had done some fancy warding on the city walls. I remember because I wanted to ask the Greaves boys about it when they next went to the big market, to see if it was anything like in fairy tales. Thorns and thickets and—" Sylvie broke off and ducked her head. She adjusted her blankets around her shoulder. "I wanted to ask, anyway."

Prior resumed pacing, having faltered as Sylvie spoke. He rubbed one arm with the other. "A mage? I've heard the same stories, but we can't afford a mage's fees. Even asking a question is beyond our budget. And Northrope?" Prior considered Fenton, lingering on his crown, his vines. He shook his head at Sylvie. "Have you another idea?"

Fenton's vines adjusted his crown, checking it hadn't sloped during the course of the day. He scratched the tip of his ear and surreptitiously nudged a bud to bloom. Perhaps the scent would be pleasing to the siblings. They were both tense, and Prior had watched him strangely all day. Humans were very odd.

"There's nowhere closer you'll find someone stronger, that's for certain sure," Sylvie said, to Prior's clear displeasure.

His mouth a thin line, Prior glanced searchingly at Fenton, like he sought a safe place to land. Should Fenton spread his arms? He held a forest. What sturdier place could there be?

"Northrope is a city," Prior told him, as if the word should convey some particular weight. "And mages aren't like us. Me. They'll want something in exchange for helping, money, I mean, or favours we can't afford. It's why I didn't mention the possibility before."

Fenton looked to Sylvie, who had not yet confused

him. "There is magic in this city? With this mage?"

Her chin trembled at the direct address and her eyes lowered, but she nodded, rearranging her skirts as she did. "Plenty, if the hunter were speaking true, and I don't see why she wouldn't've. Nothing to be gained by it. I think the mage even received a medal for their work."

"Then we go to Northrope. To this city," Fenton told Prior. His shadow curled around his feet in satisfaction at the decision.

Prior let out a gusty sigh, and rolled his eyes to the thatch. "This will be fun."

A FOX IN GOAT'S CLOTHING

One-Horn-Crooked did not care for the lanky fox and his surprisingly round-pupilled eyes. He smelled of too much metal and not enough dirt, and he lacked half his parts, and when One-Horn-Crooked told him as such, all he did was tilt his head like a witless corvid! Yet his hands were pleasing around One-Horn-Crooked's ears, and the fox found the best scratching points without needing to be butted into place. He even clawed away a bit of One-Horn-Crooked's overgrown front hoof where the iron-smelling human had missed it during the last trim.

"Have you a name for me?" the fox asked, in the human tongue. "It seems I have many more than I recall."

All goats understood the human tongue, of course, but it pleased them to pretend otherwise, and One-Horn-Crooked saw no reason to change this behaviour. Not even for the fox. One-Horn-Crooked hadn't eaten the tempting flower crown the fox wore so boldly; that should show favour enough. With a careful bump to the fox's hand, One-Horn-Crooked encouraged the fox to recommence his scratching.

Resuming his attentions, the fox's rounded pupils drifted to One-Horn-Crooked's namesake. One-Horn-Crooked stamped a foreleg with pride. That had been a battle indeed! One-Horn-Crooked had been challenged for position by Bites-Hot-Iron—a name no other goat had been foolish enough to earn—and they had butted heads in a clash to rival the epics. One-Horn-Crooked had been the victor, of course, and Bites-Hot-Iron had gone to skulk at the other end of the village.

The fox's free hand drifted away from scratching and to his temples, where his skin was smooth as a kid's, and compassion wormed in One-Horn-Crooked's breast. Yes, the fox lacked some of his parts, but the loss didn't make him less and it was folly to think as such! That trail led only to sour grass and regret.

At One-Horn-Crooked's fervent bleating, however, the fox's face creased like the iron-smelling one did before starting to bargain the herd toward the pen. He reached for his head again, and One-Horn-Crooked prepared to ram the silly fox to sense, but with a flick of his clawless fingers, the fox pulled a fat bloom from his crown.

"Would you care for a gift? Your herdmate liked these well enough," the fox said, holding the bloom out on the flat of his palm.

One-Horn-Crooked almost refused on principle—who had been associating with the fox and not telling of it? For shame!—but to refuse a gift would be the height of rudeness. Not to mention unwise, when offered by one such as the fox.

The fox's dirt scent thickened as One-Horn-Crooked lipped the bloom from his palm. As it should. Foxes needed good, rich earth. A home for lush grass and plentiful flowers. Somewhere to stretch their lanky legs— whether two or four, and whether tipped with feet or paws or hooves. Whether they had all of their parts or only some.

The fox let One-Horn-Crooked finish eating, then gently bumped his flat forehead against One-Horn-Crooked's. As a kindness, One-Horn-Crooked permitted him to do so.

PART THREE:
DON'T SHAKE THE MAGE

In a hamlet between Ashcroft and Northrope lay despair. Prior looked upon its face. Breathed it into his lungs. He could not unknow it; the sight scarred into him.

"It's the curse that's done this, isn't it? The blight." Prior rubbed his shaking hand over his mouth. "How did you know to come here?"

Fenton, crouched over a body he was studying with a dispassionate eye, didn't look up. Sunlight picked out the red in his hair and set the newly yellow flowers in his crown ablaze. "Someone told me of it. I had not thought—" He shook his head. His vines were still. "I had not thought."

For once, Prior empathised with Fenton's struggle for words.

The hamlet they had come to, a place so small it had no name, sat in a sheltered lee a handful of miles off the road that ran to Northrope from the coast. After leaving Ashcroft, Prior and Fenton had been making steady progress westward with an eye on the lowing sun when Fenton had abruptly veered from the road. He had cut through an overgrown field, the stalks seeming to bend away from him as he arrowed toward a stream and the heather-dappled crest beyond. Prior had lingered on the road for a moment before he'd cursed and followed Fenton. A mile or so past the crest they had reached a dusty square with handful of tired houses clustered around it, and silence in wait behind every door.

Prior had discovered the first body across a doorway, sprawled as if they had tripped and simply not bothered to rise again. Their features were fixed in death, though by the stench of rotten food wafting from within the open door, the corpse should have been a mess of putrefaction and insect activity. Prior had entered the house—he had been compelled by some force beyond his ken—and found two other bodies tucked in their beds, so like Sylvie had been. Neither chest rose nor fell. Eyes sunken, hands clawed around their thin blankets. The same bruise Sylvie bore smudged their throats.

He'd been sick in the boiled-dry stewpot hung over the cold fire.

Then he'd staggered to the next house. The next. Desperate for a sign that the entire hamlet hadn't been left to sleep themselves to death, for an indication someone had escaped the curse—for that was what had killed everyone in the place, as it would have killed Sylvie, as it would take everyone in the moors if they didn't break its hold. Yet even insects refused to linger in the cursed place. He found no one.

Prior had been sick again, his stomach cramping as it wrung itself. Then he'd returned to Fenton, who had not left his investigation of the first body in the doorway.

"We should bury them," Prior said. He didn't want to spend another second in the dead hamlet, but the part of him that strove to be better spoke the words.

Fenton shook his head. "We should burn them."

Startled, Prior took a step back. "I thought the curse wasn't contagious like that? You said—"

"There are other sicknesses the dead carry." Fenton unfolded to his full height, less gracefully than usual. He scratched his temple, jostling his crown. His eyes were dark. "Burning would halt the spread."

"We can't. What if someone comes back and sees"— Prior gestured, helplessly—"all of this? Everyone they love burned in their absence. What if—"

"Prior—"

"It could've been me, Fenton! Returning home to—to nothing." Prior's knees wobbled as the realisation struck him. "Gods, it could still be me."

Abruptly, Prior's knees failed him, but Fenton caught him in strong arms before Prior could meet the ground. Tears stung Prior's eyes and his lower lip trembled as despair rose in him like a dark tide, constricting his throat and clipping his breath short. He pressed his face into Fenton's chest, where Fenton's heart beat so steadily in comparison to the fevered pounding of Prior's own. Fenton's rich loam scent embraced Prior, as welcome as the strong bands of Fenton's arms and the low rumbles from his chest that Prior felt more than heard. Prior borrowed Fenton's strength and permitted himself to appreciate the closeness, temporarily heedless of their respective natures and the distance he had tried to keep between them. The distance he had needed to protect himself from acknowledging his attraction to Fenton. The distance reduced now to nothing.

"It will not be you, Prior, I swear it," Fenton murmured, pressing the words to Prior's hair.

Prior sniffed. "You can't promise that."

Fenton hummed.

They stood together as Prior's heart gradually settled from its wild rush and his knees firmed to hold his weight. No birds sang around them and no insects buzzed. Even the wind had dropped. Nothing sounded in the dead place but Fenton's steady breaths and Prior's slowing ones.

When he could bear it, Prior pushed himself back. Fenton let him go.

"We have to leave. Find somewhere to stay for the

night," Prior said.

Fenton's fingers twitched at his sides. "You wished to bury the dead."

"We can't. But we won't burn them, either." He firmed his jaw. His heart. "We're not far from Northrope, and someone might have gone there for help. If they come back, or if anyone comes here and finds nothing but a pyre..." Prior sighed. "There's a chance it might be connected to us somehow, if someone saw us passing this way. You're very, ah, memorable. I don't want to be running for the rest of my life to evade arrest for committing a massacre. Do you?"

Fenton tilted his head. "I do not understand. We did not kill these people."

"'I didn't do it' isn't a compelling argument, as these things go." Prior shifted in place and cast a look at the darkening sky. He met Fenton's eyes. "I know you don't understand, and you're trying— You're trying to help. You *are* helping. But we have to go. There's nothing we can do for these people."

Prior's chest ached at the thought of leaving, but if Fenton didn't break the curse, there could be a hundred such places before summer came. They didn't know how quickly the sickness was spreading, and with the unnatural preservation of the bodies, they couldn't be certain how long these people had been dead. The best thing he and Fenton could do would be to continue to Northrope.

After a hard look around himself, and a lingering glance at the body nearby, Fenton nodded. His vines shifted his crown.

"As you wish," he said. "Let us leave this place."

They continued west, toward the lowing sun.

Fenton did not sleep. As Prior twitched where he slept on his bedroll, a small fire crackling nearby, Fenton paced around the clearing like a dog tied to a stake. He did not understand his own behaviour as he circled again toward Prior, checked over him—head, hands, heart—and turned away again. Bats clicked at Fenton as they passed overhead, gliding through the tranquil night, and curious noses snuffled in the growth that horseshoed the clearing, but no creature approached. His agitation kept them away.

He circled back to Prior. Away again.

Fenton scratched the inside of his arm as he paced. He had thought to sleep, to use the time to replenish his strength. As night had settled, he had lain beside Prior and closed his eyes. Listened as Prior's breath and heartbeat steadied from the tripping rhythm they had played since entering the accursed hamlet. Waited for sleep.

Opened his eyes.

As he had done countless times that evening, Fenton checked on the magic that connected him to Sylvie and protected her from the blight taking further root. It held strong. She would not become as those others had. As Prior had feared enough to shake.

Fenton curled his fingers. The memory of holding Prior in his arms stained him. He had never felt as weak as he did then, able to offer nothing but platitudes and a reckless promise. His jaw flexed. His shadow flowed up from his feet to curl around his waist and pour over his shoulders, checking for wounds before seeping beneath his clothes to tighten comfortingly around him. Fenton circled again to Prior and looked down at his face, at last relaxed in sleep.

The connection to Sylvie drained relatively little of Fenton's magic. Protecting the rest of Prior's village surely would not take much more effort on Fenton's part.

Lowering himself to his knees at Prior's side, Fenton closed his eyes and opened his senses. His vines twitched. Magic flowed.

After a fitful night, Prior had set a brisk pace, both to leave the hamlet behind and to hurry onto Northrope. They'd made some headway before stopping midmorning at a roadside tavern for bread and small beer, where Fenton sat in shadow and Prior tried not to twitch at every sidelong look. Keeping good time, they had even managed to bathe in the river; Prior hadn't wanted to enter the city still perfumed with travel, and although Fenton had seemed unmoved by Prior's explanation, he'd gamely scrubbed himself after observing—entirely too closely for Prior's composure—Prior wash as best he could.

Now Northrope's walls loomed ahead. Prior and Fenton were two among many pushing toward the city, but two alone with a conspicuous lack of burden. Market day had come to Northrope, and the road heaved with traders bearing wares by hand or cart or, for the richer among them, in resplendently coloured caravans. Prior had visited Northrope's market once, as a child, and had assumed his memory had painted it brighter than in truth. In light of his current surroundings, he wondered if memory had not dulled the true splendour.

And the *smell*. There were numerous spice traders, merchants who travelled from port to palace and back again, and they were pleasant enough, but days-long travel smelled hard on livestock, and Prior tried to block his nose's experience of the tanners altogether. Ashcroft hadn't enough passing trade to support a tannery, and Prior gave renewed thanks for their loss. Yet it all added to the anticipation and novelty of the city.

Beside him, Fenton didn't appear as excited at the prospect of Northrope as Prior. Though Prior had been nervous at first—particularly regarding the combination of Fenton and a city—as they had travelled together, and especially after their experience in the hamlet, he had grown to think he had perhaps reckoned too little of Fenton. In private recompense, he had shared stories he'd heard from travellers: the mage who'd made Northrope's wards to protect the city from attack both magical and mundane, and about the founding of the city by two foxes in ancient times. Fenton had eyed him dubiously in response to that tale, but he hadn't said anything against it. Prior had wondered, wildly, if Fenton might have been jealous of some unnamed fox's notoriety.

He hadn't asked. Fenton's expression had turned rigid as Northrope made itself known on the horizon, and set more firmly into blankness as they neared. The vines in his hair had wilted instead of wending around his crown as they usually did. Prior wanted to straighten Fenton's crown like a parent might their child's clothes on a feast day, even as he worried at the sight of it. For where Ashcroft might forgive an outsider's oddities due to Prior's connection and their own indifference, a city the size of Northrope would surely entice those who knew how to convert the wondrous into coin and possessed the inclination to do so.

Worry gnawed at Prior. With a glance to the other travellers, none of whom spent more than a penny of notice on him, he beckoned Fenton from the road.

"What is it?" Fenton's eyes flitted over Prior's shoulders as another colourful cart rumbled by. "Do you need to pi—"

"No!" Prior interrupted hastily. Fenton had become somewhat fixed on Prior's bodily functions after Prior had called for a piss break on the first day, and Prior hadn't yet succeeded in explaining the concept of discretion in a way Fenton deigned to understand. It wasn't as if Fenton didn't find his own convenient trees when required. "Just— Before we enter Northrope, I want to check if you're well. You're looking, ah, pinched." At Fenton's incomprehension, Prior tried again. "Your flowers are wilting. Do you feel hale? Healthy?"

Fenton tucked a vine behind his pointed ear in a curiously nervous gesture. He watched the carts and merchants pass.

"There are many people here," he pointed out.

"Cities are like that."

"I cannot remember seeing so many before. Not for a long time."

Prior bit back the first dozen questions that landed on his tongue. "Long", as Fenton meant it, likely measured a far greater distance than for Prior. For Prior, it had been a long time since his grandmother died, nearly ten years gone and every one an ache; he suspected a decade to Fenton meant little.

But Prior's curiosity wasn't relevant. He adjusted the strap of his pack on his shoulder, where the weight dragged. He had not brought his longbow to Northrope, uncertain if carrying it would bring more trouble than it might solve. Fenton had done all their hunting on the journey.

"There'll be more people yet within the walls. If you'd prefer to wait here, or in that inn farther back along the road, I can find the mage myself," Prior offered.

"And what would you ask them?"

"If they'd come to meet you, I suppose," he said, thinking quickly.

Fenton visibly weighed the proposition, his brows furrowing and his gaze going inward. Over the past few days his body language had become more verbose, so that Prior could tell when a question was being considered, or, more frequently, when it was being ignored. Perhaps it was more accurate to say Prior could better interpret Fenton's language of gestures and expressions.

In either case, Prior saw when Fenton dismissed his offer.

"To delay further would not be in our bargain. I will accompany you into this *city*." Fenton said the word as if it were laced with belladonna.

Compressing his lips when they wobbled with a grin, Prior nodded to the road. "Come along, then. The guards are up ahead, they're the ones with the frowns and the swords. Are you able to look less— Just *less*? At all? We've been passing your ears for elfkin, but in Northrope they might realise sentient vines aren't a usual fashion among that kind." Not to mention the odd blackness that Prior had seen trailing Fenton's bare heels, inclined to climb his body on a whim. Prior couldn't conceive of a plan to conceal that event, so he'd elected to simply not think on it.

"My vines? What objection have you to my vines?" Fenton demanded, as the contested greenery rippled with thorns. The blackness encircled his throat like a choking hand and glimmered like armour.

"Nothing at all, I like them very much!" Prior hastened to reassure him, glancing over his shoulder for witnesses, and only hearing the words after they were too late to take back. Heat lit his cheeks but he blundered ahead. "They're very green! And the flowers are very, ah, fetching. Snowdrops, aren't they? Sometimes? Rather pointier now. Who doesn't enjoy flowers? But many—most—people would find them unusual. We don't want to be found unusual in Northrope. They don't care for it, historically speaking."

Covering his face with his hands, Prior cut off his babble. He wanted to cut out his tongue, but when he glimpsed through his fingers, he found Fenton's defensive features had disappeared to wherever they usually lurked. Relief and something far warmer took nest in Prior's gut at the curious expression on Fenton's face.

"Your heart beats fast," Fenton said.

Prior gasped with a laugh. He raked back his hair with shaky hands and made himself meet Fenton's eyes. "That'll be the fear."

"Fear of what?"

Adrenaline took hold of Prior's tongue. "You! You're terrifying! I thought I was going to be thorn-whipped to ribbons!"

"That— I would not. Not you," Fenton stuttered,

paling and taking a step back. He tugged at the hem of his tunic. Looked again toward the road, as if seeking assistance.

His words weren't as comforting as Prior might have hoped—they had left the horror of possibility very much on the table—but they were far more reassuring than he'd expected. Prior took a breath and blew it out, flexing his fingers at his sides as he did. He had to remember that Fenton's roots reached deeper than Prior could ever hope to guess, and touched things far darker than he'd ever want to meet.

Yet, oh, how he found himself wanting.

"Forget about it," Prior said. He tried for a grin, though Fenton wasn't watching him. "If anyone takes issue, do as you will with them."

Fenton grunted. His gaze returned to Prior. "Magic pours from that place, that *city*, like blood from a wound. At least one god has roamed there not long past. Is that not 'unusual', as you would have it?"

Prior had never heard of a god in Northrope. *Another question for another time.* "I understand what you're saying, but there are many more humans than gods. And humans generally stab things they don't understand."

"I fear no human."

Prior swallowed. "I do."

A passing horse brayed, high and sharp. Prior flinched—at the noise, at his admission of selfish cowardice—but didn't look away from Fenton. Couldn't. Humans prostrated themselves to powers like Fenton so their heads might better miss the swing of an axe.

Fenton, however, did look away, and there his attention lingered. His mouth twisted. Then, with a huff, he pushed at his crown a few times, adjusting how it sat. When he faced Prior again, his vines were no more noteworthy than any other element of his flower crown. Which, being that Fenton wore the guise of a grown man and there were no feast days for another moon, was reasonably noteworthy, but hopefully less likely to incite stabbing. Prior finally breathed out.

"Thank you," he said.

Fenton shrugged. The gesture sat awkwardly on him. "I would simply have slaughtered any who dared attack, but you seemed concerned. I would not have you worry."

Far more worried than previously, which he'd thought had been his maximum reach of anxiety, Prior nonetheless stepped onto the road toward Northrope. A shouted curse and galloping hooves froze him in place before an approaching rider, but Fenton grabbed Prior's arm and yanked him aside, even as the reckless bastard cracked the whip on the poor lathered mount. Prior trembled, heart rabbiting furiously in his chest, knees quivering beneath his weight, but Fenton let Prior clutch his shoulders as he fought to recover his equilibrium. A tree with roots set firm and Prior a nest held in sturdy branches.

The sound of laughter broke into Prior's wild thoughts and he jerked upright, the back of his neck tingling in awareness. But no one watched him and Fenton; the laughter came from a passing group, weavers by his guess, as they chatted amongst themselves. Self-conscious nonetheless, Prior cleared his throat and smiled brightly at Fenton. He received no smile in return, of course, but Fenton inclined his head expectantly.

Prior clapped his hands and thought positive thoughts. "To Northrope! Where we will present ourselves as awed country cousins on a visit, ask about their famous mage, and gain said mage's assistance in breaking a curse. Sylvie has requested sweet buns as a gift. Get all that?"

A shadow—figurative, not literal, blessedly—crossed Fenton's face. "Find the mage, find sweet buns. It will be so."

As good a prayer as any other. Prior set forward.

Fenton did not care for Northrope. People crowded every clearing, shouting to better hear their own voices, while magic bellowed even more loudly from the wards lacing the high stone walls. Fenton wanted to scrub the noise from his skin, but Prior had asked for "less", and Fenton would attempt to comply. Prior best knew what humans could accept, and Fenton did not wish to cause him harm. The memory of Prior's fear made Fenton's mind crawl in discomfort; Fenton's reaction at the perceived insult had been instinctual, but Prior's reaction had punctured him like a lung. Unless and until his human guise became stifling, Fenton would endure.

The miasma of dirty bodies, old meat, and hot metal made his nose wrinkle and his vines coil even more tightly around his skull. His shadow cringed. Endurance was indeed the watchword.

Fenton followed Prior through winding streets where buildings grew on either side like ugly trees, blocking the sky as if those trapped between their walls couldn't abide the sight of all that space. A river cut through the city's centre—a key contributing factor to Northrope's wealth from trade, Prior had explained, as if such things mattered—and Fenton paused at the crest of the bridge as they crossed, trying to scent clear air. Yet even the water smelled befouled. He scratched the inside of his wrist, where thorns wanted to break free.

"Do you sense something?" Prior asked. He had stopped when Fenton did; his awareness of Fenton resembled that of a rabbit to a fox. Fenton had not yet decided whether that bothered him, nor why it should.

Fenton pulled the cuff of his borrowed tunic over the reddened patch of skin. "Magic."

"Oh? The mage? Which direction should we take?"

"None. There is too much noise," Fenton said. Prior's face fell, and Fenton's shadow tightened around his legs. He tried again. "What plan had you?"

Prior brightened. He set off walking, beckoning for

80

Fenton to follow. "I had thought to ask after the mage at a tavern. Taverns are usually the best place for information. Betta always says innkeepers are gossips, and she would know, since she's been running Ashcroft's inn for as long as I can remember. Besides, I'm famished," Prior said as he guided Fenton toward a squat building by the riverside. He pointed. "The Trout. I overheard someone in the market say there's reasonable prices here, compared to other places in the city, and our pockets are light enough that came as a very strong recommendation. What do you think?"

Labourers were unloading boxes from a boat moored nearby and carrying them behind the tavern, working in synchronicity like ants moving berries. Their patterns rarely overlapped. Fenton watched them and the way they listened to their queen, standing on the boat with a stave in hand. Their harmony indicated good order. He considered the tavern's thatch, the drawing clouds. When it began to rain, they would be dry, and Prior would be fed.

"Acceptable," Fenton declared.

For some reason, Prior smiled. "Fulsome praise indeed! Let us hope for something equally as acceptable to eat."

As Prior started for the tavern, a chirrup made Fenton pause. He whistled at the magpie who'd called, and held out his hand so they could drop something into it: a piece of clear glass the size of his fingernail. The magpie chirruped again and Fenton bowed his head in thanks. He held the glass to the sun and admired the refracted rays; they brought to mind Prior's touch and the warmth it had engendered in Fenton, the effect disproportionate to its origin. Fenton rolled the glass between his fingers. Gifts were important. To receive, and to bestow. The gifts he traded were often small fancies—stones and flowers, things easy to carry by beak and claw—but in a life as long as his, Fenton had come to value meaning over material. Size did not matter, for favour had no size. Favour did not decay.

He had not yet given Prior a gift. Not and claimed it so. Fenton pocketed the glass and followed Prior.

The tavern smelled as strongly as the rest of the city, but boasted a large, crackling fire with an unoccupied table nearby. Leaving Prior to his business, Fenton claimed the table and two sturdy chairs. At their tavern visit that morning, Prior had explained the concept of currency to Fenton, then charged him with the task of finding an empty table and chairs—*without*, he'd stressed quite firmly, evicting anyone from them. After delivering his instruction, he'd paled and dashed off to speak to the proprietor, stinking acridly of distress.

A strange human, Prior. At times he treated Fenton as he might a kit still chasing their brush, only to recoil from his own brazenness in the next moment. Fenton had decided to treat him like one of the forest's squirrels, who used to fluff their tails at him and bully him into searching for acorns, only to hide with their tails over their faces for days on end if the mood took them. Changeable creatures. But then Prior would reveal vulnerability, as he had in the hamlet, or boldly declare his own fear, as he had outside the city, and Fenton had no model to understand that behaviour.

If Fenton chanced to meet the other god in the city, he might ask their advice on humans. For now, Fenton took a seat and watched the fire. Sprites danced in the flames but they were merely chaff of things that had once lived in the wood.

When Prior returned, his fern scent curling ahead of him, Fenton looked away from the flames. Ghostly sprites pirouetted once in an afterimage. He took the cups from Prior's hand and placed them on the table, then reached for the bowl Prior cradled in the crook of his elbow. Prior let him take the bowl, and set the other down with a sigh.

"Thank you. I definitely thought I'd end up wearing that soup," Prior said as he drew the other seat to the table. Their knees brushed together as he sat and settled his pack by his feet. Drawing two bread rolls from his pockets, he placed one beside Fenton's bowl. "Here. I have warm goat milk and slightly less warm soup for us. They didn't say the kind of soup. My guess is leek, by the smell. Honestly, I could eat day-old horse without grumbling, but if it's not good, you're welcome to try your luck with the kitchen. But be warned, the cook wielded a wooden spoon in a most intimidating fashion."

Fenton sniffed the milk and the soup—it was indeed leek—and hummed. They smelled good. He'd explained that he didn't need to eat as frequently as Prior, but doing so would be pleasant, and Prior had spent his limited coin on Fenton. It would be churlish to refuse.

"Thank you," Fenton said as he broke his roll in two.

Prior blinked rapidly. "You're quite welcome."

They shared their meal in a companionable silence, while around them the tavern grew louder as more people entered; Prior had been right about the popularity that low prices afforded. Fenton didn't wholly understand why he couldn't merely take currency from others if it were distributed so unevenly, but Prior had been adamant against the notion.

Once bowls and cups were empty, Prior tipped his chair back on the rear legs and balanced himself by bracing his foot on the table leg. Fenton rested his weight more firmly against the table to keep it in place.

"To business, then." Prior patted his stomach. "Just the thing to aid digestion."

More bodily functions. Fenton needed to learn which were acceptable to mention and which not. The longer he spent with Prior, the more gaps showed in Fenton's knowledge.

"Business," he echoed.

Prior glanced around the room, then lowered his chair to all four legs and leaned over the table. His eyelashes were very long. Fenton hadn't noticed before.

"The mage is named Nola, but the chap behind the bar

said she isn't receiving petitioners at present. None without a title, anyway." Prior pulled a face like he'd smelled something unpleasant. "I rather got the impression both her prices and airs have increased since the business with the walls. I did, however, receive directions to a herbalist working nearby who has a decent reputation. Might we try there?"

"No."

Prior sighed and rested his chin on his folded-over hands, laid flat on the table. He watched Fenton from his lowered position. "Yes, I suspected you'd say that. Look, can we— This table is sticky, hang on, let me—"

Gracelessly, Prior shoved himself upright and wiped his palms on his trouser legs, his nose wrinkled in disgust. Fenton found himself baring his teeth at the sight, amusement rumbling inside him at Prior's antics until the feeling burst out of him in a bark. The noise made Prior start. He stared.

"Did you just *laugh*?" Prior asked, his own lips curving. He raised his eyebrows and his expression turned to affront that even Fenton knew to be feigned. "Did you just laugh *at me*? I don't know whether to be insulted or delighted."

Fenton's vines tightened at the teasing light in Prior's eyes, fighting the temptation to turn toward the sun. His face felt hot and his shadow blanketed the floor of the tavern in an attempt to dissipate the heat into the flagstone. Fenton went to drink from his cup of milk but found it empty. He played the clay cup between his palms. It was easier to look at than Prior's face.

Abruptly, he remembered the magpie. Fenton flexed his fingers at his side and his shadow dropped the polished glass into his hand. He placed it gently on the table.

"Here. A gift for you," he said. His vines twitched in their binding, unable to fidget away his nerves.

"For me?" Prior held the glass up and squinted at it, as if trying to peer through, then smoothed the surface with his thumb. "Where did you get this?"

"A magpie gave it to me."

"A magpie, of course. Renowned gift-givers, magpies."

Fenton tried to explain a thing he had not needed to before. "Birds sometimes give me gifts. And other creatures, too, but they do not travel as widely. Birds bring stories to each other."

"About you?"

"About all manner of things."

"I think I'd like to hear those stories, one day." Prior's gaze flicked searchingly over Fenton's face, then he smiled and drew back into his chair. He took the glass. "Thank you for this. I'll treasure it."

Although Prior seemed pleased by the gift, Fenton knew he had failed to make himself understood. He clenched his hands beneath the table. As he opened his mouth to try again, a sudden uproar came from the other side of the room, wiping away Prior's pleased expression as he flinched and darted a look over his shoulder. A group were haranguing one another over a game of chance; there were cards scattered on the table, and on the floor. A member of the group caught Fenton's eye and raised their eyebrows in silent challenge, but rejoined their companions without commenting. Fenton watched for a moment, but when voices were the only things raised, he called his shadow back from where it had moved in preparation to attack.

Prior rubbed his face, where whiskers darkened his jaw. "Anyway. I think we should see this herbalist and hope they'll give us another avenue to try with Nola, if that's who you must meet with."

"If they would but point me in the correct direction, I can make my own way to the mage," Fenton conceded.

"You can't find the mage without guidance?"

A growl warmed Fenton's throat. "Magic surrounds this place, pouring from the walls like a waterfall into a lake. We stand inside that lake. I cannot divine one drop from another." In the spirit of honesty, Fenton continued. "Another may be able to locate the mage, but such deftness never numbered among my strengths. My sibling— I have no head for such finesse."

Fenton could follow a mouse across a forest days after the fact, but Northrope screamed with magic and muddied all subtler trails. The lingering presence of another god, the siren of the mage's work on the walls, and the immeasurable other petty workings—prayers, cantrips, charms, and superstition—altogether overwhelmed Fenton. His time in the forest had left him weaker than he'd known, and in addition, his connection with Sylvie and Ashcroft taxed his strength more than he had expected. Fenton was stretched thin. But he would not speak those failings to Prior. His deadwood heart pulsed at the notion of admitting further limitations.

"I understand. Or I think I do." Prior pursed his lips. "Well, no, I don't really, but I'll take you to the herbalist. It's important we speak to the mage, I know, but we can't help anyone if the guards throw us out on our ears, or if someone takes issue with our asking questions here."

Fenton didn't know the city. He trusted to Prior's guidance: it was Prior's sister in the balance, after all. He nodded. "As you will have it."

"So! To the herbalist, then afterward we'll find somewhere to sleep, since no one likes a late-night visit from someone asking for a favour, much less a stranger."

So saying, Prior gathered his pack and rose from the table, then gave Fenton an expectant look before heading toward the door. Fenton followed. He was growing used to the sight of Prior's strong back leading him forward.

The herbalist had been no use whatsoever, but Prior had suspected as much before knocking on their door. Herbalists and mages differed greatly, not merely due to the price of their services, but also the scope of their efforts: herbalists produced tonics for skin complaints while mages toppled courts. True, a herbalist's potion might achieve the same effect, and Prior had little doubt a mage could clear a rash, if not only by virtue of replacing the offending skin entirely, but—how had Fenton phrased it? Hedges and oaks, indeed.

By even the most generous measure, Irial measured barely any more impressive than a potted plant. One that had been carefully tended, surely, as his shop had been finely outfitted—albeit not as finely as his robe, which had sparkled—but a potted plant nonetheless. Fenton had entered the shop, circled it once, then walked right back out again, leaving Prior to hastily fabricate that they'd gotten lost on their first visit to Northrope. Irial had reacted in a markedly unimpressed fashion and Prior hadn't chanced to ask his questions about the mage.

Unfortunately, the diversion had taken them twice across the city, since Prior had in truth gotten turned about and locals were more interested in his paltry purse than bestowing directional charity, and now dark lowered its hood over Northrope. Prior corralled a wilted Fenton beneath the tattered awning of a closed shop. Ivy spread its fingers across the wall beside them, dry and brittle but stubbornly hanging on. Prior could empathise.

"Admittedly, that didn't go quite as I'd hoped," Prior ventured.

Fenton slid a flat look at him. "How had you 'hoped'?"

That we would break the curse. That Sylvie would be saved. That you might laugh again.

"Just... Better. More helpfully."

Fenton didn't rise to the bait. He'd been visibly losing energy all day, and as the evening drew in, even his vines were drooping. There had been an instant with the herbalist when disappointment had darkened Fenton's face and his fangs had flashed in a serrated grimace, as if he'd temporarily lost control of his guise. Prior's heart had stuttered in alarm and he'd braced for the impact of claws, or fangs, or whatever else Fenton might bring to bear against Prior as the source of his displeasure. Yet Fenton had simply stalked away.

"That charlatan you took me to helped not at all," Fenton said. He paced shortly from one end of the awning to the other, clawed fingers flicking outward at his sides. "I dislike this city. This Northrope. There are too many people here and not enough— *Not enough.*"

The creeping ivy burst violently into bloom at the stress in Fenton's voice, a riot of fragrant yellow and cream, only to wither immediately to dust. Fenton inhaled the ghosts of flowers in gusty breaths, his eyes fluttering shut, his mouth slightly open. He flicked his fingers again as he resumed pacing. His claws shrank, then disappeared. When he next prowled to Prior's side, his shoulders had lost some of their tension.

Prior, however, had gained tension, specifically in the trouser region. When Fenton's voice had shaded to a growl, Prior's hindbrain had surged to attention along with his cock. Desire had subsumed his fear nearly entirely between one blink and the next as Prior had learnt something new about himself. While the reaction of the ivy had been an impressive display of whatever primal power Fenton possessed, it was Fenton's *command* that had affected Prior. He had suddenly comprehended the restraint with which Fenton held himself, and with it, the notion that at any moment Fenton might lose control. Prior didn't know what might happen in that instance, and his rational mind insisted it would be horrific, but the significantly less rational part thrilled with possibilities that suffused his lusty mind like a drop of ink across cloth.

Adjusting his weight, Prior willed his cock down and directed his mind forcibly to other things. Other things still existed, surely.

"We need to find an inn or we'll be sleeping in the open, and we can't set fires in the city," Prior said, focusing on the tangible. The bed-related tangible. *Get your head together, Prior.*

Fenton grimaced. "No more people."

"I'm sorry, I truly am, but I can't walk all night. I can, however, die of exposure quite easily, and winter isn't so far around the corner that isn't a concern." Prior tried to affect a light tone as his lust flagged and his concern rose. Thus far, he and Fenton had been relatively united in purpose, if not execution, but Fenton's grasp of Prior's mortality seemed to fade in and out. Prior needed to make himself understood. "*I* need somewhere under shelter to sleep. Warm and cheap, for preference. You can go on ahead if you—"

"No." Fenton tilted his head, as if listening to something beyond Prior's senses. Then he grabbed Prior's hand in his shockingly hot one. "This way, the birds say."

"The birds?" Prior's attention locked onto Fenton's hand around his, and his mouth continued on without conscious input. "At least it's not rats, I suppose."

Trotting to match Fenton's brisk pace, Prior followed him through the narrow, meandering streets of Northrope's dock quarter. The air hung thick with fish and salt, and he cupped his free hand over his nose and mouth for the little good it did. Some night traders glanced at them from dark alleyways, but Prior didn't meet their eyes. He didn't have time, not with Fenton's unrelenting strides. He might be shorter than Prior, but Fenton's height appeared to be all in his legs.

Prior needed to stop thinking about Fenton's body.

He focused on their surroundings, which were becoming marginally fresher smelling but no more salubrious.

"Where are we going?" he asked, belatedly. "Have the birds been any more forthcoming?"

Fenton didn't answer, but he turned a corner and the answer presented itself. A mostly intact roof sloped over a sad wooden building that, to gauge by rotten hay scattered hither and yon, had once served as a stable. Squinting through the lowing light, Prior made out remnants of paint on the lopsided door: a faded yellow sheaf of wheat. He found a corresponding shape painted on a nearby building, and though the paint was brighter, the windows were dark; a closed down inn, then. Prior could guess why the inn had shut, as they were far from the market square and the docks where most visitors would arrive. Indeed, the area boasted more shadows than light.

"Are you and the birds sure about this?" Prior glanced around again. "A closed inn and yard seems, ah, inopportune."

Fenton squeezed Prior's hand and led him toward the door, opening it with a swift, metallic yank. As Prior trailed him over the threshold, he saw broken chain links on the floor. He stepped carefully around them. The place smelled musty, but not actively unpleasant. Yet it was far from an inn.

"It is dry and the birds said there are candles..." Fenton trailed off. He released Prior's hand and darted into the swallowing dark.

Clattering and clanking noises followed. Prior shifted in place and tried to match the noises to benign actions instead of face-eating creatures of the night. His hand felt cold without Fenton's in it. He tried to think of other things. That had been the thump of hay, hadn't it? And that clinking—some old chain?

Why did Fenton need chain?

A burst of light seared Prior's eyes and made him flinch. When he blinked away the spots, he saw Fenton had lit the remnants of a stubby candle and set the holder on a dusty, upturned pot. He'd arranged sacking to form a very meagre bed, and shoved what remained of various rusted equipment aside. The building had been used to store all manner of things, with hay forks and rotten barrels pushed against the wall, and deflated grain sacks in every corner.

Prior toed the "bed". He eyed Fenton, who had undoubtedly done the best he could. He'd been living in a forest, after all.

"Is there a reason we're not in the inn itself? Since it's right there?" Prior asked.

Vines moved in Fenton's hair. "The inn has guests already."

Guests. By Fenton's tone, Prior assumed he didn't want to meet said guests. Prior's head ached. He needed to sleep.

"Very well! If this is our bed you've made, let us lie in it. We'll rise early and seek directions to the mage. Failing that, we'll walk across this damn city until we find the mysterious Nola and shake her secrets loose. Figurative shaking. Don't shake the mage, please, Fenton."

Fenton tilted his head. It was not a reassuring response.

The thin sacking of the "bed" did little to thaw the cold of the flagstones, and Prior regretted letting Fenton and his birds lead him to the back end of Northrope to lie on the floor like a fool. His purse was light, certainly, but it could have stretched to more than *this*. Prior shuffled onto his side and curled his knees to his chest. He was sleeping in his boots, even. No one came to Northrope to sleep in their boots. He could've done that at home, if he'd been willing to have Sylvie shout at him for it.

Prior closed his eyes and tried very hard not to think about how near winter lurked. Like a shadow, it was. Like a promise. The lone candle painted the inside of his eyelids red.

A sudden warmth covered his body and he opened his eyes. What the—? Prior jolted to sitting, then gaped. Continued to gape.

"Fenton!" He couldn't think of another word to say.

The bed—and by extension, Prior—had been blanketed with flowers. A cheerful collection of colour and shapes, shocking in the gloom, exhaled a muddle of nearly overwhelming fragrance. The flowers were knitted together with delicate vines, much like Fenton's crown, and the amassed flowers, both familiar and strange, weighed on Prior like an embrace. He shakily ran his hands over the floral blanket. His fingertips thrummed at the variant textures.

When he finally lifted his gaze to Fenton, standing by the flickering candle, he found yet more warmth in Fenton's eyes and in the tiny smile tucked into the corner of his mouth. In the most overt act of his otherworldly power, Prior glimpsed the humanity in Fenton.

No. To assume such acts were in humanity's remit alone—the sentiment, if not the ability—was arrogance. Compassion belonged to no one.

"Thank you," Prior said, fervently. His eyes prickled. He wiggled his toes in his boots.

"Better?" Fenton asked.

"Much."

"You seemed cold."

Prior smiled. The expression felt blurry. "I was."

"You can sleep now?"

"I can. Will you?"

Fenton shook his head. Candlelight made dark pits of his eyes. "I will think on the question of the mage for some time longer. You must sleep. Good night, Prior."

Prior tugged the blanket to his chin. "Good night, Fenton."

Fenton blew out the candle. Settling onto his back once more, Prior ducked his head to smell the flower closest to him, the one with blood-dark petals the size of his thumb. It smelled like wine kissed from someone else's mouth. He breathed deep. When he fell asleep, it was to an image of Fenton's wine-stained lips.

Fenton had left Prior for but a moment. Only long enough to walk to the river in an attempt to discern a trail through the medley of magical signatures, under the hypothesis the current and the night might have cleared some of the haze. Fenton had stood at the murky banks, closed his eyes, and begun to reach his senses throughout Northrope in search of the strongest beacon of power shining in the vicinity.

He had scarcely progressed his search past the inn when a discordant, ugly pulse had reverberated behind him. Nearly immediately behind him. An owl had shrieked in hoarse outrage and Fenton had cursed himself for being no wiser than a fledgling stumbling from the nest. He should not have left Prior alone!

Fenton stepped through his shadow into the place he'd left Prior sleeping. Traces of transportation magic sparked in the air but there remained naught else besides a trampled blanket of flowers and a blown-out candle. Nothing of Prior but a few strands of hair.

Rage howled in Fenton. It surged from his body in the sharp bite of fangs and claws, and throbbed at his temples in a familiar rhythm. Thorns rippled from his vines and his shadow flowed over his body, hardening to chitinous armour. His deadwood heart cracked like the shell of a nut. Fenton roared and a city of creatures replied in kind.

Crouched over the place where Prior had slept, Fenton inhaled the story of his scent. Sleep-sweat, musk, and Prior's distinct fern smell. Another breath brought leather and metal, and the piquant tang of old blood: hunters had been here, not long before. Fenton let his mouth hang open to taste the remnants of the transportation magic, his chest rumbling at the bitter flavour. He licked it from his teeth.

Rising to his feet, Fenton followed the faint traces of the transportation magic outside, where the city instantly devoured what remained of its trail. Frustration made him growl. What an accursed place! Then his nostrils flared at a fresh scent of smoke and meat, and he noted flickering light seeping from the main inn building. He followed the scent to confirm that the hunters were inside, yet he could not smell Prior.

No matter. One or more of the hunters' compatriots must have gone with Prior, and those who remained would tell Fenton where. Then he would kill them all.

Fenton burst into the inn with a roar, the door splintering beneath his blow. The contents of the room came to him in flashes—five leather-metal-blood hunters; a firepit; a crimson jewel that whispered weak magic; dust and dirt and cobwebs. No Prior. No scent of Prior.

"Where is he?" Fenton bellowed. The elongated shape of his muzzle made the words blur. By the sharp scent of urine, Fenton reasoned he'd been understood.

One of the hunters yelled to the rest and there followed a clattering of blades, but too slow. Much too slow. The hunters moved like sap. The piss-scented hunter fell to Fenton's fangs. The next found an end in Fenton's vines, gurgling out a hoarse protestation that polluted the air as much did the stench of their voided bowels. Blood splattered Fenton's face in a hot mist when he raked his claws over the third hunter, piercing the thin shell of their jacket, but they retaliated with a swift blow of their cudgel and the shock struck his hand numb. Another hunter swiftly picked up their fallen compatriot's cudgel. Fenton stumbled backward with a hiss and circled the fire, keeping it between him and the remaining hunters.

Two of them still stood, one with the cudgel, and one with a sword. Neither advanced. Cudgel-hunter gripped the weapon white-knuckle tight. Sword-hunter shakily assumed an offensive stance, eyes searching for weaknesses Fenton did not have. Fenton would use the sword to pick his teeth clean of the hunters' flesh. He lowered his head and rounded the fire.

"W-wait!" the cudgel-hunter stammered, eyes round and bright. Prior's flowers rimed the bottom of their boots. "We only wanted coin! If he'd given us the coin we would've gone quiet-like— Shit!"

Thorns erupted from Fenton's skin in bloody bursts. He stretched until he loomed over the hunters, until his crown nearly touched the ceiling. Spiders scuttled to the corners as their webs trembled. The fire lashed tall in its pit. Fenton threw back his head and *roared*. The night answered in a thousand voices—birds, bats, the far-off howl of a wolf, a universe of chittering insects. He would destroy these hunters and pour them into the river. Give them to the sea. His shadow hungered.

Fenton started forward with death on his mind.

"Where is he?" he asked again, prowling around the fire. He stepped over one corpse. Two. The hunters retreated, though they had nowhere to go. Fenton bared his teeth. He liked this game. "Where is he?"

Sword-hunter blustered. "Whatever kind of m-monster you are, it don't matter! You can keep asking but—"

"Shut it, Mik! It killed the others without blinking. Like they was dogs!" Cudgel-hunter turned pleading eyes on Fenton, weapon loose at their side. "We only wanted your coin, for the love of the mother. Saw you at the Trout with your fella, didn't we, when you were giving him shinies like they weren't nothing. Figured you were flush, like. Flush enough for ransom."

Fenton remembered the hunters now. The group at the inn, with the card game. He'd dismissed them as of no consequence. Anger and an unfamiliar, caustic feeling, curdled in his gut until he could taste acid. Killing the remaining hunters would not bring him closer to Prior. Fenton took a shallow breath. The night waited on his word.

"The lyin' rat said he didn't have coin, but it doesn't matter now. If you don't find 'im by dawn, Raine will slit his fucking throat," Mik sneered.

Then he screamed.

Then he made no sound at all.

With a twist of his shoulder, Fenton yanked his vines free from Mik's eye sockets, his thorns scoring bloody tear trails. Mik's severed arm fell across the fire. Fenton let it burn. He caught the sloppy blow from cudgel-hunter and tossed the weapon aside, then grabbed the hunter's hands in one of his and slowly, gleefully, tightened his grip. The hunter's fetid breath—old meat and sour ale—polluted the room in shallow whimpers. Bones creaked.

"Where is he?" Fenton asked, for the fourth time.

"I-I don't know! I don't fucking *know*! I never knew— Mik was in charge!" the hunter babbled. "He's always been in charge, from years back, ever since we found that fella with the diamond around his neck. Mik said you was the same and now he's *dead*. They're all dead!"

Salt and piss and blood and *still no Prior*.

Fenton tilted his head. "You cannot help me."

"No— No!"

Fenton left what remained of the hunters for the crows.

Outside, once more in tolerably human guise, his breath steamed in the cold air. Fenton clenched his teeth together until his jaw ached. Somewhere in the wretched city, Prior waited for his throat to be slit.

Fear shook Fenton like a leaf on a branch. Dust and blood smeared his clothes and clung to his skin. Even his vines were tired. He needed to find the mage, but he hadn't been able to locate the accursed Nola even at full strength, and he was far from that now. He bared his teeth.

The sound of footsteps made him startle even as he readied his claws, but the cloaked human offered their attention only briefly; their eyes flickered to Fenton's face, ears, hands, from beneath the covering of their hood. Then they continued on their way, gaze averted and shoulders hunched. Fenton appreciated the unasked-for discretion. Then he remembered Prior.

"Wait!" he called.

The human flinched but kept walking, curling their shoulders higher. Fenton strode forward and caught up with them. He darted in front until the human had to stop or walk into him.

"I didn't see anything! I'm going about my business, same as you—"

"I require directions to the mage," Fenton said, speaking over their protests. "Quickly."

The human lifted their head, allowing the hood of their cloak to fall back slightly. Their ears were pointed. Elfkin, Prior had called that trait.

"A mage?" the elf asked.

Fenton struggled to keep his teeth even. "Nola. Might you direct me?"

The elf sucked their teeth. "You'll have difficulties seeing her. Better with the healer that sees poor folk sometimes, out near the marketplace, but she don't always answer when you call. And she's more likely to help with sicknesses, like, not..." The elf trailed off, but the flick of their eyes toward Fenton's bloodied hands made the rest of their words clear.

Not with killing.

Fenton lifted his hand to press at his chest when it ached. "I do not require a healer. I require the mage."

"Well, if you're sure. No harm in directing you."

After receiving directions, and a brief clasp to his upper arm, Fenton went with haste to the blue door at the end of the docks. Mint and lavender were the scents he had to find. He asked rats for help, those few he could divert from rutting, and quickly located the door set in one of many large, neglected buildings along the dockside. The paint on the door had faded and the walls were pockmarked with neglect. The mint and lavender plants were withered, their scents mere echoes of themselves.

Dawn threatened.

Fenton stretched the boundaries of his senses and sent his shadow through the gap beneath the door. It rebounded with a sting that made Fenton snarl. Wards. He closed his eyes and opened himself to the city, to the magic that sang in every stone. The rush threatened to overwhelm him but he fought against it, thinking of Prior.

When he opened his eyes again, he grinned. There was a garden.

Fenton flexed his claws and leapt, applying himself to the edifice. The building was tangible—stone under his claws attested as much—but its true shape had been concealed by a façade, making it seem more haggard than in fact. Climbing quickly and carefully, Fenton reached a protruding balcony, hidden by magic from the street below. He ripped a hole in the magical wards wide enough to send his shadow through and followed after in a tumble.

What greeted him justified the wards. Magic had grown a garden and it was *beautiful*. Fenton's shadow rushed ahead to learn the shape of the vast garden, glowing beneath a glass ceiling, heady with perfume and merry with the chatter of birds. A lithe fox wound around his ankles before darting away. Fenton stood beneath the embrace of a willow that whispered to a crystalline pond and listened to a chorus of nightingales. He wanted to linger. He could not.

"Not what I had expected to find when my wards were broken, I admit. Not that I expected my wards to be broken at all."

Fenton glanced over his shoulder. The mage wore close-fitting breeches and a shirt that billowed as if to compensate. Her round face showed years in the lines at the corners of her eyes, and her close-cropped hair shone silver as the coins Fenton did not have. Magic thrummed from her in a haze. She was strong for her kind. An oak.

Fenton was a mountain. Turning back to the tree, he raised his fingers so a bird might land on them. "The wards were adequate."

"'Adequate', he says. Adequate! I'm famous for them, haven't you heard? Though I suppose you wouldn't have listened, even if you had. That's what the stories say about you, isn't it? You're not one to listen," she said.

Fenton listened to the bird for a moment, then lifted his hand gently to encourage it to return to the nest. He turned fully around.

"You are the mage. Nola."

"I have that pleasure. What name might I call you?" she asked.

"Fenton. I require your help. Quickly. I should not have—" Fenton shook his head. Focused. "My— He's gone. Prior. There was transportation magic but the city confuses me. Here." Fenton withdrew the crimson jewel he'd taken from the hunters. "Can you find him with this?"

Nola's lips curved. She had scented prey. "What will you give me should I help you find your Prior?"

Fenton did not have the luxury of time. *Prior* did not have the luxury of time. Fenton had dithered once more at Prior's expense. Anxiety rapped on the drum of his deadwood heart. Though his gut twisted and a muscle flexed in his jaw, Fenton knew what he must say.

"If it harm none and be within my power to give, and in yours to receive, you may have it." He let some of his magic creep into his eyes as he spoke. If the words were not enough, he would find another way.

Nola's eyes widened and she took a step back as if Fenton's vow had landed a physical blow. Fenton almost smiled; whatever game Nola thought she was playing, he had learned long before. Nola waved her hand sharply. Rings glinted on her fingers.

"That is not— I would be honoured to help your friend, Fenton." She said his name with a strange weight. "No payment necessary. Here, give me the gem."

As Fenton dropped the stone into Nola's hand, he caught her eyes. "Please. Quickly."

She nodded. "It will be done."

When the silver-haired woman appeared in a cough of

99

smoke, a bright, broken-glass smile dimpling her cheeks, Prior knew he was about to die. His hands shook in his bonds. The other woman—Raine, he'd heard one of the bandits say—had thrown him in the dank boat cabin, kicked him in the face, and sneered a promise that he wouldn't see dawn. She'd left him with a porthole facing east, so he could see death coming.

He hadn't thought Raine would permit another to kill him, but what did Prior know of bandits?

The boat rocked in the water but the new woman rolled her rounded hips like she'd been born at sea. Prior scrambled into the corner of the cabin, for all that would help, and tried to look his death in the eye. He swallowed the saliva that rushed into his mouth. He wouldn't shame himself further. Exhaustion and fear had strangled him since he'd jolted awake to find Fenton gone and bandits in his place. But he could raise his bloodied chin, couldn't he, and hope his killer remembered his face.

But the woman stopped advancing. She glanced at something in her hand, then back to him.

"I haven't been on many rescues, so I suppose I should check. You're Prior, aren't you? Friend of the one calling himself Fenton?" she asked, arching a single brow.

"Friend of the— I'm Prior. Yes. I'm Prior," he answered, focusing on the part of her question that made sense.

Nothing made sense.

She grinned and tapped the whatever-it-was in her hand. "Excellent." Then, bizarrely, she said, "I've a delivery for you."

Though dawn's fingers were already resting their tips on the porthole, an encompassing darkness abruptly surged through the cabin like the coming of a second night. Goosebumps swarmed Prior's skin and he shuddered uncontrollably. Even the woman seemed disconcerted, and he had the impression she didn't often permit herself surprise. The boat swayed as if hit by a great wave and Prior fell hard against the wall and slumped to the floor, air knocked from him. As he gasped, he heard a cry from abovedecks—Raine—and cringed, but then he heard a sound like a branch splintering underfoot and a hand reached out of the shadows to grasp his. A warm, familiar hand. Prior let his eyes fall shut.

"Fenton." He sighed the name into the dark.

Fenton squeezed Prior's hand. "I am sorry I lost you."

"I am found."

Soft fingers traced the slope of Prior's nose where dried blood tightened his skin. "I am sorry you were hurt because of my failure."

Prior's heart did something complicated. His face hurt, his wrists hurt, his chest hurt, perhaps even his heart, but how could anything ache more than the sweet tone of Fenton's apology? Prior wanted an explanation for Fenton's disappearance, but it could wait. He opened his eyes. The darkness had retreated from the cabin to look out from Fenton, on his knees at Prior's side; Fenton's pointed face was painted with blood and worry, and as welcome a sight as any Prior had yet seen.

Prior licked his lips. "Can we—"

Before he could finish his question, the cabin door slammed open and booted feet stomped in. Prior's hand tightened around Fenton's and he pressed himself against the wall. Raine wore armour and had twin daggers at her hips, and she had laughed when the other bandits mentioned ransoming Prior. She'd said she'd known his gift from Fenton to be simple glass, not a gem as the others believed, but had gone along for the sport of it. She'd thrown the glass through the porthole after they'd emerged from the transportation spell.

"What the fuck is all this?" Raine demanded as she entered the cabin, a dagger already in her hand.

The other woman exchanged a look with Fenton, then shrugged and leaned against the cabin wall, tucking her hands behind her back.

"All yours," she said to Fenton with a sunny smile.

Raine didn't wait on etiquette. She lunged forward with a yell, her dagger raised and aimed for Fenton. Knelt on the floor, his hand still in Prior's, Fenton had nowhere to move and no time to act. Prior braced and closed his eyes like a coward. He might want to stare his own death in the face, but he couldn't bear to see Fenton's. Prior couldn't let him go.

He didn't have to. A crisp, summer-scented breeze tousled Prior's sweaty hair. A wet noise, like the slap of meat against a chopping board, sounded close to his ears and he jerked in place. Someone gagged and the sour, hot stench of vomit made Prior wrinkle his nose. Fenton squeezed their joined hands.

"You can open your eyes," Fenton said.

When Prior did, he didn't understand what he saw. The cabin walls were misted red and there were lumps of— Prior saw two daggers in the mess, their blades clean, and realised that Raine had been spread across the cabin in fleshy chunks. The cabin smelled like a charnel house.

He stared at Fenton, whose grave-dirt eyes had taken on a glossy sheen, though that might have been a reflection of the fresh blood that daubed Fenton's face. Fenton's features seemed more animalistic than usual: something in his mouth, in the broad points of his ears. Prior swallowed thickly.

"Charming as all this viscera is, I'm not staying one second longer." The woman spoke brusquely, as if to hide the shaking of her voice. She wiped the corners of her mouth with her little finger, then arched her eyebrows at them. "Do you want to dwell here until the guards or the rats find you, or do you want to clean up in my garden? I can heal Prior's injuries, if you like, as good as new. A one-time offer, in return for the strangest night of my life."

Fenton blinked sleepily at Prior. "This is the mage Nola. Do you wish to go to her garden?"

Nola? How had Fenton found the mage? Prior couldn't

have been missing for that long, surely. Feeling detached from his body, he nodded at Fenton, then at Nola. He carefully didn't look at anything else in the cabin.

"Yes, please. Anywhere away from here," Prior said.

"By transportation spell?" Nola asked, looking at Fenton.

Rather than answer verbally, Fenton rose to his feet. His clothes rasped as he moved, creases unsticking from the grip of congealing blood. Dawn inched over him and invigorated the flowers in his crown, bringing glossy yellow colour to the dingy cabin. Behind him, Fenton's sleek shadow—for at once, Prior realised that was what the blackness must be—painted his exaggerated shape on the wall.

Fenton offered his hand to Prior. Prior knew, if he took it, that things would change. Again. By taking Fenton's hand, he would travel however Fenton had, and he would know him more fully than he did in the present moment. He didn't know where the journey would next take them, but he knew he could never turn back after taking that step.

"We will meet you there," Prior told Nola.

He took Fenton's hand.

Nola muttered something unintelligible, then disappeared in a whipcrack of smoke, the boat rocking slightly in her wake. Prior saw her leave only from the corner of his eye. The hungry animal of his attention remained locked on Fenton, who helped Prior to his feet, then grinned as brightly as a boy playing pranks. His eyes crinkled and his pointed eyeteeth gleamed. Prior shivered. The cabin wasn't cold.

"I am glad you chose me," Fenton said.

Prior smiled. "I am, too."

Fenton's grin dimmed. His gaze flickered over Prior's face. "I would not give you cause to regret that choice. I will see you healed, and by gentler hands than mine." Prior didn't know there could be a touch gentler than Fenton's, but he nodded in understanding. Then Fenton gestured to the wall behind him, where his shadow waited. "We will travel by shadow. Have you travelled thus before?"

Laughter rocked Prior's shoulders. He shook his head. "I haven't travelled by shadow before, no."

Taking hold of both of Prior's hands, Fenton laced their fingers together. He walked backward, as Prior walked forward, until he reached the wall.

"Close your eyes," Fenton said. When Prior did, he continued. "Follow me."

Fenton started to walk backward again. Implausibly backward, as the wall had been behind him and yet nothing impeded their progress as Prior followed Fenton into the welcoming mouth of the incredible dark. Trust made Prior's steps firm. The fear that had been his companion through the night had shattered with the arrival of dawn and Fenton. Prior held Fenton's hands and trusted him. He walked.

He could smell flowers. Hear birds.

Fenton squeezed his hands. "Open your eyes."

Prior did, and gasped in delight. "This is wonderful!"

They stood in a garden of colour and light, a world away—possibly literally—from the dank cabin. There was a willow tree overlooking a pond, and Prior followed the bobbing flight of a sparrow until his attention was drawn to a small rabbit venturing across the grass on comically oversized paws.

Nola's voice came from behind them. "Make a move, his face won't fix itself."

Sitting on a blanket spread over the grass, cushions scattered around her, Nola patted the space beside her in invitation.

"This space for the patient." She jabbed her finger toward the far side of the blanket. "That space for the other."

Imperious as she was, Prior had the notion he owed Nola his life. He let her attitude wash over him. Besides which, they needed her help with the curse.

When he'd been waiting to die in the cabin, Prior had thought over and over of Sylvie's drawn face in her sickbed. Of the bodies in the hamlet. He'd tried to glimpse the moon from the porthole, wishing it back to a sliver, to give Sylvie more time while Fenton searched to break the curse. Whether Fenton would continue to search or not—and Prior remembered too well Fenton's words on the matter—Prior had to hope positively. He had to hope. His mind had swung between fear for himself and fear for Sylvie until sweat drenched his back.

And then Nola had appeared.

Prior sat cross-legged where Nola had indicated, though Fenton wandered off to the willow tree instead of sitting. Prior felt cold without his touch. He made fists at his sides and tried not to wriggle beneath Nola's knowing gaze.

When Prior had settled, Nola gave him a serious look. "I will have to touch your face to assess the damage in order to heal it. It will feel strange." She pursed her lips. "I'm not sure how strange, honestly, because there is other magic on you."

"There is?" Prior asked, alarmed.

Nola's gaze flicked briefly over Prior's shoulder. A complicated expression crossed her face. "I don't think you've anything to worry about," she said, and smiled at him.

"Oh."

"The magic seems new. If I were to guess, I'd say he's worried about losing you again. Can't always rely on the kindness of mages, after all."

Warmth curled in Prior's stomach. "*Oh*," he said again. All other words were out of reach.

"I'd ask for the story of how you two met, but I suspect that particular tale is not yet complete." Nola affected a lopsided grin. "Thought I had a story like that myself, once, but it transpired I was merely a passing chapter in her life. Left me *very* cross, let me tell you! Anyway, close your eyes. Let's make sure you keep that pretty face in good repair so the inevitable ballads don't have to do all the heavy lifting."

If Fenton's magic were an avalanche, Nola's was a needle: they were utterly different. Nola's magic had been honed for a purpose, by people. Fenton's magic was of the earth itself and nothing in him would ever bow to a need other than his own. Fenton was the hurricane; Nola the house clinging to its foundations as the storm passed through.

Prior would not have known to appreciate how unstructured, *unbound* Fenton and his magic was, without Nola's smaller, neater, working for comparison, and he found himself missing Fenton in a new way entirely. He sighed as Nola began to work, and thought about another's touch.

Time passed.

From far away, Prior heard voices.

"—should do the trick, if I've studied my anatomy correctly. I think I did. The naughty bits were more interesting, of course, but I'm reasonably sure I got his important parts in order."

"Be very sure."

"On my magic, I am as sure as I can be that your Prior will recover no worse the wear for his misadventure. And here"—an odd sensation, as if stroking a cat's fur against the grain, but all over—"I've cleaned away those bloodstains that were bringing down the place."

"Thank you. For the healing. The bloodstains were inconsequential."

Prior came fully back to himself with a laugh. Fenton sounded so stiff!

"Prior?"

A squeeze to his shoulder made Prior open his eyes. He found himself laid on his back on the blanket, with Fenton kneeling beside him, wiped clean of blood and dressed in a

106

fresh set of clothes. His wet hair curled at the ends, and his vines were lushly green. He smelled faintly of herbs and smoke. White flowers decorated his crown. Prior placed his hand over Fenton's on his shoulder and felt his expression soften.

"Hello again," Prior said.

Fenton's eyes fluttered shut and he expelled a sound that might have been a prayer. To whom did such creatures offer thanks?

Pushing himself to sit upright with his legs outstretched before him, Prior smiled as Fenton once more gripped Prior's hand in his. As if Fenton needed a grounding touch, or simply wanted it. Prior smoothed a strand of Fenton's hair with his free hand and tucked it behind Fenton's pointed ear, wishing that he might be able to reciprocate the thanks by his touch. Fenton tilted his head toward Prior's hand and Prior breathed deeply of the green garden. His pain and fear belonged to a fading dream. He lifted his gaze to the woman who had healed him. The mage Nola.

Reclining on a sumptuous chaise, her head propped on her hand, Nola seemed very much like a mage from one of Sylvie's story books. Confident, compelling, and draped in an attention-grabbing green silk cloak. Her lips were painted to match. When she looked between him and Fenton, her eyes narrowed in a way Prior found unsettling, but she had healed him. If he understood correctly, she'd been the one to find him and bring Fenton to the boat. He had no reason to think she would hurt them.

He met Nola's eyes. "Thank you for your help. Thank you for finding me, and likely saving my life." Prior averted his eyes as a thought came to him about the mage and her services. "However, I must confess we have no coin to pay you."

Nola barked a laugh, as if shocked. She conjured a golden goblet with a flick of her wrist and lifted it once, as if in toast. "I have already been offered payment, and I refused. It is no matter."

"It matters to me quite a bit."

"And I," Fenton murmured, without opening his eyes.

Surprise flittered across Nola's face, quickly quashed. She took a long draught from her goblet and dismissed it from sight, only to drum her hand against the rise of her hips, as if nervous. Morning shone through the glass ceiling, making her cloak glitter emerald: a jewel among the dirt. Prior wondered how Fenton had dug her up, and if he'd remembered to ask the question that had brought them to Northrope in the first place.

He squeezed Fenton's hand for his attention, and grave-dirt eyes found his.

It took Prior a moment to remember his question. "Did you ask about the curse?"

Fenton's vines flickered as a ripple of pink buds opened and closed around the stems of his crown. With a grunt, he shifted to face Nola more fully. He smoothed his thumb across Prior's knuckles as he spoke. Birds twittered across the garden.

"There is a blight and I require assistance to find the source, as there is much magical interference. I know it is nearby, but time is a concern. We came to this place to ask your advice," Fenton said, more flatly than Prior had heard him for a while. As if he were resentful of having to explain himself. Prior tried to catch his eyes, but failed.

Nola studied Fenton. "To ask? Or to demand?"

"I require only a better sense of direction," Fenton said.

Prior reminded himself that he knew nothing about magic and therefore should keep quiet, even with Fenton being unhelpfully vague. With, again, the mage who had saved Prior's life. Which Prior very much needed.

"Any help you may offer would be gratefully received," Prior blurted, before Fenton could say anything else.

For a long moment, Prior thought he'd ruined whatever fragile truce had been brokered, but then Nola let out another short laugh and shook her head. Sitting upright, she studied Fenton's face, the line of his shoulders, his hand in Prior's, and seemed to read something on him that Prior could not. She smoothed down her perfect cloak.

"I know the curse you mean, and I know the location you seek. I will even offer my assistance with cursebreaking for the individuals affected, if you wish, but to remove the source itself... You are far better suited to the task then I." Nola flicked her fingers in the air, her rings glinting in the light. "Some things are beyond even my celebrated skills. As it is, I've narrowed the source to a small area, and there's but a single estate on that land. Knowing the landowner as I do, or as I thought I once did, I'd wager that's where you want to go."

"If you have all that information, then why haven't you gone there yourself?" Prior asked, heat in his voice. Fenton pressed their shoulders together, and Prior took strength from the support.

Nola lifted a hand loosely. "No one has paid me to. Haven't you heard? Mage Nola doesn't work for free." She smirked at Fenton. "Even for you."

Her mind changed on a whim. Prior wondered why she had helped them, so instantly, for nothing, when she wouldn't help all those affected by the curse. It didn't make sense.

"What do you want for this information?" he asked. She had refused payment once, but twice? He feared what she might ask, and it made his words sharp.

Nola seemed to have been waiting for the question. "Can I tempt you to accompany me to a dance? All the great and good will be there, and I need a way to discourage more invitations. A small explosion, perhaps? I'm sure he could find something up his furry sleeve."

Though Fenton made a contemplative expression, Prior answered first. "No."

"I suspected that might be your answer. My garden, then. Have that one tend my herbs with his green fingers and we'll call it done."

Prior didn't like the way Nola spoke around Fenton, but he didn't want to start a fight with a mage, either. For one thing, he'd only have to ask her to heal him again afterward. For another, they'd never get the answers they needed.

Anger and relief fought within him. Anger at Nola knowing the source of the curse and letting it continue unchecked. Relief at the thought they might soon break it. He took a short breath and expelled it. The important thing was that Nola *would* help. Dwelling on past inaction would do nothing but stain future feeling, and he couldn't go back in time and change anything, no matter how much he wanted to.

Taking another measured breath, he nudged Fenton with his shoulder. "Can you do as Nola asks? You don't have to."

"It will be done," Fenton said.

Prior nodded at Nola and she rose to her feet.

"Then I'll return at noon, and give you the information you want. Good morning, boys," she said.

Nola left the garden through the nearby door and Prior let himself slump sideways to rest against Fenton's bony shoulder.

"Will you really be able to do as she asked?" Prior wasn't even clear what Nola had requested, in truth.

"I will check her herbs and ensure they grow true," Fenton said. He clicked his tongue, something he hadn't done before. Prior wasn't sure what it was meant to convey. "Some people need an excuse to care."

Prior's chest tightened at Fenton's quiet words. He struggled against them. "But she's known about the curse this whole time and done nothing! I can't help but wonder why we should do anything for her. I know we're exchanging for information but— It galls me, a bit."

Fenton hummed lowly, in that way he had. "The mage Nola helped you, and she did so for free, despite her words. There is much I would do if she asked."

Prior couldn't bring himself to argue again.

They remained there, side by side, for a short while, as birds sang and water ran and Prior let the scent of living fill his lungs. He looked down at their joined hands; Fenton's palm was narrower than Prior's, his fingers more slender, and his nails nearly opaque white rather than the pink Prior was used to seeing on his own hands. His hands bore no scars, unlike Prior's, which were marked by a lifetime of farming. He wondered if Fenton liked that about Prior, that he wore the earth on him. Perhaps it reminded Fenton of home.

"I lost your stone," Prior remembered. "I'm sorry."

"I lost *you*. I am sorry."

Put like that, Prior didn't feel as bad. "I suppose we should start on these herbs, then. Don't look at me like that, I've tended a garden before."

"I believe you."

"And then can we return to Ashcroft? Just for a bit. I want to see Sylvie."

Fenton nodded. "We will take her some sweet buns."

Prior pressed his grin into Fenton's shoulder, afraid its brightness would confuse the birds. "I can't believe you remembered that."

"Find the mage, find sweet buns. Simple enough."

"Anything but," Prior murmured. He again considered their joined hands, and how easy the connection felt. He'd smoothed back Fenton's hair earlier and Fenton had accepted the touch as if Prior had done it a hundred times. Prior caught Fenton's eyes. "Does this feel strange to you, how comfortable we suddenly are?"

Fenton lowered his gaze to their hands. He'd wondered the same, then, to understand what Prior meant. Fenton lifted and dropped his shoulder, the one Prior leant upon.

"Much of the world feels strange to me, Prior. You do many things that I do not understand, though I would like to. But this?" Fenton raised their joined hands. "To me this is as a seed planted in good earth. I would grow together with you, if you wish it."

Prior's chest hitched. His pressed his face against Fenton's shoulder until stars sparked behind his eyes. Had Fenton truly said all that? He couldn't have. Prior must still be waiting for dawn in the cabin. No sun could rise on such words.

He couldn't let Fenton think they were unheard.

Prior pushed himself upright. His smile trembled. He drew calm from Fenton, who watched placidly as Prior pulled himself together.

"You... You terrify me, Fenton," Prior said, and tugged Fenton down as he went to rise, his expression shuttering. "No, sit, please." As Fenton did, Prior continued, picking his way through what he wanted to say. "You do, but not only because you are... what you are... but because I've never felt this way about anyone before. I don't know if I'm feeling too strongly too fast, or if other people feel like this all the time. If this is what ballads sing about." He smoothed his thumb along Fenton's forefinger where their hands were joined. "I'm excited to see how we will grow together, but I must be honest."

"But you want this?" Fenton asked, as warmth returned to his face.

Prior ducked a kiss to Fenton's fingers. "I do. Whatever it turns out to be."

A boyish grin crept across Fenton's face and two points of colour spotted his cheeks. Prior beamed at the sight. Refraining from asking further questions—his nerves were frayed enough for one morning—Prior shifted his feet beneath him.

"Come on, then. Up with you. We've a garden to prettify."

Prior rose, and Fenton let himself be pulled to his feet. Prior glanced around the garden, searching for a bed of herbs or something more clearly tended than the flowers that occupied the majority of the space. If he were a mage, where would he put the herbs? Near water? He frowned at the sparkling pool.

"Over there, do you think?" he asked.

When Fenton didn't answer, Prior looked at him. Though their hands were still joined, Fenton's expression had sobered and a shadow flickered in his eyes as he caught Prior watching him.

"What is it?" Prior asked. Whispered.

Fenton's mouth thinned. "My sibling is— They are very strong. Whatever has changed their magic must thusly be likewise. My sibling was the one to ensnare me in the forest. For a human, even a mage, to go against them... I understand why Nola did not try to break the curse herself. She is right to be scared. As are you."

Prior licked his lips. "And you? Are you scared?"

Fenton didn't answer.

HUNTING TWO HARES
(IN VINO VERITAS)

After the god and its acolyte left her garden, Nola released a long, unsteady breath. When her wards announced the two creatures had crossed the threshold of her house, she stood, and exited the small room where she had been waiting. Not hiding—what mage would hide in their own domain?—merely waiting. In perfect silence. In the dark. Shaking.

Several layers of intricate spells unwound as Nola released their protection. The ache that had been clawing behind her eyes for hours finally eased as her magic stretched languorously out of the taut shape she had been holding it in. Knots loosened in the muscles of her back. Lanterns flickered to life as she strode along the hall toward the garden, flickering over the faces of portraits that had never before unsettled her. Their knowing, painted eyes made her skin crawl. She transformed every portrait to a bucolic scene. Cows were relaxing.

The hallway opened onto the garden. Northrope's walls had brought Nola accolades, the freedom of the city, and a messy split with the owner of the Aspinwick Estate, but the garden was her jewel. Many joyful hours had been whiled away in pursuit of clever spellwork, and in pursuit of nothing at all. Birds sang in the branches of trees she'd imported—by drudging, manual methods—via the port at Spear Bluff, carried over the vast ocean from the gardens of the world. Her herb garden rivalled any on the continent, and she occasionally sold some of the offcuts at eye-watering prices to those who wanted to boast they had a mage's own work flavouring their banal dinner party.

Nola had poured power and love into her garden.

She saw the god's pawprints on every blade of grass.

Conjuring a goblet of wine, Nola gulped it messily. Wine spilled from her mouth, over her chin, staining her white shirt in bloody blotches. When the goblet emptied, she tossed it aside in favour of a bottle, pulled from her cellar by a snap of fingers, and took long pulls until her hands stopped shaking.

A *god*. Breaking through her wards like they were parchment. Bargaining with her like the world wasn't pinned beneath one great paw, a word away from being broken in twain. The idea didn't seem to have even occurred to that vulpine brain.

Nola had been terrified and baffled by the whole situation—her mouth had run ahead of her, but she knew that refusing to aid a god would recoup nothing but death—and then she had followed the transportation magic to that sad little boat. There she had realised the truth, as the god had beheld that boy, Prior, like all the world's words were his to speak.

Banishing the empty wine bottle, Nola sat heavily on her chaise, where hours before she had played at composure. Her garden flourished prettily around her. A rabbit nosed at her slippered feet. She didn't remember ever bringing a rabbit to Northrope—animals and magic were rarely good friends—but there it sat, sniffling its pink nose.

"You are adorable," she told the rabbit, because it was. She hated it.

A bone-deep shudder suddenly shocked through her,

the magic of the garden quaking in turn. The rabbit made a startled noise and scampered away, whiskers quivering. Nola allowed herself to relax as best she could: the god had passed through Northrope's wards. She would never have to feel that enormous power scrape across her senses again. She closed her eyes and smelled the basil.

A crow called in its harsh voice. She had imported only songbirds. Nola opened her eyes, and stared at the crow perched on the edge of the chaise. Its glossy black feathers reminded her of things she had already decided to forget.

"They've gone to Aspinwick," Nola told the crow. Told herself. "It's none of my concern. None of yours, either."

The crow hopped in place.

"Don't ruffle your feathers at me, I helped as much as I could and look what I got. All this perfect damn nature nonsense. Just like I asked."

Altruism had never held appeal for Nola. Gold was far shinier. She let her head loll back and stared unseeingly toward the ceiling. How much gold would she be able to enjoy if the god and his acolyte returned? Nola didn't doubt her strength—she was, after all, one of the finest mages in the world and had the accolades to prove it—but she wouldn't deceive herself: to Fenton she offered no more threat than a twitching-nosed rabbit, without even the shield of cuteness to protect her. If he asked for something and Nola refused, she would be stewed.

"I think it might be time to relocate," Nola murmured to the ceiling. Sitting upright, she raised her eyebrows at the crow. "Time to ply my trade elsewhere, don't you think? Northrope has terrible weather, and I remember seeing an invitation from one of the southern republics. Sun, sea, and several thousand leagues away. All the worms you can eat. What do you say?"

The crow croaked a response.

Nola nodded, resolute. "Shuffle your feathers, we've packing to do."

PART FOUR:
HE OF BONE AND BARK

As Northrope's walls grew small behind them, Fenton's muscles finally unclenched. He relaxed his shoulders and flexed his hands at his sides. Dirt rounded his fingernails, as it did Prior's, but they hadn't lingered to wash nor rest, despite Nola's invitation. Fenton had thought to stay for Prior, who had recovered well from his ordeal but deserved respite, but Prior had graciously refused the offer. Keen to return home to Ashcroft, he'd said. Then he'd taken hold of Fenton's hand and started walking.

Fenton had had to navigate Prior to the exit of Nola's manse after Prior had taken a wrong turn into an alchemical laboratory, but the intent had not been lost on Fenton. No time for delay. He had thought to offer travelling by shadow, but his strength had not yet recovered. The previous journey had taken more from him than he'd expected, and Prior had not asked. Fenton would have tried regardless, if Prior had asked.

They'd continued out of Northrope with only a brief detour to purchase provisions—and sweet buns—from the market, and neither had spared the city a farewell. Though Prior had scarcely stopped speaking about it; Fenton's ears itched from listening, and his temples throbbed ferociously, but Prior hadn't yet released his hand and the touch occupied Fenton's mind so thoroughly it was difficult to care about anything else at all.

"Do you think I'd be able to grow a garden like Nola's behind the cottage? It was beautiful. You could show me how best to grow things, couldn't you?" Prior nudged Fenton's shoulder with his own. "And those birds! They adored you. Singing their little songs like ladies flutter fans. Do you understand birds?"

Fenton glanced at Prior, who smiled at him. Fenton had almost lost that smile entirely. He could not be so careless again.

"Well? Can you speak with birds?" Prior asked.

"Anyone can."

"Ah, but can anyone understand what they say in reply? That big hulking raven you were glowering at earlier, what did they say?"

Something not unlike "*piss off, fox-face, of course I'll help*". Ravens weren't renowned for their formality.

Fenton had tasked the raven to carry a vial holding a cure for Sylvie. He'd dictated instructions for its application to Prior, who hastily scrawled them along with a promise of an explanation on both the situation and creation of the cure when they arrived in Ashcroft. Nola had created the cure for the sleeping sickness the blight caused among humans, but she had reiterated that the potion addressed only the blight's symptoms. She could not offer any remedy for the dying livestock or withered crops, nor how the blight was spreading its influence unchecked. After depositing Prior in Ashcroft, Fenton planned to journey to the Aspinwick Estate and hopefully break the blight itself.

He needed to do so with haste. Maintaining the connection to Ashcroft, preventing anyone else falling victim to the blight, required a constant drain on Fenton's energy. What had begun as an almost unnoticeable trickle had grown to a steady stream of outward magical flow as the moon fattened to full. He had considered severing the connection and directing all his energies toward breaking the blight itself—but he didn't want to see Prior's face, should Ashcroft fall.

All of which meant he scarcely had the fortitude to follow a conversation, much less take part in it.

"Let's break for lunch, what do you say?"

Fenton blinked heavily at the tug on his hand. They'd stopped walking. When had they stopped walking?

Prior tugged Fenton's hand again, and jerked his chin toward an upturned log to the side of the road. "Shall we sit?"

Nodding, Fenton sat on the log. Prior released his hand to search through his pack, humming tunelessly as he did. Fenton rested his hand on the log and watched a spider nudge his fingertip, determining what the new thing was, before scuttling away again. Rabbits rustled in the hedgerow. Fenton listened with one ear for any passing gossip, but they were focused on their lunch.

As was Prior. Tearing a bread roll in two, Prior deftly stuffed each half with some crumbled cheese, and passed one half to Fenton.

"Eat," he instructed.

Fenton felt Prior's keen attention as he wolfed down the bread and cheese, then did the same with the second half when Prior passed it over. After that, he drank from their waterskin, and then another roll appeared, and more cheese. A wineskin. Crumbs covered his lap and Fenton licked his fingertip to capture as many as he could. When there were no more, he wrapped his arms around his heavy stomach and groaned. He did not *need* to eat, but perhaps he should do so more often, if it restored him thusly.

A tentative touch to his hair made him look up. Prior smiled and continued carding his fingers through the ends of Fenton's hair, careful to avoid his vines and flower crown. Their touches had grown more frequent, and each struck Fenton anew with his good fortune. The sun did not warm Fenton as much as Prior's presence did. Fenton's head quieted its clamour.

"Do you feel any better?" Prior asked, taking a seat beside Fenton.

Angling himself toward Prior, so there was no need for the stroking to stop, Fenton nodded. "Much. Thank you. I will gather more provisions to replace those I took."

"You didn't 'take' anything. The food is ours to share," Prior said, smoothing Fenton's hair back.

"But I owe—"

"No." Prior folded his hands in his lap. Fenton immediately missed his touch. "Let's not talk of owing between the two of us, shall we? You saved my sister's life. How could I ever possibly repay that?"

Fenton looked away. Their arrangement had been that Fenton would save Prior's sister, and Prior would help hurt Fenton's sibling in return. He didn't want to remind him of the reciprocal element, if Prior had forgotten. It had been only a short while since that conversation, but that version of Fenton seemed to be from very long ago. The revenge of something better left sleeping.

He was almost certain, now, that Lorcan needed his help. Prior would want Fenton to help Lorcan, if he could. Hadn't Prior done all he could for Sylvie? Surely Fenton could do no less than a human had attempted.

Perhaps he could ask Prior for assistance with Lorcan?

"I will gather more food from the tavern, the one between here and Ashcroft. We stopped there before," Fenton said, instead.

"You'll have a bother. We're not going that way this time."

"What do you mean?"

Prior pointed over his shoulder, away from the road. "I thought we'd go across country, rather than follow the road. It should take half a day or so off our journey. I wasn't certain of the route before, but I paid attention on the way here, and I've got it now. There's an old farmstead we should reach before nightfall. We can overnight there, and arrive in Ashcroft by noon, if we follow the river." He grinned. "Don't worry, I won't get lost."

Fenton would simply ask a bird for assistance if they did get lost, or use his connection with the village to navigate. Getting lost didn't concern him. Prior concerned him: already he'd suffered because of Fenton. Fenton would prefer to keep Prior in comfort, if he could, on familiar paths and with his own kind.

Then again, hadn't it been humans who'd attacked Prior in Northrope? Fenton frowned. His head redoubled its aching. There was no good choice.

But if there was no good choice, then there was no reason to argue with Prior's decision. The conclusion pleased Fenton.

"I will follow you," he said. "I trust you."

I trust you, Fenton said.

Prior wanted to hide his face in his hands and scream. Just for a moment. Just until he felt less overwhelmed. Until his fingertips forgot the touch of Fenton's hair.

Who was he trying to fool? That would take longer than a moment. The first touch had transformed the whorls on Prior's skin. He'd become someone new. Touch by touch, breath by breath, since a hand had reached out of the dark of that dank cabin and he'd recognised it as safety, he'd been changed. He and Fenton had been drawing together since they had met, like a vine growing around a stake, and Prior longed to know how they would flower as they reached together for the sky. Yet he feared the knowledge, too. Stories of mortals and gods never ended well.

He cleared his throat. No need to borrow trouble; it would arrive soon enough.

Once they arrived in Ashcroft, Prior would see Sylvie well and then sit Fenton down and ask what ailed him, for it was clear something did. The handful of days they'd known one another were enough that Prior could tell something worried Fenton; he'd become less stiff and remote, certainly, and Prior welcomed the change, if only for his own peace of mind, but he'd become paler, too, his skin and his vines washing with grey, and new lines scored between his brows. On anyone else they'd be marks of pain, but Prior hoped they meant something different on Fenton's face, as Prior didn't like to think what might cause such a being to suffer so. Perhaps their time in Northrope had worn on Fenton, and he would recover as they travelled farther from the city. Prior hoped that to be the case.

Cutting across country would reduce their travel time, and Prior could ask his questions sooner. It also allowed less time to talk himself out of the plan. Courage of this nature had never been something Prior needed to call on before, and he didn't want to open the cupboard of his soul and find it bare.

He dusted his hands against his trousers and stood. Fenton's vines twitched at the movement, and Prior untucked the vines from around Fenton's crown with a flick of his fingers. The vines had been semi-concealed since they had entered Northrope, but Fenton was a creature of the wild and he deserved to relax. Prior hadn't realised how he'd missed the expressive appendages until they were muted.

Fenton's brows furrowed, but he didn't pull away. "What are you doing?"

"You're all... Scrunched together," Prior said, not knowing the right words but meaning them all the same. He teased one of Fenton's vines around his finger, then tucked it behind Fenton's pointed ear and patted it in place. "There you go."

He stepped back and grinned. Small pink buds had emerged along the vine, blooming beautifully in Fenton's hair, as if in thanks. Prior inhaled the headiness of spring, similarly rejuvenated. Fenton still appeared worn, but they would rest soon enough. Prior glanced at the sky, then across the horizon, and considered their relative position to the farmhouse. They should reach it well before sunset.

He held out his hand. "Come on. The greater distance we put between us and Northrope, the better, don't you think?"

"I agree," Fenton said. He took Prior's hand. Somewhere, birds were singing.

Miles passed peaceably as they left the road and cut through carefully tended fields, the sun travelling behind them as they went east. Moorland rolled before them in gentle waves, with only the occasional rock or stray sheep to interrupt, and the day stayed dry and crisp. They passed through a thin ribbon of trees and Fenton lingered in the wood, pressing his fingers to one trunk after another. A sparrow alighted on the end of his upraised fingers and twittered merrily as Fenton inclined his head in solemn attention, then Fenton nodded and the bird went on its way.

If Prior hadn't already been half-infatuated with Fenton, the sight of him in the woods would have ensured his fall. Prior had been awed by Fenton from the instant they'd met, but at some point, and he didn't know when, Fenton had become someone tangible. Touchable. Prior's hand at home in Fenton's proved as much. Indeed, touching Fenton had become near all Prior could think about, despite the reason for their acquaintance being the curse threatening the lives of everyone in the moorland.

Fenton's hand was so warm. His grave-dirt eyes so kind. Prior wanted to be buried in them.

They left the woods for higher ground, a rocky outcrop that required concentration to scale. The outcrop was another reason for taking the merchant road to Northrope, but ascending it instead of going around shaved half a day off the journey, and the farmstead sat at the top. Prior and Baltair had explored this way as boys, roaming off in search of adventures and the occasional stray goat. Prior had fond memories of the place.

He did *not* remember anything about a *griffin*.

At first, Prior thought he saw a horse on the rise before the farmhouse, nosing at something in the overgrown grass. Then a shadow moved, or his eyes adjusted, and he realised three things in rapid succession: horses weren't that big, horses didn't have strange, hooked snouts, and horses *didn't have wings*. Part cat and part bird, but bigger than a draught horse and more frightening than any bandits, griffins had hunted the moorlands until the arrival of Fenton's forest had driven them north.

As Prior and Fenton stumbled to a stop, the griffin turned toward them and spread its magnificent wings in a display that chilled Prior with its sheer *size*. A single blow from those wings could easily break his bones. They were far enough away to retreat before he had to test that theory, but they needed to be quick. Prior had heard stories about griffin attacks and they were nearly all second-hand. He'd rather live to tell his own story.

Prior stumbled backward, reaching for Fenton as he did. "We need to run!"

But Fenton evaded Prior and stepped forward, putting himself between Prior and the griffin. Prior's stomach sank. He grasped for Fenton's shoulders but he might as well have been the breeze for all the notice Fenton took.

"I will request that the griffin return to their nest. All will be well," Fenton said, as if chatting with a griffin were something perfectly ordinary. "Wait here." When Prior shifted, Fenton's eyes hardened. "Wait here, Prior." Fenton strode toward the griffin with a determined gait.

The afternoon was cool, but when Prior shivered it had nothing to do with the weather. He folded his arms tightly across his chest and wished he'd brought his longbow to Northrope; he mightn't have deterred the griffin, but it would have been of more use to Fenton than panic.

Fenton's shadow oiled across the grass ahead of him.

No sign of Fenton's former tiredness showed as he crossed the distance toward the griffin. For its part, the griffin spread its wings and stood proud and tall—so much taller than a horse—and clacked its beak in warning at Fenton's approach. Fenton's head scarcely came level with the beast's chest ruff, and the griffin stood easily twice as broad as Fenton's shoulders. Prior's palms began to sweat.

Between the distance and the rising wind, Prior couldn't hear what Fenton said, but he saw Fenton gesture smoothly and point north. For a moment, Prior thought they would all three go on their way with no harm done.

But only for a moment.

With a sudden hoarse cry, the griffin reared onto its hind legs and spread its wings. Prior started running to help—Fenton was so tiny before the beast!—but the griffin's powerful scream punched through him and Prior fell to his knees. Desperately gathering his breath, he scrambled to his feet in time to see a wing smack Fenton and knock him onto his back. Another scream followed, triumph in discordant noise. The griffin's front paws rose as it reared again. If the griffin landed its weight onto Fenton, it would crush him. Prior's heart pounded in his ears. He shouted a warning as he sprinted toward Fenton's prone form, but a resounding *crack*, like a tree splitting open, ricocheted across the rise. The sound knocked Prior to the ground and made the griffin tumble backward, buffeted by the force.

Prior shoved to his knees, searching for the source of the noise. What he saw made him freeze. Where Fenton had fallen, a figure rose in his place. Kept rising. When it stood, it was on four enormous paws.

The creature matched the griffin's height, but the lines of its body were leaner and the thick brush of its tail made it seem longer. Prior had never seen a fox of such a size, but fox it resembled, with glossy russet fur, black socks, and a tail tipped startlingly white. Paws the size of serving bowls. Fangs like knives. A low, rumbling growl that made

Prior's hair stand on end and his nape prickle. Prior frowned toward the place where he had seen Fenton fall, where no one lay now, in some desperate bid by his brain to check what his heart already knew: there stood Fenton.

Prior made a noise, though he scarcely heard it over the frantic tattoo of his heart, as the griffin shrieked and began to prowl menacingly in his direction. Immediately, Fenton leapt to block the way and responded with a bellow of his own, a noise no fox had ever made. Fenton leapt for the griffin and knocked it down, pinning an outspread wing with one of his paws. The griffin beat its other wing furiously at Fenton's snout, but Fenton didn't relent. More screaming. More growling. The meaty tearing of claw through flesh, the snap of a razor-sharp beak around fur.

Prior's ears throbbed at the brutal cacophony and he swallowed around his rising gorge. He hunched small over his knees and covered his ears with his hands even as he watched the fight with stinging eyes, desperately trying to follow what his brain could scarcely comprehend.

Twisting dexterously in its pinned position, the griffin speared its beak through one of Fenton's shoulders with a sickeningly viscous sound that made Prior cringe. Fenton yelped—Prior would remember that noise until his dying day—but he didn't buckle. Instead, he jolted his weight forward, trapping the griffin's beak with his own shoulder even as the action must have caused him agony. He knocked aside the griffin's free wing with his other forepaw and managed to get his fangs to the griffin's twisting throat. Prior rose to his feet to see more clearly. Fenton's ears twitched, but he didn't turn from the puzzle of blood-spattered limbs.

Prior exhaled in relief as he saw what Fenton already knew: Fenton had the upper hand. Paw. With a heaving shudder, the griffin made the same realisation and went still.

Fenton and the griffin were a tableau of hurt, filling the air with the metallic stench of blood. The griffin glared balefully ahead. Fenton tilted his head to the side, in the manner Prior had come to know; the sight made his heart and fists clench. Prior wanted to undo the entire day. Let them begin again from Northrope's walls. He didn't want to be standing there, knowing what would happen next. He didn't want Fenton to do as he must.

Fenton breathed out long, making the griffin's feathers ripple. The griffin closed its eyes.

The ugly orchestra of breaking bones made Prior's stomach curdle. Bile burnt his throat and Prior twisted to the side as he gagged, frantically spitting until his mouth was clear. The acerbic stench of vomit stung his eyes. He rubbed at them as he stumbled over to Fenton, who had wandered away to stand with his back to the griffin's body. His white brush hung in the dirt.

"Fenton…" Prior didn't know what he could possibly say. The griffin had only been doing as a griffin did. It would have killed them both—and perhaps many more— if Fenton hadn't acted, but its death hurt nonetheless. Prior felt no relief.

He wanted to hold Fenton but could scarcely reach Fenton's torso, much less wrap his arms around the big furry body. Fenton stood almost twice Prior's height. He should have been intimidating; he smelled of the rich, deep heart of the forest, yes, but also the terrible stench of death, and he rumbled with a constant growl. Yet the sound held no anger in it. His head hung low. The growl made Prior think Fenton was experiencing some emotion he couldn't release any other way.

Prior tried again. "Is there anything I can do?"

A foolish question. He still wanted to know the answer, more than any other question he'd ever asked.

With his back to Prior, Fenton sat and curled his tail around his haunches. Sitting, now, he and Prior were of a height, and Prior could better see the wound the griffin had speared through Fenton's shoulder. Prior edged forward, intending to inspect the wound, but a strange storm-feeling rippled through the air and Fenton dropped his chest to the ground with a pained yowl.

Prior rushed forward but Fenton rolled onto his side and swept out a forepaw in a staying motion, then tossed back his muzzle and made the horrid noise again. His yowl burned into a bestial shriek as, with splintering bone and an explosion of blood, antlers burst from Fenton's skull. Prior clapped his hands over his ears and drew his shoulders up. He wanted to look away. He couldn't. The antlers stretched out and out like a rapidly growing tree, branch and twig and Fenton all coated in viscous sap that hissed as it met the air.

Fenton screamed until his voice shredded to a rasp. Prior burned with shame. What could he ever have done to help *that*? He watched helplessly as Fenton writhed in pain until, at last, the antlers finished growing. Fenton collapsed limply to his side, his ragged panting steaming in the spring air, the white fur of his chest gone pink with blood.

Prior lowered his hands shakily and inched across the grass. When Fenton didn't move but for the jerky heaving of his chest, Prior reached for the nearest paw.

"Fenton? It's me. It's Prior," he said.

Fenton's eyes fluttered open and Prior's breath caught as he saw their grave-dirt colour had been filmed with honey. A mesmerising play of brown and gold. With a chuff, Fenton rolled laboriously onto his front. Legs trembling, he pushed himself to four paws. Prior raised his hands in readiness to catch Fenton should he fall. Absurd; he'd be crushed. He intended to try nonetheless.

But Fenton didn't need the help. With a hoarse bark, he began to shrink and warp into the form of a man. It was difficult to watch and Prior's eyes couldn't fully translate the information to his mind. He saw hard-won antlers vanish to smoke, russet fur melt to pale skin, and then Fenton. Only Fenton, in his familiar not-quite-human guise, his shadow wrapped around his legs.

Once more on two feet, Fenton staggered and Prior leapt forward to catch him, adjusting his grip with care for Fenton's shoulder wound. Fenton's skin was slick with sweat and blood. His vines were limp.

"Easy there, take it slow. Can you walk? Once you've got your feet under you, we'll get you settled. The farmhouse is right there, do you see it? A few more steps. You've more than earned the rest." Prior supported Fenton's weight, far lighter than his presence, and inhaled the wild scent of him. "I have a hundred questions, at the very least, so you'll be needing your rest to answer them."

"Get them… in order," Fenton said with a wheeze.

Prior's startled laugh owed more to relief than amusement. "I will, I absolutely will. Very handsome, your other shape, by the by. Very large. Fangy." Prior had to keep talking or else he'd start to cry. "And a good thing red suits you, for you've brought it back in your hair. Steady!"

What little balance Fenton had regained was promptly lost as he grabbed for his hair and pulled a lock before his eyes, then staggered as he forgot to hold onto Prior. Prior tightened his arm around Fenton's waist and held him up, wincing at the bloody mess of Fenton's torso even as he took the opportunity to admire Fenton's changed features. To admire Fenton, in his arms and breathing. Out. In.

Fenton's eyes were newly goldened, and the tangle of his hair smouldered with the same russet as the fox's fur, making the white blooms of his crown as kisses caught in blood. The fox-like shape of his face had become more pronounced, somehow, perhaps through some subtle change to his cheekbones or the angle of his pointed ears, which were newly tufted in wisps of black fur. The sparse hairs on his chest were red, and a smattering of freckles capped his shoulders; if it weren't for the blood crusting Fenton's skin—blood he scarcely seemed to note—Prior would have been content to spend the day counting the tiny dots.

Fenton finished examining the new colour of his hair

and hummed. Then he prodded his temples and winced. Prior recalled him rubbing and scratching at the same area during the past few days. Intrigued, he tried to glimpse through Fenton's hair, but the knots and the vines didn't permit scrutiny.

"What is it? Are you cut there?" he asked. He hadn't seen a head wound, but one could be serious.

Fenton grunted. "Antlers are trying to grow."

"Of course, that should have been my first guess." Prior blanched. "It's not going to be as painful as it was before, is it?" Prior couldn't watch that again.

"No," Fenton answered, with gratifying quickness. Then he hummed. "I think not."

Prior decided against further questions. Gathering his strength and his courage, he nudged Fenton forward. "One step at a time. Not far, now, then we'll see to your wounds and you can rest." They could both rest.

The farmhouse stood on top of the rise, as it had for generations, though time and neglect showed in the pockmarked walls and the rotten beams of the roof. Yet the sky was clear and the weather mild, and no one would bother them in the night—at least, not once Prior removed the griffin downhill to deter scavengers. He would see to the griffin after settling Fenton, and before losing the light. The task would be intimidating enough without having to grapple a corpse in the dark.

With visible effort, Fenton finally got his human feet firmly under him and managed to complete the short walk, needing only marginal assistance from Prior. They managed the crooked door easily enough, as Prior and Baltair had long learned the trick of it, then Prior assessed their situation.

The farmhouse comprised a main room and a long kitchen to the rear, and had a handful of outbuildings that had long since fallen to disrepair. The main room had a partial wall that divided off a small sleep area—Baltair had used the motheaten sleep pallets for firewood one

130

autumn—while the main section boasted a stone firepit, which had been a large draw to them as boys. Over the years, Prior and Baltair and their friends had brought what they could spare for their "den"; old blankets and the ends of candles, some precious stolen mead, and all the secret things the moors had given them. The house stayed empty, as it sat on contested land, and so their childhood treasures had remained safe.

Prior hadn't visited the farmhouse since the summer before last, when he and Baltair had gotten howling-at-the-moon drunk as a goodbye to the place and the free time they'd had to spend there. The harvest had already started to dwindle then, and they'd seen the drawn faces of the village elders and knew there'd be hard days to come. Neither had spoken their fears aloud, but the mead had provided excuse enough to shout.

Perhaps Sylvie, or other moorland folk, had been by since, as the farmhouse looked no worse than it did in Prior's memory.

"Even better than I hoped!" Prior declared, though Fenton appeared sceptical. What did he know? He used to live in a forest. Prior spoke as he moved about the room, sweeping a layer of dust off the small table they'd used for games and setting his pack on it. "Baltair and I used to come here as boys, and Sylvie and her friends came later, of course. We all of us played here, and some brought company when there was nowhere else to go." Not a particularly romantic location, but the mostly-intact roof and lack of nosy neighbours spoke loudly in its favour. Propping Fenton against the nearest wall, and giving him a stern look to remain in place, Prior rummaged through the old chest tucked in the corner of the main room. "These blankets are musty but a brisk airing should see them right, and they're dry, at least."

The outbuildings had been more interesting to explore as a child—they held old, secret things brimming with potential stories—but the main room was by far the driest for overnighting. Blankets, candles, and bottle of mead someone had left behind, together with the provisions from their packs, would allow a cosy night.

Prior settled Fenton into a hastily swept corner in a nest of blankets, wary with his shoulder injury. Though Fenton didn't seem overly pained by it, and indeed the wound looked less severe than it had when Prior first glimpsed it, whatever energy had propelled Fenton through fighting the griffin had slowly left him, and his skin glistened with feverish sweat. Prior's heart twisted with the need to comfort him. To protect him—but from what? Dust?

Though Fenton grumbled, Prior cleaned his shoulder wound as best he could with water from the waterskin, and bound it with a ripped strip of cloth from the bottom of his tunic. He wondered after the poultice Fenton had made before, but when he eyed Fenton's crown, the flowers were snowdrops. Perhaps Fenton's magic didn't work like that. Prior draped a blanket around Fenton's shoulders.

"I don't suppose you can retrieve that tunic, can you? You need to be warm."

Fenton blinked drowsily, then trailed his fingers down his opposite arm as if only just realising it were bare. His eyes were big and his pupils blown black.

"Blue?" he asked.

"That's right, it was blue." Prior shook his head as Fenton visibly drifted again. "Never mind. I'm going to move the griffin, just so no wolf pack comes nosing after it and finds us here, okay? I won't be long."

Fenton refocused. He licked his lips. "Feathers. Please. Bring some feathers."

"Feathers. Okay."

"Thank you." Fenton rested his head against the wall. His eyes shut.

Prior hurried about his tasks. Moving the griffin took a great deal of effort, and several times he cursed himself for his hubris in the attempt: if Fenton had struggled fighting the creature, how could Prior expect to move even its corpse? Afternoon slid rapidly to evening as he worked. He eventually managed to shove the griffin unceremoniously downhill, and felt like shit as he did: the griffin had been protecting its territory, and now it was a crumpled sack of blood and feathers halfway down a hill. Prior rubbed his eyes. *Keep it together.*

Collecting the feathers he'd selected from the griffin's wings, Prior set his shoulders and marched back to the farmhouse, his thighs burning as he ascended the hill. As he neared the farmhouse, he saw a raven waiting before the closed door. When it noticed him, the raven croaked at Prior like a mother chastising her child and hopped anxiously from foot to foot, wings outspread.

Prior ran. He burst into the farmhouse with a curse and dropped the griffin feathers onto the table before rushing to Fenton's side, the raven cawing after him.

"Fenton? Fenton!" Prior called.

But Fenton didn't respond. He'd fallen asleep, curled on his side like a babe, and didn't twitch at Prior's entrance. With shaking hands, Prior watched until he saw Fenton's chest rise and fall, so perhaps it was a healing sleep instead of anything ominous. Fenton needed good, healthful sleep, didn't he? Prior slumped against the wall, his legs outstretched, and rested his hand lightly on Fenton's hair. Panicking over a raven like a fool. Prior knocked his head against the wall.

"You're ridiculous," he berated himself.

Blowing out a breath, he got to his feet and retrieved a candle stub from the chest, lighting it with his flint, then set it nearby. He had intended to check their provisions and make a light supper, with an eye on breakfast for the two of them. Strange, then, to find himself sitting by Fenton's side and stroking his red hair. The raven had followed Prior inside, and it clacked its beak at him, as if admonishing, but Prior hissed at it.

133

"You're just jealous."

The raven didn't answer.

As Prior continued to stroke Fenton's hair, smoothing aside his vines, he found an odd protrusion. Touching it lightly, he huffed out a laugh as he realised what it must be: Fenton's antlers. Was that what had been consuming Fenton's energy? Between growing new body parts and fighting a griffin, little wonder Fenton needed all the sleep he could get. Prior ached for Fenton. With gratitude, with pain, with— Well. He ached.

A curious caw made Prior glance at the raven. He smiled tiredly. "It's been quite the day, my raven friend. Are you the same raven that went to Ashcroft, I wonder? Nod once for yes."

The raven croaked in a manner Prior chose to interpret as affirmative, but it did not nod. He let his eyes close.

Evening bowed to night, and then the screaming started.

Prior startled awake to a flickering candle and Fenton thrashing as he fought griffins in his sleep. Prior called Fenton's name to no response. When he reached out tentatively, thinking to steady Fenton from hurting himself, vines erupted from Fenton's skin and whipped defensively at Prior, jagged black thorns bristling along their length. Prior crowded against the far wall, heart hammering, trying to avoid causing further harm or aggravation. Fenton continued to struggle, and though Prior pleaded his name, it had no effect. He had to watch helplessly as, again, Fenton fought alone.

Fenton unleashed a particularly sonorous scream and weeds punched through the farmhouse floor in violent response. Birds gathered at the broken windowpanes; the mass of feathery bodies so tightly crammed together they prevented each other getting through. Prior's raven companion chased the birds off and remained on guard while Fenton struggled and Prior dug his nails into his palms.

134

Eventually—thankfully—the screaming stopped, though Fenton's cracked whimpers were no less terrible for their quietness, and Prior dropped his head in his hands. His eyes stung with exhaustion, with powerlessness. But there was no one else who could help Fenton, not even in the limited capacity Prior had to offer.

Prior knee-walked across the uneven floor toward Fenton, who had collapsed onto his back; though he seemed at first glance to be resting peacefully, the restless flickering of his closed eyes and the pained shape of his mouth belied his rest, while the blood around his mouth and the grooves his claws had carved into the floor discredited the notion of peace. Prior hesitantly gathered one of Fenton's hands in his, wanting and needing to know he was real. When Fenton didn't react, Prior scooted closer. Ducking his head, he kissed the cradle of Fenton's dirty palm.

"In case you can hear me, know that I'm here, I'm with you. I'm staying," he promised.

Fenton didn't stir. Prior hadn't expected him to, but hope had deep roots. He dashed away a tear and settled against the wall, still holding Fenton's hand. Carefully, so carefully, he smoothed Fenton's hair away from his eyes. Fenton's forehead was clammy.

Prior glanced at the raven, at the black eyes shining in the low light. "Do you think I should go to Northrope and ask Nola for help? She healed me. She'd be able to do something to help him, surely." The raven puffed its wings and Prior nodded at the response he wanted to hear. "You're right. But who else is there to ask? Baltair is good with his goats, but I don't think this... whatever this is... is within his expertise." Prior suppressed a hysterical burst of laughter. "Wrong type of horn, for one thing."

Who could possibly claim experience of such a situation that they might be able to help? Fenton's sibling, Lorcan? Perhaps, but if Fenton couldn't find them, Prior had no chance. Besides which, how could he know Lorcan would assist, and not harm Fenton further? Lorcan was an unknown element, and lurked as a dark figure in Prior's mind. No, Prior couldn't chance drawing their attention.

He rubbed his face. What to do? Prior had sought Fenton—or the god in the forest—for aid, yet all they had found for each other was trouble. The curse remained, and Prior's worry for Sylvie had become so much a part of him he could scarcely comprehend what would happen if Fenton didn't wake—and yet Prior wanted Fenton for more than his magical usefulness. Prior *missed* Fenton. It had been only hours and already he missed Fenton's companionship, his curiosity and steadfastness, the light in his eyes. The dark had been safer with Fenton in it.

Misery threatened to settle like a rock around Prior's heart. He took a breath. Another. The raven croaked in support.

"This is something Fenton needs to do and will soon pass," Prior told the raven. "I shouldn't overthink things. All will be well and we will travel to Ashcroft in the morning. Good night, fair raven."

"—man. Hey, human!"

Prior jerked awake to find a—a *something* staring upside-down at him. A green-furred something draped in several flower garlands that shimmered in the early morning sun. The something was human-shaped, but seemed crafted by a maker unfamiliar with the model; their willowy limbs were slightly too long and their torso too short, as if lacking several ribs, and their eyes were yellow as buttercups. He stared. The something stared back.

"What's happened to his most high and handsome foxliness, then?" the creature asked impatiently.

Prior wondered if he should run. Should *try* to run. He pulled his legs under him, but then he registered the words: "his most high and handsome foxliness" had to be

Fenton. He rested on his knees and considered the creature again, trying not to gawk.

The creature had no such reservation. On gaining Prior's attention, the creature danced back and twirled on the spot, finishing with their hands on their hips and their eyebrows arched expectantly. Prior didn't know if he should applaud or be intimidated. He checked on Fenton, who remained unconscious, snuffling in his sleep. Adorable but unhelpful.

"Very, ah, very dynamic. Can I help you?" Prior asked the creature.

"Don't know, can you?"

Prior blinked. "I don't know. This feels circuitous. Who are you?"

The creature beamed and hopped in place, then gave an elaborate bow that somehow involved a curtsey as well. Their flower garlands swooped with the action. Prior could smell snow.

"Burdock is my name, human!"

"Prior. I'm called Prior, not 'human'," Prior said.

Burdock narrowed their eyes and gave a haughty sniff. "Seem human enough to me."

"I'm not—" Prior cut himself off. He hadn't had enough sleep for this conversation. Though, in truth, he doubted any amount of sleep would be sufficient.

Glancing toward the window, he saw the empty ledge where his raven friend had been perched during the night, and loss needled his chest. Silly, to get so attached to a wild creature. Prior shifted, trying to wake his numb legs, and with effort, he rose to his feet and eased into a stretch. Burdock watched him like children watched mummers' plays, wide eyed and slack jawed. Had they never seen a human before?

Prior tugged at his clothes, embarrassed by the scrutiny. "What brings you here, Burdock? Are you looking for something?"

"Not looking, but found!" Burdock twirled, as if in

emphasis. "I followed the magic. Like a storm shower it was, bright as anything! No one but his fearsome treefulness what does magic like that, I said, but my siblings didn't listen. Too busy searching for new trees, they were, so I snuck back when they wasn't paying attention. And here I am!"

Prior understood perhaps half of Burdock's story but half was enough. Apparently, they'd followed a burst of Fenton's magic, probably occurring when he changed shapes. "His fearsome treefulness" made Prior grin. He hoped he'd remember to share it with Fenton when he woke.

"And here you are," Prior echoed. He tilted his head at Fenton, curled beneath the blankets. "Whatever magic happened tired him out. He'll wake soon."

"He'll wake when he wants, and I don't see how it's any concern of yours as to the timing of it," Burdock rattled sharply, their countenance darkening like a cloud covering the sun. "You should show proper deference, human Prior."

Startled by Burdock's sudden change in mood, Prior backed toward the wall. Cool stone beneath his fingers grounded him and he slid his gaze past Burdock, through the cracked-open door, to the world outside the farmhouse. His heart beat in his ears as Burdock's snow smell made Prior think of winter. Long, cold nights with no reprieve.

The hoarse caw of a raven broke the pressure with a rush. Prior's raven friend landed by his feet and hopped between him and Burdock, flapping its wings in reprimand.

"Pfft," Burdock said, shooing the raven. "I had to check, didn't I? Making sure the human weren't taking no liberties."

The raven hopped to Fenton's side and cocked its head as if searching for any liberties Prior might have taken. Burdock tapped their foot. Prior let his eyes rest on

Fenton for one heartbeat. Two. He traced Fenton's profile with his eyes. He'd washed Fenton's face using the tail of one of his own shirts as a cloth, but blood speckled Fenton's hairline where the antlers had broken through in his other form. Prior had left the blood there as a reminder that some things were bigger than him. Fenton contained a forest; Prior would never know all of him. He'd felt silly as he made the decision but the sight reassured him now. Fenton would wake. He couldn't not.

Prior forced himself to relax, allowing the wall to support him, and met Burdock's yellow stare. "I assure you, I took no liberties. Fenton is my friend."

"Fenton?" They scoffed. "He has no friends. He is the Fox-Faced One, He Of Bone And Bark," Burdock whispered in a sing-song, as if speaking the names any louder would be unwise. "You would do well to remember."

Hearing Fenton's epithets stated boldly struck Prior like a wish spoken aloud. He'd carried the names in his heart for a long time; he'd grown hearing his grandmother's stories about those names, about the two brothers— siblings, as it transpired—and their constant fighting. Prior's chest went tight as the words repeated in his mind. The Fox-Faced One. He allowed himself to remember the white-tailed stag, the pride and power that had simmered within it, obvious even to Prior's human senses. He remembered how Fenton had been almost diminished beside the stag.

Yet Fenton *was* the white-tailed stag. He Of Bone And Bark. All the hunters that had never left the forest had gone in pursuit of prey they'd never had a prayer of capturing. But Prior had walked out of the forest with a god beside him. A god who—improbably, *impossibly*—had knelt before him.

Prior didn't realise he was smiling until he registered the tugging at his cheeks. He pressed his hand to his face, carded his fingers through his hair, rubbed the back of his neck. Continued to smile.

Old Nan had two children, and I'm falling for one of them.

The thought was more absurd than anything that had happened since he had first left Ashcroft for the forest. Falling? Fallen. Prior stifled the laughter that fizzed in his chest.

"Human Prior? Have you eaten the spindly mushrooms? They're not good for you."

Prior did laugh at that. He shook his head and slid down to sit beside Fenton. The raven hopped onto his knee and appeared content to settle there. Its slight weight was welcome.

"No mushrooms. And please accept my apologies. I meant no disrespect to Fenton. To the Fox-Faced One," Prior said, as Burdock watched him unblinkingly. He firmed his voice. "But Fenton *is* my friend, and I am his, and *you* would do well to remember that."

Burdock regarded Prior with one eye, then the other, twisting their neck like rabbits unable to see forward with both eyes at once. Then Burdock spun in place, their green fur rippling with verdant colour as light moved over them. The raven cawed in approval. Prior considered doing likewise.

"I forgive you! His ostentatious foxliness has ever had unpredictable moods. Why, last we met I thought for certain sure he'd kill me and yet here I am and there he is and see, how merry we are!" Burdock sounded delighted.

"Merry indeed," Prior said, after dismissing the first three comments that rose to his tongue. He rested his hand on the nearest part of Fenton—his elbow—and lowered his voice. "You spoke of magic bringing you here. Did you see— There was a griffin, outside. Fenton protected me from it and, in so doing, changed shape into a… A fox? Mostly a fox. With antlers." Prior indicated the sides of his head, feeling foolish as he did. Surely Burdock knew what antlers were.

Burdock nodded. "Of course, and how else would he

140

look?"

"Well, like— Like he looks." Prior gestured toward Fenton, still sleeping. "Like that."

Burdock blew a raspberry and waved their hands in dismissal. They removed one of their garlands, one with sulphurously yellow flowers, from around their neck.

"He looks how he looks however he looks," they said with a shrug. They studied their garland with a furrowed brow, passing it through their hands in inspection. "Likely his magic is just settling. It's been locked away for a while, is how the stories go."

"A while?"

Burdock smiled slyly. "Rude to talk about someone's age, ain't it?"

Prior conceded. "It is at that."

With a shuffling step, Burdock neared Fenton, their garland outstretched. Prior quashed the urge to warn them off; Burdock had offered no harm, and the raven did no more than ruffle its wings. But Prior remembered too well Fenton's screams, and he wanted to preserve Fenton's peace—his soft snuffles and relaxed features—for as long as he could. Prior's fingers twitched. Whatever expression he wore made Burdock's gentle. They shook their flower garland, scenting the air with perfume.

"I shall leave some magic behind that he might have something delicious to snack on while he sleeps. It is but flowers, friend Prior." So saying, Burdock draped the garland over Fenton's head, careful not to tangle with his crown or vines. Then they were in motion again, rolling backwards and flipping to their feet in an acrobatic display. "Always catching you sleeping, lazy fox. You didn't snatch me this time, though! Ha!"

When they delivered an expectant look to Prior, he clapped his hands together, too startled and aware of Fenton to make decent applause.

"You're welcome, you're welcome!" they said, bow-curtseying with aplomb.

The raven clacked its beak and Burdock blew another raspberry. Prior checked on Fenton—it had been a lot of activity—and already his sleep seemed easier, his eyes no longer roving behind his lids in fevered dreams.

Prior smiled at Burdock. "Thank you, for your aid. It's helping him."

Burdock threw up their hands and let them clap their legs when they fell. "Already said 'you're welcome', can't go repeating it. Be, what's the word, tautologous. Shush your thanks and be well."

With that, Burdock turned to go. Morning sun made their fur glitter. Between Burdock and Fenton, Prior felt lumpen and dull. Yet he rolled to his feet fast enough to brush Burdock's elbow as they stepped over the threshold of the farmhouse, the raven grumbling behind him. Burdock stiffened at the touch.

"Yes, friend Prior?"

Prior worked his jaw. "Friend Burdock," he echoed, surprised to find he meant the words. "If it's not too much to ask, and you have the time and inclination, might you look in on the village of Ashcroft? It's half a day's journey from here in the direction of the coast." Prior contemplated what might distinguish Ashcroft from any other moorland village. "There are goats?"

Burdock tilted their head, as Fenton often did. "Did his handsome self spend time there?" Burdock asked, flicking their gaze over Prior's shoulder to make their meaning clear. Not that Prior needed clarification on handsomeness.

"Not a long time, but recently. A few days back. He said there was magic in the village, if that helps." Prior hoped it helped.

"Between his magic and any other, I can find it true." Burdock beamed with their straight white teeth. Prior had expected fangs. "I like feeling useful! Thank you, friend Prior. I shall espy your goats with utmost meticulosity!"

Before Prior could explain the goats weren't his chief

concern, Burdock had spun in place and danced away along the hill, petals scattering hither and yon in their wake. Prior blew out a breath and watched them go. His head throbbed. Had he done the right thing, to send Burdock to Ashcroft in his stead?

With heavy steps, he returned to the cool dark of the farmhouse and slid onto his arse next to Fenton, who rolled over in his sleep. His hand inched across the stone toward Prior, then settled. Prior smoothed his new garland with care.

A god slept beside him. Prior had agreed to kill his sibling. The Night-Black Sea. The Hand That Reaches From Beneath the Waves. Awe—the true kind, ripe with dread and wonder both—filled Prior like water in a well. He brimmed with it.

He rested his hand on Fenton's wild hair. Burdock's flowers glowed a pretty yellow against Fenton's skin. "I have questions when you wake, friend Fenton. But you sleep, now. We'll speak again soon."

Fenton woke slowly, as did great trees emerge from the earth. First, a flex of roots and fingers, toes and vines. Jaw working. Spine bowing. He stretched his arms luxuriously, his joints popping. He rolled his head from side to side, enjoying the pull of the tendons in his neck, adjusting to the new-old weight of his antlers. Checking them with his fingers, he found they'd grown nearly a handspan and the tips poked through his hair; the energy the growth required had kept him sleeping. He adjusted his crown, and finally opened his eyes.

Heat rushed to his face as Fenton discovered Prior and a raven watching him. He hadn't even thought to check; he was becoming careless. He shifted upright, jostling the blankets that had been draped over him. Prior tracked his movements, his face soft, his eyes all the more luminous

143

for the sleepless red that ringed them, and his lips—which Fenton had been spending more and more time contemplating—curved in a small, disbelieving smile. He and the raven were sat near a small fire, and Prior held out meat on stripped branches that dropped ever closer to the flames, until the raven squawked and Prior came back to himself with a rush.

"You're awake! You know you're awake. How— Wait there— Just. Wait! Please." Quickly resting the sticks onto a shallow dish, Prior shooed the raven away from the food then scrambled across the room to kneel beside Fenton. "You're awake!"

"I am," Fenton allowed.

Prior pressed the back of his hand to Fenton's forehead and peered keenly into his eyes. "You feel cooler. That's a good thing, I think. To be honest, I don't know what temperature you should be, but I'm in the habit now." Prior babbled as if he'd grown used to the lack of response while Fenton was unconscious. He fussed for Fenton's hands. "You need clothes. Yours disappeared when you transformed— Is transformed the right term? I don't know. But you'd be warmer, if you had them. Here, your pulse, let me."

Panic and worry hung over Prior like a shroud, the sour strata of his scent telling Fenton the story of Prior's time while Fenton had been unconscious. Fenton swallowed a whine. He didn't experience time as humans did; a moon could last a season, or ten winters might pass like two. How long had his sleep lasted, to have layered on Prior so thickly? If it weren't for the garland around Fenton's neck—one of Burdock's, it had to be—the scent of despair would be overwhelming.

Fenton curled his hand around where Prior's had stilled. Whatever Prior had endeavoured to check, he'd stopped, and he knelt in stillness, his head bowed. Fenton couldn't see Prior's eyes. It suddenly became important to do so.

"Prior? Might you look at me?" he asked.

Prior sniffed, and shook his head. He shuffled closer on his knees. Movement, at least. By the fire, the raven hopped closer to the abandoned meat and Fenton flicked his shadow at the cheeky bird. To Prior, he only hummed. He considered the garland he wore, and stroked their limp blooms; their colour was dull and their petals frayed, which meant the dryad had likely greatly aided Fenton's recovery. He owed them a dance.

For now, there was only one he wished to dance with. Fenton touched intent into the garland and it flushed anew with rich colour. Removing it from around his neck, he held it between him and Prior.

"Might I give you a gift, then? You need not look at me if you do not wish it." He glanced aside. "I have been poor company."

Prior hissed between his teeth and looked up with a glare that pinned Fenton as surely as the griffin had. He snatched the garland from Fenton's hand and shook it at him.

"Don't give me that! 'Poor company', he says? You were *unconscious*, Fenton! Unconscious for days—"

"For—"

"And now you're giving me flowers! Yanking them off over your head when you just had a *damned shoulder injury!*"

Fenton hadn't realised it was possible to aggressively don a flower garland, but Prior managed it. Then he grabbed Fenton's hand again and shuffled closer, reducing the space between them to naught.

"Thank you, they're lovely, now stay still while I check on you in case you've done any more damage to yourself," Prior said, flushing.

Fenton let him do as he would. Prior's touches to his forehead, his wrist, the vulnerable skin of his throat, were the first burst of rain after a drought. Fenton let his eyes shut and drank them in to his roots, nourishing the wide-open crack of his heart. His vines flowered beneath Prior's attention, as obvious as a blush. Prior's fern scent had taken on the faintest, most delectable tease of rose. It nearly obliterated the older scents of his distress.

"Fenton!"

Startled, Fenton opened his eyes. "What is it?"

Prior looked away, his earlier fire banked. "Nothing. Just checking." He played his fingers over the garland. "This is beautiful, thank you, but do you not need it anymore? Burdock said you needed something to snack on." His mouth twisted as he bit his lip, gaze wandering to Fenton's hair. No, to his antlers. But Prior didn't mention them as he returned to the fire, speaking over his shoulder. "I don't have any magic, but did you want something to eat? There's rabbit. I felt rotten killing the poor things, I think they came nosing for you, but the provisions from the market ran out two days ago, so—"

"Two days ago?" Fenton blurted, jerking forward. Surely not!

Prior shrugged stiffly. "Around that. This is the fourth dawn, I think, since the griffin. Don't worry, between the rabbits and the river nearby, and my raven friend on guard, I've been well enough. Sylvie's sweet buns are but a dream, alas, but delicious they were while they lasted. How do you feel? You seemed… Did you want something to eat?"

Fenton wanted to lie down and sleep until the world made sense. Little wonder he felt rejuvenated. Little wonder Prior looked wan; their provisions hadn't been generous, considering the short journey they had planned. Four dawns meant Fenton had been more injured, and more drained by his connection to Ashcroft, than he'd realised, especially to have slept through a visit from the dancing dryad and their accompanying nonsense.

He firmed his jaw. He could do nothing about the missing days but vow to do better.

As Prior resumed tending the fire, Fenton flexed his fingers and reached into the nowhere space where his forest lived, where his fur lived. He stretched until one of his claws snagged fabric. He twisted his wrist and yanked it free. The clothes had not fared badly, considering his unexpected transformation. Fenton quickly donned them.

Prior poked at the flames with a charred stick and a fierce glower. Firelight burned his face to shadows, his eyes to embers. The meat waited in the dish. The raven had retreated to the rafters, and well it might, for hurt flowed from Prior like a river to the sea and muted his fern-and-rose scent. Fenton rubbed his jaw. Why had Prior not returned to Ashcroft? True, if Fenton died, he would not break the blight, but surely it would have been better to go to Ashcroft and learn Fenton's fate second-hand. It would have been safer.

But Fenton couldn't ask those questions, and he could not regret Prior's attentions, nor how the fussing had warmed parts of Fenton long sleeping. Fenton scratched the base of an antler, where skin remained tight around the new growth, and shuffled his feet so Prior wouldn't be startled when he spoke.

"Thank you for staying with me," he said, trying to put his gratitude into his voice. "I am sorry for worrying you. Sorry for leaving you alone. It was not my intent to do so. Sylvie is well, and the village also, as far as I am able to discern."

Prior had stiffened when Fenton started speaking, but with a soft sigh he set down his stick and turned around. His mouth trembled but he firmed it resolutely. Fenton's fingers twitched at his sides, unsure if he should offer comfort. He relaxed at Prior's smile, wet though it was.

"It's been a long few days," Prior said. His smile firmed. "I'm very, very glad you're back, and with such good news. Please, sit, eat these poor rabbits." He nodded over his shoulder. "Your feathers are over there, by the way, though you never did mention what they were for."

It took Fenton a moment but then he remembered the unfortunate creature and crossed the room to examine the griffin feathers. Prior had selected three beautiful tawny feathers, each nearly the length of Fenton's forearm. Fenton brushed the tip of one over his lips. Magic crackled over his skin, less potent than it would have been four dawns ago, but still strong enough to taste.

Prior's breath caught when Fenton carefully threaded a feather through Burdock's garland, tucking the spine to secure it.

"A small token of my thanks," Fenton said. Prior's eyes were dreamily dark. Fenton cleared his throat and looked unseeingly away. "Where is your pack?"

When Prior pointed, Fenton went and tucked the feathers among Prior's things. He considered using the nowhere space again, but it pleased him to have the feathers in sight. Besides, there was plenty of room, as the pack that had held their provisions now hosted only crumbs. Fenton did not allow his jaw to clench. He sat on the floor beside Prior, the fire warming his crossed legs. He held his hands over the flames.

When Prior offered a dish of meat, Fenton took it. They ate together in silence broken only by the crackling fire. When he'd eaten half of his share, Fenton offered Prior the dish.

"Here."

Prior startled from his meditation in the flames. He'd long since devoured his own portion. "Are you sure? You're still healing."

His lips glistened from the grease of the meat. He still wore a hard winter in his sharp cheekbones. Fenton touched his fingertips lightly to the garland Prior wore. The feather.

"Burdock's garland and the griffin—the feathers—have done what they could to sustain me. That is what I had intended, in the asking. There is magic in such things. You need more than that." He offered the dish again.

This time, Prior took it. "If you're certain, then thank you." He spoke between savouring bites. "I've seen you eat food, though. Human food."

"I require both, but sometimes more one than the other. I shall forage on the way to your village to replenish the provisions. Hunt, if you would like me to."

Prior chewed the rabbit meat slowly, the dish balanced on his leg. Fenton watched him, satisfied, until Prior hunched his shoulders and tucked his head over his food. Fenton drifted his gaze away and chanced upon one of their wineskins. A shake of liquid remained within. He offered it to Prior.

"I'd been saving that," Prior said as he took the wineskin. He upended it over his mouth and drank, but then offered it back to Fenton, smiling crookedly. "Here. Share. Seeing as I was hasty to drown my sorrows earlier with the last of the mead."

Fenton took the wineskin and put his lips to the place Prior's had been. He drank, conscious of Prior's attention, and suddenly parched. He tossed the empty wineskin toward Prior's pack, then stretched out and arranged himself with his head in Prior's lap, careful with the angle of his antlers. He tucked his hands against his chest and turned his face to the fire. Prior accepted the change of position with only a mutter about getting rabbit grease in Fenton's hair, but Fenton ignored the comment; his hair was thick with blood and dust. A little grease would hardly matter.

Time passed. The side of Fenton's face grew tight from the fire. His vines stretched and twisted, some wrapping around the base of his antlers, while others rearranged his crown as they wished. His shadow returned from exploring and pooled across the uneven stone floor, forming a crescent moon with the fire in the centre. Its chill provided pleasant counterpoint to the flames.

Prior finished eating and tossed the cooking sticks into the fire. He rubbed his fingers clean on a scrap of cloth, then added that to the flames as well. One of his hands came to rest in Fenton's hair, the other on Fenton's hip. A welcome weight.

"I was so worried," Prior whispered, as if he didn't want Fenton to hear. Confessional, as if used to Fenton not being able to respond. "I didn't think you would ever wake. I thought about leaving so often, but how could I?"

Fenton's gut twisted. Days ago, he had left Prior while he slept and not thought twice about the decision. The circumstances were dissimilar, true, and the lesson of the bandits had ensured he would not make the same decision a second time, but he had left and Prior had stayed. The difference felt fundamental.

He lifted his chin, exposing his throat, in an effort to meet Prior's eyes. When he moved, Prior turned his head aside, avoiding Fenton's gaze.

"I am sorry to have worried you," Fenton said. Perhaps Prior would hear him this time. "Sylvie is well, despite my weakness."

"As you said. I believe you, and I'm more relieved than I can express, but Sylvie isn't the only one I've been worrying about."

"I know, there is the village also. I extended my protection—"

"You did? Why?" Prior sounded strangely hurt.

Fenton searched again for Prior's eyes, and again failed to find them. He glanced at his own hands instead, where he hooked the tips together as he spoke. "You were upset. At the hamlet. At the thought that you might return to find Ashcroft thus. The notion of your distress... discomforted me. It perhaps took more of my magic than I had anticipated."

"You put yourself in danger, doing that for me," Prior murmured. He smoothed his thumb over Fenton's hair. "You didn't need to. The griffin— It could really have hurt you. It *did* hurt you."

Fenton wanted to scoff, but Prior's tone made him sober.

"The griffin came as something of a surprise," Fenton admitted. "But I am well."

Prior's hands twitched where they rested on Fenton, as if he wanted to hold on. Silently, Fenton willed him to do so. Yet Prior's hands relaxed and he scratched his fingers through Fenton's hair instead, tracing the base of Fenton's antlers. He pursed his lips and leant over to catch Fenton's gaze at last.

"Thank you. I just— Thank you." Prior gently tapped one of Fenton's antlers. "A lighter topic, I think. I hope. Tell me, what does it mean that you have these now?" he asked.

If Fenton ever had the words to explain, they evaded him. He searched the ceiling for answers, in case any were hidden in the eaves. The raven perched on a crossbeam eyed him with a beady glare. Fenton's heart beat loud against his ribs.

"They represent an unlocking, of sorts. A part of myself I had lost has been recovered. I can banish them, if you wish," Fenton offered, though he did not want to do so. But he would not make Prior uncomfortable if he had the power to do otherwise.

"I don't want you to banish them," Prior swiftly reassured him. "I only wondered. I remember the stag, in the forest. You were separate then. I didn't even realise both were *you* until recently. While you were sleeping, I kept thinking of all these questions I wanted to ask you. I shouted quite a few at you, but of course you couldn't answer. And now that you're here, awake, I find I can't think of a single one of them."

As he spoke, Prior curved over Fenton, reducing the space between their faces to a handspan. Fenton flicked his focus from one of Prior's eyes to the other, a bird searching for somewhere safe to land. A rabbit twitching in a snare. Fenton would spend his days tethered, if only Prior were interested in the hunt. If he wanted to be chased at all.

Fenton focused on Prior's lips. They seemed safer, for once.

"Are you upset?" he found himself asking.

Prior didn't answer. He traced his thumb around the socket of Fenton's eye. Over the bridge of his nose. He pressed his thumb lightly to Fenton's lower lip. Firelight played in his eyes.

"The Fox-Faced One, Burdock called you. He Of Bone and Bark."

"I have many names," Fenton said, Prior's thumb still on his lip. He wanted to kiss all of his truths to Prior's skin.

Prior tapped the tines of Fenton's antlers. "You told me only one of them, though."

Fenton snorted. "If you met Burdock, you will have heard a great many of my names." He sobered. He had to know. "Are you upset with me?"

Prior's hands stilled. Fenton went cold, despite the fire. Then, with a sigh, Prior resumed his careful stroking of Fenton's tangled hair. The raven shuffled on its perch and took to wing, flying through the broken window. Leaving them alone. Fenton sent his shadow out the door to guard them.

"I am upset, yes, but not with you. This all has become rather more of an adventure than I had imagined, and I already thought the storytellers would need many nights to tell this one," Prior said drily. "I rushed headlong into this, whatever this is, and having time to think has given me, well, time to think."

"Can I help?"

"You are. You're awake, and soon we'll move on, and something else will happen. I'm sure of that."

Fenton didn't think that sounded helpful, but Prior knew his needs best. He hummed, and allowed himself to enjoy Prior's touch.

Prior hummed back, and laughed softly. "You wear the fox well, I must say. I see him here on your ears, and painted in your hair under all this dirt, but until now I hadn't seen the stag since that day in the forest. It was the stag who chose me, wasn't it? Seemed to choose." Prior flushed. "Or have I misunderstood?"

Fenton shook his head, careful not to dislodge Prior's hands as he did. "The stag is a part of me that remained unknown, at the time. Locked in the deadwood heart of me, deep in the knot."

"Don't say that."

"It is the truth. The stag recognised you when I could not. The beast that so many had tried to kill bowed at your feet, and laid its head and my heart in your lap."

"Fenton!" Prior gently swatted his shoulder.

Fenton smothered his grin. "What?"

"You can't just *say* things like that. Do you have a head wound? I should have checked for a head wound."

Fenton laughed, and continued laughing, until he rolled over and shifted around so he could muffle his face against the side of Prior's waist, careful with his antlers. His shoulders shook until he didn't know if he laughed or wept, his breath rasping in his throat. Making a low hushing noise, Prior cupped the back of Fenton's head. The steady rise and fall of Prior's stomach offered a balm to the frantic energy coursing through Fenton, and Fenton curled in place until his own breathing came even and his eyes no longer stung. Then he lay there a while longer. With the warmth of Prior at his front, and the fire at his back, Fenton knew the peace of a fox in the earth.

The remainder of their journey to Ashcroft passed without incident, for which Prior was more grateful than he could say. Moreso when he found no further signs of the curse on the village, just as Fenton had said, and as Prior had scarcely dared believe; even Baltair's goats were happier beneath Fenton's protection, as they neglected to charge at Prior's approach and merely butted his legs in an almost friendly fashion. The worry that Prior had been repressing left him all at once, and he nearly staggered with relief. Fenton had protected Ashcroft.

It wasn't that Prior had doubted Fenton's protection, but he had imagined the guarding as something subtle, detectable only to those with magic, and as such the idea had been intangible in Prior's mind. Fallible. Yet, standing in Ashcroft, he felt Fenton's presence as the shade of a great tree. To cross the village's border was to enter a welcoming embrace. He wondered what the other villagers thought about the change. He could see folk gossiping over fences, and see others going about their business as they might any other day. If they were worried about the change, surely they'd all be indoors.

Chest warm, Prior turned and found Fenton already reaching for a goat. Prior huffed a laugh as Fenton straightened, his ears twitching almost sheepishly.

Prior pointed toward the other end of the village. "Carry on with the goats as you like. I'm going to check on Sylvie and see if she's well."

"She is," Fenton said quickly. Not to be reassuring, but stating a fact. He tilted his head. "I would have told you otherwise."

Prior knew he would have. "It's just an expression. I missed her, and I need to make sure Nola's remedy arrived safely. Did you want to come with me?"

"I must ensure there is no residue of my sibling's magic, nor any trace of other malicious efforts made in our absence. I can feel that a dryad has been here." He frowned. "Burdock?"

"I asked if they would look in on Ashcroft. I was worried," Prior said.

"A sensible precaution." Fenton glanced at the goat. "I will investigate for evidence of any other visitors. My protection may have faltered while I was... recovering."

"And you want to pet the goats, I understand."

Fenton blushed. The new red colour of his hair magnified the effect. Prior wanted to learn how to paint.

"Goats are sensible," Fenton said, primly. His vines adjusted his crown and its yellow and white flowers.

Prior relented, though one day he intended to tease Fenton into a full-body blush. His own cheeks heated as he hastily dismissed the thought before he could thoroughly distract himself.

"Go on and do as you must, and I'll see you later," he said, and waved Fenton off with a grin.

He crossed the village beneath Fenton's shade. Children called to one another, and the inn rumbled with happy noise, making the thin spring day bright. Goodwoman Hilde and her broom were nowhere to be seen. If Prior put a skip in his step, well, why shouldn't he?

He found Sylvie pinning washing to the line and singing cheerily, as if she'd never taken ill at all, and every speck of doubt washed from Prior as if it were him hanging on the line. Relief made him stumble. Sylvie's familiar tuneless singing became as a chorus of nightingales. He climbed over the wall that ringed their cottage, rather than trust his numb fingers to the gate, and staggered toward her.

Sylvie dropped her bucket of suds as she clapped her hands to her mouth. "Prior! You're back!"

He wiped his face, smiling like a buffoon. A soapy buffoon. "You look very— Umf!"

Sylvie near-strangled Prior when she grabbed him around the neck to draw him into a hug, crushing the garland he still wore. He returned her tight embrace and rested his head on her shoulder. How long had it been since Sylvie had been well enough to hug him? It felt like a year of hard seasons, yet could only have been the span of a moon. Far too long.

"Sorry about the bucket. Gods, you're soaking," Sylvie said as she released him. She swept her hair from her face and looked him up and down. "And you got skinnier. What happened on the way to Northrope that took you so long? Did you get lost?" She paled and looked him over again. "Are you hurt?"

Prior shook his head. His smile felt huge. "I'm only tired. Getting to Northrope was straightforward but we took quite a diversion on the way back. I'm so glad to see you well, Sylvie."

"I'm glad to be well. That remedy of yours—and delivered by raven, no less!—saw me straight to rights. You'll share the method, won't you? One of the Greaves boys has taken ill."

"We'll do it today, I promise," Prior said. It seemed that Fenton's suspicion that his protection had wavered was correct, but they had the remedy. The Greaves boy would be fine. They would all be fine, now.

Sylvie tugged sharply at one of the sheets. "In that case, the other half of your 'we' is welcome to supper, if 'we' would like," Sylvie said, stressing the "we" as she peered over Prior's shoulder. Finding no one there, she frowned at him. "Did you lose your shadow? Or was that a fever dream?"

"He's— Well, I'm not entirely sure what he's doing, but he'll come by if the mood takes him. He knows where I'll be. Tell me how *you* are, won't you? I can't believe how much stronger you seem."

"I am. I'm tired, too, but nothing rest won't cure," she said. Then her expression grew mischievous. "I'll set the table for four, shall I? We'll have stew."

"Four?"

Sylvie's cheeks coloured and she fussed with the sheets on the line. "Baltair will be by. He's been checking in on me while you were gone."

"He has, has he?"

Prior learned that some suds remained in the bucket.

After he'd changed into dry clothes—draping his garland and feather on a hook by the window—Prior helped Sylvie with the rest of the chores, then put together a new batch of Nola's potion to steep over the fire. He arranged the table for four as instructed and went to collect Baltair, letting him know about the more formal supper as they walked to the cottage; Baltair might have been used to coming around to the cottage, but it would be cruel to spring unexpected company on him, especially when he'd been good to Sylvie. Sylvie deserved someone being good to her.

Fenton arrived not long after the stew had been put to the fire, a goose cradled in his arms. Prior gave him a flat look until he put the bird out, then made introductions as Sylvie bade them sit at the table. Baltair helped Sylvie with serving, the two of them working together with familiarity, though Baltair's efficiency was compromised by his glances toward Fenton.

Other things happened, probably, surely, but Prior scarcely noted them. Fenton sat at the table Prior had made as a boy, with legs of uneven length and a split in the wood from an over-eager hand. Prior had long intended to make another table, but he'd never got around to it, and there Fenton sat, every part a god visiting from one of Sylvie's tales. A fox-spirit in the black tufts of fur on his pointed ears, his russet red hair, and the peculiar vulpine cast to his face; a stag-spirit in the antlers that rose from his temples, jutting proudly from the mass of his vine-strewn hair. He wore the forest in his crown, which was presently studded with white flowers and red berries. Prior could see the slick shape of Fenton's shadow undulating in the dark of the room, oiling closer to the fire. He thought he'd seen Fenton drop a corner of bread for it, like someone might sneak food to a pampered pet.

Prior wanted to kiss him. He wanted to cup Fenton's face in his hands and learn the taste of him. He wanted to lay with Fenton in a lush field of flowers and memorise the way their bodies were the same. He wanted to revel in the ways they were different. He wanted to watch Fenton ripen and bloom.

"—said, where do you two plan on going next? Prior? Prior!"

Shaking his head slightly, Prior forcibly dragged his gaze from Fenton and turned his attention to his sister. Sylvie raised her eyebrows, amusement plain on her face.

"Back with us?" she asked, pursing her lips in fake annoyance.

Prior took a fortifying sip of ale. "Apologies for my inattention, dearest sister. What were you saying?"

"More to the matter, what were you thinking about? You looked very contemplative," Sylvie said with a grin.

"The harvest," Prior blurted.

Beside him, Baltair coughed as he took a sip of his ale the wrong way. Prior refilled Baltair's cup in silent apology.

Sylvie gestured somewhat stiffly to Fenton. "Since my brother's mind is elsewhere, might you answer my question about your plans after you leave here? More adventures, perhaps?"

Fenton tilted his head to acknowledge the prompt. A good idea to acquiesce, since little stopped Sylvie when she chose to play host.

"I intend to travel to the Aspinwick Estate. Having had opportunity to investigate Ashcroft with the blight's influence muted, it has become clear to me that some force manipulates my sibling. I will find them and free them. They need my help, whether they know it or not." Fenton ran his finger along the edge of his cup. "Whether they will welcome it or not."

Sylvie nodded firmly, and Baltair echoed her with less conviction. Prior continued to admire Fenton's face, until he realised what Fenton planned. Stew splashed Prior's shirt as he dropped his bread into his bowl. He wiped at the mark impatiently. Fenton's change of heart was more important than stew.

"Just a moment. Does this mean I'm not to help you kill a god after all?" he asked.

Sylvie's eyes rounded and she darted a look to Fenton, before narrowing her glare at Prior. "You were going to kill Fenton's sibling? I can't believe you!" She swatted Prior lightly with the back of her hand to his.

"What do you mean you can't— He *asked* me to!" Prior said, swatting her in return.

"Why, you—!"

"You were going to kill a god?" Baltair interrupted, in a numb sort of voice.

Prior scowled at him, even as Sylvie continued to mutter about what would their grandmother have said. "What would you have me do? I made a *promise*."

When Fenton started laughing, the whole house smelled like spring.

TRUTH AND OTHER THINGS THAT BURN

Sylvie held her hands toward the fire. Though she had many of her and Prior's blankets wrapped around her shoulders, and more piled over her lap, not to mention the layers of stockings beneath her heaviest skirt, she couldn't quite get warm. She hadn't been fully warm since breaking from the hold of the sleeping sickness, but held to hope the cold would soon melt from her bones. Already she felt herself thawing; on that first day she had shivered until her teeth clacked together, her brain rattling in her heavy skull, but now only felt as if winter had not yet left.

Spring had come. Sylvie knew that. It sat beside her at the fire, reaching out claw-tipped hands, and watching her from dark eyes. It chilled every corner of her home.

"I didn't thank you for the remedy," Sylvie said. She spoke quickly, as if it might compensate for her tardiness. "I thanked Prior, but not you."

Fenton tilted his head at her. "Fenton". Difficult to think of a god by his first name, but impossible to think of Prior's friend by an epithet Sylvie had learned from fairy tales. The dichotomy had no easy resolution.

"The concoction was not my doing, but you are welcome nonetheless," he said, like he knew it was polite to welcome someone's thanks.

They fell to silence again. Sylvie adjusted her blankets and looked toward the door, but Prior didn't walk through.

After the strangest supper Sylvie had ever experienced, she had seen off Baltair at the door with a promise of explanation when she had it. Baltair had kissed her cheek and squeezed her hand, accepting. He had smelled like lye, iron, and goats. Sylvie could see herself living with that smell for the rest of her days, now that she had the days to dream about.

When she had closed the door behind him, she'd found Prior spooning out the brewed potion into a clean cup. For the Greaves boy, he'd explained, not wanting to waste any time. He'd gone not long after, taking the potion and recipe with him, saying he'd visit Betta at the inn after seeing the boy right. As innkeeper, Betta was best placed to both brew and distribute the potion to those who needed it, he'd said.

Sylvie had heard what Prior didn't say: he wouldn't be there to brew the potion himself. He would be wherever Fenton had led him.

Sylvie had long known her brother wanted more than Ashcroft, but she had been waiting most of her life for him to realise the same. She didn't begrudge Prior a step on his path to adventure, though she would worry for him while he was gone, and hope he would visit from time to time to tell her of all he had seen.

But did his adventure really need to include Fenton?

Fenton shifted in place. His shadow stretched along the wall. Sylvie flipped her hands over, so her chapped knuckles might feel more of the fire's touch.

"Were you in that forest long, then?" Sylvie asked. It wasn't the question she wanted answered, but she didn't know how to approach her true concern.

Fenton hummed. "A very long time, as both you and I would measure. I do not know how long, precisely."

She moved slightly to face him. Fenton echoed her

position. He wanted to make her comfortable, Sylvie realised. Did he view her as some extension of Prior, to extend his concern to her? For it was clear enough that Fenton cared for Prior. His regard showed in every look, every touch, and was reciprocated in kind; Sylvie had exchanged a dozen bewildered glances with Baltair over supper, both of them astonished at the casual intimacy shared by Prior and a *god*. Prior had chattered away as cheerfully besotted as anyone newly courting, and Sylvie had been charmed by his joy, but then she would follow Prior's eyeline and be reminded what held her brother in thrall.

If Fenton cared for Prior, Sylvie needed to know what shape his affection took.

"Hunters come through Ashcroft sometimes. All manner of folk, really, being as we're located near the Great Road and all. This probably means nothing to you, does it?" She caught his eyes; they'd been drifting. "But these hunters. They come by and they say they're going east to hunt the white-tailed stag for wishes."

Fenton had stiffened as Sylvie spoke. A muscle clenched in the sharp line of his jaw. He touched the base of one of his antlers.

"I recall hunters," he said.

"None of them ever come back."

Fenton didn't respond. The vines in his hair hung limp; they'd twisted playfully all during supper, nudging his flower crown and twining around his antlers. She'd pinched her own thigh to stop herself from staring. Seeing them motionless unsettled her, for some reason.

"Why don't they come back?" she asked.

"They die."

She swallowed. Persisted. "Why do they die?"

Fenton rocked forward, as if he would rise to his feet, but quelled the movement. He scratched viciously at the inside of his wrist, digging the points of his claws into the vulnerable flesh. Sylvie wanted to stop him but didn't know how he'd react. She cleared her throat.

"Could you pass me the water, please?" she asked, when he looked at her.

He did, after pouring her a fresh cup from the ewer. Sylvie took small sips and set the cup aside.

Fenton licked his lips. He still held the ewer, and gazed into it as he spoke. "If the hunters had caught m— If the hunters had caught the white-tailed stag, and killed it, what would have happened?"

"They would have gained their wish, I suppose, if that story is true."

"What would their wish have been?"

The hunter who had passed through Ashcroft the past winter had spoken of a wish for food, most of all. The audience at the inn had understood that desire; the moorland had narrowly struggled through bad harvests. Food was a straightforward want, for all that it evaded so many.

But Sylvie had been raised on fairy tales, and she knew that simple desires rapidly turned complex when they came close to fulfilment. A wish for food might become a wish for abundance, in all manner of things, because why be satisfied with a single meal when one could wish for all the harvests in the world? People holding "enough" in their hands looked toward the horizon of "more" and starved themselves for want of it.

Sylvie saw nothing wrong with wishing for the world. But that wasn't how stories worked. Wishes turned rotten more quickly than unsalted meat.

"I can't say what their wish would have been," Sylvie said, as she considered the question. "But that doesn't mean they had to die to stop from speaking it."

Fenton set the ewer down and picked up the poker, prodding listlessly at the fire. He chewed his lower lip. Sylvie had never seen anyone think so hard before speaking. She tucked her hands beneath the blankets and drew them to her chin, watching him.

163

"The forest was intended as a punishment." He prodded a log, breaking it into sparks. "I cannot tell you for what action, as I do not recall, but my sibling and I have long tormented one another. I am certain I have done something similar in my turn."

Despite the heaviness of the conversation, Sylvie snorted. "Yes, I'm familiar with that particular game."

Fenton grinned, a quick gleam of teeth, before sobering. He set the poker aside.

"I did not recall that I was being punished. For moons upon moons I slumbered, deep in the roots, and woke only in flashes." He tilted his head. "Yet the white-tailed stag remained awake, and together with the forest it— It defended me, you could say, vulnerable as I was in my slumber."

"So you're *not* the white-tailed stag?"

"It is very difficult to explain these concepts in words. None have ever asked me these questions before, Sylvie."

He said her name like she was a constellation. Sylvie didn't know what to do with the feeling it evoked in her. She curled her toes beneath the blankets.

Fenton continued without her prompting, as if he wanted her to understand. As if he wanted to understand himself, perhaps. "When the hunters came, I—this incarnation of me, sitting with you by your fire—did not act against them. The forest and the stag worked together in my stead, in my defence. With each new energy absorbed into the forest, I woke further." He ducked his head, seeming almost boyish. "I did not know what to do with my waking until Prior arrived."

Sylvie couldn't process the quiet affection in his latter statement. She focused on the danger instead. She *had* to focus on the danger.

"You fed on their lives, you mean?" She wanted to spit the question, but kept her tone even.

"As you like."

Sylvie *didn't* like. Her stomach rolled. Her brother had

entered that forest in search of a wish. He could have fed
Fenton, just as those hunters did. Sylvie would never have
known what happened to him.

She studied Fenton's pointed face, his elegant hands
draped between his bony knees, the strong line of his back.
Antlers and ears and crown.

"Would you have 'absorbed' Prior, too?" she asked.

Fenton's eyes flashed. "Never."

Before Sylvie could challenge that assertion, the door
creaked open and Prior walked in. He stomped his feet to
knock dust off his boots, and clattered the door closed
behind him,

"Hoo! Betta had a hundred questions, none of which I
could answer, so we'd better take the long way out in the
morning, Fenton." Prior unwound his scarf from around
his neck and hung it on the waiting peg. "The Greaves kin
send their thanks, by the by. The youngest got took with
fever too, but there was enough remedy to share. No one
else has fallen ill. Betta is already brewing a second batch."

As Prior began relating the conversation he'd had with
Betta, detailing her planned distribution for the potion, he
bustled around clearing the supper plates Sylvie hadn't got
around to washing. Sylvie nodded in the right places, but
her attention stayed on Fenton: the god watched her
brother like a flower unfolding toward the sun, his eyes
brightening, his vines reanimating, and even the ugly creep
of his shadow adjusted to a more accurate resemblance.
Prior patted Fenton's shoulder as he passed, and Fenton
raised his clawed hand to touch the same spot, as if he
wanted to savour the warmth.

As she continued to watch the two of them, Sylvie
realised that she could question Fenton for years on end,
but no resolution would ever be found. Whether man or
fox or white-tailed stag, he remained beyond her
comprehension. The Fenton that had sat at her table and
shared her bread was but a human guise stretched over the
bones of something Sylvie could never understand.

Something that had entranced her brother.

Sylvie made herself smile as her brother joked about one of the geese chasing Goodwoman Hilde. Beside her, Fenton chuffed a laugh, and Prior gently tweaked one of the vines that entreated him.

She had thought to ask Fenton whether he understood anything of human affection. If he could comprehend how Prior felt for him, the way growing love shined from Prior's eyes for all those who cared to see. When she had beckoned Fenton to sit by the fire, Sylvie had planned to ask if Fenton were able to reciprocate Prior's feeling. Fear had weighed heavy in her chest but for Prior she would have asked for the world. Wished for it.

Yet now silence held her tongue, and truth stuck like gristle betwixt her teeth. The truth was thus: Fenton was not human, and Prior did not wish him to be. Fenton returned Prior's love like a dog to its master. Like the wolf that waited behind the hound's eyes, he watched Prior with hungry rapture.

Sylvie tugged the blankets closer around her shoulders, taken with a sudden chill.

PART FIVE:
IT MUST RUN IN THE FAMILY

Prior observed the Aspinwick Estate from where he and Fenton huddled behind a half-crumbled wall, part of a folly arranged on the nearby rise. The folly boasted a useless bastion, only slightly taller than Prior's cottage, with narrow, inaccessible, apertures dotted around the walls in a way that Prior assumed would make the structure seem imposing and defensively sound when viewed from inside Aspinwick House. A wall ran alongside the bastion, slumping and covered with shrubbery, with a few rocks scattered artfully nearby. Overall, the folly gave the impression of genteel ruination, despite it having been built scarcely a decade past. Prior remembered his grandmother muttering about the whims of landed folk and their bottomless purses.

Prior felt somewhat more generously toward Aspinwick now, as the folly provided shelter for his and Fenton's spying on the estate. No shelter from the weather, however: wind bit Prior's cheeks and chapped his knuckles, and he'd ducked his chin to snag the folds of his scarf over his nose and mouth. The rise allowed a view over the grounds of Aspinwick, while the cover provided by the wall and bastion kept he and Fenton hidden. They had retreated from the cold night and slept inside the bastion, with Prior snug beneath a blanket of flowers and Fenton's avid promise to guard Prior's rest. Prior had never slept so soundly.

A heartbeat after Prior had opened his bleary eyes that morning, Fenton had said he was off to Aspinwick. Prior had scarcely grabbed his shoulder in time to plead for caution. The rising sun could do little to burn away the frigid air that had settled between them since. As Fenton again rose to a high kneel to peer over the wall, the last of Prior's patience finally rattled out between his chattering teeth.

"How many times must I explain that you can't simply wander in there, you horse's *ass*," he hissed at Fenton. No one was around to overhear but grazing sheep, yet Prior kept his voice low. He poked Fenton's leg. "Get down!"

"It is not my intent to 'wander'," Fenton said sullenly. He sank down to rest on his haunches beside Prior, his legs buckling in a manner to which Prior had yet to become accustomed. As Fenton explained it, since leaving the forest—and predominantly since his transformation at the farmhouse—his magic had been returning in force, and his body was adjusting to the energy as best it could without abandoning human guise altogether.

Since leaving Ashcroft the day before, Fenton's legs had altered to more resemble the backwards knees of a fox, his ankles and feet shifting to accommodate the change, and his antlers grew more prominent day by day. They currently spread half an arm's length from his temples, and nearly that again in height; Fenton had claimed the antlers would eventually stop growing, but he hadn't clarified when "eventually" would occur, nor how unwieldy the antlers would become before then. He hadn't been clear on much, all told, though his ambiguity seemed due to a lack of knowledge rather than contrariness. Prior had stopped asking.

When they had been around people on the Great Road,

Fenton had quashed the changes to don a more human appearance, but the strain had been visible in the tight corners of his mouth. Back in the moors, with only Prior to witness, Fenton had relaxed into his altered shape. Prior had wanted to tell him he didn't need to hide, that Fenton deserved comfort wherever he was and hang the consequences, but part of him enjoyed being the only one privileged to know Fenton's true shape. Also, he didn't want to see how quickly a mob could form.

Fenton shifted. His gaze was fixed on the Aspinwick Estate. "There are trees aplenty to climb, and shadows to disguise my form. I am familiar with the concept of discretion."

"Discretion? You have antlers! Yesterday you snapped your teeth at a crow for flying too close. You almost caught feathers!"

Fenton jutted his jaw and his vines flickered in a pattern Prior recognised as impatience. While at first Fenton had seemed as distant and unknowable as the moon, during their time together Prior had begun to learn Fenton as a traveller learned a new road. A road, after all, was a road was a road, and only the heading ever altered. Prior need but stay the course.

Unless Fenton rushed into Aspinwick and got his fool self captured—or worse.

The current owner of the Aspinwick Estate was a mage and a particular former friend of Nola's, and Nola had shared her confidence that the estate held the source of the blight. After seeing Sylvie settled and leaving Ashcroft, Prior and Fenton had travelled across the moorlands with Fenton's senses focused on the trail of his sibling's magic. Once they'd arrived at Aspinwick, he'd confirmed that Lorcan's magic tangled so thoroughly with the estate's that he could scarcely tell where one began and the other ended. Prior didn't fully comprehend the implication, but the grass about Fenton's feet had leached of colour, and his shadow had unspooled from him like dropped thread.

The reaction had been enough.

Aspinwick occupied as much land as Prior's village and boasted a clear brook running through it, feeding into elaborate water gardens that fanned out on the far side of the manor house. The brook held no fish, Fenton had said, with conviction Prior didn't question. Fenton had gone quiet after that.

Tall stone walls encircled the house and gardens, interrupted by the archways that allowed the brook, and a broad wooden gate that met the road to Northrope. The gate bore the family crest: a wyvern, if Prior remembered his grandmother's lessons correctly. Liveried guards occupied the gatehouse, and were armed with swords, crossbows, and an unfortunate level of professional diligence. More guards patrolled the gardens, and domestic staff crisscrossed the grounds as they attended to their tasks. There had been no sign of the mage, which was all to the good, but Prior's heart sank nonetheless: before arriving at Aspinwick, Prior had hoped to sneak in unseen. That possibility had become progressively unlikely the more Prior observed of the estate's activity.

"Are you certain Lorcan is within those walls?" Prior asked, not for the first time.

"I am indeed certain Lorcan is within," Fenton said, also not for the first time. His vines twisted in agitation around his antlers. "I need only get closer and I will be able to locate them more precisely."

"And in getting closer, what danger do you expose yourself to? No," Prior said firmly. "We're not doing that. If someone can influence Lorcan, what's to say they can't capture you as well? I can't rescue you from that kind of magic. Not from any kind of magic!" Prior didn't know to make his fear any clearer. Frustration made his voice tight. "*Please.* We need a plan. We at least need an exit."

Fenton frowned and rearranged himself to sit with his back to Aspinwick. Prior sat beside him, stretching out his legs. Dew-damp grass had soaked through his trousers where he'd been kneeling; undoubtedly he'd have a wet arse in short order. He rocked his booted feet from side to side, tapping Fenton's bare, beclawed foot as he did. Fenton curled his toes. Prior repeated the motion until Fenton met his eyes.

"I'm sorry about this. About making demands on you, I mean. I'm not sorry about not wanting you to be captured, or have whatever's happened to Lorcan happen to you." Prior chewed the inside of his lip. "It's just... We started out with an agreement to kill your sibling, and I can't help but worry this rescue, if that's what it is, will somehow change again—"

"I was wrong." Fenton's eyes glowed gold. He did not blink. "Prior, I was wrong before. I had spent a long time in the forest, so long that I had started to think it was the only world that mattered. In my injured pride, I thought that Lorcan must die so I could live." He raked his fingers through his hair, yanking sharply when they tangled. Prior eased Fenton's hand away and held it. Fenton's mouth twisted wryly. "But there is more to the world than pride. I remember that now." He looked at their joined hands. "Lorcan needs my help. I am certain of it."

Prior's heart ached. "I believe you, I do."

"Yet you wish me to wait."

"I wish you to be *careful*. There must be another way to enter Aspinwick, without running headlong into who knows what," Prior said.

Fenton suddenly twitched his head, making Prior start. Before Prior could ask what had happened, Fenton flicked his hand at the creeping ivy: it had tried to knot around his antlers. Prior snickered, louder when Fenton let out an amused huff and patted the ivy back into place with exaggerated care. Affection melted the chilly tension between them. Prior wanted to curl up inside it for as long as he could. He leaned against Fenton and rested his head on Fenton's sturdy shoulder. Closeness thrilled in him.

"I do not wish to delay," Fenton said, his voice

unusually gentle.

"Nor do I wish you to delay. I know you're being... Indulgent, of me. Of my worries." That Fenton hadn't simply taken off to do as he pleased made Prior's chest sweetly ache. Fenton could, of course, do as he liked, whenever he liked, but his willingness to hear Prior's concerns meant more than Prior had courage to explain.

Fenton squeezed Prior's hand. "Your worries flatter me. I could do no less than return the concern you have shown."

Prior had no idea what to do with such words. He wanted Fenton to say them again. He stared furiously at his boots and Fenton's clawed feet.

"I-I think we should— What's that?" Prior twisted around to rise on his knees and peek over the wall, toward the road leading to the estate. "There's a carriage coming up the road."

Led by finely plumed horses, the glossy blue carriage swung low over its wheels, scarcely jouncing over the uneven road. Laden. Prior squinted, trying to distinguish the emblem painted on the door of the carriage, but his vision fared poorly over such distance.

"Who do you think that is?" he asked, albeit rhetorically. Fenton would hardly know. "I can't make out the shield."

"The image resembles a feather over a loaf, if that holds meaning for you. I do not recognise the bird from whence it came," Fenton said. He'd sat on his heels with his chin resting on top of the wall. He made a distressingly adorable sight.

Prior forced himself to contemplate the question of the carriage. A feather over a loaf wasn't the symbol of any noble family of the moorlands or along the Great Road. A merchant, most likely; perhaps a baker. Prior's grandmother had diligently taught he and Sylvie the symbols of noble families in case someone of import should pass through Ashcroft; a loathed lesson that had transformed into a protection Prior came to appreciate as he got older. If the carriage on the road belonged to a merchant, it was one doing rich business, to judge by the prime state of both carriage and horses.

"I don't know who they are, but let's watch for a while. If more carriages come, we might be able to sneak along the road and board one somehow," Prior said.

To his relief, Fenton nodded and settled into a comfortable waiting position. Tendrils of ivy reached for him and Fenton looped his fingers through their stems like someone might tease the hair of a lover. Prior tore his gaze away and concentrated on the question of the estate. He needed to find a way to get Fenton safely in—and out again, and past any protections the mage might have put in place.

The morning passed and brought numerous carriages to Aspinwick, each as rich in appearance as the first, and each instigating a flurry of activity from the estates' staff. Although they were on a rise, which enabled a limited view into the grounds, Prior became frustrated with the restricted viewpoint gained from behind the wall. He crawled into the ivy-covered bastion and there considered the structure more thoroughly, now he had the light of day. He eyed the narrow apertures, the type that archers could have used if the bastion hadn't been a sham: the tower was hollow, without even crumbled stone to suggest a functioning staircase had ever been present. The only archers able to shoot from the folly's top windows would have to be twenty feet tall.

Behind him, Fenton hummed. He'd followed Prior; silently, of course. "This structure is odd." Fenton pressed his fingers to the nearest wall, then licked his fingertips. His vines twitched. "What is the purpose of this place? Does someone inhabit it?"

"No one lives here. No one does anything here. The folk of Aspinwick admire it from the windows of their big house and tell their friends about it, and that's all," Prior said, aware of the bitterness in his own voice. The coin spent on building the folly could have fed Ashcroft for seasons. But Ashcroft was not so pretty as the folly.

"Then it is not a defensive fortification?" Fenton asked.

"For decoration only. It's called a folly. Pretty to look at but without any other purpose." Frustrated, Prior gestured toward the top windows. "We'd get a good view over the grounds from up there, but"—he let his hand fall— "there's no way to see out. Unless one of your raven friends is about. Are they?" He wasn't being entirely facetious.

Fenton hummed again as his gaze flitted across the apertures. Then he tilted his head at Prior. His eyes were bright. "We do not need a raven."

Before Prior could ask what *that* meant, the answer began to reveal itself as Fenton splayed his hands in the tangle of ivy on the nearest wall. Pressure built in Prior's head and he took a judicious step away from Fenton, watching as the ivy began to grow and wend around the interior of the bastion. Fenton grunted and pulled one hand away from the wall to make a beckoning gesture at the ground, from which green shoots—resembling Fenton's vines, but far larger—began to rise and crisscross through the ivy to form a supportive net. Prior followed the progress with his eyes, tracing their journey all the way to the bastion's roof, until at last the vines settled with a sigh. The apertures had been left uncovered.

Fenton pulled away from the wall and scrutinised his work, as the vines in his hair adjusted his crown. He ran his hand along the snaking curve of greenery as someone might stroke a beloved pet.

"Much better than a raven," he said, with satisfaction. He looked expectantly at Prior. "Do you not agree?"

"I'm not certain what I'm agreeing with, if I'm honest," Prior said.

"You wished to see from above."

"Yes, but— Oh!"

Prior fell silent as he watched Fenton cross toward the nearest section of vines and start to clamber up like they were a ladder. Hand over confident hand, sprays of pink flowers blooming in his wake, Fenton climbed until he reached one of the uppermost apertures. There he stopped, one hand and one foot supported by winding vines, the other hand and foot free, and beamed at Prior. The sight made Prior's stomach flip in a complicated tangle of fear and attraction.

"Pretty *with* purpose," Fenton said, proudly and not a little smug. He patted the vines with his free hand.

Prior licked his lips. "I can see that, yes."

Flushing slightly, Fenton pulled himself toward the wall and peered through the narrow window slit. "There is more movement in the grounds." He beckoned Prior. "You can watch from here as you like."

He was so *pleased* with himself. Prior tried to gauge the height of the bastion. He probably wouldn't die from a fall of that height, would he?

Fenton wouldn't let him die. The conviction arrived in Prior fully formed. As if it had always been there, waiting to be consciously thought. Prior didn't question the truth of it.

And he really *did* want a better view of Aspinwick's grounds.

"All right, I'm coming up. Don't— Don't say anything, please. I need to concentrate," Prior said, unwinding his scarf and setting it aside. Just in case.

"I shall not speak." Fenton grunted. "*Now*, I shall not."

Despite his nerves, Prior smiled as he selected his starting spot. Then, carefully, steadily, Prior started to scale the vines. He progressed more slowly than Fenton had, but Prior had climbed trees as a boy, and his confidence returned as the vines assisted him by providing easy footholds. Fenton's silent support. Climbing became enjoyable, almost, so long as Prior didn't look down.

He was careful not to look down.

Prior focused on one hand, then the other. One hand, then the other. Until, at last, he found himself tapping Fenton's foot instead of another vine. Prior wobbled as his momentum faltered, but Fenton clasped his outstretched hand with a comforting strength, and Prior found himself drawn to a position on the other side of the aperture to Fenton. Vines arranged themselves beneath Prior's hands and feet, and one particularly robust vine wound itself firmly around Prior's waist and tugged him close to the wall. The security of Fenton's touch, his hand and his vines and his focused attention, made the last of Prior's nerves ebb away.

"It doesn't seem so far now I'm up here," Prior said, glancing down. He let out a nervous laugh. "Far enough, though." Looking toward Aspinwick, Prior was pleased with the view into the estate grounds. He smiled at Fenton. "Thank you for this. It was very clever of you."

When Fenton didn't respond, Prior squeezed their joined hands. "Fenton? Are you well?"

"You will not be distracted if I speak?" Fenton asked quietly, his vines twisting around the base of his antlers.

Prior wanted to kiss him. Very much. But that last distance between them might as well have been leagues. He didn't know if he could cross it. He didn't know where to *start*.

He squeezed Fenton's hand again. "Please, speak to me. I'm sorry I wasn't clear with you. I was scared I would fall, before. That's all."

"Do you fear falling now?"

Prior already had.

He shook his head. "I know you'll keep me safe."

Fenton made a soft sound, like he'd been struck, and lurched forward to press his face into the crook of Prior's neck. He hooked his free leg around Prior's to draw himself closer, making inarticulate noises that shocked through Prior in a direct line to his cock, as Fenton crowded against him so tightly it seemed he wanted to climb inside Prior's skin. Prior wanted to help him. He wanted Fenton as close as they could get. Daringly, his heart thumping with adrenaline, Prior unwound his hand from the vines, trusting the one around his waist to hold him, and smoothed back Fenton's hair. He received a wet kiss to his throat and lifted his chin to give Fenton better access.

He caught sight of Aspinwick through the window and his hand stilled in Fenton's hair.

They had to stop.

Prior didn't want to stop. He wanted to kiss Fenton still—had never wanted it more—but they were suspended at the top of a bastion they had climbed to spy on a mage's estate. To stop a blight.

"Fuck," he said, with feeling. Fenton froze, and Prior immediately resumed stroking his hair. "No, no, not— We had a plan. Didn't we? We were working on a plan." Fenton said something that Prior didn't hear. "What was that?"

"I *said*"—Fenton lifted his blotchy face from Prior's throat—"ten curses on your plan." He tugged at one of his vines and tucked it behind his ear. "Very well. As you wish."

With a smile, and an unsubtle adjustment of his breeches, Prior relaxed into the grip of Fenton's vines to watch Aspinwick from his new vantage point. As the sun rose toward its peak, staff began to work in the gardens, assembling wooden structures and draping them with awnings and colourful bunting. Fenton left, then, to go foraging as best he could, while Prior continued to watch the estate until he thought he had the shape of things. Then he turned his back on Aspinwick and climbed to the ground. The downward journey went significantly easier than the upward, not least because Prior allowed the vines to do most of the work.

Fenton had returned by then, and unsurprisingly, his best efforts at foraging were very good: he'd produced ripe fistfuls of berries and an arrangement of mushrooms to accompany the flatbread from their pack, along with two fat wineskins Prior didn't remember bringing from Ashcroft. He didn't know that berries or mushrooms were in season, either, but reasoned that was Fenton's prerogative.

"The essentials?" he asked with a smirk, indicating the wineskins.

Fenton nodded solemnly, settling at Prior's feet with his legs crossed. "Just so."

They divided the provisions and Prior settled in to explain his findings. "My guess is there's to be some event at Aspinwick, and soon, seeing as they've been loading up on food and plenty of it. There were blocks of ice, even. I've never seen anything like it! Looks like it'll be quite the party, and going on either tomorrow or today would be my guess. Might be we can enter along with the guests. They'll be a good distraction while you sneak around doing whatever it is you're planning to do."

Flicking a berry into the air with his thumb, Fenton caught it with a snap of teeth and chewed thoughtfully, leaning back with one hand braced on the ground. A magpie swooped into the bastion and landed by his hand, bobbing its head and letting out a chirrup when Fenton tore a piece of flatbread and crumbled it in his palm for the bird to peck. Prior's chest went tight. He only remembered to exhale when the magpie chirruped again and took off, blue feathers bold against the sky.

"Here." Fenton dropped something on Prior's leg. "A gift."

A feather. Prior picked it up with faintly shaking fingers. He wanted to brush it against his lips. "Thank you. And thank your bird friend as well."

Fenton smiled faintly, then tossed and caught another berry. Vines moved in his hair, readjusting his flower crown. Prior ran his thumbnail along the edge of the feather and thought about nothing at all.

"The event?" Fenton prompted, eventually.

Prior cleared his throat and set the feather carefully aside. "Yes, absolutely, the event. We should sneak in with the guests, but if the mage is as strong as Nola says—"

"Hartling," Fenton sneered, his shadow flickering across his throat.

The corner of Prior's mouth pulled in a brief grimace. He'd been trying not to think of Lady Hartling's name; a leftover fear from his grandmother's stories, that a mage might hear their name and turn their sight his way. It was a silly fear, but he had learned it young, and the scars of youth bedded in firmly.

According to Fenton's investigation, and Nola's knowledge, Lady Hartling—the current owner of the Aspinwick Estate—was responsible for the blight, and for Lorcan's imprisonment. Nola hadn't shared details about their previous relationship, simply stating that Lady Hartling owned the property and had enough magical knowledge to be dangerous. Prior could not bring himself to ask further questions from one who had offered more assistance than he'd dared expect, and Fenton hadn't displayed curiosity for anything other than the location of his sibling.

"If the mage is that strong, then undoubtedly there'll be wards in place to protect against intruders, and there's definitely guards besides. That could be messy for us," Prior said.

"Guards do not concern me."

"I'm sure they don't, but I'd prefer no one get hurt if we can avoid it."

"You keep saying 'we'." Fenton tilted his head. "Do you intend to accompany me?"

Prior nodded. "I do. I made a promise, didn't I?"

Fenton looked away, his mouth twisting, but then he hummed. Prior slumped back. He hadn't wanted to argue the point with Fenton—not least because Prior wasn't sure of the reason for his own insistence—and he was glad to return to the more important matters of finding Lorcan.

"Very well. Then what is your suggestion to enter this place?" Fenton asked.

"The brook?"

Fenton shuddered. "No. It is dead."

Whatever made Fenton reject the brook likely meant Prior shouldn't swim there, either. Prior tried to think around the problem. They didn't know what the event was, nor when it was being held; if it were to occur that evening, they would have no other opportunity to find a discrete route inside, and Fenton would have to take his chances. Delay wasn't an option worth discussing. But the magic wards—currently hypothetical, but almost certainly actual—presented a problem.

Magic wards.

Struck by excitement, Prior rolled forward onto his knees and drew closer to Fenton. He grinned. "Who do we know who gets invited to all sorts of fancy events, and must surely have received an invitation to this one? Or at least might acquire one for us?"

"… Baltair?" Fenton offered, hesitantly.

"Baltair? It's not a party of *goats*, it's— Nola. Nola! She must know what's happening here. She's Northrope's famous mage, isn't she? And didn't she want you to, what was it, explode something so she didn't have to go to a dance? That might even be for here! It's perfect."

"But Nola does not wish to come here."

Fenton wasn't wrong. Nola had expressly stated her disinterest in the Aspinwick Estate but that didn't mean she'd been struck off the invitation list. If Prior understood anything about such matters, her reluctance would surely make her a more alluring guest, in addition to the fame she had procured from warding Northrope's walls. The only potential hiccup Prior could see was that Nola might have been removed from the list, but they wouldn't be any worse placed than they were now, and Northrope wasn't far to travel to check.

"Nola doesn't have to come with us, she need only help us get inside." Prior tapped Fenton on the knee with the magpie feather. "Trust me on this. I know I'm right."

For a long moment, Fenton stilled so entirely it appeared he stopped breathing. He did that when his thoughts required his full attention, Prior knew, and it accentuated Fenton's singularity moreso than even his appearance did. Every creature required the vitality of breath. Every creature save Fenton. Prior found it compelling. Found Fenton compelling.

Prior chewed his lower lip as he watched. If Fenton didn't agree, Prior could do nothing but follow him and hope. The thought didn't distress him as much as it should.

Finally, Fenton inhaled. He touched Prior's chin, raising his gaze so their eyes met. "I trust you," he said.

Prior swallowed. He nodded. "To Northrope, then."

Fenton had not intended to ever return to the wretched city of Northrope, but Prior had requested it, and thus they were once more within the wards that prickled his nape like so many biting flies. He tugged his hooded cloak—Prior had insisted—more firmly over his head and tried not to inhale too deeply, lest the myriad stenches of Northrope find home in his lungs. His cloak stretched as he bade it; Fenton's shadow disguised the compressed shape of his antlers better than any fabric could attempt.

"Her house was this way, wasn't it? I think it was," Prior muttered, answering himself and leading Fenton through the city streets. "We've lost so much of the day already, even with your *very* quick method of getting us here." He glanced back at Fenton. "Are you sure you're well?"

"I am as expected," Fenton answered, smoothing the lines of his cloak. They had travelled by shadow to a spot just outside the city walls that Fenton remembered from their previous visit. They'd nearly landed on a fornicating couple, but fortunately the couple had been too distracted to notice their entrance.

Prior accepted Fenton's answer and continued on. "If you're sure. Let me know if anything changes, won't you?" He blew out a breath. "I hope the Aspinwick thing happens tomorrow, or after, or else someone will be picking my teeth from one of those fountains after I follow you over those walls and get beaten half to death by a guard in the attempt."

He was wrong, of course, since Fenton would simply consume anyone that dared approach Prior with violence in their heart. Prior had already come to harm through Fenton's negligence, and Fenton did not intend to permit a second incident. Much of his magic had returned to him, and Prior walked with protection shimmering over his skin for those who knew to look. Not true wards, for those required more time to construct and more conversation to implement, but the relatively simple cantrips would summon Fenton if he were needed.

Mistakes were an inevitable part of accumulating experience, but Fenton didn't like making the same ones twice. Or at all.

He tapped Prior's shoulder to gain his attention, then pointed toward the blue door of Nola's residence. "There, ahead."

Prior firmed his jaw. "Let's hope she's home, shall we?"

If Nola were away, she would surely appear once they triggered her wards, as she had when Fenton had climbed into her garden. Fenton followed Prior and waited as he rapped a rhythm on the door. Smoke and sweat perfumed the air.

Prior shifted in place when no one answered the door. "Should I try again? Where else do you think might she be?"

With a nudge of effort, Fenton extended the claw on

182

his forefinger. He scratched a line into the door, flaking away the paint to reveal naked wood, then crossed that line with another. He lowered his arm.

"Knock again. She will answer," he said.

Prior raised his eyebrows dubiously, but knocked again. Only once. As soon as his knuckles touched the wood, the door blew backward off its hinges and collapsed in a puff of dust and splinters. Spluttering, Prior wafted his hand in front of his face, then he slowly dragged his gaze to Fenton.

"Did you really just—?" he trailed off, his shining eyes wide.

Fenton bared his teeth in a grin and crossed the threshold, letting his shadow reclaim its place at his feet as he did. Wards broke over his body like gossamer. "We had not the time to wait."

The door opened into an airy five-sided room with closed doors on every wall, and a single large window that showed the meditative waves of a sea that Northrope did not contain. Light glowed from the hundred candles of an ornate chandelier, which Prior craned his neck to examine. The candles did not leave smoke trails, nor did their flames flicker. Fenton wrinkled his nose. Beside the door, a golden table held a single, long-stemmed red dahlia in a tall glass vase. Fenton poked the flower with his claw. Fake.

"I mean, it certainly was effective, I can't say otherwise. However, I can't help but notice that Nola didn't actually *answer*, as such. We've more… invited ourselves in," Prior said. "How do you think she lit all those candles?"

"Magic," Fenton said.

Prior gave him a flat look. "Strange how they never say how funny you are in the tales." He shoved his hands in his pockets and chewed his lower lip. "I thought Nola would show by now. I'm not sure what to do next. Which door should we choose to look for her? *Should* we look? It seems rude."

Nola's absence disturbed Fenton also, though rudeness

did not concern him. He could sense no presence in the building other than theirs, not even— His vines went still.

"Her garden is gone. Nola will not return here. We must leave. We should not have tarried," he said and turned for the door.

Prior sidestepped to block his way. His eyes narrowed. "How will we get into Aspinwick? This is the best choice, and you know it."

"There is no one here!" Fenton gestured sharply.

Suddenly, the waves in the window shuddered as, beyond the room, something crashed. A rumble trickled through the building from the top down, like the first stones tippling from the top of a mountain. Fenton's shadow climbed to his waist in readiness for armour. The floor shook. Prior locked his gaze on Fenton.

"What's—"

"Down!"

Snake-quick, Fenton tugged Prior away a beat before one of the inner doors blasted into splinters. Heat seared across Fenton's face. The wall behind where Prior had been standing rocked with the impact, the stone cracking and spitting shards that beat Fenton's back as he twisted to take the brunt. Prior gripped the front of Fenton's tunic, clinging so close Fenton could feel the rabbiting beat of Prior's heart against his own chest.

Glass shattered—the vase—as the building trembled again. As the air filled rapidly with dense smoke, Fenton made for the door that opened onto the docks, pulling Prior with him. Fenton's vines twisted in agitation. What was attacking? He sensed nothing beyond general threat. Nola remained absent.

Prior coughed. He pressed his face to Fenton's chest. "Wh-what's happening?"

Broken wards and spite, if Fenton were pressed to guess. Clearly Nola had warded the building before leaving Northrope, either against intruders in general or Fenton and Prior in particular. It didn't matter which. As he herded Prior toward the scent of water, Fenton's ears twitched as he listened for another ripple of magic. The door was farther than it should have been. Fenton held onto Prior's shoulder as he gently but firmly directed Prior; he took strength from Prior's solidity, from the curve of bone beneath his palm.

"I can't see the door," Prior said, voice reedy.

"It is before you. Can you smell the air?"

Prior took a breath. "I-I think I can. Almost there. Almost— Fenton!"

Another door combusted into shards behind them, and the remaining doors rattled in their frames. The building creaked. Wind whipped through the room, briefly clearing the smoke, and Fenton shoved Prior toward the exit, then dove aside to avoid a lash of magic. Hearing Prior's cry, Fenton twisted onto his back and his eyes went wide: the chandelier and its hundred tiny lights teetered on its mooring. As one, the candles screamed into tall, bright flames. Fenton's shadow roiled.

"You have to move!" Prior shouted.

"Why are you still here?" Fenton snapped.

Smoke obscured Prior's face, and his response, as he spluttered. Snarls roughed Fenton's throat as he scrambled upright, meaning to go to Prior, but there came an ominous creak from above. If the chandelier fell on Prior it would kill him. Panicked, Fenton yanked his shadow from where it had been suppressing the magic-born flames so they did not engulf the surrounding buildings; a burning city would not solve their problems. But if the choice was between Northrope or Prior?

Let Northrope burn.

The chandelier plummeted into the inky pit of Fenton's shadow, which swallowed flames and smoke and metal alike. Power surged through Fenton. He howled with it. The petty magic of the remaining wards broke against him like spray against a cliff face. He raised his hands and grasped for more: more magic, more power, whatever he could dig his claws into and *consume*.

Something caught hold of his claws.

Fern and rose. Fenton's nose twitched. He glanced down. The smoke had cleared and left Prior's eyes reddened. Fenton blinked. Voices shouted nearby. He concentrated on Prior's.

"—people coming. Difficult to ignore a building setting on fire. We need to go before they get here."

"You wanted an invitation," Fenton said, as much a reminder to himself as to Prior.

Prior snorted. His gaze skipped from one corner of broken stone to another. "That isn't a good reason to destroy someone's house."

"It was the wards. It—"

The floor exploded. Fenton grabbed Prior and twisted mid-air so that when they hit the wall—when they went *through* the wall—it was Fenton that took the brunt, his shadow braced for impact. Plaster and stone burst and showered around them. They collided with a table, loosing a flutter of paper, and a pot of ink splashed across Fenton's chest. They stopped. Fenton sprawled in the mess, Prior panting atop him. Fenton would move in a moment. In one moment. His foot twitched as one of his deeper lacerations sewed itself shut.

"We definitely— We need to go." Prior shuffled in place. Grunted. "Fenton? You're alive, aren't you? Fenton?" Moving jerkily, he put his weight on Fenton's chest, then cursed when Fenton wheezed. "Sorry, sorry, I'm— Say something, please." Tears rumpled his voice. "I can't do this again."

Prior's panic punched Fenton harder than any blow. With a grunt, he pushed to his elbows. "I am well. Bruises, only."

Prior sniffed and glared through red-ringed eyes. "You better not be lying."

"I would not."

"No. No, I suppose you wouldn't." Settling on his

heels, Prior looked around the small room in which they had landed. "She'll need to redecorate her study after this." He rubbed his face. "What a mess."

Moving carefully, pleased he had broken no bones—or none so badly his healing could not fix them—Fenton pushed to his feet. His shadow flexed around his legs. "Magic will tidy it well enough."

Prior snorted. "Pragmatic of you." His attention drifted to the mess of paper. "We broke into her house and sort of... exploded it... and now I'm going to"—Prior grabbed something, then tucked whatever it was into his pack—"steal this. Come on, I know you're the big bad fox, but we need to go before someone starts asking awkward questions."

"We were not to blame."

Prior's eyes narrowed. "Is this *your* house?"

"... It is not."

"Exactly." Prior took hold of Fenton's hand. "Let's go."

"I can return us to Aspinwick, if you wish?" Fenton offered, already readying his shadow for travel.

Prior shook his head. "We need some things from the city, if we're going to make this thing work. Baths, for one, and with soap, not just a splash in some frigid river."

"'This thing'?"

"I'll explain as soon as I can. We need to find somewhere to stay, first. And to get past the crowd outside."

That would not be a problem. Though he did not understand Prior's delay, Fenton had trusted him thus far, and would continue to do so. Leading Prior toward one of the outer walls, Fenton uncoiled his shadow until it stretched as another door. Warmth seeped from it, brushing Fenton's face and making his vines twist.

Prior frowned. "I said I didn't want to go back to—"

"Do you trust me?" Fenton asked, squeezing Prior's hand.

Prior smiled softly. "You know I do."

"Then come with me."

They stepped through shadow and into the alley outside. Prior laughed. "I should never have doubted you. I'm sorry. Now, let's go, quickly."

Their shortcut enabled them to evade the curious onlookers studding the docks, and in silence they made for the centre of the city. With the sun fully set, darkness painted every corner, scarcely thwarted by the weak street lanterns, and enhanced by the narrow wend of the alleys. Cloaked in his shadow once more, Fenton watched the crowds as he followed Prior.

"We need somewhere to spend the night," Prior muttered, leading them toward a small market square, the stalls empty, a central fountain burbling lowly into holes in the ground. An inn dominated one side of the square. "Here, what do you think? It looks reasonable." Prior grimaced slightly. "The roof is intact, at least."

Fenton considered the inn. The roof was indeed intact. A sign carved to resemble a rearing horse swung in the slight breeze, while light glowed through the small windows, and the scent of cooked vegetables wafted from within. Fenton could smell no blood, nor fear, nor befouled magic.

He tilted his head at Prior. "Reasonable."

"Strong praise."

After deftly negotiating for a room and bath, Prior handed his money to the innkeeper resignedly, then led Fenton upstairs. The innkeeper watched after them with only a cursory glance, more interested in the coin offered by another patron waiting for their glass to be refilled. The indifference soothed some of Fenton's tension.

"It won't be much," Prior said, as he fumbled with the key. A candle on a nearby sconce flickered as he sighed. "So don't hold your— Oh. Well. That's not ideal."

Fenton peered over Prior's shoulder. The small room offered a narrow bed tucked into the corner, two tired wooden chairs, a tall screen patterned with a lumpy peacock, and a window overlooking the square. Several unlit candles were placed about the room and a fire simmered in the hearth. A dented copper bathtub sat in the corner.

"The bathtub is empty," Fenton pointed out as he followed Prior inside. He caught the key Prior tossed at him and locked the door while Prior lit a candle with the provided flint. Fenton's shadow dropped to pool around his feet.

Candle lit, Prior moved to the next. "The innkeeper will send the water once its heated."

"Then what is not ideal?"

Prior flushed. He struggled with the flint. "There's only one bed."

Fenton tilted his head. "I see no issue with that arrangement."

"You see no— One moment!" Prior interrupted himself as a knock came at the door. He made an odd gesture at Fenton, as if— As if pulling up a hood. Once Fenton's shadow cloak settled in place, Prior unlocked the door to admit two members of the inn's staff with buckets of steaming water.

Several trips were used to half-fill the copper tub, and the staff gave Prior and Fenton a sliver of lye soap and two thin drying cloths before leaving. The astringent scent of the soap stung Fenton's nose and he suppressed a sneeze. His shadow rippled and slid down his shoulders, sinking to the floor.

"You don't have to use the soap if you prefer not to, but the bath isn't optional," Prior said as he moved the peacock screen between the tub and the rest of the room. He retrieved his pack and stepped behind the screen. "I'm taking first bath, by the way, hope you don't mind," he continued, raising his voice, though such a negligible barrier did not impede Fenton's hearing.

"I do not," Fenton replied at his usual volume.

Then there seemed nothing to do but perch on one of

the chairs and wait. The injuries Fenton had accumulated at the mage's building continued to throb and sting, but the vast amount of magic his shadow had consumed from Nola's manse had boosted Fenton's natural healing. Much of the magic had surged toward Sylvie and Ashcroft, following the thread of his connection, but enough had been retained to make a difference. A night without battle should see to the rest of his healing.

Rustling from behind the screen drew Fenton from his thoughts. A soft splash, followed by a larger one; Prior lowering himself into the water. Fenton's vines rippled and he shifted on the chair.

"Gods that's good," Prior muttered. He raised his voice again. "Do you want to guess what I found in that study?" Without pausing, he went on, "An invitation! I recognised the crest from the one on Aspinwick's gate. It transpires that the *extremely* venerable Aspinwick Estate has cordially invited a mage of our ever-more-strained acquaintance to a masquerade party tomorrow evening, to be held in honour of the lady of the manor and her poor taste in stationery. Peach on cream. I can scarcely read it." A scratching sound, then a soft curse. "Dropping it in the bath doesn't help, of course."

Fenton snorted. "I imagine it does not."

"I know, I should've waited, but let me just— There. Anyway, that's why we need the baths. Got to look fancy for this sort of thing. Wash your vines, buff your antlers." Prior sighed. Water moved; perhaps he had stretched out his legs. Fenton's ears heated. "Turn your brain to think how we might find some appropriate clothing, will you? We'll need to sort that in the morning. Preferably for free, since I'm very much light on coin."

Fenton tired of the notion of coin.

"We are not the mage, though," he pointed out, instead of saying as much.

"Sometimes people send emissaries to events in their stead, so it's like attending without *actually* attending. I'm hoping we can brazen it out. Besides, who would be so bold to steal a party invitation from a mage?" The scent of lye deepened. Water splashed. "We know she won't be there, after all." A pause. "Well, we can be reasonably certain. It's worth a try."

Fenton hummed. Other avenues remained to breach Aspinwick, if Prior's preferred, peaceful, method failed; they had not been very peaceful thus far, after all. Fenton traced the shape of the peacock with his eyes, as if he might see Prior beyond it. His shadow lurked near the screen and Fenton yanked it to heel.

As Prior continued to bathe, Fenton closed his eyes and leant back on the chair. Worry gnawed at him, flourishing in the deceptive tranquillity of the small room. Lorcan and the blight were an ever-present stain on the fabric of Fenton's mind. No bath in the world could cleanse him until resolution was found.

Prior padded around the screen. "Your turn. I hope you don't mind sharing water?"

Fenton opened his eyes. Redressed in only his trousers, Prior scrubbed at his hair with one of the cloths. Water dripped down his chest, and Fenton followed the trails as they split over the curves of Prior's ribs, the harsh divot of his hip. Fenton wanted to fell a deer and feed it to him piece by piece until Prior's hard edges softened. The blight had altered Prior's landscape; Fenton would tend to him as he had every other garden.

"Fenton?"

Fenton yanked his gaze to Prior's face, and found a smile there. Prior tilted his chin toward the screen.

"Go on, before it gets any colder," Prior said, his cheeks pink.

Fenton went.

He washed quickly but thoroughly in the cool bath, listening to the noises of Prior preparing for sleep on the other side of the screen. That noise—he had turned back the sheets. Now he climbed into bed, fabric against fabric as he settled. Fenton scrubbed dirt and dust from his hair and the base of his antlers as he listened. Prior sighed softly. Did he wait for Fenton?

Fenton sent a wave over the lip of the tub as he surged upright from his half-doze. *One bed.* Surely the ideal amount of beds?

No. Fenton chastised himself. He would not—he could not—bother Prior with his attentions while they had so much in the balance. Not to mention the possibility his affections were unreciprocated, though Fenton did not think that to be the case, but affection took many forms. Many forms that did not require a bed nor bed-like object.

Closing his eyes with a pang of pain, Fenton ducked his head beneath the surface of the water, in hopes the dunk might cool his sudden ardour. Petals stuck to the sides of the tub, shed from his crown and blossoming vines. The air smelled like summer. He dunked his head again. His antlers clonked the tub with a peculiar noise.

Finally, with a grunt, Fenton levered himself out of the tub, then dried himself roughly with the remaining cloth. He tapped his ears lightly to loosen the water inside and fluffed the fur on the tips. Summoning his shadow to cover his legs, uninterested in dressing in heavier fabrics for sleep, he nudged his crown to bloom over his damp hair. Then, taking a breath, he rounded the screen.

Sitting against the headboard on the far side of the bed, Prior watched Fenton with a heavy-lidded gaze that made Fenton feel like fox and stag both. His vines flickered. Prior licked his lips, then suddenly shook his head. He covered his face with one hand and flicked back the top of the sheet with the other.

"Get in," he said gruffly.

Fenton paused in place. "I do not need to sleep in that bed. I do not need to *sleep*."

Prior peeked through his fingers. "Don't be silly. You crashed through a wall today, you're not staying up all night."

"The floor—"

"No." Prior lowered his hand entirely. A furrow darkened his brow. "I thought you saw no issue with this arrangement," Prior said, repeating Fenton's words from earlier.

Heat crawled to Fenton's face. "I had not considered the implications."

"And you've considered them now?"

Implications tormented him. They threatened to consume him. Fenton swallowed. "I fear I shall be haunted by them until the day I return to the earth. This, too, is an arrangement with which I see no issue."

"If you don't get into this bed this instant I'm going to throw a pillow at you," Prior said, his eyes very wide. "You— Saying things!"

Fenton crossed the room more quickly than any human could, and had one knee on the bed when Prior raised his hand.

"Just to sleep, tonight, if that's all right? I want you close, I do, but… Gods, this shouldn't be so humiliating. Just sleeping."

"As you wish," Fenton readily agreed. He could think of nothing finer than sleeping with Prior.

They negotiated the narrow space until Fenton lay on his back, his antlers scraping the headboard, with Prior curled on his side beside him, the blanket tucked beneath Prior's chin. Fenton's left side was bare, but he saw no reason to mention it. He closed his eyes.

Prior shifted. "The candles—"

Fenton's shadow snaked the room and snuffed every candle, plunging them into darkness, before returning to cover his legs.

"That's handy," Prior mumbled. He resettled, but his breathing did not steady.

Opening his eyes, Fenton contemplated the water stains on the ceiling. Another peacock? Perhaps. As Prior remained awake, and Fenton knew him to be so, the sliver of space between them seemed charged with heat, until Prior shifted. The muscles of Fenton's stomach jumped.

"Are you comfortable?" Fenton asked, craning his neck to meet Prior's eyes.

Prior huffed. "It's a narrow bed, is all."

And Fenton took up too much of it. That was easily remedied.

Fenton shuffled sideways in an ungainly fashion until he lay at the edge of the bed, and braced himself with one foot on the floor. Behind him, Prior aborted a delicately hurt sound that nonetheless speared Fenton's chest like a thorn. Fenton needed to prevent the sound happening again. He reached for Prior's hand and gently tugged Prior closer, his grip loose enough that Prior could draw away should he wish; Fenton meant his touch to be an invitation, not an imposition. Sighing easily, Prior curled around Fenton's side, his arm snaking across Fenton's waist as if to prevent him from falling. Fenton would not fall, yet neither would he discourage the warm curve of Prior against him. It reminded Fenton of being cradled in the earth.

Fenton did not intend to sleep deeply—he trusted neither the city nor its denizens—but he could doze and heal in Prior's embrace. He would permit himself that.

Prior's thumb swept soft arcs over Fenton's hip. He nudged Fenton's shoulder with his nose. "This is perfect. You're— This is perfect. Good night, Fenton."

Fenton smiled. "Good night, Prior."

Morning washed Northrope deceptively clean. Birds sang and stallholders bellowed and Prior managed to evade all suspect puddles as he and Fenton made their way toward the city's clothing district; surely the city was a paradise by any other name. If their breakfast of watery porridge had been meagre, at least it had been cheap, and the morning—nearly afternoon, in truth—was warm, and Prior had woken with Fenton in his arms, having fallen asleep the same, and could scarcely concentrate on anything for the memory. Yes, they had to return to a cursed estate and somehow break Fenton's sibling free in order to release the moorlands from a killing sickness, *but also,* Prior had spent the night with Fenton in his arms.

He wanted to spend every night the same way for the rest of his life.

No. No, that wasn't true. He would be open to being held by Fenton instead, if Fenton wished. A terrible hardship, but Prior could endure. He eyed Fenton, who had drifted a few paces ahead of Prior, and though his cloak covered him from antlers to feet, Prior's memory supplied the shape of him. Definitely big enough to hold Prior.

Prior pinched the bridge of his nose. *Get a grip.*

He forced his attention to the shops they were passing. Not all had windows, as glass was expensive, but most had signs swinging above their doors to indicate the goods or services that could be found within. Prior slowed as he checked each shopfront. He'd explained to Fenton that they needed appropriate clothes before returning to Aspinwick, but he'd been able to tell that Fenton hadn't understood. And why would he? Forests didn't care about couture.

Fenton returned while Prior was looking into the window of a dressmaker's shop, where faceless mannequins modelled fine doublets and splendid gowns. A golden doublet, decorated elaborately with brocade, had commanded Prior's attention, the fabric alone a hundred harvests out of Prior's budget.

"Here, do you see this?" Prior asked Fenton. "This is the kind of thing we need."

Fenton tilted his head at the window, then scrutinised Prior's clothing. Prior shifted, aware his clothes were long past their best, but Fenton didn't relent; he peered closely at the laces at Prior's neck and lifted Prior's arm to exaggeratedly examine the seams at his side, at which point Prior realised Fenton was teasing. He flapped his hand free hand at Fenton.

"Stop being foolish," he said through his grin.

Fenton lowered Prior's arm and tangled their fingers together. He considered the window again.

"Your clothes are less shiny?" Fenton ventured.

Prior nodded. "Precisely. We need to be shiny for this event." He chewed his lower lip. "But we can't afford it."

"What do the clothes matter? You shine like stars."

The way Fenton just *said* things like that— Never mind stars, Prior's face must have been bright as the sun itself. "Th-thank you. For saying that. But others would disagree."

"Then 'others' are incorrect," Fenton said, like the conclusion was obvious. Perhaps, to a god, things were that simple. Prior envied Fenton his conviction.

"Incorrect or not," Prior said, forcibly returning to the topic at hand, "there are expectations."

Fenton grunted, his eyes dark beneath his hood. He stared hard at the window before his gaze drifted to the sky, then to the surrounding buildings and the people passing by. Suddenly, he tugged Prior away from the shop, and around the corner. He led Prior on a wending path through the tangled streets of the clothing district until Prior could scarcely find his arse with a compass.

When Fenton stopped, they stood at the head of a dead-end alley. Broken crates clustered against a tall fence that stank of stale piss. A cat hissed at them. Fenton hissed back. The cat scampered away.

"Where are we?" Prior asked, his nose wrinkling.

"Here," Fenton said. He pulled at the hood of his cloak with his free hand. The slick mass warped and flowed along his arm and down his body, pooling briefly at his feet, before sinking away into the ground. Prior stared. He raised his eyes to Fenton's.

"Dare I ask where it's headed?" He hadn't seen it do that before.

Fenton's lips quirked. Reaching out, he smoothed back a stray strand of Prior's hair, where it grew overlong, and searched Prior's eyes. Prior let himself be seen. He felt brave, for once.

"I would give you the world. You need only ask me for it," Fenton said, in that way he had.

"The world isn't yours to give," Prior pointed out, his chest tight.

Fenton hummed. Prior smiled. Then Fenton disentangled their fingers and reached behind himself. His shoulder moved oddly, though the intensity of his gaze didn't falter, and with a flash of teeth he stepped back and raised something between them. A golden doublet shimmered in Fenton's hand.

A very familiar golden doublet. The one from the shop window.

"This is mine to give," Fenton said, with a triumphant expression.

"I don't know what—"

Fenton began to reach behind himself again. "I have many others, should you prefer a gown, or else a—"

Prior laughed and caught Fenton's hand before Fenton could produce who knew what. "I believe you! This is— I don't know what this is. Wonderful. You're wonderful." Impulsively, he pressed a kiss to Fenton's cheek. One of Fenton's vines stroked Prior's brow and the soft touch made Prior burn. "Thank you."

For a moment, even Fenton's vines were still. Then his fingers flexed around Prior's and he tilted his head. "Anything. As I said, you need only ask."

Increasingly, Prior feared he might. He pushed the thought aside. The crux of the issue was thus: they needed to enter Aspinwick. To have a chance of entering peacefully, they needed to present themselves as viable emissaries for a rich mage. Otherwise, Fenton would tear the place down stone by stone. Prior knew that, as he knew each further delay frustrated Fenton, and only his... affection... for Prior had stayed his hand thus far.

Besides, they could return the clothes later.

Prior grabbed the doublet and jerked his chin behind Fenton, where his shadow painted the wall.

"Let's go."

Fenton grinned.

Stepping through Fenton's shadow, which became more familiar every iteration, they landed by a thicket near the folly tower. The sun crested high above them, signalling noon, and Prior squinted toward Aspinwick's walls, beyond which staff were bustling to put the finishing touches on the grounds for the party. The golden doublet and a small pile of other clothes—breeches, a chemise, even shoes—were folded neatly beside him. Fenton had taken complete outfits from several mannequins, he'd explained, which gave them plenty to choose from.

"We've time to watch a while longer, then we can dress and try and get in. What do you think?" Prior asked.

Fenton nodded. Then, to Prior's astonishment, he curled on his side on the ground, and for all appearances, fell asleep. His shadow covered him like a blanket.

"Well, that's that, then, I suppose."

Prior settled in to wait. He'd gotten good at that over the past few days.

The afternoon dragged by as carriages flowed along the road and Aspinwick's gardens were made resplendent in anticipation of the evening. Fenton woke briefly to forage, returning with apples—definitely out of season—and mushrooms, pressing them on Prior when his nervous stomach protested. Then Fenton fell asleep again. Prior envied his rest.

He ate the apples and watched Aspinwick.

He nudged Fenton awake when the sky began to darken and the road grew thick with carriages. They dressed in tense silence, leaving their old clothes behind, and crept toward the road, where Prior drew them to a stop while they were still under cover of the trees. Prior briskly dusted off their borrowed—fine, stolen—clothes, smartening their appearances as best he could before they attempted to enter Aspinwick.

They'd done well with the theft. Prior's golden doublet, white breeches, and golden satin shoes fit reasonably enough, though the armhole of the doublet kept pinching his biceps, and the waist of the breeches hit in an odd place. So long as no one looked too closely, he should fade into the background without comment.

The same could not be said of Fenton, who, by chance or magical intervention, appeared to be the man the clothes had been designed to adorn. Prior's attention kept flitting from the open neck of the forest green tunic to the heavy leather belt that made Fenton's waist seem almost delicate to the tight black breeches outlining powerful thighs. Vines twisted Fenton's red hair into messy plaits, while his crown bore tiny golden flowers in addition to the snowdrops he seemed to prefer. More flowers decorated the tines of his antlers.

Prior couldn't look directly at Fenton. He couldn't look away.

"Masks," he blurted. "We don't have masks. I mean, you have your whole... Antlers. And all that. But what do I have?"

If their entire plan fell apart because Prior didn't have a mask, he would scream. Then lots of other people would scream, most likely, as Fenton tore his way into Aspinwick. Prior's gut churned. He couldn't consider that outcome. He refused.

With a thoughtful expression, Fenton pressed his palms together in front of his face, twisted them from side to side as if rolling something between them, then drew them apart. The world seemed to tremble as something appeared in the space between Fenton's hands. Prior recognised the rough texture of wood, and what looked disconcertingly like flashes of bone, but surely couldn't be. He squinted. It was like looking at a reflection in the back of a spoon, until with a flick of his wrist, Fenton flipped the thing over.

"A— That's a fox," Prior stammered, eyes locked on the mask in Fenton's hands. "You made a fox mask. Out of—"

"Bark and bone," Fenton said, lifting his chin.

"I'm incredibly impressed, but I don't see how... that..." Prior trailed off as Fenton held out the fox mask to him. Prior's heart tripped in his chest. "For me?"

"For you."

A fox mask from the fox-faced god. Prior's hands shook as he took it. The way the light played over it made the mask seem to smirk. What would it mean, to wear Fenton's name so boldly? Would anyone recognise it? With a thick swallow, Prior realised it didn't matter. *He* recognised it. Fenton did.

"Thank you. It's beautiful."

Fenton shook his head. He twisted his fingers to produce a thin vine that he coaxed to knot at the small holes in the edges of the mask Prior still held. Their fingers touched over the curve of the mask. Fenton captured Prior's gaze.

"What it will cover is beautiful," he said.

Prior couldn't respond.

In comfortable silence, they joined the growing crowd streaming through the open gates of Aspinwick, and proceeded along a path toward another gate that led to the inner gardens. Evening had drawn firmly in, but the gardens were lit by flickering lanterns hanging on ropes between the poles that lined the paths. The friendly glow made the evening seem warmer than in truth. Manicured lawns rolled from either side of the path, regimented with flowerbeds from which grew tall, lonely flowers. In person, the grounds were even vaster than when viewed from the folly. Doubt stitched threads through Prior's gut. He tugged his clothes. Would they pass muster?

He glanced sidelong at his fellow interloper and heat swamped his face. It was absurd. Prior kept waiting for somebody to notice his clothes didn't fit perfectly, to spot the impostor in their midst, but why would anyone pay attention to him when Fenton looked so otherworldly beautiful and so thrillingly *dangerous* in his own stolen clothes? Perhaps Fenton's nature made it possible. Another ability the stories had failed to note.

Fenton ended his contemplation of the lawns and met Prior's eyes. He glanced at the group ahead, myriad figures in startling costumes and masks, then back to Prior.

"Are you well?" he asked, in a low voice.

Prior nodded. "Just, you know, thinking about the night ahead."

"Worry not. I will protect you."

Prior went to duck his head, overwhelmed, but Fenton lifted his chin with a touch. A man in a vermillion tunic sniffed haughtily at them as he passed. Prior would have commented—he recognised Irial, the herbalist, and could have conjured a few choice insults—but Fenton's fingertips remained on his chin, four hot points of contact that demanded complete attention.

"What is it?" Prior asked, alight with the way his jaw pressed into Fenton's fingers as he spoke.

Fenton reached with his other hand to subtly adjust Prior's mask. His eyes smouldered with internal fires, as if he'd unveiled his magic for the night, and the sight made Prior feel short of breath.

A last adjustment made Fenton smile in satisfaction. "There, as you should be. Fox-faced."

He trailed his thumb along Prior's uncovered jaw to the corner of Prior's mouth, and there stopped, his caress reducing the rest of the world to ash. The world became

Fenton's touch. His eyes. Prior's heart thudded in his throat as if it, too, reached for Fenton. Prior's lips tingled. Fenton's gaze locked on Prior's mouth. His thumb twitched.

Someone cleared their throat loudly as they passed, speaking to their companion about "appropriate behaviour", and the moment shattered. Prior jerked and licked his lips unthinkingly, and immediately lost all "appropriateness" when his tongue caught the pad of Fenton's thumb. A bolt of heat shot through Prior's gut as Fenton gasped. Their eyes locked on a world of two. Then Fenton stepped away, turning for the inner gates, his hands flexing at his sides. With a subtle nudge to his breeches, Prior stumbled along behind him.

Passing several groups of guests, they joined a queue behind a small group, waiting as a liveried guard inspected each group's invitations with a furrowed brow, at length returning the invitation and allowing the guests to pass. The process seemed simple enough.

Their turn. Prior strode confidently forward.

"Invitation?" the guard asked in a bored tone.

Prior handed their stolen card over. It had fared well despite its brief dip in Prior's bath. Beside him, Fenton waited with his hands tucked behind his back.

"You are not the Mage Nola," the guard said, after reading their invitation.

The moment of truth. Truth or violence. Prior tried to keep his nerves from betraying him. "We're her emissaries. She did not wish to compound insult by ignoring such an invitation, but could not attend herself." Prior lowered his voice. "There has been some high feeling of late, as I understand it."

Frowning, the guard studied the invitation again. Prior slid his gaze to Fenton and found him looking back, a muscle clenched in his jaw. Slowly, Fenton tilted his head toward the guard. One of his vines flicked subtly in question. Prior's chest tightened. He didn't want to answer.

"Either let this riffraff in or have them removed, but cease your dallying! Some of us are expected!" someone shouted from behind them.

Prior glanced over his shoulder and saw Irial and his vermillion tunic among the waiting groups, looking irritated. Prior couldn't be sure it was Irial who had spoken, but he wouldn't have been surprised. He suppressed a snort.

"It would seem there are some impatient attendees this evening," Prior said to the guard.

Behind him, another member of the waiting crowd tittered. The guard's face somehow became blanker still. Then they blew out a hard breath from their nose and handed the invitation back to Prior.

"Mage Nola's emissaries to be admitted," the guard said, and stepped aside with a stiff bow.

Prior glanced at Fenton, who tilted his head. "After you."

Trying to project confidence, Prior stepped through the gate that led to the inner part of the estate. Two liveried guards stood at attention on the other side of the gate, but they showed no especial interest in Prior or Fenton. Prior tried not to betray his relief as, chin high, he led Fenton past a group of guests and toward a path that curved around a series of staggered stone steps that led to Aspinwick House itself. The path was one of many lit invitingly with lanterns, which cast the guests' masks into grotesque relief. Some guests peered toward Prior and Fenton, their gazes lingering on Fenton's antlers, but most people were loudly admiring the gardens to each other. Apparently the fountains were a fine example of their type.

Crunching over the gravel path, Fenton caught up with Prior. "I felt us pass through the wards," he murmured.

Prior matched his tone. "Are you able to get a sense of Lorcan's location now we're inside the gates?"

"Not precisely. They are here, I know that. Not within any of the groups we have passed, but somewhere…

Somewhere behind. Near water, perhaps."

"From what I've seen, Aspinwick is near big as the whole of Northrope. I saw water gardens from the folly, and there's the stream running through as well. There might have been other features on the far side of the main house, I can't say for sure."

Their conversation paused as a laughing trio passed in the opposite direction, and Prior made himself smile and return their wave. Glad of his mask and the growing dark, Prior was nonetheless self-conscious of the types of people invited to such events, compared to the type of person *he* was. He reminded himself sternly that he and Fenton had come to Aspinwick to find Lorcan. They weren't out of place; they were precisely where they needed to be.

They followed the path farther into the inner gardens, passing clusters of well-dressed guests gathered in pockets of conversation under the pretty awnings, while smartly attired waiting staff flowed from one group to another with trays of food and drink. Subtle music threaded through the air, almost beyond the edge of hearing, though Prior saw no musicians.

"We don't need to hurry. No one is paying attention to us," Prior muttered, as Fenton tugged him along the path by their joined hands. Lantern light turned Fenton's red hair to flames.

The same fire shone from Fenton's eyes when he caught Prior in his fierce gaze. "Had you walked past me, dressed in riches as you are and yet more precious than any stone these humans feign to value, I would pay attention to naught else. You are the sun, Prior, and to pretend otherwise is base foolishness."

Prior's mouth went dry, his mind similarly parched of response. When Fenton moved on, he drew Prior with him like the tail of a comet.

Though intimately aware of Prior's presence at his back, Fenton returned to the reason such distracting fashion had been required: Lorcan, and the mage who held them. Within Aspinwick's wards, the toxic presence of Hartling's magic bothered Fenton like the bloody gap of a newly missing tooth. He would become hardened to the noxious magic, only to be stung afresh as he encountered a new working—a charm on the lanterns, or a spell on the stones. Aspinwick was riddled with Hartling's work, so much that he couldn't determine the mage's actual location, nor if Hartling and the source of the blight were in the same place. It might be that he would have to destroy everything within the estate to ensure success.

Fenton warmed at the thought.

Yet some spells could be arranged to self-destruct if challenged, and extinguish all that remained within them. Fenton had to find Lorcan first, interrogating the mage if required, and *then* destroy Aspinwick.

The tasks seemed simple. Fenton knew they would not be.

He redoubled his concentration as he and Prior progressed along the path until it opened onto a wide, paved courtyard. Several other paths led from the edges, and an elaborate stone fountain in the shape of a horse and rider dominated the centre. More lanterns cast a merry glow in the drawing evening, stinging Fenton with their magic, and long tables of food perfumed the air with spices and savoury scent. Groups of guests milled together and reminded Fenton of birds in the forest; bright plumage and eager song, flitting from nest to nest with news. Some of the humans with drabber plumage— waitstaff, Prior called them—moved between the groups and tended to the long tables. No one was eating.

"Do you think they're waiting for a dinner bell?" Prior asked quietly. He looked around. "A signal?"

"Perhaps they do not hunger."

"I hunger," Prior muttered.

As he crossed the courtyard, he pushed his mask to rest on top of his head. When he reached the nearest table, he tore a piece of bread from a loaf and stuffed it in his mouth, brusquely wiping away the crumbs that fell onto his clothes.

"Their own fault if they're too busy posing to eat," he said, as Fenton joined him.

Some of the guests frowned at Prior as he took a handful of berries and a glass of wine, making him hunch his shoulders defensively. Fenton offered him a plum and bared his teeth when the guests attempted to extend their displeasure his way. They suddenly found other things to observe.

Prior snickered. "Causing quite the stir. We'll be struck off the invitation list for next time."

"I am certain the loss will not cause us undue suffering," Fenton said.

"You needn't expend the extra effort on impressing anyone, you know. You're the most spectacular person here." The comment made Fenton's head feel light. He tugged the bottom of his tunic. Then Prior continued with a teasing note in his voice, "In fact, the only guest anywhere near as impressive is that striking figure in the teal doublet. What do you think that set them back? The colours move like water, do you see?"

Following Prior's gaze, Fenton went cold, and not from Prior's divided attention. He pushed the heel of his hand to his chest, bruisingly hard, in hope his bones might cage the tangle of thorns that threatened to burst free. The name tasted like blood in his mouth.

"Lorcan."

"The Hand That Reaches From Beneath The Waves," Prior whispered, unsettlingly reverent, his eyes fixed on Lorcan. "Of course."

Clad in human guise, Lorcan held court at the edge of a large group, and their shimming blue-green tunic did indeed resemble water as light passed through it. Lorcan's pale hair—like the froth of a wave—had been drawn into a high queue, allowing the display of the scar-seeming gills on their throat and the storm-dark scales that dappled their jaw. Their half-mask resembled a bird, and its beak exaggerated the downturn of their mouth. Fenton had seen them sneer and smile and mock and scowl, but that expression was new to him. When the woman beside them laughed, Lorcan echoed her amusement like ripples in a pond. As soon as the woman looked away, they went still.

The instinct to transform and steal Lorcan away rose in Fenton like a shoot through soil. His claws lengthened and fangs crowded his human mouth. His shadow boiled. With effort, Fenton commanded himself to calm. Prior had requested he attempt not to kill.

Nausea roiled in Fenton and the thorns tightened in his chest. They scraped his throat as he swallowed. He hadn't seen Lorcan for—for a very long time. He had scarcely recalled their existence until leaving the forest, and then only as a foe to hunt. To kill, if he could. Even as he had realised Lorcan was involved in the blight, and then that some other force had tarnished his sibling's magic, Lorcan had been merely a concept. A name scratched into the back of Fenton's mind.

As he watched the wan figure of his sibling, whatever arguments the two of them had in the past became as distant to Fenton as the bottom of the ocean. He folded around the heel of his hand, still pressed to his chest where it hurt, and dug his claws through his tunic, into his skin. He wanted to yank out the knot that had grown beneath his bones and burn it to ash. There would be no stones to mark its passing. No wheat. Nothing would grow in its place.

"Fenton? You're hurting yourself. Can you hear me? Come back to me now, please."

The tender voice beckoned Fenton from the trap of his mind. Blinking hazily, he discovered that Prior had led him away from the main part of the courtyard, and into a secluded, ivy-covered corner tucked near the steps leading to the main house. A stone plant pot squatted in the corner. Prior held one of Fenton's hands in both of his. Fenton's claws were bloody and he frantically scanned Prior for sign of injury, but Prior shook his head, his mouth a thin line.

"I'm fine. Your tunic is a bit of a mess, but the colour should hide th-the bloodstains." Prior tried to smile, but quickly abandoned the attempt. He stroked Fenton's knuckles. "You scared me."

Fenton's throat hurt. "I am sorry. It was not my intent."

"No, I know. I know that."

"I had not expected that seeing Lorcan would affect me thus," Fenton tried to explain. He rested his eyes on their joined hands. "My mind knew them, but it was as if my body remembered only now, and all at once. It— It hurt, to see them. It *hurts*, Prior."

"I know it hurts, and I'm so sorry."

Still holding Fenton's hand in his left, Prior cupped Fenton's face with his right. The grounding touch helped settle the wild storm of Fenton's emotion as his focus narrowed to Prior's skin on his skin. To the peace of Prior's eyes. The promise of his lips.

"We'll get them back, Fenton," Prior said, vehemently, almost viciously, and Fenton recognised himself in the curl of Prior's lip. For a moment, he imagined he saw fangs. Then Prior cleared his throat and drew away, as if his own reaction had alarmed him, and he paced back and forth as he spoke. "Okay. Okay! How do we do this? What's our first step? Second step. Perhaps third. What step are we up to— What are you doing?"

Fenton continued to coax the flowers within the pot to climb the wall and join with the creeping ivy until roots and stems combined to create a low bench, bolstered by the stout strength from the curious roots that had been nosing through the flagstones. Suspended partly by the ivy, the bench would support Prior's weight.

"Here, sit," Fenton said, and gestured toward the bench. He glanced anxiously over his shoulder—Lorcan remained in place—then frowned when Prior didn't move. "What ails you?"

Prior stared from the bench to Fenton. "You just— You created that from sad little peonies! The vines were one thing, but *peonies*?"

"They are hyacinth." Fenton petted the nearest pink flower. "And they are not sad."

"The mood of the flowers wasn't really my point—"

"Please, Prior. Sit," Fenton bit out.

Prior's eyebrows rose but he sat without further hesitation. He smoothed his hands down his thighs as Fenton took to one knee before him. Fenton inhaled the sweet perfume of Prior's scent, to capture it in his memory.

"What step is it we're up to, then?" Prior asked, his voice almost as hushed as the music threading through the air. When Fenton didn't answer, Prior smiled sadly. "It's the step where you leave me here, isn't it." It wasn't a question.

Fenton pressed a kiss to Prior's fingers where they rested on his thighs. He didn't dare take hold of Prior's hand, because he couldn't trust himself to let Prior go.

"I ask that you please remain here while I retrieve Lorcan. Can you do that? Will you wait for me?"

Licking his lips, Prior nodded. He raised his hand and cupped Fenton's cheek again. Fenton felt as if he had learned a human guise solely that Prior's hand might have a place to rest. He leaned into the touch as Prior drew his thumb across Fenton's lips.

"Of course I will wait for you," Prior said. His eyes darkened. "Might I ask you a favour, before you go? In case— Might I ask?"

"Anything."

"Kiss me."

Immediately, Fenton kissed Prior's thumb, savouring the salt of Prior's skin. He nipped at the pad and grinned when Prior gasped and shifted.

"Fenton, that's not what I—"

Surging upright, Fenton drank the rest of the words from Prior's lips. He braced himself with one hand on the wall and his knee on the bench by Prior's hips, crowding Prior between his legs, and leaned his kiss into Prior's plush mouth. He kissed Prior as he had not the night before, when he had lain awake in Prior's arms and yearned for better timing. Prior grabbed Fenton's hips and met him with matching hunger, a moan escaping him between kisses. Desire burned in Fenton like a forest fire, scourging him that he might be made anew. He cradled Prior's face and shared the heat as best he could, pressing himself into Prior's mouth and greedily drinking Prior's delicious noises until they drew apart.

Fenton rested his forehead on Prior's, panting lightly, his fingers playing with the hair at Prior's nape. Prior's fern-and-rose scent filled the air, and Fenton wanted to taste it from Prior's skin, almost as much as he wanted to blanket Prior with Fenton's own scent that all the forests of the world might know who walked in them. His own possessiveness startled him, even as he watched Prior lick his kiss-bruised lips and decided he had to taste the blood beating in them.

When Prior opened his mouth, Fenton ducked his head and snared another kiss. He nipped Prior's tongue, making Prior jolt and groan, then gently push Fenton away. Fenton allowed himself to be moved, and the cold night air and thread of music shocked him from the haze of lust.

"Enough, enough!" Prior said with a laugh as he adjusted himself in his breeches. Fenton swallowed and took another step away. "A kiss, I said. Not a public devouring." Prior sobered, though his eyes were blown black. "Go now, that you may come back to me all the sooner."

Fenton opened his mouth and reached for words—of comfort, of promise—but all he could taste was Prior. He closed his mouth and ducked his head.

Fenton turned, and went.

His mind foggy with Prior—his touch, his taste— Fenton reached the group of revellers at the top of the courtyard before noticing Lorcan had vanished. As Fenton stumbled to a stop, eyes darting for any sign of his sibling, he heard a thready whimper. Only when a passing guest looked askance at him did he realise it had escaped his own throat.

Fenton scratched the inside of his wrist. His ears twitched. He could return to Prior.

And then what? The question asked itself viciously in Fenton's mind, as if the part of him that was fang and claw had been given voice. Should he leave Aspinwick with his tail tucked between his legs? Leave Lorcan and the blight and all else to fate and seclude himself in the forest? Things had been simpler there, but Fenton hadn't any memories to use as comparison. Whether that had been a gift from Lorcan or intended as a further taunt, Fenton didn't know. But he *did* know, now, what he would leave behind.

With renewed will, Fenton set his shoulders and forged along a canopied path that led deeper into the heart of the gardens. Fewer lanterns spotted the secluded trail, and low laughter emanated from small groups gathered in alcoves that branched from the main path. Music wove through the air.

Fenton could smell water ahead. Skirting a large group that were dancing in intimate embraces around another fountain—this one a dryad, and not at all accurate to life— he descended a short series of steps and passed a groomed hedge. The severe lines made him itch, and doubly so as the filigree of spellwork brushed against his own power. Fenton's eyes hardened. He sent his shadow ahead to track the scent of water; water was ever Lorcan's domain, and if the mage wanted to utilise Lorcan's strength, it made sense to situate them near a source. To do so courted hubris, but Hartling did not strike Fenton as humble.

A thin reasoning, perhaps, but Fenton needed a way to narrow his search; Lorcan's soured magic lay over the Aspinwick Estate like mist. It rasped as bitter as shame in Fenton's throat. He loped onward, each stride a promise: he would find his sibling; he would destroy the blight; he would leave with Prior. Find Lorcan. Destroy the blight. Leave. There could be no room for doubt.

At length, his shadow pooled at his feet in a dark puddle, and Fenton learned where Lorcan had gone. Moving with purpose, Fenton progressed along the dark path and deeper into the garden. No lanterns guided his way, but the stars had always been enough. Sounds of revelry faded, and quiet shrouded the garden as he reached a small outbuilding in good repair. The building smelled of green earth and the insidious poison that tainted Lorcan's magic.

Fenton stretched his senses. No life nearby but the night's creatures, and Lorcan. Somewhere. Bracing himself, Fenton cautiously entered the outbuilding, easing open the door on silent hinges. Yet, aside from bags of fertile soil, well-kept gardening implements, and a pile of cloth and sacking, he found nothing of note. Mice wiggled their furry noses from a crack in the corner, then squeaked and fled when Fenton snapped his teeth in frustration. Taking a sharp breath, Fenton shook off his claws and sent his shadow again to hunt. Lorcan was *here*. Fenton *would* find them.

A door. His shadow thrummed.

Whirling on his heel, Fenton rushed to circle the outbuilding. Tucked on the ground close to the wall, and nearly hidden by the bramble of look-away cantrip, an innocuous hatch sat within a neat stone border. If any stumbled across it, they would likely suppose it were winter storage. Perhaps they would not note it had neither handle nor hinge. The cantrip would dissuade curiosity. Even Fenton could feel his attention sliding from the hatch. His vines pricked his ears with thorns, reasserting his focus when it strayed.

Fenton dropped to his knees on the damp earth and lowered his head to sniff at the stone, where someone might grasp for balance as they lifted the hatch or lowered themselves down. Or, failing that, where old stone might recall what young grass could not. Fenton licked the stone, his tongue rasping into the porous grooves. Lifting his head, he spat, and scraped the taste away with his teeth, relief and regret making an acidic mixture. Lorcan had been through the hatch, and recently. Their saltwater magic was unmistakable.

For all he wanted to smash the hatch and launch himself within, the cantrip made Fenton wary. He tried to send a tendril of his shadow through a seam in the wood, but progressed no deeper than the surface. A growl warmed his throat. Frowning darkly, he tried again, and again progressed no farther. Snarling, he leapt to his feet. The cantrip pushed at him, but Fenton planted roots. He held out his hand, palm up, and opened himself to the garden, to the green things that had been bullied into neat lines and straight edges; trees with unsettlingly uniform height, flowers with leaves clipped and faces turned from him. He gathered all of Aspinwick's thwarted potential until a quaking orb of magic coalesced in his upraised hand, scarcely contained by the prick of his claws. Then, with a powerful twisting motion, he attacked the hatch with a blow of pure, living strength.

The hatch broke. Of course it broke, shattering into splinters, and the surrounding stone wall bulged inward under the force of the strike. Fenton's antlers creaked in the wake of his display, absorbing the remnants of power. Birds called raucously through the dark. A fox yowled nearby in confused celebration. Too far to hear the humans, Fenton wondered if they had noticed a thing, or if the wild had left them too long ago for his magic to touch them.

The mage would have noticed.

Setting his jaw, Fenton took hold of a sturdy root and lowered himself into the dark throat that held his sibling. Hand over hand over hand, until Fenton's palms rasped with blood from the abrading root, until at last his boots met firm ground with a splash. He waved off the root, which whipped away. The speed made Fenton start and look up in alarm, just in time to watch a new hatch seal itself over the opening, delivering perfect darkness to the perfect prison Fenton had perfectly, recklessly, trapped himself in. Magic crackled as the seal reasserted itself, and though Fenton thrashed his shadow against the door he gained no purchase. He winced. He was trapped.

Prior might laugh.

Fenton hoped to tell him the story someday. He scratched the inside of his wrist then flicked the thought away. No matter. He had opened the hatch once, and would again.

After he found Lorcan.

Straining his eyes, Fenton tried to see—well, anything. His night vision had never failed him before, but the blackness was so complete he might as well have been human. His nape prickled as his boots shushed in the scrim of water that coated the ground, announcing his progress as he ventured deeper into the consuming dark. His shadow tightened around his torso, forming protective armour. Spit pooled in his mouth.

Abruptly, light blistered Fenton's vision. He flinched bodily and raised his hand to shield his watering eyes as he squinted toward the source. The single flickering candle was followed by a searing arc as high-set lanterns illuminated in a blaze of magical harmony, making Fenton recoil as magic and light scraped across his senses. Rubbing his eyes with his fist, he peered at the figure revealed by the light. Despite the taut, angry lines of their face—without a mask, their eyes smouldered like the blue heart of a fire—Fenton could not remember a more welcome sight.

"Lorcan," he sighed. He smiled.

Lorcan's eyes flashed. They hurled a rock through the air.

Fenton knocked the rock away, almost without seeing it, and he jerked back, but he couldn't dodge Lorcan's lunge, and they collided, landing hard on the ground. Water splashed as they struggled with one another, Lorcan wrestling with a ferocity that Fenton tried to combat defensively, rather than meeting like for like. His hesitancy gained him a crack to the jaw that made blood burst in his mouth, and a blow to the kidneys that made him grunt. Lorcan squeezed Fenton's throat, their nails raking in bloody gouges as Fenton struggled to free himself without hurting his sibling. Twisting sharply had no effect, and Fenton resorted to battering Lorcan with one of his antlers, stunning Lorcan enough that Fenton could wriggle free of the chokehold. His skin smarted with welts from Lorcan's fingernails. At least they hadn't thought to use their talons.

Crudely fighting fist to face seemed more malicious than throwing mountains at each other. Fenton didn't care for it.

Hand raised to forestall another attack, Fenton swallowed, bruise-thick. "What are you— Lorcan!"

Words and breath blew away when Lorcan kneed Fenton hard in the gut. His shadow softened the blow, but Lorcan hadn't withheld their strength. Taking advantage of Fenton's disorientation, Lorcan tried to grab Fenton's antlers, but vines lashed their hands and Lorcan yelped, falling back. With a hiss like water boiling, they dropped to the ground and kicked Fenton's ankle in a vicious snap, trying to knock him down. Fenton twisted aside and shoved Lorcan when they advanced again. Lorcan stumbled to their knees, whatever energy that had fuelled their attack beginning to visibly seep from them. Sweat dripped down their face and over their wild eyes. Fenton pressed his advantage and used his shadow to swiftly bind Lorcan, sacrificing the protection of armour for a chance to speak with his sibling without getting a fist to the face. Lorcan still wore the attire from the party, all but their mask, and fine silk clothes rippled as Fenton's shadow restrained Lorcan's limbs.

Fenton crouched, hoping proximity would help his sibling hear reason. "Lorcan, I—"

Fenton's fangs clacked together when Lorcan headbutted him in the jaw in almost the same spot as previously. Fenton would be bruised purple. He shoved Lorcan's face away as Lorcan snapped their teeth, like they intended to chew their way through Fenton, and he scrambled to pin Lorcan between his knees, his shadow fizzing as Lorcan's magic attempted to dislodge it. Lorcan continued straining their neck and trying to bite Fenton, their eyes fevered, their legs thrashing. The air stank of sweat and rancid fear.

Exhausted, Fenton bent forward to headbutt Lorcan gently on the chest, and let his head rest there. Let Lorcan chew on Fenton's antlers if they wanted. He panted as Lorcan continued to writhe and fight against the hold. There wasn't *time* for this nonsense.

"Calm yourself," he said, trying to be heard over Lorcan's hissing. "We must leave this place before the mage returns. There is no time for this— This *fussing*."

Lorcan stilled completely. Fenton froze in kind, readying for a trick.

"'Fussing'?" Lorcan spat, the first word Fenton had heard from them since he could remember. "'*Fussing*'? How would you I should react to this intrusion? Shall I ready the bread and salt?"

"Before the mage returns, we must—"

"Oho! Are you not here by that one's leave? No bread for you!"

216

Fenton snapped his teeth. "Will you stop talking and please *listen* to me, for one cursed second!"

Lorcan kicked their heels against the floor. Their yell rumbled through their chest like a storm gathering over the water, straight into Fenton's skull. "Listen to you? *Listen* to you! As you kill me, I should pay perfect attention, is that how you'd have it?" They bumped one of Fenton's antlers with their chin, then again, when Fenton failed to react. "Might my agonising death come by these weapons attached to your face, perchance, dearest brother? Or had you planned on using some other trick of yorn, fox-face?" Lorcan kicked ineffectually at Fenton with their bound legs. "Listen, he says, as he rushes in to murder me in my bed."

Fenton remembered, all at once, everything about Lorcan. He closed his eyes. "You are not in your bed, sibling. You are in a— I know not where this is."

"A trap, you fool," Lorcan said, and finally went limp.

For a span of breaths, Fenton waited, kneeling in the muck, to learn whether Lorcan feigned submission as they awaited another opportunity to strike. Tentatively, he loosened his shadow's hold on one of Lorcan's arms, ready to reassert the binding if Lorcan went for his eyes. As he did, his vines readjusted his crown from where it had been crushed against Lorcan's chest. The sensation must have irritated Lorcan, for they swatted—instinctively, it must have been—at Fenton's shoulder, making a pleased noise when they found their hand free. Fenton braced himself for further attack, but Lorcan only began poking his vines as if to hurry the process along, mumbling indecipherably. Fenton waited for them to mumble themself out; Lorcan's heartbeat had finally begun to slow, and Fenton allowed himself to believe the fight might truly be over.

"We must leave, Lorcan," Fenton said as his vines settled, his voice muffled by Lorcan's doublet.

"There is but one door, and it is locked tight against both thee and me," Lorcan murmured.

Silence lowered on them like the lid of a tomb. Fenton buckled beneath the weight of it. This had not been in his plan.

It was possible he should have spent more time on forming a plan.

"We can leave together," Fenton insisted, though he knew the thought to be futile. His shadow had not made a dent on the door, and he couldn't access the energy that he had used to break it open: Lorcan's cell offered death in every direction. If Fenton let himself notice his severed connection to green things, the loneliness would chew his mind to shreds.

"At full strength, yes, we would already be berating one another on the surface. But you're missing half your parts—don't bluster, I can see the spaces—and I…" Lorcan trailed off. Their heavy sigh moved Fenton like a wave. "Let's say that I haven't remained here because I enjoy the ambiance."

"The mage? Hartling?" Fenton asked, to have it confirmed.

Lorcan hissed. *"Say not that name."*

"All the more reason we should leave, before she—"

"All the more reason we are stuck in place!" Lorcan shouted. They subsided with a slap of their hand to the floor. "After parading me to her guests, she delivered me once more to these delightful surrounds with the indication I would not be called upon until dawn. Some working or another, I imagine, but I have long since ceased inquiries in favour of gratitude for the reprieve. Did you happen note the sun?"

"Not yet a thought on the horizon."

"Precisely." They tapped Fenton's shoulder. "Now then, do shift your enormous head. For one so averse to reflection, your skull certainly makes a cumbersome anchor."

Lifting his head, but remaining in place, Fenton eyed Lorcan warily. The lantern light carved deep shadows into their face and made dark pools of their eyes, and their pale hair had gone grey with muck, while their scales were without lustre. Lorcan had appeared well in the courtyard; surely the fight had not been enough to exhaust them so? Fenton urged his shadow to further lessen its hold, concerned he had exacerbated Lorcan's condition.

Lorcan didn't move, though they must have felt Fenton's shadow shift. "Yes, yes, I've had better days, no need to mention it. Besides, you're hardly pristine." Lorcan's expression grew sly. Familiar. They arched their eyebrows. "Though you're more bipedal than last we met, so that's in your favour. Are you any easier to reason with, I wonder?"

The stag, they meant. They'd last seen Fenton when they ensnared him in the forest, however long ago that had been.

Whatever expression crossed Fenton's face made Lorcan wrinkle their brow. "Do you— You do remember that? Me?"

"You're my sibling," Fenton said, woodenly.

"Do you remember what we fought about?"

He had been trying not to, dismissing the details as unimportant, but trapped with Lorcan in their cell Fenton admitted to himself that he was afraid to know. Being at the whim of a mage didn't scare him—that would only cause pain, or death if he were careless—but somehow, the idea of learning what he had done to deserve such banishment... It made Fenton's cracked-open heart quake.

Turmoil flooded his chest and Fenton shoved himself away from Lorcan, surging to his feet. With a grunt, he wrenched his shadow back and released Lorcan entirely. His vines twisted into knots, making his scalp sting as they snagged his hair in their agitation. Fenton pulled in a shaky breath. *Free Lorcan.* Flexing his fingers, Fenton paced back and forth in the confined space, water splashing over his boots. *Free Lorcan.* His skin felt tight. *Free Lorcan.* His head throbbed.

"Now then, brother, I was merely asking a question," Lorcan said, rising to their feet in a crackle of joints. "Forget I asked, if you like, there's no need for all the ruckus. We've precious little space for your loping." They started to fiddle with one of the lanterns, affecting nonchalance even as their shoulders drew a stiff line.

Suppressing a growl, Fenton halted his pacing with a splash and balanced on one leg, fumbling for his boot. Giving as the leather was, if his claws grew again, the boots might get stuck on his feet. Lorcan didn't need an excuse for teasing. With a yank, Fenton tossed the freed boot aside, then made to switch legs. Turning from what they'd been doing, Lorcan let out a cry.

"No! Don't—"

Too late. Fenton plunged his bare foot into the cool scrim of water. For a heartbeat, he did not understand Lorcan's fear; it was only water. But then he understood. Vomit rushed to his mouth. He gagged and recoiled, grabbing for the wall to brace himself as he tried to balance on one foot as wading birds did. For the water was not water at all, but Lorcan's shadow, reedy and diminished as the ocean caught in the cup of a hand. How had Fenton not realised? It was anathema. Fenton glared at Lorcan through the blur of his tears.

"Call it back!" he demanded, wavering in place.

"I *can't*," Lorcan gritted out. Amusement had fled their face. "It is the work of the mage. It is— Let me fetch you a chair, you look ridiculous."

Lorcan retrieved a chair from the far corner of the bleak room, where it had sat beside a lopsided table and a miserable, narrow pallet covered neatly with one thin, threadbare blanket. Beyond those few items and the magical lanterns, the room contained naught but scratches carved into the stone walls. In the scratches, Fenton recognised Lorcan's talons at work.

"Here. Sit." Lorcan watched as Fenton awkwardly lowered himself onto the chair, and crossed his bare foot over his knee. They made a moue of displeasure at Fenton's pose. "My shadow won't eat you, you know."

"Do I know that?" Fenton was far from certain. Without grappling to distract him, touching Lorcan's shadow made Fenton's skin crawl. He did not understand how he had not noticed before, for now it was the only thing he could think about.

Lorcan flashed their teeth, humourlessly. "You have learnt caution, I see. Fear not, I wouldn't be so crass to attack an ally."

"You— Lorcan, you attacked me scarcely minutes past. You attempted to throttle me."

"I didn't know we were allies then, did I? It was a passing fancy, I assure you."

"And if the fancy passes this way again?" Fenton asked.

"Want you an apology? You will not have one."

"Remind me. You are the elder of us, are you not?"

Lorcan brayed a laugh, even as they rolled their eyes. "You recall the important details at least." They took a seat on the pallet, one leg drawn beneath them, the other stretched long and splashing lightly in their shadow. "Tell me, if it is not to fight, then what is it that brought you here?"

Fenton worried the thigh of his breeches with his claws, unpicking a thread. "I learned of a blight in the moorlands, taking livestock and killing villagers. Dryads have left for new grounds, and they do not abandon territory without cause. I even encountered a griffin damaged by the effects." The thread came free and Fenton flicked it aside. "I came here to destroy the source."

"I am, in fact, intimately familiar with this so-called blight." Lorcan's mouth twisted. "But what care you for humans? Last I recall, you were deep in your forest and content to remain there until the ages turned again. And how is it you came to leave the forest? Did you learn your lesson, I wonder?"

"My 'lesson'?" Fenton growled and leaned forward in

the chair, nearly putting his bare foot down to lunge, before his shadow snaked around him in warning. With a hard breath, he leaned back and canted his chin. They had fought already. To do so again would achieve nothing. "This incarnation does not hold all my memory. What lesson is it you were so intent I should learn?"

"Missing half your parts, I did mention—"

"Bold talk from one ankle-deep in their own shadow," Fenton goaded.

Anger lit Lorcan's face and darkened their scales to tempests. They leapt to their feet and jabbed their finger at him. "You were being an *arse*! As you ever are, you fork-faced malcontent! You banished me to the darkwater as a prank, and when I crawled from the ocean depths an epoch later I found you charming rivers—"

Fenton suddenly remembered. "They looked lonely—"

"As you said! And we fought over words you scarcely understood and no longer remember and— You lost. That is all. You lost and I pulled the forest from you and shoved you in it and there you remained." Lorcan's heat faded as they ranted, and their posture lost its rigidity until finally they threw their hands in the air with a huff. Resuming their seat on the pallet, they pulled up both legs to sit cross-legged and rested their hands on their knees. Their hair half-covered their face. "I did intend to help you discover the way out again, had you not done so yourself. Eventually. But here you are, and well done to you! Do stop haranguing, brother. Tis bygones, after all."

Fenton bit back the urge to point out only the offended party were able to claim if bygones were bygones. The vestiges of his anger, already borrowed from an incarnation he remembered only in glimpses, disappeared entirely at the delicate shaking of Lorcan's hands on their knees, the faded lustre of their scales, the atavistic horror of their severed shadow.

There were other memories, rich and raw, that Fenton had resisted dwelling upon. Fenton permitted himself to recall Prior's gentle touch to his face, the heated grab to his hips when they had kissed in the courtyard.

"Bygones," he agreed.

Lorcan's head jerked up, disbelief writ on their face before they regained control of their expression. "Very noble of you. I'd voice doubt you were truly my brother, but the overcompensating antlers and garish crown are something of a giveaway. Why *are* you here? Truly?"

"To rescue you."

"Rescue—"

"Or to kill you," Fenton added, in the spirit of honesty. He wiggled his bare toes. "But I had already decided on the former, even before our bygones."

Lorcan opened and closed their mouth, then smiled tightly. They flicked one of the tassels on their sleeve. "Candidness suits you. Amuses, if nothing else. Why were you never thus before? I might've— I might've done a hundred things, it's irrelevant. I'm certain we'll cover numerous topics in full as we while away the days. There's precious little to do but talk to oneself." Lorcan grinned. "You will make a pleasant change."

"It is not my intention to spend any longer conversing," Fenton said, with conviction.

So saying, Fenton sent his shadow for his abandoned boot, then jammed the boot on. Steeling himself, for now he knew the truth of it, Fenton plunged both feet into Lorcan's shadow. His own shadow clung to his torso, becoming an underlayer beneath his tunic, as Fenton crossed to the wall behind Lorcan's pallet. Bitter magic had soaked into every pore in the stone; designed to impede Lorcan, and well, but the prison had not been secured specifically against Fenton. He splayed his hand on the wall and hummed lowly, letting his eyes drift shut.

"I know that face. That's the face of someone with a scheme," Lorcan said. They began moving about, splashing and thumping, hopefully in useful endeavour. "A scheme! How long has it been since—"

Fenton let Lorcan's chatter fade from his perception. Eyes closed, he pressed his hand to the stone until his claws chipped and scraped, and the heel of his palm rubbed raw. The physical strain helped direct the stretch of his senses as he combed the estate grounds for something that might hear his call. Though the gardens were lush, and had responded to him previously, the stone had been crafted to dampen magical efforts and it was as if Fenton bellowed to the gardens from the bottom of a well. Beneath a mountain. That didn't like him.

Perhaps he and Lorcan were in truth beneath a mountain, or in some other place out of the world. A pocket, like his forest had been. Fenton hadn't sensed transportation magic at work as he climbed through the hatch, but Lorcan's stone crypt played on the senses. Fenton redoubled his search. Blood trickled hot from his ears.

At last, at the very edge of his influence, almost beyond his reach, a single root twitched. Thorns rippled across his vines and his teeth grew to fangs in his muzzle as he lost hold of his more human façade. Beneath Fenton's paw, the stone shifted—

A startling blow of power crushed Fenton to his knees and shredded the fragile grip of his influence. He bellowed in pain as a scalding hand grabbed him by the scruff and shook him like an errant cub, making his brain rattle in his skull, then hurled him into a wall. His shadow clenched around his body, preventing his ribs from shattering to kindling, but the impact still punched into Fenton's side with stone fists. His fangs clacked through his tongue and blood spattered his chin. Head ringing, his vision spotted with dancing suns, he collapsed to the floor beside a trembling heap of blue silk.

Lorcan was hunched almost double as white whips crackled around their body, holding them in place, though they were utterly limp. As if used to the pain. Beyond it. Yet their eyes were locked wide and their fear stank more pungently than did Fenton's blood. Fenton held his ribs as he swallowed back the bile scalding his throat. He turned his unsteady gaze on their attacker. When he went to push himself upright, Lady Hartling—for it must have been her—clenched her fist, and Lorcan screamed.

Fenton slumped back in the perversion Hartling had made of his sibling's shadow. Seeing his defeat, Hartling loosened her hand. Lorcan panted and spat. Hartling didn't spare them a glance. She directed her disdain at Fenton alone.

"A herbalist associate did mention some low-calibre guests had slipped through the gate but I thought he had merely spent too long at the trough. Imagine my surprise, after I had left this dreary place for more pleasant diversions, to find myself called back when my wards were violated. I thought my pet had slipped its leash again, but here *you* are, pretending to be Nola's emissary," she said, sneering at Fenton from the far side of the small room. Unsettling shapes warped across the walls as silvery light encased her with magical protection.

Her magic tasted like death. The blight seeped from her like pus from a wound.

Fenton didn't know if she wanted him to reply. He flattened his lips and tried to place her face. A small woman in a big dress, her tall hair studded with gemstones, Hartling held an amber rock in her outstretched hand and a diamond-tipped staff in the other. He had seen her laughing, and not cruelly. Where had it been?

Apparently, his response had not been required, as Hartling continued. "From the stories, I had believed you two were forever at each other's throats, but instead I find you cooperating? *Getting along.* I am most disappointed. Have you anything to say for yourself?"

The woman beside Lorcan at the party. He had been so *close.* Fenton pressed at the sorest point of his chest in an attempt to pierce the shame knotted beneath the hurt. He should have known then, in the courtyard. He should have gone immediately for Lorcan. He should have slaughtered a path through Aspinwick. He had been a fool. He would not learn his lesson in a thousand forests.

"I will kill you," he promised Hartling. He would break free and then break her.

Her disdain deepened, becoming almost palpable. "Don't be absurd. You have all this power"—she clenched her hand around the amber—a magical focus, it had to be—and Lorcan whimpered, horribly—"and you can do nothing. Don't you see? You have done *nothing*. In but a handful of seasons, I have claimed this entire region as my own, beyond anything a titled prick could ever claim, and I used only that one's ill-fitting magic to do so. I am not a slippery creature of water," she said, showing she knew nothing at all of Lorcan or their power. "I am a mountain, and I have scarcely begun to work. A region? A single scrap of land?" She scoffed. "With the two of you in my grasp I will have the world."

Hartling jabbed forward with her staff, making the diamond tip flare with a bolt of light that speared Fenton's chest. He heard his sternum crack, and then he heard himself scream. Light prised between the shattered puzzle of his chest and burrowed in like a tick, incising a noxious trail that ate through Fenton's flesh and bone in acidic lances. His shadow thrashed as something sought to peel it from the deepest delves of his being. Wolves gnawed him. Carrion birds pecked his living corpse. He tasted blood and salt. He tasted ash from the burning heart of him.

When at last something other than agony eased into Fenton's perception, it was the gentle shushing of waves against the shore. No—it was blood beating through a sturdy heart. Fenton held his breath to better listen, and then in short order realised he had breath, and lungs, and a body to keep them in.

Strong hands held him as his nerves howled a chorus of distress.

"—ton. Fenton! Steady, you're hurting yourself—

There. Can you focus on me? I'm the dashing rogue playing nursemaid."

Lorcan. Fenton forced his eyes to meet Lorcan's instead of staring sightlessly at the glittering scales that arced over their jaw. Saltwater tracks were drying on their cheeks. They'd been crying. They'd been—

Jerking in alarm, Fenton tried to rise from his vulnerable position, to defend against further attack from Hartling, but Lorcan easily held him in place.

"Steady, I said. She's gone through one of her portals. Vile things, like licking the inside of an eel. Don't ask me how I know that. Here, let me help you sit," Lorcan said, putting word to action. They tutted as Fenton floundered. "You must extend my apologies to your tailor, you've taken quite the tumble from grace."

With Lorcan's assistance, Fenton sat tucked in the corner of Lorcan's pallet, his legs splayed out in front of him. Two legs, ten toes. A strong start. His ribs protested as the movement jostled the dislocations and breaks, still tender, though he could feel his healing working, and his shadow bound his torso tight. He swallowed blood. Lorcan sat on the edge of the pallet, elbows braced on their knees and their head in their hands. Their back to Fenton.

"I'd offer you water, but there isn't any," they said, lightly.

Fenton curled his toes. One of his claws had snapped off. "She will return, then."

Lorcan sighed. Exhaustion bowed their shoulders and reduced the proud line of their back to a tired slump. When they spoke, it was to the murky puddle of their shadow.

"Indeed, she will return. She always does. That display was merely a taste of her proclivities. There's something in the walls here, I'm sure you can feel it, that smothers attempts to connect to anything outside this place. Blood and hate in the very foundation. I don't know whether she built this place or discovered it by chance, but the longer you remain here, the weaker you will become. And you will not notice your loss." Lorcan rubbed the lines on their throat. "I forget the sea for days at a time."

Fenton worked his jaw, trying not to taste the rotten seeds of his fear. "How long have you been trapped in this place?"

"I don't know. Long enough I regretted putting you in that forest."

Bygones. Fenton exhaled slowly, grunting as one of his dislocated ribs snapped into place. "How is it she came to discover you?" He remembered Lorcan quick as a wave dancing from the shore.

Lorcan groaned and hunched their shoulders. "Must we?"

Another rib cracked into position. Fenton gagged, then levelled a flat look at the back of Lorcan's head. "We must."

"Persistent as pox." Lorcan moved around, to sit with one knee on the bed. "If you *must*, then I had been out enjoying the current, as is my wont, dallying hither and thither with— Do you remember the merfolk?"

"Pointy. Noisy."

"An accurate summation, albeit unflattering." Lorcan flicked their fingers. "There I was, dallying, when a tempest rudely blew me leagues off course. Mages doing something or other. Mayhaps there was a war." Lorcan shrugged half-heartedly. "In any case, some time later, and after a bit of extended unpleasantness with a bespelled harpoon—may those mages have every pox visited upon them—I crawled in an undignified manner out of some unsavoury estuary and was set upon by bandits—"

"Humans?"

"Don't give me that face. I'd recently had a harpoon through my chest, I was distracted."

"Lorcan…"

"Hush." Lorcan waved their hand. "Anyway. They beat

me in a very thorough fashion, robbed me of a trinket I'd been playing with, and gifted me to the mage. Let's not dwell on it."

Fenton studied Lorcan's face. The thing they were not saying. He narrowed his eyes. "Tell me of the trinket."

He watched Lorcan's intent to dissemble cross their face as clearly as a cloud passing over the sun. Yet then it cleared and Lorcan ducked their head, picking at their silks.

"You've seen it. A toy in my hands, or your paws, but a weapon where it now sits atop the good lady's staff," Lorcan said bitterly.

Fenton rubbed his face. He thought about asking for further details, but rationalised the point was moot until and unless they escaped. Without Hartling's poisonous magic ripping through him, his own magic had begun to heal his injuries, and Fenton suspected that to be her design: if he expended energy healing, he would deplete his magic that much more quickly, and be unable to restore his reserves as the prison stone drained him in turn. Presumably, Lorcan had been fatigued the same way. Fenton wouldn't ask. He didn't truly want to know.

The pallet, like Lorcan's silks, was stained with Fenton's blood. Disgust shuddered within Fenton at the notion of even a small part of him forever trapped in Hartling's oubliette. He longed for fire.

When Fenton asked no more questions, Lorcan flopped backward onto the bed, narrowly missing Fenton's leg. "This isn't how I thought I'd die, if I'm being honest."

"How did you think you would die?" Fenton asked, despite himself.

"Naturally, I thought you'd kill me."

Fenton's vines tugged at his crown, though its dishevelled state was beyond such brief assistance, and Fenton didn't have the energy to spare on grooming. Another rib popped into place. He nudged Lorcan with his foot.

"I can kill you, if you would like."

Lorcan shot up to their elbows. "Kill me? We're not yet that desperate, are we? And anyway, who's to say it wouldn't be *me* killing *you*? I'm the eldest!"

"Then you have lived longest—"

"And thus you will miss life less, you enormous furry fool! *I* say you must—"

"Do not *tell* me what to *do*!" Fenton roared.

Something exploded and they both froze, then scrambled to their feet, for all the good standing would do against Hartling's next attack. She would only knock them down again, and even more easily. But it was not Hartling.

"Hello!" Prior said, his head poked upside-down through the hatch in the ceiling. He threw down a rope. "Anyone for escape?"

Prior had secured the rope with a pitchfork that he had driven deep into the welcoming soil, then he had braced his weight on the pitchfork and wound the rope around his body. He'd had to act quickly, and he wasn't confident his hasty plan would succeed, but there had been no time to seek an alternative. Lady Hartling could return at any moment and Prior didn't think she'd believe his story about being an emissary.

"Any moment now," Prior reminded the siblings below, his voice tight with desperation. He glanced around the dark garden again, ears straining for the booted tromping of liveried guards or the silken steps of courting lovers. Or griffins. Could there be griffins?

He considered the lantern near his feet. Perhaps he should snuff it out.

A tug at the rope: someone was ascending. Prior readied himself. All he needed do was hold on. He could do that. He *would* do that. The rope went taut.

When Fenton had gone investigating, Prior had waited

for the length of several vanilla cream pastries, two glasses of sparkling wine, and a soggy quiche. He'd watched the large group at the bottom of the courtyard as they dispersed in dribs and drabs, with the woman holding court in the centre waving them off—to drink, to eat, to dance, by her various motions of the staff she held in one hand. She'd laughed and smiled and simpered until the final guest departed her company, and then her amiable expression had dropped and she'd turned on her heel, taking the same direction as Fenton. Prior had grabbed a lantern and followed.

Whatever other powers Lady Hartling might possess, confidence numbered high among them; she'd strode alone through the dark garden without looking about her nor betraying any sense of unease, light softly glowing from the tip of her staff. No guards patrolled this section of the garden, and the guests were long left behind. Prior's pulse beat in his throat fit to make him sick, and twice he'd ducked into hedges, cupping the lantern's light, paranoid Lady Hartling would turn and blast him away. But she hadn't. She'd gone directly to an outbuilding, rapped her staff upon the ground, and vanished. Prior had still been blinking in confusion when someone had started to scream.

Shortly after the screaming had stopped, Lady Hartling had reappeared and marched off into the gardens. Prior had dismissed the idea of following her. Instead, he had waited until his hands no longer shook, then wiped away his tears, spat out the taste of vomit, and gone to see if he could help. The hatch had been easy to find thanks to the stones scattered about and the solicitous bramble that snagged the fabric of Prior's breeches; Prior had carefully petted the nearest leaves and thanked the plant on Fenton's behalf.

The hatch had seemed entirely without access, at first, but as Prior knelt down and ran his fingers across the surface—searching for a way to prise his fingers beneath—

the strangest thing had happened. His inner arms had begun to itch ferociously, impossible to ignore even through his panic, and Prior had raked at his flesh with his fingernails until the inside of his forearms had wept blood. He had forgotten his task and sought only relief from the terrible, consuming itch.

Then the roses had appeared.

Petals as purple as heather had emerged from the wounds in Prior's wrists and had pushed outwards, at first like they were escaping, and then like something drew them forth. More and more petals, relentless, until the heads of flowers as big as Prior's palm were growing from his skin. Horror had ensnared him; his own body had become alien. He had stretched his arms away from himself, as far as he could, yet the roses had kept appearing—impossible, incredible—and their stems had followed, each peppered with thorns that had exacerbated the messy ruins of Prior's wrists. Blood coated him from palm to elbow but he had been in a place beyond pain. Horror had given way to a fascination that turned him numb. Was this his body? Was he dreaming?

Roses upon roses had emerged from the garden of Prior's body. They extended from him like Fenton's vines did, and moved as independently. Prior had trembled at the night's cold breath on his wounds. *What now?* he remembered thinking.

In response to his silent question, the roses had prised around the hatch, scraping wood and stone and shattering magic that Prior had felt break over him like a wave. The roses had pummelled the hatch until it exploded into shrapnel.

Then they'd disappeared, leaving only dried blood, unbroken skin, and intricate purple rose tattoos behind.

More tugging on the rope. Prior dug his heels into the earth and thought strong thoughts. His palms burned and his biceps strained and his shoulders felt as if they would tear loose from his body, but *there*, at last! A pale hand grasped the stone ledge that squared the hatch. A second hand joined it, knuckles bleaching with strain. Prior sagged with relief and he scrambled forward to take hold of the hands and *heave*. Every muscle protested the effort.

He fell backward onto his arse, nearly clonking himself on the head with the pitchfork tines, but he didn't care. He'd got one of them out! Prior laughed shortly as his lungs struggled for air and his arms quivered with exertion. He blew out relief to the starry expanse above, and fancied that the winking stars approved of him.

From Prior's perspective, Fenton seemed tall as an oak. As distant as the curve of the moon. As beautiful. Prior wanted to reach for him, wanted to be held by him, but they didn't have time. He pushed himself to his feet, waving Fenton off when he came near.

Fenton stepped back, hands tugging at the sides of his breeches as if reminding himself not to touch. "I smell blood. You are— Are you hurt?"

Prior didn't know how to begin explaining about the roses. He shrugged instead. "I'm well enough. Nothing that can't keep."

Humming lowly, Fenton inclined his head, but his eyes remained troubled. Prior opened his mouth to speak—to say what, he hadn't the faintest notion—when Fenton suddenly glanced over his shoulder, as if he'd heard something. His vines rippled. Prior tensed. His forearms prickled.

"Lady Hartling?" he breathed the question.

Fenton shook his head and a smile flickered in the corner of his mouth. He returned to the hatch. Jagged rents tore his fine tunic, and something dark matted his hair, mud or blood or some other misery. The ghost of screams echoed in Prior's ears.

Gathering the rope, Fenton looped it around his leg and over his elbow, crooking his arm. His shadow crept up his legs and set like tar. Fenton leant over the hatch.

"You can climb now," he called.

If a reply was made, Prior didn't hear it, but Fenton stepped back and braced himself. The rope rippled as someone took hold of the other end. Hurrying, Prior lent his weight to the pitchfork, and stood on the rope closest to the tines. To his alarm, the rope started to fray.

Prior whispered harshly, "Fenton!"

When Fenton looked over his shoulder, Prior pointed to the rope. Fenton nodded, apparently unconcerned, and resumed his task. Another yank on the rope exacerbated the fray and the rope started to unravel. Before Prior could panic, a familiar slick blackness, darker than the surrounding night, darker than the space between stars, oozed along the rope beneath Prior's feet. Like wax pooling over a lantern base, Fenton's shadow encased the rope and hardened into a shell. The rope locked into place, scarcely rippling with the weight on the other end, until at last another hand reached over the lip of stone. Fenton heaved his sibling onto the grass in a tangle of limbs and panting.

"That... was horrendous," Lorcan grumbled, and swatted weakly at Fenton.

Fenton barked a laugh. Prior's lips curved as he watched the siblings tussle like puppies, with Fenton trying to rise, only for Lorcan to pull him to the grass, and then receive the same treatment. Were it not for the... everything... Prior would have been content to watch them play, but panic made every delay a blow to his composure.

"Please," he said, casting an anxious look around the garden. "Please, we must go before the good lady returns."

"She is not *good*," Fenton spat, as he got to his feet.

"On that we agree," Lorcan muttered, as Fenton heaved Lorcan to their feet beside him.

The two were similarly built, though Lorcan was the broader, and while both shared an ease of movement, Lorcan bore the palpable weight of exhaustion and lacked the otherworldly air that of late limned Fenton like stardust. Notably, too, Lorcan had no antlers.

While Prior had studied Lorcan, he'd clearly been studied in return. Lorcan gestured toward him with a flick of their fingers.

"Who is this, then, brother?" they asked as Fenton tugged them forward and indicated for Prior to take the path to the courtyard.

Reluctantly, Prior walked ahead. He left the lantern and rope behind and tried not to think of the light as a beacon calling for someone to examine what he'd done. Surely escape could not be so easy.

"That is Prior. He is— He is my friend," Fenton said.

Prior ducked his head, though no one could see his blush.

"I see. One more friend than I recall you having," Lorcan said, perhaps not entirely teasing.

Prior wanted to throw a rock at Lorcan, but Fenton only snorted.

"I owe a dance to a dryad, should that gain me any further credence. When we are far from here—"

"When we are—? No, Fenton, stop."

The serious tone of Lorcan's voice brought Prior to a halt, though he hadn't been included in the conversation. He looked back. Fenton and Lorcan faced each other on the path, lit only by moonlight. Prior strained to read the sober lines of Lorcan's unfamiliar face.

"I can't go with you," they said. The way they touched Fenton's elbow was straightforward with regret.

Movement in Fenton's hair: his vines, expressing agitation. "Of course you can. Prior freed you—"

Lorcan scoffed. "Think you not I have climbed from that place before? There was once a ladder, you furry fool."

"But the stone?"

"The stone weakens me. It drives me from my mind, true enough, but I have seen these gardens a time or two."

Fenton's hands clenched and unclenched at his sides.

"Then what must I do?" He sounded almost childish. "How can I free you?"

It seemed to Prior as if Lorcan were taken aback by the question, but he didn't know them well enough to be certain. Then Lorcan smiled widely and released Fenton's elbow. They flicked the ragged ribbons of their sleeves and tilted their head toward Prior, who drew back at the unexpected attention.

"Prior, was it?" When Prior nodded, Lorcan continued, still smiling. "Did you happen to see the good lady's staff? Ugly thing, nearly as tall as I, with a fist of a gem atop?"

"I did." He'd thought it an affectation of privilege.

The noise Fenton made was nearly a whine. "What of it?"

"Do keep up, brother. Without that gem I cannot leave the bounds of Aspinwick." Lorcan jabbed a finger toward the ground. No, toward Fenton's feet and the shadow that rippled across the grass beneath them. When Lorcan spoke, their voice lashed like a whip. "For your shadow is here at your feet, but mine? The heart of *my* shadow is in that woman's stolen rock."

Fenton growled and gooseflesh prickled over Prior's skin. That growl was a warning. A promise. Fenton's lip curled and he seemed to grow as night and shadow fed into him like a star turning inside-out. Lorcan grabbed Prior's sleeve and tugged him away from Fenton, who had started to shake. His shadow boiled. Prior could smell burning. His eyes stung at the outpouring of magic.

"Where's a pond when you need one?" Lorcan muttered, nonsensically. "Little brother is *cross*."

"Little"— Prior almost laughed, but Fenton's growl reached a feverish pitch, and, as if recognising a cue, Lorcan yanked Prior to the grass and covered him with their own body. Fenton's growl cut off as a blast of frigid air buffeted Prior and the night swallowed what little light moon and stars afforded. A pulse beat through the earth. Prior's arms throbbed. Lorcan groaned.

"I certainly hadn't missed *that*." With a grunt, Lorcan rolled off Prior and onto their back. They coughed. "Dramatic."

Moonlight tremulously reasserted itself. Rising carefully to his feet, Prior found himself unsurprised by the sight that greeted him: Fenton in his fox form, though substantially larger than the last—only—time Prior had seen it. Prior's head didn't even reach the cream fur of Fenton's chest. When he stretched to touch it, the fur was soft as down.

Prior craned his neck to meet one of Fenton's eyes. "Hello again."

Fenton lowered his great head—his antlers were bigger than Prior!—and pressed his muzzle to Prior's hair. He smelled like flowers Prior didn't recognise. And like blood. Prior patted him under the chin. In the back of his mind, he wondered if he should fear the fangs that were long enough to chomp straight through his spine, but he couldn't conjure any alarm. He patted Fenton again and stepped to Lorcan's side. Fenton's shadow flowed over his fur like a dark wind.

"Go on, then," Prior said. He made a shooing motion at the giant antlered fox with the aura of old blood and ancient power. Lorcan made a high-pitched noise. Prior grinned at Fenton, who tilted his head to the side, jostling his crown. "You've got a mage to squash, don't you? We'll meet you there."

Fenton's tail lashed from side to side and he shifted his weight, then with a deep bark, he leapt over Prior and Lorcan entirely. Prior whirled around, stumbling into Lorcan as they did the same, and they steadied one another as they watched Fenton bound down the path toward the main house, his tail a comet whipping through the night.

Lorcan cleared their throat, as if they would speak. Then they stopped, shook their head, and smiled; a small, real smile, unlike their earlier baring of teeth. Prior at last saw familial resemblance. Before Lorcan could break the fellow feeling—Prior suspected they were very practised at deflection—Prior offered his elbow.

"I heard there's a party up ahead. Shall we join it?"

Wryly amused, Lorcan slid their hand onto Prior's elbow. They inclined their head. "I'd be delighted."

Rage pounded in Fenton with every beat of paw to ground. His shadow urged him to speed; experience urged him to caution. Fenton's ears rang.

How long had Lorcan been without their shadow? The watery anathema had not followed them from the pit and Fenton had tried not to stare at the absence. The abhorrence. Then to discover Lorcan had been bound by such an integral part of their nature—bound by a scrap of a human, no less! Fenton's veins burned with the knowledge of the affront. He would flense every strip of skin from Hartling before he finally permitted her to die.

Night cloaked him as Fenton loped through the garden. Nocturnal creatures chittered excitedly as he passed, but he remained focused on the scent of Hartling ahead. He would know her unto the earth, now. The blight spiralled from her like breath in the cold, and though the entirety of her demesne had been poisoned by it, Fenton had become forcibly attuned after having had Hartling's magic seared into him. He knew the core of her lay ahead. He ran.

Fenton burst into the courtyard. In this form, he could access his sense of magic, which showed the place smeared with a fresh tangle of spells, and he halted sharply to avoid being snared in the web. Someone screamed: the masquerade had continued in his and Prior's absence, and guests continued to mill in the courtyard, though it seemed most had gone elsewhere. The few remaining guests brushed against Fenton's fur as they fled through his legs and he tried to ignore their panic, to concentrate instead on his hunt. He lifted his muzzle. He could sense Hartling, but where— He twisted aside to deflect a bolt of silvery light. It scorched along his flank, filling the air with the pungent scent of burning fur. When it landed on the courtyard, stone ruptured. People screamed.

Another blast nearly took out Fenton's hindlegs, and only a quick dodge enabled him to avoid injury. One of the surrounding walls exploded instead. He danced aside as one of the bolder guards stabbed at his paw with their sword, and collided with the fountain, knocking the stone figure aside. Water geysered from the broken spout. Finally, he spotted a small figure in a golden dress, posed arrogantly on the stone stairs as her guests fled, shrieking and crying. Drawing his shadow tight to his centre, protecting it, Fenton bounded forward, intent on the staff in Hartling's hand. *Free Lorcan.*

He expected her to shout. To run. To gloat. To send another bolt. She stood in place as he neared. Frozen like a fawn before the fang. Fenton would break her in twain. His tail whipped behind him as he leapt.

Then, with magic loaning her speed, Hartling drove her staff into the ground, making the flagstone splinter. The stone atop the staff glowed. The stone that contained the heart of Lorcan's shadow, and thusly everything Lorcan was or would be.

Light streamed from the stone atop the staff, carving Hartling's face into a garish mask of fury. Fenton's fur singed as light raked across him. He leapt—and too late, noticed the amber stone in Hartling's other hand. The focus for her own power. Where she stored the blight. Where she had pulled the magic to trap Lorcan.

She twisted, and shoved the amber into his chest.

Someone shouted.

Something burned.

Fenton fell, and kept falling.

A thrash of waves. "The rivers are not yours to charm!"

"They are not anyone's. They were lonely." Wind susurrating in the leaves.

A clap of thunder. "Was this your plan all along? To send me away and take everything for your own?"

"We own nothing, sibling. Do not boil and froth so, it is unmannerly." The first rumble of stones on a mountaintop.

"You know well what I meant, don't twist my meaning." The rush of rapids. "I don't care for this incarnation of yours. It's all bite and no bark. How many times must I tell you to get your enormous furry feet *out* of my waters!" A lightning strike. Another.

The movement of a wolf in the tall grass. "Is that a challenge?"

"If you cared about a single thing other than yourself, there may be purpose in challenge. Do you?" A green flash, far on the horizon. "Can you?"

Fenton woke in a forest. Blackened trees reached crooked fingers from the scorched earth. No grass grew. An icy wind churned grey ashes in dismal eddies. No birds sang. The red sun smouldered low and offered no warmth. Fenton pushed himself to human feet and stumbled, his centre of gravity altered without the weight of antlers to steady him. No shadow offered aid and he dropped to one knee on the wretched ground, impact making his teeth clack. He shivered as the wind scourged his bare skin. He plunged his hand into the dry soil but nothing answered his call. Nothing lived in the grey land but him.

"You could have been so much more than this. Every name they hung on you like garlands, and in the end, all you are is a scrawny man trapped in his own empty head."

Hartling's voice came from everywhere and nowhere. Fenton searched for her on the horizon, but nothing moved in the deadwood besides the wind, and the skeletal trees offered no shelter. He pushed himself to his feet, unwilling to be weak before an enemy.

"Where am I?" he asked, the words scraping his parched throat. "How long have I been here?"

"You have been here all your long and wasted life. And here you will remain."

With a hoarse bellow, Fenton reached for fur and fang, for hoof and horn, intending to rip the world apart until he found Hartling and peeled her face off. His muscles shook and his head throbbed and his sweat-slick skin prickled with effort—but he remained human shaped. Restricted.

Hartling's laughter was a crack of lightning that set one of the trees aflame. Heat billowed toward Fenton as another tree caught, then another. He watched the grey flames rise until embers hit his skin in a hot spit of pain and he scrambled away, newly aware of his vulnerability with no shape nor shadow to aid him.

"Where will you run, little dog?"

Away.

Fenton turned tail and ran.

The grey land stretched in an endless smear of dead things. Not in the process of decaying—not gifted with even that much life—but frozen in a timeless end. Fenton stumbled through the forest, if such a place could be given that name, from copse to clearing, until he reached a pool of flat grey water with a spindly willow kissing the surface. He realised, then, where he'd been condemned to: not any of the forests of the world, but his own, the one that lived within him. Where Lorcan had banished him.

Where he had let himself remain banished. The white-tailed stag, the part of Fenton tired of fighting, had taken the uglier parts of Fenton's incarnations and refused to return them. They had become trees, Fenton remembered now. Oak and hawthorn. Birch and yew.

Fire crackled in the forest. Fenton circled the pool, passing through the space that had once held wheat, that had once known the summer hunter. He let himself remember the rich fragrance of wheat; the summer hunter had started the process of his awakening, after he'd spent years in slumber, and as he inhaled, Fenton realised he had scented the first hint of the blight, then. On the hunter's skin, in her hair.

Would she have killed the white-tailed stag if she had found it? What would she have done on learning there were no wishes to be had?

Fenton briskly rubbed his bare arms. If the fire didn't take him, the cold would. He glanced at the eerily still pool, the surface like obsidian. Perhaps drowning.

Drifting his fingers through the memory of sunset flowers, Fenton moved to stand at the pool's edge and considered his reflection, as he had in the forest. He raised his hands to his face and pressed the ridges beneath his eyes, the protruding banks of his collarbone. No muzzle. No beak. No vines in his hair nor crown on his head. No shadow at his throat. His fingers rested on the hard slash of his mouth. He tilted his head. No kisses.

Fire ate across the forest, the noise of the flames so loud it seemed to sizzle within Fenton's skull. Heat dried his skin. The willow at the side of the pool crackled as fire transformed it into a flickering candle. Sparks rained on the pool and made Fenton's reflection shiver. He licked his lips.

He could— Could he smell fern and rose?

The willow tree cracked in half and crashed into the water with a mighty hiss. As the water sloshed, something glimmered in its murky depths. Amber, bright as a slap in the face.

Fenton dove into Lorcan's shadow and swam down.

Down.

Down.

Fenton opened his eyes to the deepest blue sheet of night and the bright flash of lightning. With a grunt, he rolled aside to avoid the strike, pulling his tail out of the way at the last instant, then surged to his feet. Scorched stone cracked beneath him, but his shadow protected his sensitive paws. He turned in place to locate Hartling to prepare for a new attack, but then he saw the thorn-studded vines crisscrossing the courtyard. He paused. Had he done that?

His distraction nearly cost him everything, as the second strike cracked against the base of Fenton's spine and crushed him to the ground. Only his shadow saved him from paralysis, and Fenton reached for every green thing in the garden—for ivy and hyacinth, for fern and oak, for the smallest wildflower hidden among the tended grass—to feed the rapid healing of the damage to his spine. The thorned vines shuddered at his call. He panted and watched Hartling move closer.

"I didn't think you'd make it out of there. You're brighter than I thought," Hartling said as she advanced toward him, her feet floating inches above the broken flagstones.

They were alone in the wreck of Aspinwick. No guests. No guards. No Prior and no Lorcan, to Fenton's mingled relief and worry. He grunted as his shadow pulsed around his vertebrae, resetting the alignment. Pain shocked from his spine through his body like a rock thrown into a pond.

Hartling continued with a sneer. "But then, I don't think much of you."

Sweat and mud painted Hartling, and a wound on her forehead trickled blood over her face. She leant heavily on her staff, as if one of her legs troubled her. Her protective spells were so faint as to be almost transparent; she had been substantially weakened, but he could not have been in her spell for longer than an hour. The rotten stench of the blight coated nearly every scrap of her own magic. To Fenton's opened senses, Hartling wore the blight like a second skin. She would never be free of what she had invited into herself.

Fenton inhaled. He smelled fern and rose and saltwater. Raising his muzzle, he tried to find Prior and Lorcan but he couldn't see them. Fear dug hot claws into his heart. A whimper broke through his clenched teeth.

When she reached him, still craven on his belly, Hartling looked at him like gods looked at humans in those stories people used to tell around campfires. Fenton had overheard so many of them he'd begun to think they were true.

"Nothing to say?" Hartling sneered. "You're just like the other one. All this power"—a *crack* of magic blistered the fountain beside Fenton to rubble—"and you run from it! All this!" Hartling raised the staff and water rose with it, twisting in shapes that made Fenton sick to see. Lorcan used to do that. Hartling gestured, and the lance of water rushed for Fenton. Her eyes flashed. "What are you but flowers and fangs? You are *nothing.*"

Bracing himself, Fenton let the water-spear impale his shoulder. A high whine escaped his clenched fangs at the sickening impact, one heard more than felt. Then the water burst out of his back, and his foreleg buckled as bright pain took hold of his nerves and crushed them together. The coppery stink of his blood thickened the air. Fenton panted and let his antlers draw his head downward.

Hartling laughed, dark and low. Fenton watched the diamond on the tip of her staff from beneath his lowered lashes.

Approaching him, her staff and stone held ready, Hartling scoffed. "Useless," she declared. She closed her hand again over the amber stone, its lustre dimmed.

Fenton braced his weight. Something flickered at the corner of his eye and he stilled as Prior and Lorcan dashed behind Hartling. Relief nearly buckled his legs.

Hartling raised her staff. The diamond sparkled as power coalesced inside it. "I think I shall take your shadow, and whatever is left of your skin. I have no need for the rest of you." She paused. "Is there a message you'd like me to pass on? Any final words for your sibling before I return them to where they belong?" When Fenton made no response, Hartling clucked her tongue. "Rude. It must run in the family."

The diamond flared like a star. Hartling took a breath.

Before she released it, Fenton lunged forward and pinned Hartling with his good front paw, breaking her magical protection with the blow. Baring his fangs, he bore his weight down until Hartling spluttered, her face red and damp with spittle. His paw spanned her torso and pinned her in place, trapping both hands beneath his outspread claws. Sparks bit and nipped from her gemstones as she wheezed, then, with an almost admirable will, collected herself. Her eyes flashed and her hands tightened around her weapons.

"Do you think I cannot kill you as well from here?" Hartling shredded her skin on his claw as she wrenched her arm free, holding the amber stone aloft. Avarice lit her eyes.

With a nimble dip of his muzzle, Fenton bit off her hand. Bone splintered between his fangs. Saltsweet flesh and hot blood filled his mouth. He crunched palm and fingers and the burning amber until they were shards, seasoned with Hartling's delicious screams. He swallowed. Licked his chops.

Lowered his head for her other hand.

Struggling wildly, her bloody stump painting the stone as she flailed, Hartling managed to yank the staff partially free. The diamond—the heart of Lorcan's shadow—rested against her throat. Grey-blue smoke writhed within, like mist off the water.

"You want this?" Hartling asked, her voice shrill with pain. "Take it! Enough magic to glut yourself, you hungry beast!" The gem trembled and Hartling managed to grin savagely even through her obvious agony. Whatever blast she released would kill them both and she didn't care.

With a gleeful snarl, Fenton spread his toes and bore his weight down. Muscle and flesh, bark and bone, every seed that had ever stretched its way from earth to sky, the trees that whispered and the mountains that sang—Fenton pressed their combined weight inexorably onto Hartling and her stolen shadow like the judgment of ages come due. He took his time. Hartling writhed and twisted beneath the crushing force as her taunting dissolved to blubbering pleas and then, as the creaking of her ribs gave way to cracks, her wet breath scraped into gasps. Blood splattered her lips. Fenton trembled as something gave way beneath the pad of his paw. His claws scraped the flagstones.

Movement made him whip his head around. Prior. He stared at Fenton with wide, sad eyes. He smelled like blood.

"Fenton, she's dead," Prior said, his voice the cool breeze from a long-ago summer.

Behind Prior, Lorcan stood as stone. When Fenton caught their eye, Lorcan nodded once, grim.

With a deep, resounding bark, Fenton reared onto his hind legs then *slammed* his paw onto the crushed mess that had once been a mage. His claw speared the grey-blue stone. A spiderweb crack splintered its face. Fenton tore away the limp sack of Hartling's remaining hand and tossed it aside, baring the staff and its diamond eye. Power thrummed from the stone. A high tone warbled, almost beyond his hearing, and Fenton's shadow clenched around his throat as a rush of power not his own rippled through his fur. The crack in the diamond widened. Saltwater tang touched his curled-back lips. Lorcan started to laugh.

The unleashed magic tore through Fenton from nose to tail and he heard nothing but thunder.

Fenton crumpled into a lump of bloody fur as the sky

rent open with a sudden deluge of rain. Prior dashed across the ruined courtyard, nearly tripping over ruptured flagstones as magic in the few remaining lanterns flickered and died. As Lady Hartling had. Somewhere—a world away—he could hear someone calling his name. Lorcan. Prior ignored them as he skirted the mess beneath Fenton's huge paw, unable to reconcile the nearby soup of flesh as a once-living human being, and instead turned his attention to the... hopefully-still-living... giant fox-stag-person.

To Fenton. Prior wanted to sink his fingers into Fenton's fur and cling until everything made sense again. Rain drummed Fenton's unmoving body, making pink rivulets stream across the courtyard. Prior clenched his hands to fists, unsure if he should touch, though he could scarcely think of anything but. Fenton had been badly hurt. Prior needed to mind himself.

"Fenton?" Prior inched closer. Even sprawled as he was, Fenton was taller than Prior. Prior raised his voice. "Fenton, it's me. It's Prior." The triangular ear closest to Prior flicked toward him. Emboldened, Prior edged around to Fenton's side, using his big body as a buffer against the lashing rain. "It's pissing down, I don't know if you've noticed, but if"—Prior cleared his throat when his voice cracked; "if" held a world of conditions—"if you can move, we might get under shelter and tend to your wounds. The guests and staff all bolted, which is fair enough, really, but there might still be wine. Watered down, but still..."

Prior trailed off when nothing more moved than that one ear. Chewing his lower lip, he darted a glance at Fenton's eyes, but they remained closed. With a sigh, Prior slowly rested his forehead on the nearest part of Fenton and inhaled the scent of wet fur. Rain flattened his hair and dripped down his nape, his fine doublet no defence against the elements, and he pressed his face more firmly into Fenton's fur. He wasn't going anywhere. He refused.

They would stay in the rain and the rubble until Fenton opened his eyes.

His forearms ached. They had wept roses.

"He's not dead after all that, is he? No. There'd be crying if he were dead," Lorcan corrected themself as they approached.

Prior wanted to ignore them, but he called upon what strength remained to him and turned to rest against Fenton's side. He crossed his arms over his chest.

"He's not dead," he said, sniffing wetly.

"No, I know, I was trying to alleviate the snuffling," Lorcan said, drawing closer. Unaffected by the rain, Lorcan had from somewhere gained fresh clothing, and now wore a buttery yellow tunic and clinging dark blue breeches, with a matching yellow ribbon tying back their long silver hair. Blue-green scales curved from the arch of their cheeks to their jaw, and Prior glimpsed more scales on the blade of their hand when they gestured toward Fenton. "If he were dead, we'd be meeting the rest of my family and answering extremely awkward questions, not passing the time chatting. He does look like something a cat coughed up, though. Do you hear me, brother?"

"The rest of..." Prior murmured, beneath Lorcan's taunting of Fenton. He hadn't even *considered*.

He shoved the thought firmly out of his brain.

"Anyway," Lorcan said. Something squelched beneath their foot and they grimaced, daintily toeing a meaty glob aside. They stepped around a puzzle of viscera, then suddenly bared their teeth and, turning, spat viciously at the remains of Lady Hartling. "Should've believed me when I said I wasn't the mean one."

Fenton snorted and Lorcan flicked their fingers, dismissive, then frowned at their hand. Cupping it, they caught raindrops, regarding them as if somehow offended, though until then the rain hadn't touched them at all. They turned their frown on Prior, lingering on his wet hair.

"This is dismal, isn't it? I know indigestion isn't the

most fun, but there's no call for this dreariness," Lorcan said, incomprehensibly, peering over Prior's head toward Fenton.

Behind Prior, Fenton rumbled a growl, as if in response. Lorcan clapped their hands together. Prior had no idea what was happening.

"I thought as much," Lorcan said. A bright grin slashed their face and they snapped their fingers. The rain stopped. Prior blinked. Lorcan waggled their eyebrows. "Like falling off a log. You're welcome. Alas, I can't do anything for the smell of wet dog, but by the way you're clinging to my brother, I can tell that doesn't bother you."

"I thought you weren't the mean one?" Prior found himself asking, though he couldn't argue. Fenton did smell like wet dog, and it didn't bother Prior at all.

Lorcan fussily straightened the collar of their tunic. "We're very competitive."

With a grunt, Fenton started to shift his weight. Rushing around to Fenton's front, Prior raised his hands.

"Wait! I'm very glad you're moving, but your wounds are still, ah, oozing. Might a smaller form be better?" Prior didn't enjoy calling attention to Fenton's injuries, but they were hardly subtle. There was a hole in one of Fenton's shoulders the size of Prior's head. He had been trying not to see it. "Two-legged, perhaps?"

"He can't shift until he's digested that pretty little rock," Lorcan said. "Isn't that right? You bit off more than you can chew, and your fangs are as long as my—" They grinned. "Arm."

Letting the comment pass, Prior moved onto the more salient point. "What rock? I thought your rock broke. There was an explosion. I definitely remember that." He couldn't forget.

Lorcan shook their head. "Not my diamond. That's stardust, now. No, I mean the other one, where the magelet stored her magic, and sent out her poison to the world. The one she had an eye to fitting our mutual acquaintance into." Seeing Prior's incomprehension, they elaborated. "The amber stone was the source of your blight, among other nastiness, and the big furry fuck here ate it."

"You *ate* the blight?" Prior asked Fenton, his voice high.

Fenton flicked his ears and huffed. Then, moving slowly, he covered his eyes with one massive paw and hunkered down, curling the messy brush of his tail around his enormous body. Blood drying on his fur, human flesh smeared beneath his breast, and big as a coaching stable he might be, but Prior nonetheless desperately wished to gather Fenton in his arms and cradle him close. Something in Prior's heart had cracked open. He didn't intend to stitch it shut.

"How long will the... digesting... take?" Prior asked Lorcan, his attention mostly on Fenton.

Lorcan waved a hand airily. "As long as it takes."

"That's remarkably unhelpful."

Their expression darkened like gathering clouds. Wind whipped their hair and bit Prior's exposed skin. Lorcan curled their lip. "You might have tricks up your torn sleeves but I would suggest you not test me. I am not my brother."

Fenton's ear twitched. The air thickened with the scent of the ground after rain. Prior's chest tightened as he looked from one sibling to the other and nervously realised he stood between them. Then Lorcan exhaled dramatically and tossed their head, making their hair flick. They levelled a look at Prior and their lips quirked.

"I have a strong desire to burn down Aspinwick and piss on the ashes. Would you care to join me?" they asked. When Prior hesitated, Lorcan tapped Fenton's nose. "Boop! Tell your human he can set fire to things with me. We'll bond. You'll regret nothing."

Lowering his paw and opening one eye, Fenton found Prior with his gaze. Warmth shone from him as it did the sun.

"Steal all... her gold..." Fenton rumbled. He closed his eye again.

Laughter cracked Prior's dry lips and relief filled him with light. He pressed a kiss to Fenton's cold nose. Then he motioned for Lorcan to lead the way.

"Let's steal her gold and then you can show me how gods celebrate victory," he said.

Lorcan grinned.

As smoke began to billow from the broken windows of Aspinwick House, sometime around dawn, Fenton felt a jolt as the lump of cursed stone in his gut finally dissolved and released its hold on the land and his shape. The garden sighed around him as the blight dissipated. Effects would ripple out from the Aspinwick Estate, as they had when the blight had first struck, but the resolution would work much faster. Prior's village might be free of the effects entirely before the next moon. Relief soothed Fenton's aches. He had kept his word.

Moving carefully, he tried to stand, testing his recovered strength. Eating the stone had been an act of impulse, but with its influence removed, his own magic was free to focus on healing. He dared not draw more power from the estate's garden, damaged as it was from his efforts against Hartling, and from her own poisoned work over the years.

When he managed to stand with only minor wobbling, Fenton chuffed in satisfaction. He nosed at his shoulder wound and found his muscle had knitted together, though his skin and fur had yet to heal. The damage to his spine had been completely healed; his magic would have targeted the greater wound first. All in all, it could be worse. Much worse.

Something collapsed in the house, making Fenton's

ears twitch. He concentrated. He could access his other form now. He took a breath. Another. The scent of fern and rose drew near, and Fenton smiled as he closed his eyes and folded himself carefully inward, as did the sunset flower when dawn approached. He would bloom again.

When he opened his eyes, the ground was much closer and his shadow had moved to form trousers, while vines bound his injured shoulder. Pale morning light trailed across the courtyard, and Prior stood in a pool of it, a bottle of wine in his hand, a smirk on his dusty face, and a gold necklace with a glittering green stone hung around his neck. Fenton stretched out his senses, alarmed, but no extra magic emanated from Prior or the stone. He let himself relax.

"If I'd known you'd transformed, I would've brought glasses," Prior said, shaking the wine bottle to make clear his meaning. He perched on the rim of the fountain, one of the only parts that had survived intact. "Join me?"

Tilting his head in acquiescence, Fenton sat beside him, close enough to feel heat rising from Prior's body. Prior had found new clothes at some point, plainer fare than the ones they had taken from Northrope. Unfortunate, as the gold had made Prior look exceptionally fine. Fenton wondered how many clothes Prior's new necklace might buy.

"Not as fancy as the doublet, I know, but needs must. Do you think the tailor will accept gold as recompense for our theft?" Prior asked, with a wry grin.

Fenton pretended to consider it. "Gold and a goat? It seems a worthy trade."

"You and your goats!"

They fell to a silence heavy with exhaustion. Fenton breathed Prior in. Prior considered the label of the bottle in his hands.

"Lorcan is—"

"Might you—"

They spoke at the same time. Prior gestured with the

wine bottle.

"You first," he said, and took a swig.

Fenton hummed. "I wondered only if you intended on returning to your village. The blight has been broken, you have acquired a very pretty necklace—"

"*Many* necklaces, and rings," Prior interrupted, gleefully.

"Just so. Then you need for nothing. I-I would thank you. For your assistance." Fenton grasped for the comfort of ritual. "If it harm none and be within my power to give, and in yours to receive, you may have it freely in thanks for your aid." The old words tasted bitter.

Pursing his wine-stained lips, Prior nodded, then kept on nodding, drinking from the wine bottle as he did. He continued to nod, his eyes going distant, before he abruptly heaved the bottle back and hurled it in an overhead throw. The bottle shattered in a glorious noise against the flagstones of the courtyard, joining the rest of the rubble. Then Prior turned his glare on Fenton and Fenton worried he'd be thrown in a similar fashion. To judge by the fire in his eyes, Prior had determination to make an attempt, at least.

"No! You don't get to—to fucking *thank* me, Fenton, like we're merchants at market!" Prior shouted as he rose to his feet, distress in every vibrant line. "I don't need 'nothing'! No one needs *nothing*. There's plenty of things I need, and from you specifically. Things!" Prior pinched the bridge of his nose with a mutter, his anger punctured. "I am so bad at this."

Fenton hurried to his feet. He touched Prior's hunched shoulder and drew him around, startling when Prior lunged forward, only to relax as Prior's arms snaked around Fenton's waist in an embrace. Prior pressed his face into Fenton's throat, nuzzling him.

"You know, we didn't even get to dance," Prior mumbled.

Dancing. Fenton hummed, and began to sway softly in

place. He draped his arms around Prior's hips. "I remembered dancing when I saw you in the forest. The idea of it, of two bodies as complementary creatures."

Prior made a surprised noise into Fenton's throat and pulled back so their eyes could meet, stopping the swaying. "Because of me?"

"Just so."

"I don't know what to say to that."

"You do not have to say anything." Fenton shrugged one shoulder, then tentatively ran his fingers through Prior's hair. Plaster dust and shards of glass fell free as he did. "Will the house last the day?" he asked, amused.

Prior's shoulders shook. "Not if your sibling has any say in it."

"Lorcan is very good at what they choose to do, that is true. As are you," Fenton added. He pressed a kiss to Prior's temple. It tasted like soot. "Tell me what you desire and I will get it for you. You need only ask."

Prior stiffened and Fenton closed his eyes, pained. He'd spoken poorly again.

Then Prior's tension seemed to turn to hunger as he pressed his face more tightly to Fenton's throat, his lips moving against the sensitive skin. Kissing. Prior trailed a line of kisses to Fenton's jaw, as far as he could reach without dislodging Fenton's hold.

"This," Prior said, kissing the word into Fenton's skin. "I want this. I want *you*."

The green scent of living things filled Fenton's nose as the last scrap of his deadwood heart cracked to splinters and a riotous blossom of love bloomed in its place. It took root. Spine and stem, bone and bark.

Fenton pressed a kiss to Prior's hair, then nudged his chin until Prior untucked his flushed face from Fenton's throat. Prior's eyes were wet. Fenton kissed the tears from his dirty face, following the tracks over the curve of his cheek, the slope of his prickly jaw. Prior's breath quickened and his hands tightened on Fenton's waist. His eyes flickered to Fenton's and past, to his antlers, perhaps, or to his twisting vines, before resettling on his lips. Though excitement coloured Prior's face, and hunger lit his gaze, he didn't move.

Fenton would move the earth for Prior. Yet an inch seemed impossible.

But Prior had been bold. Fenton could match that.

"With the breaking of the blight, we are released from our vows to one another." When Prior looked to speak, Fenton stroked his thumb over the promise of Prior's lips. He smiled. "I make another to you now."

Cupping Prior's face, Fenton leaned in to kiss his oath to Prior's lips. Prior tasted like wine and ash, and he clung to Fenton like a tree in the heart of a storm. Then Prior's boldness returned and the kiss became hungry. Prior thrust his thigh between Fenton's, making Fenton groan thickly into Prior's mouth. Laughing softly, Prior retreated from their kiss to plant more across the bridge of Fenton's nose, the corner of his eye, the tip of his ear. He bit lightly around the point. A low ball of heat grew in Fenton's gut and he jerked against Prior's thigh, receiving another husky laugh for his efforts.

"You know, I think there's probably a room Lorcan hasn't set fire to yet," Prior said as he stroked carefully over the curve of Fenton's good shoulder. His skin was blessedly cool.

Fenton swallowed. "Oh?"

"Or at least we might find a couch somewhere. A bench. A flat surface."

Oh.

"What about my-my antlers—"

"I adore your antlers—"

"Or my vines. Do you want I should"—Fenton's voice hitched when Prior scratched his blunt human nails across Fenton's back and pressed his thigh up at the same time— "should dismiss them?"

Prior claimed Fenton's lips in a kiss that bit, and

grinned with all his blunt, human teeth. "You can keep the vines," he said.

EPILOGUE

Prior had been heading toward Aspinwick House, though smoke and crashes still emerged from within, but when he saw the glint of glass he changed course and tugged Fenton across the ruins of the courtyard. They sidestepped sheared flagstones and a snake of frigid water still spilling from the broken fountain. Prior's soft slippers were soaked through. He caught hold of Fenton's hand and walked faster, hoping he'd find what he suspected sat tucked behind the main house.

When they arrived at the gabled greenhouse, Prior squeezed Fenton's hand, looking at him sidelong. "A greenhouse, and still in one piece. Like it was waiting for us, don't you think?"

Fenton only raised his eyebrows, so Prior led him by their joined hands through the unlocked door. Ceiling lanterns lit as they entered, seemingly unaffected by the loss of Hartling's magic, and they cast a warm glow across the large greenhouse; their magic made Prior shiver, like cat claws prickling over his skin. When Fenton glanced at him, Prior shrugged: he didn't know how to explain about the roses, yet, or what he'd say when he tried. He took a deep breath. The greenhouse smelled like summer in full bloom, and the muggy air made Prior languorous. He knocked his shoulder into Fenton's bare one and pressed it there.

"Well, what do you think?" he asked.

As Fenton gave their surroundings careful scrutiny, Prior followed the line of his gaze. There, long benches were dotted with pots boasting healthy seedlings not yet ready for planting. Beyond, a colourful corner where geraniums reached to the glass ceiling for dawn's first blush. Along the near wall, neat shelves showcased fragrant herbs in rows, while vials and pipettes and other alchemical equipment lurked on a well-used desk nearby. There were notes stacked on the desk; Prior would burn them later.

The other side of the greenhouse, closer to them, appeared to be an area for relaxing or entertaining. Two cushioned chaises angled toward a single, tired rattan armchair, and a horseshoe of twilight-coloured chrysanthemums provided an audience. The promise of morning stretched beyond the glass panes. Somewhere, Lorcan was setting fire to things.

Perfect.

Prior nudged Fenton again. "Well?"

Fenton nodded, very seriously. Then he grinned, sly as one of his namesakes. "I see a flat surface."

Before Prior could react, Fenton had scooped him into his arms like he was readying to carry Prior over a threshold. Prior laughed, shocked, and slung his right arm around Fenton's neck, lightly swatting him with the other. If his hand lingered on Fenton's bare chest, all to the good.

"What are you doing? What about your injuries? Let me down— We're already inside!" Prior protested through his laughter.

"My injuries will heal. I like you here," Fenton said, simple and sincere. He jostled Prior in his arms like Prior weighed no more than a sack of flour. The casual display of strength shot straight to Prior's hindbrain.

Lifting his chin, Prior twirled one of Fenton's vines around his finger. "I like being here." He tugged. "Now kiss me."

At once, Fenton ducked his head and captured Prior's lips in an easy kiss, taking sips as Prior sighed into his mouth. Fenton's fingers pressed firmly to Prior's thigh and around his ribs, while his arms provided secure bands around Prior's back and legs. Prior carded his hand though Fenton's hair to keep him in place as they kissed, angling Fenton to better chase his taste. He stroked the furred tip of Fenton's ear with his thumb, making Fenton lean his head into the touch.

Prior felt Fenton start walking, but it didn't matter. Nothing mattered other than the welcoming pillow of Fenton's lips and the growing desire in Prior as his blood rushed to his cock. When Fenton's fingers twitched against his thigh, Prior moaned into Fenton's mouth and pressed closer, his neck straining, until he realised Fenton was drawing away. Prior's gut lurched and he drew back.

"What is it? Are you well?" he asked, ardour rapidly cooling.

Fenton moved in place, so Prior could see the chaise waiting nearby. "I can put you down but..." Fenton trailed off. One of his vines scratched his nose.

Prior couldn't recall seeing Fenton embarrassed before. He smiled as he played with the hairs on the nape of Fenton's neck. "Tell me. I would give you what you want, if I can."

"I want to be under you," Fenton said in a rush.

"I don't know how to explain how little I object to that plan," Prior said, once he could speak again.

After setting Prior onto his feet—Prior only wobbled once—Fenton cleared his throat, then took a seat on the nearest chaise. He laid flat, his antlers skimming the cushion of the upraised end, and planted his feet with his legs spread either side of the couch, leaving a Prior-sized space between his thighs. His bare chest heaved and his cheeks darkened in clear evidence of his desire. The vines binding his shoulder wound were the only sobering element, but even those were trying to entice, buds opening along them as they did his crown in pretty floral kisses. They didn't need to work so hard; Prior had long since been snared by the god before him.

Prior watched Fenton for a moment, because he could. Because Fenton wanted him to look, on display as he trailed his fingers down his own chest, thumbing one of his pebbled nipples and making his breath catch. Immediately, Prior wanted to bite and suck a path from one of Fenton's nipples to the other, until they were reddened. Would Fenton enjoy that? Prior licked his lips and inched closer.

"You are so beautiful. Are there any stories about how beautiful you are?" he asked.

Fenton shook his head, his colour deepening.

Prior nodded, like that was perfectly sensible instead of a crime. "You're right. How could any story possibly capture you like this?"

"Prior—"

His name from Fenton's tongue tasted like nectar. Prior let himself be drawn closer by Fenton's eager hands, and rested one knee between Fenton's open legs as he claimed Fenton's lips in a searing kiss. Fenton grabbed hold of Prior's tunic and arched his neck to meet the kiss in kind. Tongues met in an indolent slide; they had all the time in the world to learn each other. To learn Fenton's taste, the texture of his skin, the low rumbles Prior drank like sweet wine. He would become drunk on Fenton.

In his breeches, Prior's cock made the case for urgency. Prior reached to adjust himself, but Fenton touched his wrist and stopped him. When Prior broke the kiss to look at him questioningly, hunger had narrowed the planes of Fenton's face, making him more fox-like than usual. Prior's hips rocked, unbidden.

"May I touch you there?" Fenton asked, cupping his hand over Prior's, where Prior cradled his cock, to make clear his meaning.

"While you're under me?" Prior clarified.

When Fenton nodded, Prior moved to straddle Fenton on the couch, pinning his narrow hips between his thighs. The breeches he'd found in the main house were loose enough that Fenton could slide his hand inside with little effort and cradle Prior's hard cock with his clever fingers. Prior's eyes squeezed shut as Fenton took hold of him, Fenton's thumb swiping over the damp head as if he instinctively knew how Prior preferred to be touched.

He opened his eyes and nearly lost control again when he found Fenton staring at him with inky eyes.

"This isn't going to take long, I'm afraid," Prior said, with a shaky grin.

Fenton licked his lips. "I want you to spend on my skin."

Prior's hips jerked. With a heroic effort, he managed not to come immediately. "I— Oh, *fuck*, this isn't going to take long at *all*."

As if taking the words as a challenge, Fenton hastily tugged Prior's breeches down until Prior's cock sprung free. Eyes fixed on his goal, Fenton coaxed Prior to move farther up his body, to straddle his waist. Every movement shot to Prior's cock and he barely clung to his control, breeches banding tightly around his thighs. He could have removed them, but that would have meant pausing for perhaps as many as ten seconds and so was completely unthinkable. Panting raggedly, he settled as Fenton directed, his hips moving in small, irrepressible waves.

Fenton licked his palm, and Prior had a searing vision of Fenton's mouth filled with cock. Fenton licked everything, didn't he? In his current state, Prior wouldn't last long enough to make a sucking worthwhile, but he thrilled at the notion.

As though the image had travelled from Prior's brain to his, Fenton's grin grew filthy. He took hold of Prior's cock with a firm, confident grip and started to stroke, spreading his other hand across Prior's thigh and kneading the muscle beneath the thin breeches. The two touches drove Prior closer to his peak as he fucked Fenton's sure fist, his own hands gripping his hair as his scalp prickled with nearing orgasm. His panting rasped in his ears and was matched by Fenton, who rocked his hips to meet every movement of Prior's.

Fenton swiped his thumb over the tip of Prior's cock and smeared wetness down the shaft, making the glide slick. Prior grunted, moving faster. It took him a moment to hear Fenton's low mumbling over his own higher moans.

"—to taste you. Want to feel you on my skin. Want to wear your scent. Want to—"

"*Fuck!*"

Prior came in hot pulses, painting sticky stripes over Fenton's chest. Fenton panted and arched like it was he who had come, growling throatily, and Prior's cock gave another jolt at the sight.

At last, with a weak groan, Prior nudged Fenton's hand away. Fenton made a low, disappointed sound. Prior claimed a kiss, then pulled his breeches up and tucked away his sensitive cock. With a dreamy expression on his face, Fenton rubbed a streak of Prior's come into his skin, his pupils completely overwhelming the grave dirt and honey of his eyes. He hummed as he stroked, his other hand squeezing and releasing Prior's thigh in a teasing, perfect rhythm.

"This is a thing with you, isn't it? Scent? And— Yes, there it is, the licking," Prior said, watching Fenton lick Prior's spend off his thumb.

Fenton's hips rolled in small motions as he trailed his fingers across his chest, utterly daubing himself. Part of Prior wrinkled its nose at the stickiness, but the majority desperately wanted to paint Fenton again to prolong his blissful expression. Prior's cock twitched, though he couldn't get it up again so soon, despite his extremely fervent longing.

He shuffled down Fenton's body, then rethought his approach, and they rearranged with Fenton sitting upright against the end of the chaise and Prior planted firmly in his lap. Prior had no objections, especially as he now had access to Fenton's cock. The interruption to his artistic endeavours had made Fenton's expression sharpen from its far-away state and Prior intended to see that face again as soon as possible. He tapped the waistband of Fenton's trousers.

"Can I take these off?"

Fenton nodded, and… vanished his trousers, startling Prior to a laugh.

"That is *very* convenient," he said, and let himself admire the skin newly revealed. More freckles, some silvery scars, and Fenton's cock. Curving slightly from its thatch of deep red curls, the plump head dark with blood, wetness already welling from the tip; the view made Prior's mouth water.

"Will you remove your tunic?" Fenton asked, interrupting Prior's priapic contemplation.

Quickly—though not as quickly as *vanishing*—Prior yanked his tunic over his head and threw it aside. When he resettled, his hands loose on Fenton's sides, something had changed. Prior's eyes flicked over Fenton's face. Fenton's eyes were as dark, his lips as wet… but every flower on his crown and vines had turned purple as heather.

Fenton swallowed. "Prior, your arms."

It wasn't until Fenton trailed his hands dreamily—as dreamy as when he'd been rubbing come into his skin—up Prior's arms that Prior realised what had grabbed his attention: the rose tattoos that wrapped Prior's forearms. As Fenton traced the design with featherlight touches, prickles rushed over Prior's skin like the return of blood after numbness. Like thorns. He shifted in place, unsure of the sensation: was it pain? Fenton pressed his thumb firmly against one of the thickest lines and Prior gasped as he got his answer. It wasn't pain. Nothing like it. Heat hooked into Prior's gut and he rocked his hips, brushing Fenton's hardness and making him gasp.

"Can I?" Fenton asked, his hands slack around Prior's wrists. Vines twisted in his hair.

Prior nodded. Fenton could. He absolutely could. Prior's cock mightn't be ready but whatever Fenton wanted— A gasp tore from Prior's lips as Fenton plucked a petal from Prior's arm. Prior stared. Fenton hadn't even touched him. He had made a pinching motion in the air, brushing one of the lines of Prior's tattoo, and a petal had appeared. Glossy and purple, as big as Prior's thumb. Fenton twirled it between his fingers and Prior's chest heaved as he panted. He wanted to smother Fenton in petals, as he wanted to paint Fenton in come. The two ideas crossed in his mind and Prior didn't care to untangle them. He licked his lips, swimming in the pools of Fenton's eyes. He would drown there.

"Again," he said.

Fenton flashed his teeth. This time, Prior registered the crackling of magic rushing into his veins when Fenton plucked another petal. The lines of Prior's tattoo shimmered at Fenton's airy touch like light touching the surface of a pond.

The second petal was as perfect as the first. With a hungry look, Fenton pressed one of them to Prior's lips and chased it with a kiss. Power sizzled on Prior's tongue and sparked behind his closed eyes. He swallowed and watched as Fenton placed the other petal on his own tongue as if it were sugar, or one of the powdered drugs some of the travelling merchants traded. Would Prior thusly become a part of Fenton, as surely as the reverse was true?

Prior's gaze drifted to the sticky trails on Fenton's chest, and then lower, to the flushed head of his prick. When Fenton caught the direction of Prior's attention, his hips jerked. Prior met his eyes.

"I want to watch you come. Can I touch you, like you

did me?" Prior would lose himself to the task if he sucked Fenton off, and he wanted to see how Fenton looked when he came. This first time, at least. He'd get his mouth on Fenton sooner or later, if Fenton wanted.

Fenton nodded. When he spoke, the petal flashed in the dark of his mouth. "I would like that. Please."

Shuffling back to give himself more room to work, Prior considered Fenton's cock and decided simple would be the best approach. He licked his palm, though Fenton was leaking enough that it would ease the way unaided, and wrapped his hand around Fenton's blood-hot cock. Fenton moaned, syrup-thick, and lifted his hips to meet Prior's rhythm.

"That's it, you're doing so well," Prior murmured. Fenton's responsiveness made Prior's head light. His voice rasped in his throat. "Let yourself feel it."

With a bitten-off cry, Fenton arched and tossed his head, his neck craning over the back of the chaise. The long line of his throat was an invitation. Prior wanted to sink his teeth in until Fenton bruised in the shape of Prior's mouth. The urge arrived in Prior like a siren song. Firming his stroke, he lunged forward and pressed his face to Fenton's throat, breathing deep. Sweat. Blood. Ashes. Come. What did Fenton smell from Prior's skin? Prior wanted to know. He wanted to know how Fenton saw the world. He licked a stripe up Fenton's neck and sucked the taste from his teeth. Fenton keened and Prior bit back a curse at the sound.

He drew away. Levelled his gaze. "Look at me, Fenton."

Immediately, Fenton snapped his head forward. He panted lightly, and kept dragging his eyes open as he watched Prior from beneath increasingly heavy lids. His hips moved in a constant wave and Prior snuck his free hand between Fenton's spread legs to roll his heavy sack. When Prior pressed his forefinger lightly behind Fenton's sack, the resulting groan hitched into a whine and Fenton moved his hips sharply.

"You're almost there, aren't you? I can see it." Prior fixed his eyes on Fenton's face. "Let me see you come."

After a few more strokes, Fenton came with a shout that made the lanterns flicker and every plant in the greenhouse bloom. Prior kept stroking, trying to memorise Fenton's sweaty, perfect face, until Fenton slumped back, trembling with aftershocks, his eyes hazy and half-lidded. Satisfaction curled in Prior's chest. Someone could pluck it from him like a petal. He stroked his cleaner hand over Fenton's hair and cupped his face, pressing a kiss to the slope of his cheek.

"Very well done. Thank you." When Prior shifted to wipe his hand on his breeches, Fenton's hand snapped out and grabbed him. Prior startled. "What is— I should have guessed."

Fenton licked his spend from Prior's hand, his tongue flicking over the web between Prior's fingers and sucking his fingertips until every drop was gone and Prior's cock almost hurt from its efforts to stir. Prior shifted on Fenton's lap. Fenton smiled lazily, twining their fingers together.

"I like you," he said.

Warmth flooded Prior like the sun had chosen to look only at him. He swallowed. "And I you."

With a pleased hum, Fenton released Prior's hand. With some rearranging, they managed to lie together on the chaise, with Fenton in his original position and Prior sprawled on top of him, his legs out long and his head resting on Fenton's good shoulder. One of Fenton's sturdy arms slung around Prior's waist, keeping him secure. Prior had one hand tucked beneath his body, but the other lay across Fenton's chest as Fenton traced the roses outlined on Prior's skin.

Fenton nudged his hand beneath Prior's and lifted it, pressing their palms together. He slid his fingers through Prior's, from side to side, and tapped his fingertips in a playful pattern; his claws had reappeared, but they didn't worry Prior. Prior tapped back, making Fenton's chest rumble with a pleased noise. As Prior moved closer, seeking to alleviate any potential strain on Fenton's shoulder from the tapping game, Prior's stolen breeches clung in the wrong places to his legs and he thought suddenly of Fenton's peculiar trousers. He chuckled into Fenton's chest, and received a deepening rumble that sounded like a question.

"It's a silly thought," he explained. "A post-sex wondering."

Fenton caught Prior's fingers gently between his. "I would wonder with you."

Pressing a kiss to the nearest patch of skin, Prior asked the question that had been bothering him for days. "Where do your trousers go? The black ones?"

Fenton's barking laugh shook his entire body and made Prior laugh in turn as he held on, until they were wrapped in each other even more tightly than before. It had been a silly thought, as Prior had said, and he hadn't expected an answer, but Fenton trailed his claws feather-light on the small of Prior's back and hummed, the way he did when he was thinking.

Thoughtfully, he drew his thumb along Prior's arm, making the hairs rise, then smoothed his palm back to Prior's hand. In the wake of his movement, a slick black sleeve caressed Prior's skin in a cool wave, the same fabric as Fenton's trousers and, when Prior pressed his memory, the cloak Fenton had worn to Northrope. It felt like nothing. It looked like everything.

"It is my shadow. A very useful thing to have, a shadow." Fenton made a grabbing motion in the air and the shadow-fabric transferred to his hand, then disappeared. He resumed tracing Prior's tattoos, his touches nearly reverent. "Mayhaps you will have your own shadow in time."

"Do you know what they mean? The roses?" Not a silly

question, but one so serious Prior spoke it before the intention crossed his mind.

"Not entirely. This magic is new to me," Fenton said.

"They appeared when I came to find you, you and Lorcan."

Fenton's hand stilled. "I do not understand your meaning."

"After following the-the mage to that building, I knew I needed to break the hatch, but it was magically sealed and I didn't know what to do." The remembered panic made Prior tense. "Then from nowhere my arms started to itch, horribly, like I'd fallen in poison ivy but worse. Unrelenting. I've never felt anything like it. I scratched my skin to shreds, there was blood everywhere—"

"You do not have to explain yourself," Fenton interrupted, as he stroked Prior from wrist to elbow in comforting motions. His vines brushed against Prior's hair.

"No, no, I want to, it's all right." Prior contemplated the impossible roses tattooing his skin. The impossible being tracing them with his claws. "They appeared then, the roses. Dozens of them. Scores, or maybe more. They came out of my arms and attacked the hatch and the magic— I can see some magic now, I should have said, but it's not like seeing, is it? More like seeing with the eye of your mind." He tapped Fenton's chest. "Anyway, the roses and thorns broke through the hatch and then disappeared, with only these tattoos to make me believe any of it happened. And you, of course."

"I thought— Did I see your work in the courtyard? Thorned ropes."

Prior curled more tightly to Fenton's side. "When Lorcan and I arrived, you were so still. I thought— And then the roses ripped free to drive her back. Lorcan did something with the water but it took all their strength. We kept having to run and hide." Prior sniffed. "I don't want to think any more about it now."

"You were very brave. You saved my life."

The warmth of Fenton's voice soothed Prior, and he stretched up so they could kiss again. Their kisses would always be "again", now. The notion made his chest feel full. They would kiss in greenhouses and in gardens; in dark corners and bright streets. Every place two mouths could meet. Prior wanted to discover and share every type of kiss two people could enjoy. Two perhaps-not-people.

As Prior resettled, Fenton carded his other hand through Prior's hair. Prior felt the familiar hum reverberate through his chest. "I have been scenting roses on you for some time. I am honoured to have learned what they meant."

"And what do they mean? Will you tell me?" Prior asked again. "Not entirely" hadn't been "no".

"I am not certain—"

"Of the two of us, I think your best guess will be far closer than my panicked imaginings," Prior said dryly.

"You have been chosen by the forest. By..." Fenton trailed off. He tapped Prior's hand and Prior waited for Fenton to find his words. "Old Nan has two sons, you said to me once."

"Two siblings."

Fenton hummed. "Just so. Yet there are more siblings in the world than merely Lorcan and I, and more Old Nans besides. The world is a big place." He traced one of the roses. "My world is bigger, now."

"How big?" Prior asked shakily. The other questions Fenton's words had prompted were too enormous to yet voice. Fenton spoke of gods like they were goats, and goats like they were gods. Prior didn't know if he'd ever become used to it.

Fenton's chest shook as he laughed. "I know not. But I am excited to learn together with you, if you will have me."

Prior answered with a kiss that Fenton deepened, rolling over to cage Prior between his arms and legs, safe from falling. Wrapping his legs around Fenton's waist, Prior reached for Fenton's antlers and held on. Vines wrapped around his hands, holding him in turn. Hunger pooled in Prior's gut. One day, he would learn how his roses worked, and then he and Fenton could spend every night tangled together in a thicket of sex and flowers. They could build their own forest.

Just as Prior was giving thought to asking Fenton what exactly he could do with those vines, something exploded outside, making the windows of the greenhouse rattle in their frames. One of the chrysanthemums fell over in a spray of soil. Stilling, Prior cast a wary glance to the ceiling. To the walls. All of them made of glass.

He met Fenton's eyes.

"Perhaps we can start our learning outside," Prior said.

Fenton tilted his head, and grinned.

ACKNOWLEDGEMENTS

With thanks to my editor Misha Fletcher for removing the god from the machine, and to April for betaing this manuscript during its metamorphosis from a short into the beautiful butterfly now in your literal or metaphorical hands.

The beautiful cover artwork is by Tiferet Design with illustration by Mar Espinosa, and I couldn't possibly adore their work more than I do. I would like to eat the cover. The highest compliment I can give!

Honourable mention here to The Witcher 3: Blood and Wine DLC, for providing a much-needed holiday during These Times. Toussaint is lovely every time of year. (Apart from… all the murder…)

Anyway. I'm not quite sure what happened in or to 2020, but I'm grateful to have stumbled into Ashcroft. I hope you enjoy your stay.

ABOUT THE AUTHOR

Parker Foye (they/them) writes queer speculative romance and believes in happily ever after, although sometimes their characters make achieving this difficult. An education in Classics nurtured a love of heroes, swords, monsters, and beautiful people doing foolish things while wearing only scraps of leather. You'll find those things in various guises in Parker's stories, along with kissing (often) and explosions (messy). And more shifters than you can shake a stick at.

Parker lives in Oxford, UK, and travels regularly via planes, trains, and an ever-growing library.